COLD ROLLED DEAD

COLD ROLLED DEAD

A NOVEL

PAUL D'AMBROSIO

DOWN THE SHORE
PUBLISHING
West Creek, New Jersey

Box 100, West Creek, NJ 08092
www.down-the-shore.com
The words "Down The Shore" and the Down The Shore Publishing logos are registered U.S. Trademarks.

Book design by Leslee Ganss

Printed in the United States of America
10 9 8 7 6 5 4 3 2 1
First printing, 2007.

Library of Congress Cataloging-in-Publication Data
D'Ambrosio, Paul, 1959-
  Cold rolled dead : a novel / Paul D'Ambrosio.
     p. cm.
  ISBN-13: 978-1-59322-035-8
  ISBN-10: 1-59322-035-9
  1. Police--New Jersey--Fiction. 2. Murder--Investigation--Fiction. 3.
Nuns--Fiction. 4. Political corruption--Fiction. 5. Atlantic Coast
(N.J.)--Fiction. I. Title.
  PS3604.A4397C65 2007
  813'.6--dc22
                              2007020469

For my parents

Prologue

For a fleeting moment, the caress of her kiss sent a chill through every fiber of his being. He strained to look pat her serene silhouette, to the distant glow that he could no longer see.

He closed his eyes, and softly wept.

In the dank corner of the warehouse he knew his time was at an end. Through the throbs of pain, the torment, the betrayal, he wondered how long it had been. Was it hours or days? He couldn't be sure as he fought the haze of his memory. He drifted in and out of consciousness. Slowly, he opened his eyes to gaze at the far wall, wondering if his salvation was at hand.

It was the light, that brilliant light, which seemed to offer a singular shred of hope. The yellow hue flickered wildly in the darkness, far beyond his grasp.

He reached for it, but realized he could no longer stand. As his strength drained from his legs, he tumbled forward to a chortle of delight.

"Look at him try to dance," said a gruff voice.

"Poor pumpkin," a woman's voice whispered in a soft, apologetic lilt as he sat on the cement floor. The words, once so soothing, burned as they echoed in his mind. The tender pads of fingers brushed unhurriedly across his damp brow and down his fractured cheek. Poor pumpkin.

As quickly as the fingertips left his face, her lips touched his once more. Then the voice turned firm.

"Now."

The distant glow became brighter, its heat overwhelming.

Through the fog of a waning consciousness, he struggled to focus on the light. Instinctively, he turned away.

Too bright. Too bright.

And then, darkness.

DAY

Sunday, July 2

ONE

A cool sweep of air embraced Lester Lewis as he drew open the heavy oak doors to the sanctuary.

The air conditioning offered a respite from the morning heat, which seemed to grow in intensity with every passing minute. The breeze was enough to divert his attention from the dull ache in his arthritic hip, the pain a constant reminder that his once-spry jaunts were now hobbled to a measured pace. He tugged absent-mindedly at his dark blue sports jacket to shut out the unexpected chill.

He had come this morning to Saint Sebastian's Church, nestled deep in the green, lush Pine Barrens of southern New Jersey. The house of worship was a cozy remnant of a speck-of-a-town that was quickly passing into oblivion as the hamlet's eldest members faded away.

Lewis, now just a visitor, had shunned the church for years. The long shadows of the early morning hour ensured that the few remaining communicants were nowhere in sight. He scanned the hollow vestibule and then looked forward, toward the last of the wooden pews. Father Caden, a sandy-haired priest several years Lewis's junior, sat with his hands folded and head bowed as he rested on the worn, rigid kneeler.

The deep rumble of the giant oak door closing told Father Caden that he was no longer alone.

"Good morning, Les," Caden said without looking up. "I was surprised by your call. It's been awhile."

"Yes, Father," Lewis said. He winced in pain as he genuflected before the altar and turned into the pew. "After all these years, I still can't see you with that collar."

13

"We each find our own path, Les," Father Caden said as he pulled himself slowly to a seated position from the kneeler. "How long has it been? Ten? Fifteen years? Has retirement from the police force been good to you?"

"Don't bullshit me, Caden," Lewis said. "You know our friend has told you all about me."

"I left that world a long time ago."

Lewis lowered his voice to intone his impatience.

"C'mon. You got rich, we all got rich from it," Lewis said. "You couldn't stay away if you tried. You ran away to this godforsaken place, and you still couldn't stay away. Tell me, how do you explain to your flock about your nice house, your nice car?"

"I say nothing," the priest said quietly. "They assume I inherited it from a distant relative. I do try to keep my vows to be honest."

"And the women... there are still the women, aren't there, Caden?" Lewis scanned his quarry as if he were a viper about to strike.

Caden closed his eyes as he pinched the bridge of his nose. "There are no longer any women, Lester. Why are you here? Did you come to blackmail me for a few dollars? Is that what your poor life has come to?"

Lewis paused and looked away, unsure what to say next, unsure how to begin. His hard features softened faintly as he reflected on the priest's carefully chosen words.

"I am so tired," Lewis said. He turned again to face Caden as the priest moved to meet his eyes. "So tired."

"Your spirit is weary. I can see that," Caden said. He slowly reached to clasp Lewis's hands in his own. Caden felt a slight tremble as he offered a reassuring squeeze. "Do you wish to offer your confession?"

"I do," Lewis said. "You know it has been much too long. You know what I have done; the terrible things that I have done."

"Yes."

"Forgive me, Father," Lewis said as he bowed his head. "Forgive me."

"Go on, Les."

"I am here because of another," Lewis said. He raised his eyes to see a mixture of puzzlement and alarm on Father Caden's face. He felt a rush of adrenaline through his body, one that caused his left eye to twitch.

"I... I don't understand."

"Our friend," Lewis said. "Our friend was here to see you. Was it... yesterday?"

Caden was caught off guard. A minute stutter gave Lewis the reassurance that he needed. "I'm not sure that I can talk about this, Lester."

"I know he was here," Lester said in a flat tone, his eyes meeting the priest's gaze full on. "I know he talked to you. I know that he told you."

"I cannot talk about this," Caden said. He instinctively pulled his hands away, trying to inch away from Lewis, but was stopped by the solid edge of the pew.

"You know, don't you?" Lewis said, sliding closer. "Tell me if you know."

"You must leave, now," Caden said, his voice rising to a harsh whisper. "I cannot talk about this."

Lewis grabbed the priest's wrist, locking it in a tight grip. "The temptation for one more score was too much, wasn't it, Caden? You couldn't live without just one more taste, isn't that right? You need to tell me what you know."

"I know nothing," Caden said. "Your grip. Let go. Let *go*. You are hurting me."

"Do you?" Lewis pulled closer, lowering his voice. He looked around to ensure they were still alone. "Do you know about it?"

"About what?"

"The Khimer-A."

Father Caden's eyes widened and then darted toward the vestibule. Lewis could see that the reaction was the final affirmation; he had found what he had come for.

"The Khimer-A? I don't know what you are talking about. What is it?"

"I'm sorry, Father," Lewis said, relaxing his grip to offer an easy assurance of calm. "The pain... I sometimes become too anxious because of this damn arthritis."

Father Caden eased his rigid spine, a sign to Lewis that he no longer feared him. With his free hand Lewis gently caressed his aching hip. With the slightest of movements, he moved to the hollow of his back. His fingertips danced lightly over the reassuring coolness of the brass, then removed the hammer's dark and dimpled wooden handle from its thin custom holster.

"Forgive me, Father," Lewis said, exhaling. "Forgive me, Caden."

The heavy brass flashed from behind Lewis's back into a high arc. With a soft sound, like a paper cup being crushed, the ball peen dug effortlessly into the top of the priest's head. Caden slumped forward. His motion was momentarily halted by the kneeler. As the weight in his lifeless body shifted to the right, the priest slid silently into Lewis's lap.

Lewis knew they were alone. He had no need to hurry. From his jacket pocket he withdrew a thick, black trash bag. He quickly wrapped it around the dead priest's head and made sure, as he had done countless times before, that no specs of blood dripped on the floor. The hammer had a way of stopping the blood flow; the trick was never to take it out before the heart stopped beating.

Lewis thought about offering another apology to his old friend, but knew it was useless. Whatever forgiveness he sought, it was too late now. With the bag secured, Lewis yanked the priest's body to an upright position. Even with the medication, the pain shot through his hip like a knife. He let out a small yell, but he would have to endure it. There was little time for self-pity. Once outside, he knew he would have to move quickly to put the body in the trunk of his car to move it to its final, hidden place. Caden could not be found, at least for the next three days. It was all the time Lewis needed.

It was all the time he had before the Khimer-A arrived.

TWO

Even in sleep, Matt Forge could not shake the past. Rising from his forgotten youth, the specter of his terrible mistake — a hair's breath hesitation — could never be forgotten.

It returned to him each night. It shattered his mind's best defenses like a bullet shot through glass. Each night he told himself — promised and begged himself — he wouldn't let the dream return. As if wishing it away would somehow magically end the torment.

The dream was patient. It waited for his body to pass the point of no return, where he was forced to capitulate to fatigue, that heavenly rest his weary muscles and soul craved but seldom enjoyed.

Then the dream came. It tore past the fleeting barriers of self-defense, the walls of hope, the fractured pillars of esteem, until it hit the sweet spot of despair.

It was the same each night. Cold sweat in the summer heat. Restless thrashes. The cruel sense of helplessness.

This night, though, the dream would be cheated. The trill of the cell phone at his side startled Forge awake.

At first confused, unable to distinguish between the real and the surreal, Forge stared at the phone as it started a jig on the top of the worn nightstand.

He turned to the red digits of his alarm clock. *6:47.* He blinked his eyes to will himself back to reality. *6:48.*

He rose and walked past the annoying device. He had seen the name flash in bright green on the caller ID. He didn't want to deal with him, at least not yet. The remnants of the dream still had its tendril wrapped around Forge's mind. He needed air. He needed to clear his head.

The early morning salt mist had fogged the sliding glass door on The Shack.

The house — he always used that term loosely in conversation — was a ramshackle fishing hut perched on pilings that were too high and, after too many nor'easter storms, much too crooked. Forge had to be careful as he stepped past the dying potted plants and the debris on the floor; the slant was never to be taken lightly. He likened his living conditions to working on his father's boat — one hand for you, his father always warned him, and one hand for the boat. If you let go, a rolling wave will knock you flat on your back.

With a two-handed grip, Forge yanked the sliding glass door open. From his vantage at Mire Point, he could barely make out the water towers and sweep of mansions on Long Beach Island, two miles across the shallow Barnegat Bay.

The view was about the only saving grace of The Shack. Out of money, out of his house, out of a wife and nearly out of a job, Forge was thankful for the good graces of an old school chum who had loaned him the use of the place when the friend abruptly moved — to New Jersey's Bayside State Prison.

Grabbing a canvas bag and slinging it high over his shoulder, Forge stepped carefully down the twisted wood steps that led from the porch to the sand-strewn landing. He knew which broken steps to avoid, which steps he needed to carefully balance his weight on. Two hundred pounds for too long in the middle of any tread was a duel with gravity that Forge had no desire to lose.

Forge lingered on the edge of the bay. The tide was at its lowest. That was good. The black and brown muck and tall reeds of the bay's shoreline were exposed; the odor of decaying sea grass and algae filled the morning with a thick air of long-forgotten scrambled eggs. Forge didn't mind. He didn't even notice the stench much anymore. It was nature; it was the way things were supposed to be.

He waded into the warm water, gingerly pressing his toes into the spongy bottom. Something solid — a rock, he knew from experience; too hard, too wide. He ignored it. He moved cautiously into deeper water until his elbows touched the surface. A few feet to the left and his toes found what he was looking for. Breakfast from the bay.

Forge bent over to pluck the sizable mollusk from the bottom and deposited it into the canvas bag. A few more bobs and he had a half-dozen clams.

On shore, he shook the water off of his legs like a damp dog and pulled a stubby, worn shucker knife from the side of the steps. With a sharp scrape and a flick of the wrist, Forge cut the white, sinewy muscle to release its stubborn seal. Closing his eyes, he popped the exposed beige flesh into his mouth, making a gentle slurp as he drained the mollusk of all its salty juices.

Forge took the climb back to the top of the porch and walked into the living room that doubled as his bedroom and kitchen. On a small black-and-white television, precariously balanced on a chair in a corner, a fuzzy, silent picture fluttered wildly.

Forge slapped his hand around the floor until he felt the phone. It began to trill again. He knew it was the same caller. Reluctantly, he flipped it open with one hand.

"It's me," the agitated voice on the other end started. "Where the hell have you been?"

"Fishing."

"Bullshit. You don't have a fishing rod."

"Clam fishing."

"Christ." A pause. "We've been fishing, too. Wait till you see what we caught."

"A floater?"

"Sort of."

"I don't do floaters."

"You're going to want this one." .

"Why?"

"I don't want to ruin the surprise."

"Call the Coast Guard."

"Don't be a loser. This is right up your alley."

"Where is it?"

"The sisters."

"Where?"

"The sisters. Y'know, the convent."

"What is it? Tell me."

"It's your ticket. Your ticket back."

THREE

By the time Forge had showered and jumped into his faded blue 1981 Jeep, his watch read 7:25. It was the Fourth of July weekend, the worst time of the tourist season for getting quickly onto the island over the Causeway Bridge. Even at this early hour, traffic was backed up north toward New York City, and west almost 70 miles to Philadelphia.

It was one of the few times Forge actually considered that being a cop had its moments. He rode the shoulder of Route 72 to the causeway, but had to sit through traffic across the first leg of the narrow three-bridge span. Forge was forced to crawl along with all the visitors who were unable, and unwilling, to

18

make a path for him.

Once on Long Beach Boulevard, Forge banked left and sped north to Harvey Cedars and the Sisters of Mercy compound. There, he saw a haphazard arrangement of police cars and a boxy white truck marked with "Ocean County HAZMAT Response Team" in reflective gold lettering.

Forge exited the Jeep and strode toward the crest of the dune, where he saw several nuns peering curiously at the action below.

At the top of the dune ramp, a patrolman, sweating profusely, watched Forge meander his way toward the beachhead.

The uniformed cop parted his mouth slightly to offer a perfunctory greeting to the approaching detective, but quickly had second thoughts. Best not to poke a stick into the lion's cage. What does one say to a detective cast from Mount Olympus? Forge appeared as if he had slept in his clothes for a week, then rolled on the floor to press out the wrinkles.

"Good morning, patrolman," Forge said, startling the officer. "Busy keeping everyone away?"

"Not much foot traffic today, sir," the patrolman responded. "No media, no tourists. A few nuns and a priest, but it is their place, isn't it?"

Forge nodded. No media was good. Reporters were always clambering for instant answers: what do you have, who did it, what happened to them, when are you going to make an arrest? The best one he heard was from a New York TV tabloid reporter who wanted to know just a singular fact about the dismembered remains of a female murder victim: what color was her underwear? The tease for that 11 o'clock news report must have been a real hoot.

"Hey, loser," a voice cried from the sand below as Forge crested the dune.

Forge saw Duroc Fry towering over everyone along the surf line. At six-feet six-inches, with a chiseled Gulf War-hardened physique to match, Fry was not a man easily missed. They had grown up together, surfed together, and joined the police academy together. Fry opted for the relative solitude of the island police after his tour with the army's mechanized division in the desert sands in Iraq. Forge remained home, driven by an innate force he could never fully describe. Colleagues and superiors saw his determination as naked ambition; to Forge, his spectral quest pushed him toward an unknown end. Each case was harder than the next, and solving each became his sole passion. His successes propelled him to the top of the County detective roster — until, a wrong twist of a foot in the minefield of county politics, Forge's career and life instantly fragmented into unrecognizable pieces.

During Forge's heyday, Fry had jokingly dubbed him "Loser" to offset his volcanic rise. It had become a modest term of endearment between them for years.

But after his meteoric fall, Forge amused himself by noting that the term now accurately described his purgatory. From top county cop specializing in computer forensics to a two-bit detective on the Long Beach Island beat, his day involved a weary range of crimes, from preteens snatching iPods on the beach to senior citizens shoplifting aspirin at the Ocean Pharmacy. Could hell be any worse?

"Forge," Fry thundered across the beach. "Get your sorry ass down here."

Forge trudged carefully through the sand, heat rippling from its grains. The HAZMAT team was wrapping up its examination of a metal cylinder, a quarter of which was stuck in the sand and pointing at a lazy thirty degrees toward the dunes. The calm knee-high ocean waves made a slow and rhythmic *thap-thap* against the container.

Forge squinted into the sun to see Fry walk toward him in the shifting sand.

"We've been here since 6:15," Fry said. "One of the nuns was jogging on the beach and came across that down there." He motioned with his open hand to the surf line. "It's your standard, run-of-the-mill, fifty-five gallon drum — but with a special treat inside."

"You dragged me here for an oil barrel, Sergeant?" Forge said, his eyes locked on the drum.

"It's no ordinary can," Fry said, stringing Forge out as much as he dared. "Take a look." He plucked a smoky flat of plastic film from the cardboard folder under his arm.

"Hazmat used their portable X-ray to take a look inside," he said. He held the film to the blue cast of the northern sky.

Forge looked at it once, blinked, and looked again. He quickly snagged the film from Fry's hands. Forge's eyes widened a fraction. He couldn't believe the image.

"It's a... a..." Forge didn't have time to finish the sentence.

"Yep," Fry interrupted in his irksome way, eager to steal the words from Forge's lips. "It's a man in a can."

FOUR

Morning came hard for Dominick Tolck.

The sour stench of cigarette butts simmering in the dark, windowless room was so familiar to Tolck that he could barely smell the rancid air anymore.

"Boss." A firm hand gently nudged Tolck from his hazy sleep. "Boss. C'mon,

Boss. We have business."

Tolck sat upright in his brown leather high-back chair and half-heartedly brushed the thick strands of his silver mane from the front of his face, straight back to the top of his head. At fifty-seven, Tolck loathed being roused, even if his pillow happened to be the blotter on the top of his smoked glass desk. His bright orange short-sleeve shirt was puckered enough to be mistaken for seersucker cloth.

"Yes, my dear," Tolck said, regaining his composure.

As best as Tolck could recall, he had dozed off in his cluttered office around four in the morning. That was generally when the clientele outside became too intoxicated to care much if the music was still playing. He had made his usual rounds through the customers, looking for the creeps and the marks. To the rapacious Tolck, there were only two types in the world — those who could make money for him, and those who got in the way of his making money.

His cold blue eyes were the sole giveaway that he was not the genteel, grandfatherly persona that provided the first impression for strangers. Hidden behind his eyes was a bit of death.

Tolck, tall and lean as a seaside post, stood and licked his upper lip as he moved toward the mirrored liquor cabinet. On the topmost shelf were three crystal bottles of $7,000 Hardy Perfection cognac. The other two shelves were haphazardly littered with two-dozen pill bottles, both large and extra large.

The middle shelf offered a pharmaceutical potpourri of club drugs that ranged from common speed to a yellow psychoactive hallucinogenic tablet simply known as "Tripstasy."

It was the bottom shelf that most concerned Tolck. He grabbed for the first bottle of Fragmin, popped out one pill, and then fished around for the Mavik, Lasix, and lithium bottles. Tolck's drug partying days were long gone. He had left those times for his son to enjoy. The prescription pills he needed were designed to keep him alive, or at least stop the chest pains that were coming all too frequently now. The lithium put a foul metallic taste in his mouth, as if he were using a Jefferson nickel as a never-ending lozenge. It was the price he had to endure to sooth the demons of his sweeping moods.

He flipped the fragile stopper off of the 140-year-old cognac, slopped out a shot of the golden liquid into a dirty white coffee cup, and tossed the pills to the back of his throat.

"Here's to your health, kid," Tolck muttered to his mirrored image as he downed the drink without letting the liquor traverse his taste buds.

Tolck grinned at Consolina for rousing him from his fitful sleep.

Consolina smelled of a cocktail of expensive perfume and cheap cologne. She had just changed from her entertainment wear to cuffed khaki shorts and a too-tight silk blouse that formed a "V" shape, deliberately highlighting her cleavage by pushing her ample breasts together, the best that Tolck's money could buy.

"What's the business?" Tolck asked.

"Modibo," Consolina said as she placed his breakfast of three eggs, fried over-easy in bacon fat, on his desktop. "Do you want to see him now, or wait?"

"Show him in, dear," Tolck said as he returned to his desk. "My father always said it is best to deal with bad news first before it deals with you later."

"I am not happy, Tolck," the man started as soon as Consolina led him into the room.

"Councilman Modibo, how kind of you to drop in at this early hour," Tolck said, wiping a yellow dot of egg from one corner of his mouth with the linen napkin tucked under his chin.

"Cut the shit, Tolck," Modibo said, leaning over the desk so far that he had to balance himself on his two hands. "I got you the building permits you wanted."

"Yes, that is true."

"I want my money."

"I know."

"Today."

"I know."

"Now."

"Please, Modibo, sit down. There is no reason for such agitation. We have had a little problem with the building inspectors. Some were not privy to our relationship. They were not performing, shall we say, up to par."

The firmly built councilman, a man in his late twenties, towered over the seated Tolck. Modibo bared his oversized, bleached white teeth to reinforce the point of payment.

"The county inspectors are your problem," Modibo said. "I did my end of the bargain."

"There is no reason to raise your voice," Tolck said, using a sterling silver butter knife to gently slather the spread onto the last slice of toast on his plate.

"This is bullshit," Modibo said, slapping the glass table with his hands and moving to within a breath of Tolck's nose. "I will have my cops on you so fast you will think it was yesterday if I don't have my money now."

"How much is it?" Tolck asked, not looking up from his plate.

"You know what it is. Five thousand. Here," Modibo said, poking the center of his palm. "Give it to me. Now."

Tolck silently contemplated the amount as he chewed the last piece of his egg. He replaced the fork on the table with his left hand. Modibo did not see the movement on the right.

Tolck had never released the butter knife. With a speed and power that belied his age, Tolck thrust the dull blade deep into Modibo's left eye.

Modibo recoiled backward and onto the floor. He opened his mouth in a feeble attempt to scream. Tolck was amused that all this monster of a man could utter was a faint, almost inaudible, high-pitched child-like whimper. With one hand, the councilman weakly tried to feel the silver handle that protruded from his eye, the blade throbbing inside his fractured socket.

With one knee bent, Tolck grabbed the hair at the top of Modibo's head and jerked him upright. Tolck leaned in close to the man's ear to ensure each syllable was heard.

"Do not fuck with me," Tolck whispered. "In my world, you are nothing but a piece of shit; a necessary piece of shit, but a piece of shit nonetheless. You are in charge of a department that I need to get my houses built. You think you're king of the hill because you got a few lousy votes? You think you can boss me around? No one tells Tolck what to do. I got you elected. I tell you what to do. Do you understand that?"

Modibo, his remaining eye scanning Tolck in terror, nodded as much as he could under his attacker's rigid grip.

"Good. That's very good," Tolck said. "You're young. You will see better now with one eye than two. Accept this as a life lesson. The more you suffer in this life, the greater your reward in the next, or so they tell me. Now, what are you going to do for me?"

Modibo's mouth opened and closed as if he were a fish tossed onto a wharf. "I will help... you...?"

"Yes, exactly. And for my troubles today, what will you pay me?" Tolck turned his head so that the councilman's lips came as close to Tolck's ear as the protruding handle of the sterling silver knife would allow.

"Five thousand ... dollars?" he said weakly.

"Yes, exactly right," Tolck said. "You learn quickly, Modibo." Tolck released the man's head so that it dropped to the hardwood floor like a bowling ball. Modibo quietly wept as he cupped his hands around his wound.

Tolck shuffled back to his seat and dipped the last of his toast into the remaining yolk on his plate.

Without looking up, Tolck motioned to Consolina with a flick of the hand. "Get Lewis in here to clean him up and get him out."

"Anything else?" Consolina asked. She was amused that Modibo had the strength to crawl into a fetal position in a far corner of the room.

Tolck thought for a moment. "Be sure to get my butter knife back."

Tolck motioned to Consolina to follow him into the counting room across the narrow hallway. He pressed the touchpad of the electronic digits, and magnetic seals on all four corners of the two-inch-thick reinforced steel door unlatched with a soft hum. The entryway swung open.

Inside, a mountain of crumpled cash, mostly one- and ten-dollar bills, rose from the center of a long steel table. A box of credit card receipts sat neatly in the rear of the room.

"It looks light for the Saturday night before the Fourth of fuckin' July," Tolck said. "Did Costa scrape all the girls after each show?"

"Absolutely, boss," Consolina said, looking away to hide her lying eyes. "I checked the closed circuit myself." She avoided mentioning that much of her attention had been focused on flirting and finally engaging in a series of sexual romps with two bouncers in the men's stall of the cramped bathroom.

"He may be my son, but Costa is still a thieving son-of-a-bitch if you don't keep an eye on him," Tolck said.

To Tolck, Consolina was different from other women. In her early thirties, her brilliant red hair softened the faint age lines that had sprouted at the corners of her eyes and lips. Not as statuesque as his regular dancers, she still was a solid performer that the loyal customers flocked to. Most of all, she had a rare business talent that Tolck needed.

"Get Hal in here to start sorting and counting the money," Tolck said. "I can't wait for the day the girls strap on credit card machines."

Tolck and Consolina walked to the dimly lit customer area and the show floor, which wasn't much brighter. On center stage, a petite brunette was having trouble unhooking the front clasp of her star-spangled bra as she twirled around the brass dance pole, hopelessly missing the beats from the blaring music.

Tolck was the overlord of The Paradise, a strip joint off the main highway to the Shore in the middle of the New Jersey Pine Barrens. It was the type of place that no one talked about but everyone knew. It was a hard find at the end of a long, unmarked, sandy road, but Tolck had no shortage of customers from all walks of life.

The business was also an efficient washing machine for illegal money of any ilk. He dealt with loan sharks as well as uptight lawyers laundering kickbacks for even more uptight politicians who had won office on the pledge of keeping their campaigns clean of illegal contributions.

And, best of all, because his showgirls took all their clothes off the state of New Jersey left him alone. If he wanted to legally serve alcohol, he would have two immense problems: his girls couldn't dance naked and the Alcoholic Beverage Commission would regulate the hell out of him, assuming he could pass the criminal background check. To avoid that, The Paradise was, on the books, a twenty-four-hour, seven-day-a-week juice bar. Orange juice, grapefruit juice, mango juice, lime juice, mixed fruit, even exotic passion fruit were the top drinks on the menu, all at ten bucks a glass. But most of the regulars knew enough to order off menu. Tolck bragged that he indeed did have the juice, but it wasn't from a tree. He relied on his sophisticated supply chain to bring in cases of everything from cheap beer to fine wine, tax free. Each customer's palette was satiated, as long as the money flowed freely from his pocket.

Squat and nondescript on the outside, The Paradise offered a lavish but worn look inside. Recessed lights in the ceiling provided dim spotlights for the red cloth tabletops. On stage, three brass poles and a horizontal chin-up bar provided ample opportunity for the strippers to engage in gymnastics never imagined on Wide World of Sports.

It was Costa who ran the joint. His goatee and slicked, blond hair gave a menacing look to his close-set eyes and flat nose. Costa was the business manager and booker for the shows. Since there were scant "star" quality strippers in the area, he had to ensure the girls in his stable rotated on a frequent basis in order to stoke the customers into coming back to see new bodies. Costa didn't care where he found the talent, be it some co-ed at the local community college looking for money for her next rent payment, a hooker from up north whose drug habit had yet to waste her away, or a Russian teen trying to pay off the mob for smuggling her parents in from the old country.

Most of the talent lasted about two weeks, three if it was during the busy summer months. The money was good. A newcomer performing during the prime overnight hours could easily pull in $1,200, more if she danced for private parties in the "shoeshine booth," a secluded room off the main hall that could handle up to seven guys at a time.

At night, Costa's main task was to scrape the girls as soon as they left the stage. A stripper walking off had no place to hide her tip money other than under her thin silk garter belt. Costa had each girl line up before him on the second ledge of the steps at the rear of the stage so he could "scrape" all of the greenbacks from the tight elastic band. Only then was a girl allowed to put on her robe and head back to the confined, dilapidated dressing room. Costa usually stuffed the money into the pocket of his brown leather jacket, recorded his estimate of the take in a palm-sized ledger book, and then deposited the net amount in the counting room.

Tolck dubbed the business his beehive; no matter where they were, politicians would always find their way to the sweet honey he offered.

Tolck stopped in the hallway to admire his prize display of native grasses, brushing the tops of the leaves gently with the back of his hand. As he turned his palm down he noticed that a droplet of milky vitreous fluid from Modibo's eye had dotted the corner of the thumb. Tolck brushed the gel onto a thick blade of a green and turned to Costa. He pulled him to the dim side of the hallway. "You talk to our candidate?"

"Yeah."

"No second thoughts, right? I mean, you read his face, not the fuckin' words coming out of his mouth?" Tolck asked.

"Yeah. He's in for the whole dollar," Costa said. "He knows the business. He knows that the less people who know, the better it will be for all of us. He just wanted to know if we're still on target."

Tolck scanned the area once more and leaned closer to Costa. "Tell him," Tolck said in a lowered voice, "it will be the best Fourth of July he will ever see."

FIVE

On the beach, Forge muted his expression. His first reaction was disbelief, and then petty annoyance; he didn't want to give Fry the satisfaction of surprising him.

"A man in a can?" Forge said.

"Look here." Fry held up two more exposures of different parts of the drum. A thighbone could be seen clearly in one. A blur of a knee was exposed on the second plate. "What do you think?"

"I think we can rule out suicide."

"Damn," Fry said. "I was looking forward to an easy Sunday."

"No ID on the can?"

"None. It looks like the serial number was filed off."

"You run the missing persons reports?"

"Hundreds. We won't know what we have till we get a can opener and pop the top." A pause. "Not much use here for all your fancy computer gizmos, huh? But this is still right up your alley. Where do you think you are going to start?"

"What makes you think I want the case?" Forge said.

"I thought this would be a notch up from sitting in your shack and counting the dots of bird shit on your car."

"Bite me," Forge said. He stretched both syllables as far as he could with one breath.

"Don't hold back, buddy. Share those feelings," said Fry, grabbing Forge's shoulders with both hands.

"It's one of my many talents, really."

"So you're telling me the best detective in the county doesn't want a case like this? It has serial killer written all over it."

Forge refocused on the can. "There is no sign here of a signature crime. There's never been a report of a body in a barrel, and even if this was a serial crime it doesn't have any of the traditional hallmarks. The thrill is in the ritual killing of the victim, not in the disposal of the body. It would take at least two if not three men to move the body into the can and dump it on the beach."

"Ah, now I got you hooked."

Forge stopped. Fry had pushed him into dissecting the case. His mind was looking for the keys to unlock the doors of the crime, but he felt himself fumble. Was he rusty? Out of play too long? Maybe he hadn't been getting enough sleep. God knows when the last time was he felt rested. He couldn't wrap his mind around a plausible crime theory, at least not yet.

After twenty years in police work, Forge thought he had seen it all. Harvey Cedars was one of the wealthiest and one of the smallest towns in the state — three blocks wide from ocean to bay, and a half-mile long. Blink as you drive and you'll miss the borough. As best he could tell, the drum washed in with the tide, but it hardly looked like it had been in the water for more than a day. The black paint was intact and there was no telltale sign of algae.

"Look here," Forge said as he walked around the can in a semicircle and finally thumped his thumb on the black lid until it made a deep, hollow echo. He pointed to a silvery glint on the rim and ran his index finger lightly across it. "It's fresh."

"A fresh weld?" Fry asked.

"Yeah. Nice and neat. The joints are fused shut, enough for a very tight seal; a watertight seal. Looks like they took their time. They must have been out of sight for a while."

"They did it in someone's basement? Where the light won't shine out?"

"Basement, garage, warehouse — anyplace prying eyes won't see you. Where would you want to weld a can shut?"

"Car shop? Boat yard? There a hundred places that use welders."

"How many want to dump their prized work on the beach?" Forge said.

"That's what you're here for. We need your best kung fu."

"The top is sealed shut on a brand-new can. I'm going to hazard a guess and say the bottom has no holes, cracks or seams that would let seawater in. The serial number of the can has been carefully filed off — careful enough so we can't trace it back to its place of manufacture, or to make it a weak point in the steel."

"Right," Fry said slowly. "If you want to get rid of a body in the ocean, you put a few cinder blocks in the can, pop holes in the top and bottom, and let gravity do the rest. If you go far enough out, chances are no one would ever find the barrel.

"So why drop the barrel in the laps of the good sisters? Not the best karma, if you know what I mean."

"It is a public beach here, isn't it?" Forge asked rhetorically.

"Yeah, but no one uses it other than the nuns of Maris Stella. It's their convent."

"Did anyone see how the barrel wound up on the beach?" Forge asked.

"No. One of the sisters found it stuck in the sand around 5:30 this morning on a jog," Fry said.

"Where is the sister?"

"Inside the dining area. We had a uniform take a statement, but I thought you might want to talk to her, too."

"Yeah," Forge said. "Have the barrel wrapped and sent to county. We'll take it apart there."

SIX

At the Maris Stella cafeteria, the sister kept herself busy by wiping down a plain, heavily varnished pinewood table. Forge and Fry walked in from the kitchen entrance, trying not to let the well-weathered wooden screen door slam close.

"Sister, you remember we met outside? I'm Sergeant Fry. This is my partner, Detective Forge."

The petite nun tried to hide the tissue she was using to dab a tear from her eye. Forge was taken aback by how young and radiant she looked, a woman perhaps no more than thirty, with a perfect oval face and tender features that framed emerald eyes. Her feathered-back dark brown hair seemed to float lightly above her shoulders. Instead of the stereotypical black-and-white polyester habit that would swaddle a nun of a more traditional sect, she struck a pose of that of any other tourist in an "I ♥ Long Beach Island" tee shirt, worn jeans, and white running shoes. The only outward sign of her sisterhood was a small, scallop-edged gold cross pinned to the top left of her tee shirt.

"Is it true?" she asked. "One of the officers told me there was a person inside that drum."

"We believe so," Forge said. "We won't know for sure until we look inside further. We just ask that you do not mention this to anyone."

"Of course," she said.

"Sister, I do hate to intrude, but if you could give us a moment of your time, I just have a few questions to ask," Forge said.

"Yes, of course," the sister said, gently placing a fresh Marlboro cigarette between her lips from a pack on the table.

Her hands were simple and unadorned save for white-tipped, manicured fingernails and the band of silver on her left ring finger. To a commoner, the ring was the venerable sign of marriage. But in the sisterhood, it was a symbol of a union with Christ.

"My name is Sister Maris," she said. Her voice was both firm and melodic. "Sister Maris Stella."

"Sister Maris Stella of the Maris Stella convent?" Forge said. He tried not to sound confused or surprised, but failed at both.

"Yes, I get that a lot," Sister Maris said as she flicked a gold lighter and touched it to the cigarette she pressed to her lips. She took a long drag; the tip lit cherry red, then faded to dark amber. She held in the nicotine for a second before exhaling upward, being careful not to run the white smoke past the officers' faces. "And it's a retreat."

"A retreat?"

"Yes, a retreat, not a convent. Even the workers of the Lord get a little time off every now and then. This is a retreat for my order in north Jersey. We come here for a couple of weeks of R&R and then return to our, shall we say, saintly duties. There's a small pastoral church near the beach for us, and bungalows for lodging, but this isn't a nunnery or convent. It's been here since 1959, surviving storm after storm. Look out the window."

Forge turned to follow Sister Maris's finger.

"It's the most narrow part of the island and we are on both sides of it," she said. "In front of us is the Atlantic Ocean. Behind us, just a block away, is Barnegat Bay.

"My parents vacationed at the Shore before I was born and became fond of Maris Stella and, apparently, the name," Sister Maris continued as she sat down. "They named me after the retreat. Do you know what the name means, detective?"

Sister Maris focused her gaze on Forge as he pulled the spindle oak chair out from the table to sit next to her.

"It's Italian, isn't it? Sort of sea star?" Forge asked.

"You're halfway there. It's actually 'Star of the Sea,' " Sister Maris said.

"May we start?" Forge asked.

"Of course. That is our connection."

Taken aback by the comment, Forge looked at Sister Maris for further explanation. None was volunteered.

"How's that?" Forge asked.

"There is a purpose for everything, detective," Sister Maris said. "There is no such thing as coincidences. Only connections that we have not yet seen, or cannot yet understand."

"I don't follow," Fry interjected. "It happened. It was here. Someone would have found it. It just happened to be you."

"I'm sure at least you really believe that," the sister said as a thin wisp of smoke from the cigarette in her hand drifted toward the ceiling. "We are all connected, in stranger ways than we can understand."

Forge's eyes searched Sister Maris's face for any sign of doubt in her words. He found none, as her eyes seemed to gaze straight through his own. Cops weren't supposed to flinch, but for a fleeting moment, Forge looked past her eyes and down to his notebook.

"When did you discover the barrel?" Forge asked.

"I start my jog from the top of the sand dune each morning and each evening around sunrise and sunset," Sister Maris said, pointing outside the window. "This morning I started at about 5:20. As I made my way down the dune, I saw this black object at the surf line and decided to run past. As I got closer, I saw it was a barrel. It actually looked like a crude oil barrel, so I called the police. The rest you know."

"Did you see anyone else on the beach?"

"No, no one. At that hour, just the seagulls are stirring. There is only one road into the retreat, and that is the road to our chapel. There were no trucks or cars in the lot that I didn't recognize. We would have heard anyone pull up during the night. It is that quiet here."

Forge pondered the scenario. Then he found himself thinking about Paul Revere. *One if by land, two if by sea.* Sand is treacherous to walk on, especially in the dark. It's always slipping around your feet, causing you to lose your balance. He knew that was especially true as he looked out the window and heard a clutch of officers and forensic specialists grunt as they attempted to haul the barrel up the dune and into a waiting police van.

The barrel and its contents weren't especially heavy, maybe 250 pounds, but it took the men two tries to learn how to keep their gloved hands on a wet cylinder in the loose sand.

"Jesus. Jesus H. Christ!" one distant voice on the beach boomed over the roar of the surf. "I'm losing my fuckin' grip!"

"DON'T DROP IT! DON'T DROP IT!" another shouted desperately. "Ah, shit. Get it. It's rolling down hill."

Sister Maris furrowed her brow as she shot a glance of displeasure toward the window facing the beach.

"I'm sorry, Sist ... ," Forge started, unable to finish as Sister Maris swiftly rose to her feet and strode toward the open window.

"YOU! Yes, you!" Sister Maris exclaimed with both hands around her mouth to amplify her message to the closest uniformed officer she could see at the top of the dune. "Please tell those good policemen that this is holy place of worship. We do NOT tolerate the Lord's name being taken in vain. I've had a rough morning, but if I have to, I'll come up there and POUND somebody to get that message across."

Sister Maris calmly returned to her seat at the pinewood table before she detected Forge's and Fry's stunned looks.

"I'm really no good until I get my tea in the morning," she said.

Sister Maris was perplexed by Forge's unblinking, wide-eyed expression. "Please, officer, I really don't have virgin ears. I grew up in Newark, so I've heard my share of expletives."

"I'll be sure to note that," Forge exhaled.

"You didn't see anyone on the beach this morning," Fry asked. He moved to put the interview back on track.

"No, not even last night when I took my evening jog," the sister replied. "I saw an elderly couple walking their dog, but they would not be in any shape to roll a barrel."

"What about boats?" Forge asked. "Did you see any ships close by last night? A pleasure boat or a fishing boat?"

Sister Maris flipped the cigarette pack over in her hands a couple of times. Forge knew that the sister had a shred of a memory embedded in her subconscious. He had to tease it to the surface.

"No," she said. "I don't think so."

"You never saw a boat? Or are you not so sure?"

"Wait, let me reflect," she said as she folded her hands tightly in front of her and closed her eyes. "I don't recall any boat at sunset. I definitely would have remembered one if I saw it, because I would have wondered why it was out so late and how it would get back to dock in the dark. The nearest marina would be in Barnegat Light, which is five miles north and through the inlet."

"Yeah, you don't want to go through the inlet in the dark unless you've got great lights and balls — ah, nerves of steel," Fry said, correcting himself.

"But I do remember something later on," Sister Maris said. Both detectives leaned closer to her.

"After Leno was over, I walked up to the top of the dune to feed Fred," she said.

"Fred? Is that your cat?" Forge asked.

A diminutive smile crossed Sister Maris's face. "No, no. He's a fox, a small red fox," she said. "He's no bigger than a miniature poodle. He sleeps during the day and wanders around the beach at night, looking for bits of trash, small birds, maybe a nest of eggs. He's become our mascot of sorts. I feed him to keep him out of our trash cans, and we've become good buddies."

"How did he get here?" Fry asked.

"It's one of those mysteries," she said. "I don't think he walked over the Causeway Bridge or swam across the water. All I can think of is he wandered across the bay ice last winter from Island Beach State Park to the north. They have a large, natural habitat for foxes, birds, rabbits, everything that used to be here on this island, but aren't anymore. Maybe a few of them crossed together. Maybe he's the last of his kind here. He's still shy, but he has become accustomed to people. We spot him sometimes scratching at our windows, like he wants to come in and watch TV or play cards."

"When you were at the top of the dune, what do you recall seeing, exactly?" Forge asked. "Other than Fred."

"I usually look north and south to see how many house lights are still on. It was far away, but I saw faint green and red lights on the horizon out that way." She motioned with her hand toward the north.

"Bow lights, like those on the front of a boat?" Fry asked.

"Yes, exactly. It's becoming clear now. The lights weren't in front of the retreat though, where the barrel was found. It was maybe two or three blocks further north. It wasn't there for long. I just remember seeing the lights. Then a spotlight came on, like it was scanning for the beach, but it flashed on the houses for a second. In a moment, that single light and its running lights blinked off. Then I heard the roar of engines fade away."

"You didn't hear the boat pull up?" Forge asked.

"No. It was all very quiet until the end. It sounded like the boat was in a hurry to get away, especially in the dark. I don't understand why its lights went out."

Sister Maris quickly stood up and moved to a laminated aerial map of the thin, 18-mile-long island on the wall.

"Here," she said, thumping her finger over the "Harvey" in the words "Harvey Cedars."

"This is where we are now," she said. "As best as I can determine, the boat was parked here. She moved her fingers slightly north. Forge could tell it was about six or seven blocks as she skipped over two of the rock jetties on the map.

"How did you know how far it was from the retreat?" Fry asked.

"I don't. On the ocean, you have no perspective. I can only guess how far away it was by the faintness of the lights and roar of the engines," Sister Maris said.

"What's your best guess as to where the boat was?" Forge asked.

Sister Maris took a long draw on her cigarette and focused on the map before she exhaled.

"Loveladies," she said.

"Loveladies?"

"Yes. It was far enough up the road and I could see some of the lights from the mansions there. You know, where a fixer-upper starts at $3 million."

Forge struggled. If the boat owners were indeed the ones who dropped the barrel and its unfortunate contents into the ocean, why would it have ended up here? Why even drop it in Loveladies in the first place? What's the point of having the container found?

Forge's head started to ache from the smoke of what was now Sister Maris's third cigarette.

"Don't you know those will kill you?" Fry said.

"We all have our vices," she said coolly. "I choose to keep mine in the open. It is so difficult to repress one's sins without it affecting your inner soul."

"What about those of us who don't have a vice?" Fry interjected.

"We all have our demons," the sister said, looking scornfully up and down at Fry. "Our only choice in this world is to acknowledge and accept them or try to ignore them."

"Is this why you say we can't change who we are or what we do?" Forge asked.

"I never said you couldn't change who you are, Detective. All I said is that you cannot help but cross paths with certain others in your life. What you choose to do with that encounter is entirely up to you. That is the essence of being an individual. Your life is what you want to make of it."

Fry subtly motioned with a slight twist of his head that it might be time to leave.

"Here," Sister Maris said, grabbing Forge's left hand and prying it open. "There are many pathways to the soul, Detective. I can see through your eyes that you are troubled, and not just about this case. The palm provides markers to what has happened, and what lies ahead."

"You're gonna read his palm, Sister?" Fry asked. "Isn't that a bit unorthodox for a nun?"

"First, I am a religious sister, not what you think of as a full-fledged nun. I'm sure the distinction is lost on a man of such grand superficiality, but it means a lot to us. We are not secluded like traditional nuns. We are part of the community.

"Second, it's not palm reading in the sense of crystal balls and white turbans, Sergeant Fry. There are many facets to our spirituality, and our physical being sometimes allows us to glimpse the soul," Sister Maris said, returning her gaze to Forge.

Sister Maris adjusted her chair so she could see Forge's palm as he saw it. "Here," she said, and pointed to the long crease from the base of his wrist to the start of his middle finger. "That is your line of destiny, your fate line."

She lightly drew her right index finger along the line, which sent a chill down Forge's neck.

"The first half of the line shows your youth was troubled, almost turbulent. Your self-determination was interrupted by a tragic event. But this had an unanticipated benefit. Your fate line veers away from your life line, here," she said, slightly twisting Forge's hand to show him the curve of another crease that led toward his thumb.

"That means what?" Forge asked.

"That means you knew at a very early age what you wanted to do. Your fate shaped the outcome of your career, but it was your choice that you became a police officer," she said.

"As your fate line entered adulthood here," Sister Maris pointed to the middle of his palm, poking her finger into the dead center, "you felt a need to right a wrong, to avenge the tragedy that befell you in your youth. But you are, you are still looking for the right markers, the right path to take you to the end of your journey."

Forge instantly closed his hand and pulled away.

"What do you know about me, Sister?" Forge said. "Have we met before?"

"I do not think so," Sister Maris responded, as she quietly coaxed his closed hand open again. "I am a sister from Newark here on a holiday retreat. I come here every year and seldom stay for more than two weeks. I don't think we would have met at any of the church ice cream socials." Forge broke a small smile and surrendered his palm again.

"Your lines are very intriguing," she whispered. "Your adult life is — complex. Your lines show that you will be betrayed by one that you trust, and you will suffer another loss."

"Like a marriage?" Forge asked.

"Sadly, no. That is a different part of your palm. I am sorry to see here that your marriage ended quite abruptly," Sister Maris said. "See this line at the far edge of your palm?" She pointed to a faint fold about half an inch below Forge's little finger. "This is your marriage line. It is very short and forks as it spreads into your palm. That means your marriage was brief and was not meant to be. Fortunately you had no children."

"Hey, I thought palm readers were only supposed to give good news," Fry said. "You're not perking up my buddy here."

"Sssh!" Sister Maris said, as if she were scolding a preschooler. "As I said, I am not a tent gypsy clinking finger cymbals and reading fortunes for a few pieces of silver. Looking into a soul is serious and, I am sorry to say, sometimes unpleasant."

Fry looked down as Sister Maris refocused her gaze on Forge's palm.

"There will be another," she said. "You will find another love."

"Finally," Fry muttered. "Are we done? We actually have bad guys to chase down."

"Yes and no," Sister Maris said, folding up Forge's hand and placing it against his chest. "You will find out that you are going to need me more than you think."

"I seriously doubt that," Fry said. "But, what the hell. Since we're doing sideshow entertainment, how about reading my palm? I think we have a few extra minutes."

Sister Maris took Fry's palm with her left hand as she lit another cigarette with the right.

"Well," Fry asked. "What does it say?"

"It says you're an idiot." Sister Maris smirked as she dropped Fry's hand on the table. She plucked the Marlboro out of her mouth to blow the smoke over his head. "If you don't believe, you don't deserve to have your palm read."

"Great. Wonderful. That's just super, Sister. Thanks for the insight," said Fry as he adjusted his shoulder holster and turned to Forge. "Let's hit the Coast Guard. Maybe they'll have a trace on the boat."

"They won't tell you anything," Sister Maris Stella said.

"How is that," Fry said.

"It's a federal facility. They are not going to give you the time of day."

"It's a murder case."

"I'll make a deal with you, Sergeant Fry," Sister Maris said. "I don't much like you, but that's something you can't really help. But Detective Forge, I'll help him. He looks like he needs an angel on his shoulder, at least for a while. When the Coast Guard tells you — please excuse my French — to go pound sand, come right back to me. I'll get the answers that you need."

"With prayer?" Fry smirked.

Sister Maris carelessly flicked the butt of the cigarette with her thumb to discharge the ash to the ground. "This is why you and I are never going to be best friends, Sergeant Fry. You disparage what you cannot see. I believe in what I cannot see. You have to have faith."

"Faith in what?"

"Faith in that I am good friends with the coasties."

The lower edge of Fry's mouth twitched as he let out a grunt of annoyance. "Let's go. The body isn't getting any warmer."

"Thank you, Sister, you've been of assistance," Forge said as they moved toward the door. "The boat sighting was a valuable piece of information."

"Yes," Sister Maris said. "May I ask one question, Detective?"

"Of course," Forge said.

"Will you follow the markers?"

SEVEN

"Matty, Matty." His father's calloused hand tenderly roused the youngster from his deep sleep. It felt like worn cardboard, but the familiar touch brought comfort to the young Forge. "It's time to get ready."

Seven-year-old Matt Forge groggily wiped the sand from his eyes and hastily recalled the special day that would soon be upon him. Even at 4:30 in the morning, his enthusiasm quickly soared beyond the excitement level of a child on Christmas. Forge knew this would top any holiday gifts. This was the day that he would walk in his father's footsteps. He would become more than a child, more than a son of a fisherman. He would become a bayman.

After weeks of badgering, Forge's widowed father had given in to his growing desire to see his son take to the bay to learn the trade of clamming, crabbing, and oystering. He had started Matty slowly in the trade. From the dock of their West Creek home, John Forge showed Matty how to rhythmically knead the giant shinicock rake in the calm shallows of the lagoon.

"Don't tug too hard," the elder Forge quietly told Matty after he struggled to pull the twelve-foot-long rake handle too far and too fast across the bay's sticky bottom. "Gently works better for you and the clams. Just give it a little tug, like you're pulling a kite string. That's it. Tug, tug, tug, tug, then lift. Now you're getting the hang of it."

John Forge had earned his living for the last twenty years on the bay. He had learned the trade from his father, who learned it from his. Great Bay between the mainland and Long Beach Island was a cornucopia of riches for those who plied the waters in the early days of the European settlers.

The shinicock rake was little more than a wide-mesh steel basket with an aluminum T-handle attached to its top. It was an efficient tool for a clammer: dunk the basket into the water, give it a few tugs as you dragged it across the bottom, and then drop the dozen or so clams in the boat. The heavy, black muck quickly washed away as the basket was lifted upward.

Matty had been on his father's boat countless times since birth. His father was fond of telling friends that Matty was born with a rudder in his hand.

The boat was a weatherworn, drab-green, flat-bottomed wooden garvey with a small-bore, 1950 Ford six-cylinder engine mounted mid-boat. At twenty-five feet in length, it gave the senior Forge plenty of room to store his rakes, clam tongs, commercial crab traps, and even a couple of fishing rods to relax with on his days off. It was his office. It was his joy. It was his life.

As Matty and his father climbed aboard the garvey, the dull haze of the sunrise formed just beyond the island. His father's unhurried speed sent lackadaisical ripples across the glass-like bay as the two moved east into the sun.

The mist was heavy this morning, and they fought the chill from the damp air. Sipping hot coffee from a thermos cup, Matty's father held his son close.

"Do you see them, Matty?" his father asked.

"No, Dad. Where are they?"

"They'll be out there. They haven't moved all winter. I don't think they are in the mood to move now," his father chuckled.

Matty stared into the mist for a long time.

"There!" Matty shouted. "It's there!"

In the distance, Matty pointed to a faint, blinking green light of a channel buoy that marked the outer limits of the deeper waterway. It was the main highway for boat traffic, and its markers provided the best way to determine your place in a foggy bay.

"Do you see the next one? Do you see the next marker?"

"No, Dad. Where is it?"

"It's out there. You know these waters. Just imagine drawing a straight line from us to the green buoy. Do you see it, do you see it?"

"No, I don't see it.... Wait, I think I see the red one."

"Yes, Matty you got it. Remember, you will never get lost if you follow the markers."

EIGHT

Fry snapped his fingers in front of Forge's face.

"Hey, watch it," Fry said with annoyance. "You're driving like a tourist in a trance. And it's my car."

"Sorry," Forge said. "I was thinking... about my dad."

The two of them sat silent for a moment, Fry unsure what to say. Forge wondered if he would ever brush away the cobwebs.

"Look, Matt, the sister of Perpetual Attitude got you spooked because she had a pretty good time guessing at who you are. I could have told you everything she said without even thinking about it."

"Yeah, but you know everything about me."

"Look, to anyone who just met you, they can tell right off the bat Sharon left you. You wear it on your face. Hell, you still got a tan line on your finger where your wedding band was. A blind bastard can see that."

"It's not that," Forge said. "How did she know about my dad?"

"She didn't say anything about your dad's death," Fry said. "She said you suffered a tragedy at a young age. YOU filled in the blanks. She used broad words that you could shape any way you wanted. A tragedy to me was I didn't get a GI Joe for Christmas. It's all in how you look at it."

"Maybe."

"Maybe you have to start rewiring your life," Fry said. "You're a fuckin' wreck. You look like shit, you look like you haven't slept in a year. You're the most instinctive detective I know. Your work on the Cranshaw case put the FBI serial killer profilers to shame. You not only know where the needle is in the haystack, you know the color of thread that's in it. And what has it gotten you? You were on your way to the top and you blew it. Now you spend your days pining over a woman who left you and who ain't ever coming back."

Forge tightened his jaw as he started a slow burn. Forge and Fry had never talked about Sharon and the divorce. Even before Forge married, Fry had dropped hints that Sharon was a climber who saw Forge as her ticket to a higher plane. Forge rejected that depiction out of hand. They were in love and he didn't have to explain what that meant to Fry.

"Don't go down that road," Forge said.

"She wasn't any good for you."

"Shut the hell up."

Fry paused.

"Forget her," Fry said. "She has forgotten you."

Forge jammed on the brakes so hard that Fry's shoulder harness strained to keep him from slamming face first into the dash. Forge veered the car onto the sandy shoulder and threw open the driver's door so quickly that Fry thought it would break off of the hinges. He had never seen Forge so explosive.

"Get out. Get the hell out now," Forge yelled as he stood in a police stance behind Fry's door.

Fry unbuckled his seat belt to step out of the car, but kept his eye on Forge. He didn't want to hurt him, but he didn't want to fall victim to a sucker punch, either.

Fry towered over Forge, even at a good arm's length distance.

"You better back off before you get mad," Fry said. "And if you get mad, I'll have to kick your ass. Then I'll feel real guilty in the morning."

In a moment, Fry saw that his comment had disarmed his partner. Forge unclenched his fists and slumped against the rear tire of the car.

"She was everything to me," Forge said softly.

"It was a blind spot," Fry said, putting his arm around Forge. "You see everyone else's clues except the most important ones about yourself. I kept quiet and maybe I shouldn't have. But maybe this is the time that you need to recharge yourself. For the past year, you're life has become a series of small miseries. Turn it around. Make it a series of triumphs."

"You know what hurts the most?" Forge said. He expected no reply. "She said she left because she wanted more. 'More of what?' I asked. She couldn't answer me. She just kept saying that she needed to do more with her life."

"Maybe to her 'more' really meant 'different,'" Fry said. "'More' to her meant she wasn't satisfied with the house in the suburbs, the white picket fence and the green lawn. Her tastes were always, uh, eclectic. Didn't she like collecting things, little porcelain figurines of kids and dogs, the kind you see around the house during the holidays? What did she do with them when she got them home?"

"She liked displaying them, but we ran out of room on the mantel, in the china closets. Then she just started packing them away, collecting items that she wouldn't ever see again. The attic was full of all her mementos from when she was a kid till after we were married." Forge paused, lowering his voice as he looked downward. "Christ, I was just another collectable. She got me, she displayed me and then she packed me away. She got everything — the house, the boat, even my fishing gear. I just left it all there.

"If I wasn't such a selfish bastard, if I didn't get wrapped up in all these damn investigations, I would have been home more often. But I had to put the case first, that's what she always told me. She wanted to be first and I didn't see that."

"Every cop is like that," Fry said. "You got to make the case in the first forty-eight hours or it's lost. She knew that before she married you. She didn't seem to mind when you were gone a week and then got your face splashed over TV after you broke the Gallito hit. You know as well as I do she used that excuse to bail."

"Yeah, but I never told you the best one," said Forge. "As she's kicking me out, she gives me a hug at the door and says to me, 'I still love you.' So I'm thinking she's having second thoughts, that she wants me to stay, that everything will be OK again. My heart was skipping beats. And then... and then the other shoe drops. 'I still love you,' she whispers to me, 'but I'm just not *in* love with you.' Bam. Like the whole marriage was a sham, like she had to force herself through it."

"After Parker, that son-of-a-bitch prosecutor, ran you through the ringer, that's when she started twisting the knife in you," Fry said. "You should have seen how she looked at you after he shipped you back to the island PD; you were like a china doll with a big chip in its face. She was embarrassed to show you off. She had to throw you away. So what is she doing now, huh?"

"She went back to get her MBA."

"Well, ain't that just grand," said Fry. "That's what the world needs more of, another freaking accountant. She'll be getting more of nothing in that kinda job."

Forge offered silence. The frustration had abated, at least for now. Fry hoped that Forge could finally focus his energy on the case, as bizarre as it was.

Both men returned to the car, and a palpable emptiness sat between them for the ten-minute ride north along Long Beach Boulevard to the Coast Guard station at the Barnegat Inlet.

The white building, with its traditional diagonal red stripe of the Coast Guard emblem, dwarfed the fleet of fishing trawlers and yachts docked on the bayside of the inlet. A half-mile away was the 172-foot-tall Barnegat Lighthouse, built in 1859 after the sea claimed the first two. Old Barney was the grand old man of Long Beach Island, a towering icon. Its majestic red-and-white tapered form saved windswept ships for decades, until it fell dark from obsolescence. It was eventually transformed into a tourist hub for the small tip of the state park that occupied the northernmost part of the island.

Forge and Fry chatted amiably about the area with Coast Guard Commander M.A. McGill for a few minutes, but were surprised when he pulled open his bottom desk drawer to pour himself a shot of twelve-year-old scotch.

"Pardon my manners," McGill said. "I should have offered you fine gentlemen a drink, but I know you must be on duty."

"It's 8:30 in the morning," Forge offered.

"We work around the clock here," McGill responded as he poured another double into the shot glass etched with the single-star Arizona flag and the state motto, *Ditat Deus*. "When my palate tells me it's happy hour, I'm not about to argue."

"We told you about the body in the can," Forge said, trying to divert McGill from drinking himself into a coma. "We wanted to see if your station had any intel on boat traffic last night."

"We sure do," McGill said.

Fry and Forge looked at each other. They waited for his offer of assistance, but none was forthcoming.

"Could we look at it?" Forge asked slowly.

"No, sir. No can do," McGill said as he sat down at his desk. "Federal regulations."

"Regulations to impede a murder investigation?" Fry said sharply.

"Now, now, girls," McGill said, his western drawl strengthened by the 90 proof. "There is no reason to get your skirts in a bunch. I don't write the rules. I gots three missions here.

"My job is, one," he held up his right index finger, "to watch over all the little itty-bitty tourist boats so we can pluck Aunt Betsy out of the water when a sailboat boom wacks her in the noggin like a mule kicking in a barn door. Two," the middle finger popped up, "to stop those nasty drug runners from corrupting the youths of tomorrow, and, three" — Forge saw that McGill was having trouble extending his ring finger without bringing the pinkie along with it — "to run interdiction operations.

"Interdict — you know what that word means, right boys? It ain't got nothing to do with your Yankee dicks. It means we got to stop all those American-hating, bomb-carrying, turban-wearing terrorists from blowing up our beautiful beaches."

McGill leaned back in his chair as he propped his feet on a small writing table. "There ain't nothing in my orders that says we got to have a good ol' time helping local cops clean up beach trash."

"Now hold on one goddamn minute, you rat bastard," Fry shouted, jumping to his feet and leaning over McGill's oak desk until he came within inches of his nose. "We got a body, and you don't want to help us because you're too damn lazy to get off your fat ass and punch up a few buttons?"

"Whoa, now. Those are fighting words," McGill chuckled, as he casually cocked his head to one side and placed a thick hand under his chin to apply just enough pressure so his neck bone cracked with the prickly sound of two walnuts crushed together. "No one comes into my station and tells me what to do, let alone call me a fat ass. I'm telling you boys real nice, we can't help you because we got a lot of secrets here that we just can't share with the world."

41

"Or what?"

"Or all those American-hating, bomb-carrying, turban-wearing terrorists will blow up our beautiful beaches," McGill said as Fry silently mouthed the words. "See, now y'er getting the message. Well, I thank you boys for coming in and warming up my Sunday morning, but I gots work to get back to."

With that, McGill spun his leather chair to gaze out his bay window as he savored the sips of his drink.

Outside the station, as Fry paced, Forge offered Plan B.

"Sister Maris said she could help," Forge said.

"No way is a nun going to do my work for me," Fry said. "We can go to county and get a search warrant."

"It's federal. You know state courts have no jurisdiction. Besides, even if we can get to federal court in time, no judge is going to pry the lid off of their anti-terrorism secrets."

"I hate you."

"You're going to hate me a lot more by the time this is over."

NINE

Thirty minutes later, Fry had begrudgingly picked up Sister Maris and deposited her in front of Forge at the Coast Guard station.

The three of them entered the station not through the front door, but by the dock area in the rear. Forge could see that the berth for the forty-four-foot cutter was empty, but the smaller thirty-two- and thirty-six-footers were securely tied to the floating docks and bulkheads. The aluminum-hulled ships were watertight from the command cabin to the engine room, and their diesel generators were powerful enough to blast through gale winds and over hurricane-driven waves. The ships were designed to not only survive the pounding from one-hundred-ton waves, but also for temporary submersions. If a wave slammed into the side and knocked it over like a toy in a bathtub, the boat would automatically rotate 180 degrees underwater and right itself like a rubber duck.

A security guard at the rear gate stopped the two officers at gunpoint. He then saw the smiling face of Sister Maris, and eased on his assault stance.

"Good morning, Sister," the seaman said. "Odd to see you out here today."

"Oh, Jerome, we missed you at mass last week," Sister Maris said. "Were you on duty?"

"Yes, ma'am," Jerome responded. "Twenty-four hours on, twenty-four hours off. I hope to get to church next Saturday afternoon."

"Well, don't be a stranger," she said. "Where might I find Wilson?"

"He's inside at the command center," Jerome said, eyeing her two companions. "Would you like me to buzz you in?"

"If that wouldn't be a bother," Sister Maris said. She gave a quick wink to the guard. "These are two of my good friends."

Forge was stunned. Was she flirting with the guard? And, he had to admit, she did have a way of flowing around obstacles. Who was going to suspect a nun of being an American-hating, bomb-carrying terrorist?

"My pleasure," Jerome said as he held up his hand to give the secure signal to the control officer behind the blast-proof window inside the building. "Any plans tonight, Sister?"

"Just a date with the Lord, Jerome," she said casually.

The steel security fence snapped open with a buzz and Sister Maris walked in as if she had strolled through a dozen times before. The two detectives quickly followed her in as the gate clicked shut.

"Wilson, how have you and your lovely wife been?" Sister Maris said as she took the hand of the beefy young man and squeezed it warmly. "Any babies yet?"

"Not yet, Sister," the officer-of-the-day said. "But we're hoping any day now."

"Well, let's hope it's not immaculate," Sister Maris said. "We want you to be the father. We all miss you up in Newark."

"I'll get back there one of these days," he said. "My tour is up next year and I'm not sure if I'll leave or re-up."

"I know you'll make the right decision," she said. "Your mother always said you had a good head on your shoulders."

"Thank you, Sister," Wilson said, as he noticed Forge and Fry in the background. "What can I do for you today?"

"Well, honestly, my friends here are from the Long Beach Island Police Department and they are in search of some kind help from the men in uniform," she said looking over at the two detectives. "Your commander was much too busy to assist them. They are in such a hurry to solve a rather unpleasant misdeed."

"Ah, professional courtesy," Wilson said with a nod of understanding. "I suppose I could help them out for an old friend. What can we offer you?"

"You once told me about something called Hifsaw? Do you still run that?"

"You mean HFSWR? You found the man. I monitor the unit from here."

"What's HFSWR?" Fry asked.

"Oh, please excuse my manners," Sister Maris said. "Wilson, this here is officer

Fried."

Fry loudly cleared his throat. "It's Fry. F-r-y. Not Fried. That's what they do to chickens."

"Of course, how absent-minded of me," Sister Maris said. "Officer Fried here and Detective Forge are trying to see if a boat was in the vicinity of our humble retreat last night. Do you think your little gizmo would be able to help?"

Wilson walked to the floor's control panel, which was studded with fewer dials and buttons than Forge thought there would be. Rather than looking like the bridge of the starship *Enterprise*, the gleaming metal and video screens were more akin to a home video entertainment system.

Looking at the top of the panel, Forge read out, "High Frequency Surface Wave Radar," which was stamped on the center pane.

"It's a very fascinating piece of equipment," Sister Maris told Forge.

"This here is your state-of-the-art ship-and-wave detection system," Wilson said. "We set up a series of antennae all along the East Coast. There we can get real-time intel on ship traffic, and spot any giant waves that may be generated from earthquakes or subterranean volcanic eruptions. Here, let me show you."

The high-resolution color screen showed the outline of Long Beach Island as a small, wispy string in the far left corner. The markings indicated that the radar was scanning one-hundred miles east, into the Atlantic Ocean and well beyond the range of ordinary surface radar.

"You see, regular radar stops at the horizon, about three miles offshore," Wilson said as he thumped the glass with his index finger at the first marker line on the screen, "as the microwaves scoot on out into space. HFSWR works by hugging the surface. It literally crawls over the water like a bug and sends back exact images of what is out there."

"OK," Forge said. "That's good for us, isn't it? We can trace where a boat came and went?"

"Let's give it a shot. What time do you want to look at?"

"Right after sundown yesterday."

"That'll be about 8:30 or so." Wilson tapped a few keys on the console that pulled up a monthly calendar. With a couple of clicks of the mouse, he accessed the radar archives for the last 18 hours and slowly scrolled to dusk.

The screen was filled with red, blue, and green dots that looked like the aftermath of a child's marble game.

"You're seeing a snapshot of all the traffic in the area last night — small crafts are blue circles, low-flying airplanes are green triangles, and unknown targets are in red."

"There are a lot of red dots," Forge said.

"That's not unusual, especially this time of year. It's civilian traffic, and we have no reason to suspect them of illicit activity if they come out of our ports. The system is smart enough to follow a slow-moving craft and determine where it came from and where it is going. This one here" — he zoomed in closer — "is a commercial trawler coming back from the Bahamas. It's Captain Sorensen, a good friend to the commander."

"Can you pull in closer to shore?"

"Sure. How about five miles."

"Closer. Say one mile."

The sliver of Long Beach Island expanded past the limits of the screen: The northern part of the island filled the left side, with the expansive ocean to the right. On it Forge saw myriad red dots.

"This is at sunset. Here, watch what happens when I speed up the time frame."

Wilson dialed up the time-elapse meter so that minutes flew by in seconds. The dots started a waltz of sorts, dancing around in circles before most headed north. By the time the clock had hit 9:30, only the overnight party boats remained, all anchored and showing a slight wobble south in the drift of the current.

The clock ran past 10 and then 11, and Forge saw no signs of activity. A small private plane zipped across the screen as a green triangle, its transponder code flashing, and then it was gone.

"Here we go, a new day. We're passing midnight now," Wilson said.

"Hold it," Forge said. He saw a red blip zip across the top of the screen and disappear. "Back up and zoom out."

Wilson took the monitor back to 12:30 and pulled the image back slightly to show a two-mile radius rather than one mile. "Here, I'll run it again slower."

At about quarter to 1, they all saw the small red dot emerge from the Barnegat Inlet at the top of the screen and motor to about the one-mile mark.

"It's too small to be a midnight party boat, you know, the one that takes fifty or sixty people out for night fishing. But the driver seems to know what he is doing. The tide was running out, so he hooked further out to sea to avoid any of the shoals near the island."

"What's happening here?" Fry asked, pointing to the dot.

"He looks like he stopped, maybe getting his bearings. It's not the smartest thing to run in these waters at night, but yesterday was calm and with GPS the captain can easily find where he is."

"Or where he wants to go," Forge said.

The dot quickly scurried in a straight line to the shore off Loveladies, taking about three minutes to come within inches of the shoreline, at least on the screen.

"He really opened it up," Wilson said, scrubbing his chin with his free hand. "It looks like once he got his bearings he knew where he wanted to go. Look here."

Wilson zoomed in to about a five-hundred-foot radius. The dot had stopped about two hundred feet east of the rock jetties.

Just as Wilson finished his analysis, the red dot headed back north at a rapid rate and turned to go into the inlet. The time: about 2:10 a.m.

"Quick nighttime jaunt," Forge said. "Can you trace were they went after they entered the inlet?"

"No can do, sir. The HFSWR only covers the ocean surface. We are only interested in folks coming in from other waters, not going out."

"Wait," Sister Maris said, pointing to the screen. "What's that?"

A small red dot flashed on and then off and then on again near the spot where the unidentified boat had stopped.

"That would be a bogie," Wilson said. "It's an unknown, too, but it's not a boat. It's acting like a wave."

Wilson switched modes and the screen changed from a dull blue to a rippling bright green. The monitor no longer showed boats but the rolling waves.

"I think that would be our man in a can," Fry said. "It's bobbing up and down like a fishing line."

"Let me speed it up," Wilson said. As he clicked the clock to compress the time, the sporadic dot came and went as it quickly drifted south along the shore. At about 4 a.m. it disappeared completely from the screen.

"That's the limit of the radar," Wilson said. We can't see anything closer than twenty feet to shore. But you get the idea."

"Very well done, Wil," Sister Maris said as she kissed the top of the seaman's head. "You are going to go far in this outfit."

"Glad to be of help," Wilson pulled Sister Maris closer as he eyed the two detectives. "And if you can keep this between us and not tell the old man, I would be grateful."

"My lips are sealed," Sister Maris said as she looked up at the towering Fry. "And so are yours, aren't they officers?"

"Of course," Forge said.

As they left the building, Sister Maris sprinted in front of Fry and stopped to hold her chin up. The oversized Fry being stopped by the petite sister looked comical to Forge.

"As much as this is un-Christian like, I just can't resist," Sister Maris told Fry with a cheerful lilt in her voice as she stood on the tips of her toes in a vain effort to meet Fry's eyes. "You should learn to listen to me."

Fry made sure that he took the driver's seat for the ride south. With his foot pressed to the accelerator and flashing his high beams at anyone in the left lane, Fry hit sixty-five mph on the thirty-five mph roadway. In less than five minutes, Fry skidded to a stop on the sandy path outside the cobblestone walls of the Sisters of Mercy retreat.

"End of the line, Sister," Fry said. "Pardon me if I don't walk you to the door."

"I am quite sure I don't know what you mean," Sister Maris said as she calmly leaned forward from the backseat and placed her folded arms over the empty space on the blue vinyl bench in front of her.

"Please excuse me if I didn't make myself clear," Fry said as he jammed the gearshift into Park and turned to face her. "Pull up on the handle and exit, ma'am. Please."

"C'mon, Fry, be nice to the sister. She did help us out with the coasties," Forge said. "Here, let me walk you back to the dining hall."

"I would much prefer to stay with you," Sister Maris said, leaning over the front seat to grind the stubble of her cigarette in the dash ashtray. "It is, after all my vacation, and I would enjoy a tour of this beautiful area with one of the island's finest officers. Not having a car, I don't really get out much — vow of poverty and all that. I'd like to think of it as Ocean County on zero dollars a day."

"You mean Ocean County's underbelly on zero dollars a day," Forge said. "Nothing here, and I mean nothing, is what it seems. Beneath the sand, suntan oil, pretty girls, and BMWs is the darkest side of humanity you will ever see."

"That," Sister Maris said, "is exactly what I do want to see."

"Please, Sister, this is a murder investigation, not a bus tour," Fry said. "We ain't going to be taking you to the zoo. We have a lot of work to do and we can't have Sally Fields following us around all day thinking this is the *Sound of Music*."

"Now, that really hurts my feelings," Sister Maris said. "Everyone knows Sally Fields was *The Flying Nun*. Nothing about that show was real, except the habits."

"I don't want to have to remove you, but if you insist," Fry said as he unbuckled his seatbelt and motioned toward his door.

"I want to help you and you've seen how I can help in the most unusual ways," Sister Maris said to Forge, unfazed by Fry's movement. "I promise not to get in the way. And if you have to go *Mannix* on someone — see, Fry, you're not the only one who watches retro '60s reruns — I swear to look the other way."

Sister Maris made an elongated "X" over the red heart icon on her tourist tee shirt. "Cross my heart."

"No way, no way, no way," Fry said as he pounded on the steering wheel with an open palm. "No way."

Sister Maris folded her hands tightly, closed her eyes and silently moved her lips.

"What now?" Fry said. "Are you saying a freakin' prayer for divine intervention?"

After a second, Sister Maris, slowly opened her eyes and saw that Fry's right temple vein was throbbing hard. She thought the officer might succumb to a stroke at any moment.

She gradually closed her eyes again, and in a low but audible voice directed toward Fry, uttered a singular plea: "Please, dear Lord, just this one day, give me the power to suffer fools."

TEN

The "man in a can" had been delivered to the county morgue by the police van ninety minutes ahead of the two officers.

"Who do you think is in it?" Forge said as they pulled up to the hospital.

"I'm dying to find out," Fry said. "If he hasn't been dead too long we may be able to get a good set of fingerprints off the body, or even a good facial shot to match to missing people."

"Who's on call today?"

"Oh, as the Lord is my witness, I'm praying it's Dr. Ammerman."

"That would be a real treat for you," Forge said.

"Who's this Dr. Ammerman," said the small voice from the backseat.

"Just about the best pathologist in the state," Forge said. "I've worked with the doctor many times in the past. But Fry is president of the fan club."

"Sister, I thought we agreed that you would stay in the back and be quiet," Fry said.

"No, that was your promise to me," Sister Maris said. "You specifically said, 'You're not going to say nothing, right?' and I said, 'Yes, if you insist, I won't say nothing.' That's a double negative, Sergeant Fry. That means I'm now compelled by my promise to say anything that comes to mind."

Fry slapped his forehead hard. "Do you think we are in Sunday school? We're not fu... freaking kids. You have got to listen to us or we're going to drop you at the nearest Salvation Army outpost."

"Sergeant, what is your first name again?" Sister Maris asked.

"Fry. It's just Fry."

"Now, now. Not your surname, but your Christian name. Everyone has a Christian name, even you."

Fry mumbled softly.

"I didn't quiet catch that," Sister Maris said.

"I said, Duroc."

"Duroc?"

"Yes. It's an old family name. I just don't use it anymore."

Sister Maris took another long drag on the Marlboro and slowly exhaled out the rear window that she had cranked down an inch for that purpose. "Duroc... Duroc... Duroc... If memory serves me right, isn't that the breed of a certain animal?"

"Not really."

"Oh, you are too modest. It's a very special breed of, what kind of animal is it, Sergeant? Oh, yes. Isn't it a... pig?"

"It's a boar."

"Yes, yes. A red boar. I do remember reading that somewhere. It's a very meaty sort of animal. You should be very proud of your name. Did your family develop the breed?"

"Yes, from upstate New York in the nineteenth century. Can you just call me Fry?"

"A boar named Fry," Sister Maris mused. "That is quite... different. You must be a big hit at luaus."

Fry said, "When you're not at the retreat, are you in charge of church torture or something? What do you do when you're not reading palms? Whack kids on the knuckles with rulers?"

"Jokes about the sisters will not be tolerated," Sister Maris said, "unless they are amusing. As a rule, ruler jokes are as old as this rusted vehicle you call a car. And I'm not a teacher. I'm a psychologist."

"You're joking. A psychologist?"

"I've made mincemeat of you all day just for sport," Sister Maris said. "I know it's like fighting an armless boxer, but I've got to make the best with what I have. I do special counseling for the troubled and the ill at our Sisters of Mercy hospital. I have seen many of the devil's incarnations over the years, so do not dismiss me as some genteel little nun. I can hold my own with the best of them. That's why you need me here. I want to find out as much as you why our pristine retreat was desecrated by a horrible murder."

ELEVEN

Fry parked outside one of the least-obtrusive government buildings, Ardmore Hospital. The largest medical facility in the area, its entire basement level was actually a morgue. Here a team of coroners processed the two thousand or so un-attended deaths each year to determine if the dearly departed had been shuffled off this mortal coil with a little extra push.

Fry punched the down button on the staff elevator and entered the security code for L4, four levels below street grade. It was the lowest point in the entire county.

The doors opened onto a sterile-looking, lime-colored hallway. Sister Maris made the sign of the cross and said a small prayer for the departed souls that would soon come before her.

Forge could never get used to the odor. For a holiday weekend, the body count seemed low. There were only two motor-vehicle-accident victims resting on stain-less steel autopsy tables in the far corner. From what Forge could tell, the bodies belonged to a man and a woman, both in their seventies, perhaps husband and wife. They likely entered traffic too soon, causing an all-too-common T-bone collision with an SUV or another tank-like vehicle.

The room smelled like a mixture of human fluids and isopropyl alcohol, the kind of tang that instantly set your nerves on edge and triggered your basic fight-or-flight instinct, although you really didn't know why. Forge felt his pulse race slightly and his nostrils flare as a small bit of adrenaline pumped into his blood.

"Where's the package?" Fry asked, looking toward a rotund attendant busily using his two thumbs to tap an e-mail message into his BlackBerry. The atten-dant's long hair hid the tiny ear buds plugged into the iPod in his blue shirt pocket.

The attendant, who didn't notice Fry, kept on typing. Fry crossed the room in three strides.

Fry slammed the palm of his brawny hand as hard as he could on the top of the metal desk. The "*WHAMP*" sound was loud enough that it made Forge and Sister Maris jump. Startled, the attendant leapt out of his chair, sending his BlackBerry across the room.

"Jeez, you could have given me a heart attack," the attendant exclaimed.

"You would be in the right place then," Fry said, lifting the attendant's name badge with one finger. "And I have to tell you this now, Ralphie; regardless how many shades of blue you turn, I ain't gonna give you mouth-to-mouth."

Fry pulled his face as close as he could to the recovering attendant, who was starting to break into a cold sweat.

"Where's my barrel?" Fry asked.

"You mean the guy in the can?" Ralph said.

"Yeah, the can man. How many drums with dead guys do you get in here every day?"

Ralph looked as if he was starting to entertain the notion.

"It ain't a question, chubby," Fry said. He enunciated each word slowly and firmly. "My buddy and I had to get up real early this morning and we haven't had our danish and coffee yet. It's hot outside, my car doesn't have air conditioning, and I'm now stuck here talking to you when I would be better off asking Betty Boop on that slab over there how her day was. So, needless to say, we're in a really pissy mood and we want to get this show on the road."

"OK, OK," Ralph stammered. "I thought you guys might be here for something else. The other guys got here before you."

"What other guys?" Forge asked slowly.

"You know, county. The detectives from County. They got here about fifteen minutes ago and took custody of the barrel. The delivery van dropped the barrel off, I signed it in, and the two guys came and signed the chain of evidence, so now it's their barrel."

Forge and Fry were momentarily stunned, which gave Ralph a small amount of satisfaction.

"What are their names?" Fry asked through gritted teeth.

Ralph flipped hurriedly through the clipboard on his desk. "Ah, Jack something, y'know, from county homicide. Real neat dresser. Here it is. Jack Dewall and his partner, George Steers, detectives first class, Ocean County Prosecutor's Office."

"Where are they now?"

"They're in Ammerman's office. The first assistant prosecutor asked me to set up an immediate autopsy," Ralph said, licking the tiny droplets of sweat that had started to bead on his upper lip. "You know how Scratch hates to have a body sitting in the locker too long."

"Shit," Fry said.

Sister Maris loudly cleared her throat.

"Sorry, Sister," Fry said. "But I'm trying to get in touch with my inner Mannix."

Forge looked at Fry's distressed face as the two pondered the next move.

"We knew County was going to come in on this sooner or later," Forge said. "They are going to have to prosecute the case in the end. It's standard procedure; they have to be in the loop."

"Yeah, but not this early. I was hoping at least to get a look in the can before we got those two hacks crawling up our ass. Especially pretty-boy Jack."

"I'm the last person who's going to vouch for Jack," Forge whispered. "But they are here, there isn't much we can do to get rid of them, and we are going to have to grin and bear it until I can get in to see the first assistant tomorrow morning."

Forge alluded to Hendrick "Scratch" Hudson, a career prosecutor who had steadfastly built his reputation for the last ten years. He had gone toe-to-toe with some of the best sharks from New York City, the kind who had clients that didn't mind paying $800 an hour to a lawyer to walk in the door with a hot cup of double mocha hazelnut blend in one hand and a briefcase full of motions in the other.

Hudson used his charisma, which had won over scores of jurors, to maneuver himself to become the *de facto* head of the one-hundred-member prosecutor's team.

The only man above him was Randolph Parker, the chief prosecutor and a political appointee. The courthouse joke was that Parker's best asset was his brother-in-law, a state senator who happened to be good friends with the governor.

"Where's the can?" Forge said to Ralph.

"It's in the forensics lab," Ralph stammered. "We're waiting for one of the tech guys to get here to laser it."

"Let's go see it," Forge said. "I think I'm starting to get attached to the thing."

Ralph, sweating profusely, led them through two oversized swinging stainless-steel doors into another hallway, this one tinted yellow with well-worn wheel marks along the pathway. After a few paces, Ralph turned left, fumbled for his key ring, and unbolted the padlock on a door that Forge could only guess was an oversized meat locker.

The inside of the room looked more like a warehouse with twelve-foot high ceilings and racks of metal bunks lined row upon row for about fifty feet. Forge felt a strange twinge that ran a chill up the back of his neck; at first glance the bunks, three high, looked as if they had a couple of dozen adults sleeping in them. In another setting, it could have been mistaken for army recruits resting after a long hike, with drab green sheets pulled over their heads. But they weren't recruits, and the sheets weren't sheets. The bunks were filled with occupied body bags, the nametags of the departed affixed on the tag of the zipper and to a D-ring at the foot of each bag.

The room was kept at a constant forty-two degrees and ten percent humidity. It was enough to drastically slow decomposition, but not enough to make bodies too frozen to autopsy.

In the middle of the floor, about five paces from the locker door stood the black barrel, wrapped in clear, heavy plastic and sealed with yellow evidence tape.

"It looks bigger here," Fry said, kneeling at the foot of the drum as he peered through the plastic. He pushed the oversized baggie toward the barrel to try to get a closer look at the metal.

Forge ran the flat of his palm along the topside of the barrel until he felt what he was looking for. The rough grooves in a patch of metal about the size of a wallet made it apparent that someone had taken pains to cover his tracks. The serial number, as Forge had suspected at Oceanside, had been filed off. The long streaks indicated the job was done in a hurry with a long metal file.

As the two became engrossed in examining the barrel, Ralph quietly left the room and then ran to Dr. Ammerman's office, where the two county detectives were waiting.

Inside, Dewall sat on the plush leather couch reading a year-old copy of *Forensic Magazine*. He had thumbed through the technical articles and focused on one of the glossy advertisements for a product that promised guaranteed detection of gunshot residue. Steers was a bit more restless; he had gravitated to the far corner of the room where a full-size human skeleton hung, propped up by a steel rod that emanated from a wood base and ran along the spine.

"Do you think this is real?" Steers asked more of the skeleton than Dewall.

"Of course it's real," Dewall said. "Christ, we're in a body chop-shop. That's all the spare parts they couldn't fit back in."

Ralph pulled open the door, rattling the window's mini-blinds.

"They're here," Ralph sputtered. "They're down with the barrel."

"You asshole," Dewall said. "I told you no one was to go near that barrel."

Dewall jumped to his feet, brushed off his gray suit jacket, and straightened the tight knot of his lavender silk tie.

"OK," he said to Steers. "Let's go clean this up."

The three walked a brisk pace to the cold storage room. Dewall thrust open the door with the intention of startling Forge and Fry. The partners turned slowly away from the barrel and locked stares with Dewall and the trailing Steers.

"What the hell are you guys doing here?" Dewall said, as if he were a high school principal catching two freshmen smoking in the boys' locker room. "Shouldn't you be out writing parking tickets?"

"That's real tough talk from my favorite metrosexual, jack-ass," Fry said. "I'm surprised you could take time away from shopping for your Brooks Brothers suits. Just keep this in mind: You ain't our boss. This is our case. You assholes are not going to step all over it."

"Let's see, when was the last murder case you had on the island," Dewall said.

"Oh, yeah. Never."

"Tough talk from a pansy. Forge dug your ass out of so many cases when he was in county that I'm surprised you can still find it."

Dewall changed his focus to Forge, who had moved to the front of the barrel in a protective stance.

"Oh, I didn't see you there, Matt," Dewall said, as he smoothed the protruding fold over his monogrammed pocket-handkerchief. "How have you been?" He waited for a response, but Matt wasn't about to bite. "We miss you at county."

Forge narrowed his eyes and moved toward Dewall, but Fry beat him to the mark.

With both hands, Fry picked Dewall off the floor by the lapels of his suit and slammed him with such force against the wall that a couple of nearby bodies shook. Within a second Fry had his forearm squeezed against Dewall's windpipe. Dewall started to turn purple as his dangling feet desperately reached for solid ground.

Steers instinctively whipped his right hand around his back to feel for the butt of the service pistol under his blazer. In the split second that it took for Steers to unclip the leather safety from the heel of the weapon, Forge tackled him to the ground.

"Now, that's not playing fair," Forge grunted as he yanked Steers's hand away from his back. Steers had more than a sixty-pound advantage over Forge and, after a couple of pushes, flipped Forge halfway off his body.

Fry dropped Dewall on the ground like a sandbag to grab Steers by the collar. He dragged him to his feet, flipped him around like a doll, and disarmed him in a single motion.

Dewall, still on his knees, coughed a couple of times to clear his nearly crushed throat. Out of the corner of his eye, Fry saw that the crippled detective was no threat and refocused on Steers, who now had terror in his eyes.

"Were you going to pull a piece on me, asshole?" Fry yelled as he shook Steers. "No one — do you hear me — no one pulls a piece on me."

As Steers's collar began to tear from the stress of his massive weight and the torque from Fry's ham hocks, both men were suddenly engulfed in an icy, white mist. Fry coughed violently, dropping Steers to the ground. Fry found himself both disoriented and feeling as if he had walked into the arctic.

"Chill," a woman's voice calmly echoed through the hallway. "No one trashes my lab."

All four detectives froze in their tracks as they gazed at the petite woman striding toward them. In her hands was a full-size, bright red CO_2 fire extinguisher with wisps of white smoke dissipating from its black discharge nozzle.

She dropped the spent canister to the tiled floor with a hollow clatter, giving it no more thought than if she had discarded a tissue.

"What the hell are you guys doing?" she said. "I prefer my detectives to be alive and the victims to be dead. At least until quitting time."

Dr. Ammerman stood waiting for a response in her crisp white lab coat, her title and name smartly stitched into her left breast pocket. Her large, round electric-blue glasses and tightly pulled-back blonde hair gave her face a cherubic look.

"Hello, Lulu," Fry started, as he dusted the last bit of evaporating permafrost from his shirt. The other detectives softly chimed in with sheepish greetings.

"Who's the guest?" Ammerman said, pointing to Sister Maris, who stood silent against the wall, her hands folded.

"A witness," Forge said. "Sister Maris, this is Dr. Ammerman."

"A nun?" Dr. Ammerman said, eyeing the small cross on the sister's tee shirt. "It's not like we get a lot of requests for last rites down here."

"I almost thought I would have to arrange them for a couple of the detectives," Sister Maris said. "Is it always this — unusual?"

"Only when the testosterone mixes," Ammerman said.

Lulu Ammerman was a rarity among medical examiners. Her youth and diminutive stature gave her a schoolgirl appearance. But as a Harvard medical school graduate, she was one of the brightest minds among forensic pathologists on the eastern seaboard.

"What exactly do we have here, guys?" she said to the four detectives. "And why are you fighting over it?"

Dewall spoke first. "It's our case and it's our floater."

"It's an odd-shaped body," Ammerman said, looking at the container.

"The guy is inside the can," Fry said. "LBI PD found him. That makes us the primaries on the case."

"Enough," Ammerman said as the four men moved from the cold room into the warmth of the hallway. "I don't want to hear another word out of you guys unless it's, 'Yes, Lulu, I'll do what you say, Lulu. Can I get you a cup of coffee, Lulu?'"

At that moment, Ammerman heard the security lock on the main hallway door softly unlatch and the entranceway swing toward them. At the end of the hall, Navdeep "Kevin" Singh walked in wearing a sunflower-bright tee shirt, Bermuda shorts, and — Forge had to check twice — leather sandals. Singh pulled a wheeled tote behind him that made him look more like a tourist on the way to the airport than a forensic fingerprint expert. The only thing missing was a Hawaiian lei.

55

"Hey, y'all," Singh said to no one in particular as he continued to chew a wad of mint-flavored gum. "Where's the thingamajig?"

Forge pointed into the locker and Singh, who could have been no more than twenty-five, walked into the chilled room without missing a stride.

"I'm guessing this little ol' barrel here is my job for today," Singh said, looking back over his shoulder at the group for confirmation. Ammerman gave a short nod. "Okee-dokey then."

Singh unsnapped the bungee cord holding an assortment of black boxes onto the tote, and lined the boxes up to his side, one by one. He popped open the nearest one, which looked like a fishing tackle box, and flipped out a hardware-store razor knife, clicking the blade out as he moved toward the plastic.

"Who's going to take notes?" he asked, his blade stopping inches before the plastic. "Huh?"

"I guess I will," Steers said, slowly pulling out a pocket pad.

"Alright, you are the man today," Singh said, giving a thumbs up. He was relieved that he would have one less task to do this Sunday. With any luck, he could finish his job in an hour and be back on the beach catching the next wave on his red-and-gold, tri-finned surfboard.

He pinched back the heavy plastic around the can and sliced into it with the blade. The top lifted off with a rustle and he casually tossed it to the side. Singh then slit the remaining plastic around the can from top to bottom, so it would lay at the base as a drop sheet.

"OK, chief," Singh told Steers. "Write this down: Object is an apparent fifty-five-gallon drum, black in color, no apparent rust or other markings. Object was retrieved — don't write this — where was it found, guys?"

"Harvey Cedars, in front of the Sisters of Mercy retreat," Forge said.

"Cool. Awesome surfing action there, and I like the symbolism," Singh said, and then turned to Steers. "OK, write down what he just said, but without my two cents."

Singh eyed Sister Maris in the background and suspiciously looked her up and down. "Who do we have here? She looks like a...."

"A nun?" Sister Maris teased. "Yes, I get a lot of that. But I'm really a religious sister."

Singh nodded his head. "Okee-dokey then. A newbie. I'm fly with that."

Singh continued to slowly move around the can in a circular motion, his face about a foot away from the metal. "Signs of minor dents and pitting, apparently from the jetty and its soft landing on the beach. Top appears solid and fixed, no hinges, yet signs of a fresh weld. Physical exam done, proceeding to laser."

He briefly scanned the outside again, and shook his head. "No way are there any prints on this. It's been too wet too long. But never say never. Let's just make sure."

Singh popped off the lid of a cold-cream-size jar and stuck a wide-tip camel hairbrush into the dusty contents. The brush picked up ultra-fine particles of fluorescent red magnetic powder, one of the basic tools of the fingerprint trade for decades. Working from memory, Singh lightly dusted gray powder around the lid, an area he suspected might have had a latent print.

He removed the laser unit from one of the black boxes. Handing red goggles to all except Ralph, Singh screwed a flexible tube into the power pack and uncapped the flat tip of the wand. He sent the argon laser to 525 nanometers.

"Sorry, dude, outta goggles for you," Singh said to Ralph. "You're going to have to leave. I don't want you to go blind, at least not from this."

Ralph shrugged and left the room to return to his BlackBerry.

"OK, hit it," Singh said.

Ammerman clicked off the lights and Singh pushed the trigger of the laser, which shot an intense emerald glow against the barrel.

"Gotta love green. This here is the Luke Skywalker light saber of forensics," Singh said. "The high-intensity argon laser light can be focused and clicked to different wavelengths to bring out even the most latent prints that we can't see by ordinary light alone."

Singh squinted at the splotch for a minute, focusing the laser on its center, and then moved clockwise around it until he was on the outside fringe. "Wow, that's really interesting," he said.

"What is?" Dewall asked.

"There is nothing here," Singh said, still focusing his attention on the beam. "Like I thought, it's a big old smudge."

"Great," Dewall lamented. "What do we do now?"

"Gee, I don't know. How about a can opener?" Forge said. "All the evidence is inside the can, unless you hadn't thought about it."

The task was easier said than done. The barrel lid was thick enough to hold its contents securely but not thin enough to pry open with a screwdriver.

Ammerman held the X-rays to the ceiling lights that she had just turned on.

"The victim's head is about six inches from the top of the can," she said. "It looks like he is in a comfortable fetal position, so we can saw the top of the barrel right off and pop him out."

After running upstairs to the hospital floor, Fry returned with a maintenance worker holding a gasoline-powered diamond saw used to cut concrete.

"I really don't want to be here," the worker, Willie, said, looking around at the stacked array of bodies.

"You'll be out of here in no time," Fry said, grabbing him by the shoulder and leading him to the barrel. "Think of this here as a giant soup can and you as the can opener. We want you to cut along the outer ridge as close as you can to the top. Can you do that?"

"It shouldn't be a problem," Willie said, placing cone-shaped protectors into his ears. "Stand back. This may get noisy."

With a sharp jerk on the starter cord, the saw roared to life. He gunned the finger trigger on the engine three to four times to make sure the saw was up to speed.

Willie touched the tip of the blade to the top of the can. Hot flecks of metal shot across the morgue. The room glowed orange for about thirty seconds, and then the fiery display ended as suddenly as it had begun.

"All done," Willie said, reaching out with a gloved hand to pop off the top that was now hanging onto the barrel by a slim metal hinge. "What's inside?"

"Hey, thanks for coming," Fry said, grabbing Willie by the arm and leading him away from the object. "I'll let your supervisor know what a team player you are."

"That'll be real nice of you," Willie said. "Let me give you his name. He's... "

Fry slammed the door and turned back to the barrel.

Singh and the four detectives struggled to lift the barrel onto an oversized hand-truck, then gingerly wheeled it to Ammerman's main examination room.

Ammerman motioned to Fry, Dewall and Steers to the far corner of the room to retrieve a body hoist, used for easy movement of the deceased from a coroner's gurney to the tabletop.

She held Forge by the arm as the others walked away.

"I'm sorry you're not with county anymore," she started. "It was a real pleasure working with you on cases. What happened, really?"

"I zigged when I should have zagged," Forge said.

"Don't be so cryptic," Ammerman said, touching Forge's forearm gently. "I heard you pissed off the wrong person."

"The wrong person for the right reason," Forge said.

"So why exactly did you get busted down?" Ammerman asked, trying to get at the root of her original question.

"Let's just say I made an impolite comment."

"Don't tease me."

Forge was about to start another artful dodge when the threesome loudly wheeled the hoist over to the barrel. Together, all four men moved the barrel onto the canvas straps and slowly actuated the lift until the barrel tilted at a forty-five-degree angle, the nearly sawed-off top pointing upward.

They raised the barrel so that its base was parallel with the rim of the stainless-steel examination table. Ammerman then took control of the device, gently moving the can until its dark opening was just a foot over the counter. With a sharp twist of her hands, she pushed up on the bottom of the barrel. With sound of a truckload of wet fish being dumped on the side of a dock, the body slid onto the table.

A full minute passed before anyone could utter a sentence.

"What the hell," Forge said.

"Where in the hell is more like it," Ammerman said. "Where in the hell is his face?"

TWELVE

The afternoon sun stung Tolck's eyes.

He had stepped out of the back of his heavily tinted, stretch gold limo fifteen minutes late. Tolck had to tend to his business, even on a Sunday afternoon, but this was a part of the business that he had grown weary of long ago. Nevertheless, he accepted the dog-and-pony show as a necessary part of the job.

"Ladies and gentlemen, thank you all for coming today," the mayor of Tucker Township began. His voice boomed from loudspeakers as he spoke to a group of two dozen investors, buyers, and the curious seated before him. "It is my great honor today to be here with one of our community's upstanding businessmen, a man of great talent and undying loyalty to the building industry, Dominick Tolck. Let's hear it for Mr. Tolck."

Mayor Everett Preston began to clap loudly, and the audience joined in with a brief, polite round of applause. Preston pulled Tolck to the stage and pressed a pair of oversized scissors into his hand as the two stood before a large ribbon with the words "The Woods" emblazoned across the front.

"Folks, thank you all for coming today," Tolck started, reciting a version of a speech he had given countless times before. "We are here in the beautiful New Jersey Pine Barrens today because of the elegance that surrounds us. I'm proud to say that with this development, 'The Woods of Tucker', many families and children will now be able to enjoy the beauty of the pine forest up close. Today marks the groundbreaking of 'The Woods', a sixty-unit, fifty-acre planned single-family development close to the Jersey Shore and only minutes to the Parkway for easy commuting.

"These designer homes by my company, D & C Builders, will make 'The Woods of Tucker" the premier residential spot in this county. We have built many developments, but none like this. There will be nature trails into the surrounding woods, and a goal of preserving as much as a fifth of all the trees on the development lots. This will truly be a community of the woods for 'The Woods'." The audience clapped politely as the mayor and Tolck shook hands and together cut the opening-day ribbon. Tolck and Preston posed momentarily as a photographer from the local weekly newspaper shot off a series of pictures.

"Please, if you are interested in pre-purchasing an estate here, see one of my sales associates to the side." Tolck motioned to two of his bar's strippers, who had donned business suits and tamped down their make-up for the event to look more like working mothers than working girls. "We are accepting ten-percent deposits today, certified check or cash, with another twenty percent when building starts."

Tolck quickly did the math in his head, as he had done countless times before. Each house was listed for between $500,000 and $700,000. He expected two-thirds of the lots to be sold today, and the remaining third by the end of the month. At $50,000 to $70,000 per down payment, that would give him an easy $2 million. He would use just a tenth to hire subcontractors to plow under the trees and install drainage, streets, and lighting.

After work got underway, he would use the next $200,000 to start building houses. As he closed on each deal, part of the money would be put into the next phase of the development. The rest would go into his pocket. By the end of the year he was looking at an easy profit of $25 million to $30 million. And by the end of the year, "The Woods" would have no woods left in it.

Not bad, he thought, for a few women and $5,000 in bribes.

Tolck was building in the most restricted area of the state, virgin Pine Barrens, on top of the largest reserve of fresh water on the eastern seaboard.

In the distance, a small set of eyes from a nearby tree cautiously scanned the scene. Fearful of the unknown, it moved slowly away.

The small Pine Barrens tree frog instinctively sensed a new danger to its homeland.

A quilt of old-growth forests, tannic-colored streams, hamlets, iron bogs, and forgotten colonial towns, the Pine Barrens — named for the swath of needled evergreen trees ubiquitous to the sandy loams of the area — had long been the bane of developers. A recognized preserve in the heart of South Jersey, the Pinelands was twice the size of Rhode Island and took up nearly a quarter of all the land in New Jersey. Its 1.1 million acres, spread over seven counties, encompassed an amazing ecosystem unlike any other in the world.

Yet the birth of this preserve proved difficult. In the 1970s, as casino gambling was poised to reshape the desolation of Atlantic City's once grand hotels, developers saw the pine forests as the suburbs for the next Las Vegas. Although the decade's sluggish economy killed these initial plans, the growing environmentalist movement had developed enough clout to attract the attention of state politicians. Their basic argument was simple: The Pinelands sit over more than 17 trillion gallons of some of the purest water in the world. If potable water became scarce in the future, wouldn't it make sense to save this area as a way to ensure the survival of the state? As a unique habitat, the Pine Barrens needed to be preserved as much as Yellowstone, the Everglades and the Alaskan wilderness.

The delicate nature of the emerald green tree frog had made it the icon of the Pinelands and the heart of the preservationists' argument. At about one to two inches long, the tree frog could sit quite comfortably in your hand, if you are fortunate enough to find one willing to leave its perch. Despite its evolution over the millennia, the tree frog was an exceptionally fragile creature. Even in the small confines of a shallow rain puddle no bigger than the average car, the tree frog could face a daily struggle for survival: The slightest change in the acid level of the water — either too much or too little — would doom the amphibian.

Even tree frogs located miles from the nearest house could find itself awash in diluted, but still deadly, chemical fertilizers that would eat away at the delicate covering of its skin.

Landowners saw it differently. They had invested millions into the Pine Barrens, and now the state wanted to keep them from profiting from it? Maybe in communist Russia the state could take land away from private owners, but this was America. This was New Jersey. This is the not the way to do business.

With two-thirds of the land privately owned, the state faced a thorny task of passing a state law that would protect the ecological balance of the region but not destroy the rights of landowners.

The Pinelands Protection Act was the compromise. Landowners could keep their land, but would be severely restricted in development. The core area of the Pinelands, about 300,000 acres, would be off limits. The fringe areas, which encompassed many small towns, would be limited in growth.

But wiggle room was left in the law. Since there was no outright ban on development, a commission was set up to interpret the legislation. As time went on, politicians began to feel the heat from developers. Campaign contributions from homebuilders outstripped those from environmentalists a hundred to one. And the public began to lose interest.

Well-connected law firms, usually employing a political powerhouse or two, evolved to work around the commission and the law. Moderate and then pro-development politicians slowly replaced staunch protectionists who sat on the Pine-lands Commission. Funding was cut, staffing reduced. The commission became a paper tiger.

Still, the commission had the legal obligation to go through the motions of holding hearings on building projects. The pressure became so intense for new developments in the bucolic Pine Barrens that some commissioners got the idea that they could get rich off their votes.

Tolck was more than happy to oblige. During one uneventful preliminary caucus hearing to discuss water drainage with a few of the commissioners, Tolck began to probe. He looked for signs of weakness in one or two who could be convinced that greater rewards awaited them in this life rather than the next.

He set his sights on the chairman. An Army quartermaster who took an early retirement at age fifty, the chairman was frustrated in his professional and personal life. His wife had left him years earlier, tired of the constant traveling and reassignments as her military husband sank deeper into drink. A jovial backslapper by nature, Colonel Jesse Grant had a knack for ingratiating himself with his superiors, only to have a scathing falling out later over an issue as minor as forgetting to order a shipment of brass buttons.

Grant turned his talent for gab into politics. Out of boredom from retirement, he had joined former Governor Baylock's re-election effort as a local fundraiser. His first foray into the grip-and-grin parties of the ward's elite proved so lucrative for the party that he was soon promoted to regional fundraiser.

Here he quickly learned the political trait of trading. In between embellishing Army stories and backslapping donors as if they were long-lost buddies, Grant found that businessmen wanted something in return for as little as a $500 campaign contribution.

"Can I meet the governor?"

"Will I be invited to the Governor's Ball?"

"I want to talk to the governor about a project of mine."

The demands all sounded the same after a while. But Grant found the more he said yes, the more money he could extract from them. And the more money the party would kick back to him as a "finder's fee."

With a little coaching from the top fundraisers in the party, Grant developed his own silky way to woo a wavering donor.

"I've known this governor for many, many years," Grant would lie. "The governor is a man of his word, and a man who appreciates his friends. If you can find your way to stand side-by-side with him in his re-election effort, I know he will find a way to repay your loyalty."

Grant had his set fees: $1,000 would get you a telephone call from an aide;

$10,000 would entitle you to one meeting with a cabinet-level official in the department of your choice; $40,000 would get you in the room with the governor, usually with other donors vying for his undivided attention; and a $100,000 check to the party, with a separate $5,000 cash payment to Grant for his facilitator duties, would get you just about anything you wanted.

Tolck had met Grant once at a $37,000-a-plate party fundraiser years earlier, and briefly recalled talking to him about coastal development. Now was the time to test the waters again.

As the caucus hearing broke up, Tolck reintroduced himself to Grant and slowly pressed for a sign that he could be bought.

"I hope you remember me," Tolck said. "We met a few years back at the governor's support dinner."

"Of course, of course," Grant said, offering a flattering rebuttal. "You were a good friend to the governor and that makes me your good friend — unless you start supporting the other side." They both laughed.

"Well, I have a small project coming down the road that I would deeply respect your input on," Tolck said. He locked on Grant's eyes for any twitch, any dart to the side that would signal nervousness. He saw none.

"Mr. Tolck, it wouldn't be proper for me to talk to an applicant before he files the paperwork," Grant said. Like Tolck, Grant probed the man's eyes for any sign of retreat.

"No, I respect that," Tolck said softly. "I don't think I will be building in your neck of the woods, so to speak. I have a project that is very complicated and would benefit immensely from a different perspective. I have lawyers, I have engineers, but I don't have any outside people who would look at this from a political view."

Tolck felt they had clicked.

"Ah, you would like me to look at this as a consultant, no strings attached?" Grant asked. His eyes were now focused on the whole of Tolck's emotionless expression. Good poker face, Grant said to himself.

"Of course, no strings attached. It would be between you and me, no government filings that let anyone know you are doing a favor for an old friend," Tolck said. "Of course, you would be compensated for your time and travel. I wouldn't want you to go out of your way." His long-awaited sign of acknowledgment came in an almost unperceivable nod from Grant.

"I hope you are free tonight," Tolck said. "I run a tavern not far from here and we can talk quietly in my office." Another nod from Grant. "And there are some ladies I think you would enjoy meeting."

THIRTEEN

The silence inside the lab was deafening.

"It's gone," Forge said finally. "His face is burned off."

There, on the cold stainless steel of the autopsy table, the remains of what was once a man lay curled, clad in a sweat-stained, green short-sleeve shirt, blue jeans, and brown leather boat shoes.

The man, about 180 pounds with a middle-age spread evident around his waist, showed deep black charring that had bubbled the flesh into an unrecognizable mass of goop. The lips, nose, cheeks and forehead were burnt down to the bones. The black mass appeared to be uniform throughout the man's face, but as Ammerman peered closer, she noticed that the skin in some areas had been totally vaporized and the bone cracked from the intense heat.

"Look at this," Fry said, pointing to the man's hands. "The fingertips, they've been burnt off, too."

Ammerman glanced south of the face, not surprised that the fingerprints had been destroyed.

Taking a small metal probe from the top drawer of the table, Ammerman gently tugged at the black remains around the mouth. With each prod, the rock hard flesh crinkled as if someone were slowly crushing a piece of burnt toast.

"Look at this," she said, motioning to the detectives to pull in closer. "It looks like... "

In the back of the room, sudden dry heaves could be heard. Ammerman looked up to see Steers vomiting into a nearby sink with Sister Maris gently comforting him as she stroked his back. Steers deposited much of his breakfast onto his jacket before running out of the room.

"What's his deal?" Singh said to Dewall. "Is he one of yours?"

Dewall sighed. "Public relations. He's on loan from PR. He did five years in local school safety and then got onto county. I don't think he's ever seen a body."

"As I was saying," Ammerman said. "Look here, in his mouth. He doesn't have any teeth. Or more precisely, his teeth were broken out."

Ammerman focused the high-intensity overhead light directly into the now-empty cavity to show her impromptu class the jagged remains of the man's dental work.

"Someone went to great lengths to erase his identity. No fingerprints, no teeth, no face," she said.

"So why dump him on the beach where anyone could find him?" Fry asked. "It makes no sense."

"Nothing about this case is making sense," Forge said. "We only have the first piece of a very large puzzle."

"OK, from here on in, no one touch the body," Ammerman said. "There could be trace evidence we can use to help find out who this guy is."

"What's this?" Forge asked. He pointed to the foot of the corpse.

"That isn't from the body," Ammerman said. "It's not organic."

Singh placed his nose over the half-dollar size dollop of tan goop and sniffed. He jerked his head up in a gag reflex.

"Smells like alcohol, but stronger," he said.

"Yeah," Forge said. "It smells like the inside of my high school biology lab."

"Or a funeral home," Ammerman said. "My guess is it's some variation of formaldehyde. It's a preservative for bodies."

"So they tried to pickle this guy?" Fry asked.

"Doesn't seem like it," Ammerman said. "I didn't notice any formaldehyde in him. Once it is in you, it doesn't come out. It shouldn't be in the barrel."

Forge snapped on a pair of rubber gloves and tipped the open end of the barrel into the light so he could get a better look inside.

"There's a little bit inside at the bottom, and apparently some along the sides of the can," he said, his voice echoing inside the barrel. "It may explain what the barrel is. It had to be something before John Doe here was tossed in. It must have been filled with formaldehyde, emptied, and filled again, this time with a half-baked man."

"But that still doesn't answer the original question," Fry said. "Who is he?"

"Leave that to me," Ammerman said. "Everyone back up."

At the start of any autopsy Ammerman demanded silence. Her best tool was not the saw, scalpel, or rib spreader, but her eyes.

Ammerman started at the foot of the corpse, leaning down to examine the extremity from every angle. She pulled a rectangular magnifying glass from her other coat pocket and flicked on its lighted rim. Painstakingly for the next 20 minutes, she worked inch by inch around the body, searching for clues that were not yet apparent to her.

As she worked up the left arm, she stopped and hovered.

"Kev, look here." She motioned to the forensic technical. "See the red spot?"

"Yeah, yeah. It could be," he said.

"Could be what?" Sister Maris asked, trying to look over their shoulders.

"A mark, or fingerprint," Ammerman said. "It's tough on bodies. Unless it's a real fresh corpse, the fingerprint could get lost in the decomposition process."

"You mean to tell me you can pull a print off of a body?" Dewall asked. "How can you do that? There's nothing smooth for the print to lay on."

"*Au contraire, mon Capitan,*" Singh said. "Some parts of the skin are extremely smooth, like the neck and underarms. You're basically looking for areas with little to no hair."

"It may not have been a good idea to put this guy on ice," Ammerman said. "The condensation may have wrecked the print."

"I still think it's doable," Singh said. "How long would you say he's been dead?"

"Less than fifteen hours, give or take."

"If the print was made around the time of his death — and I think it was — that would be good for us," Singh said. "Once a fingertip touches the body, the body's oils and glands go to work trying to erase it. The guy starts to sweat, he rubs it, he puts a shirt on. That chews up the evidence. But with a dead guy, all that stops. The amino acids and sugars in the fingerprint sit there like they are on vacation. Deep down, on a crazy chemical level, it's almost like his body wants to tell us who the killer is. It's just up to us to be smart enough to find it."

"Sure, but how do you do it?" Fry asked.

"We glue him," Singh responded.

"Glue him?" Sister Maris asked.

"Yeah, cyanoacrylates, y'know, what you regular folks call Super Glue. We use it to freeze prints, to make them rock hard so we can pull better images off of objects. It's an acrylic, like nail polish."

"You just dunk him in a vat of Super Glue?"

"Not exactly. We expose him to a fine mist of cyano vapors. As the vapors cool, they grab onto anything sticking up off the skin, even if it's a millionth of an inch."

The technician turned back to his portable lab on wheels and popped open the largest box on his dolly. Inside he carefully unfolded a thin plastic tent that was threaded with an elastic band around its bottom. Fry at first thought it looked like a hairnet for a giant. Attached to one side was a short plastic hose about an inch thick. It simply dangled from the bag as if it were ready to be blown into.

On the side of the largest box lay a bundle of thin metal rods. Like a prodigy child building the skeleton frame of a dinosaur, Singh quickly attached the rods at their tips, and sprung the contraption so that its six legs were positioned around the body but not touching it.

Singh handed the corners of one end to Forge and Fry, then gently tugged the plastic taut. Together, they carefully pulled the tent over the metal frame so that it hung just inches above the highest point of the body. With a yank of the elastic string, Singh closed the bag around the edge of the steel table. It didn't have to be airtight, just tight enough to contain the fumes.

From another compartment of his box, Singh extracted what looked like a coffee cup warming plate, a bottle, and a small black box with a tiny fan covered by a mesh screen.

The technician screwed the end of the hose on the tent into the box, and plugged the unit into an outlet under the table. He flicked on the red power switch to test if the fan was running properly. After a few seconds, Forge could see the limp plastic of the tent slowly puff with life.

"Ready to see the magic?" Singh said.

He twisted off the top of the bottle of liquid cyanoacrylate, quickly filled a small reservoir at the top of the warming plate, and shut the cover. On the blower, he flicked another switch that said "Heat." Within seconds, a small mist of white smoke poured from the tube into the tent.

Forge watched as the acrylic fog moved across every spot of the twisted corpse. The smoke soon covered the entire body, making it nearly invisible to the observers. Singh, who was timing the smoking on his watch, flicked off the heat switch. The white smoke vanished, revealing a body covered in a microscopically thin — and eerie — layer of white crystals.

"Awesome," Singh said to no one in particular. "You just never get used to seeing this. Super Glue is amazing. It's activated by water, so whenever it hits a fingerprint, it locks on to the little bugger. Now comes the easy part."

Like pulling a sheet off of a bed, Singh yanked the tent off in one motion and tossed the spent plastic into the trash can. Everyone in the room winced as the acrid remnants of the fumes stung their eyes.

Singh returned to his bag of tricks to pull out a jar of black magnetic powder and a large feather duster.

"You're going to clean house?" Fry asked. "What happened to your fingerprint brushes?"

"Don't need them, *Kemosabe*," Singh said. "Standard procedure is to use very little powder so you can see the print clearly. The camel-hair brushes add a bit too much powder, so the feather duster is the next best think. It adds only the powder that you need to see the results. It's really amazing how many household accessories we use in this business."

Singh and Ammerman focused their attention back on the corpse and the left arm. Singh could immediately see that the red mark was a print of some sort, and dabbed a bit of gray powder around it. The print instantly stood out, but seemed blurred.

Singh used Ammerman's magnifying glass then grunted a soft *"Damn."*

"It's smudged," he said. "I don't think it's usable. Maybe one or two points, but not enough for a computer match."

Forge leaned over and grabbed Singh's arm.

"Hey, hands off, unless you buy me a drink first," the technician said.

"No, no," Forge said. "I'm trying to see what happened to our mystery guest. Here, stand up."

Forge again grabbed Singh from behind by the arm. His fingers locked on to the short sleeves of Singh's shirt, but Forge found the grip less than sturdy. The fibers would allow the victim to wriggle too much. It also didn't match the marks left on the skin of the dead guy.

"Here, let me try again," Forge said, as he pushed his hands under Singh's shirt to directly grab the flesh. "Ah, much better. A nice positive lock on the victim."

"We still don't have a good print off of him," Singh said.

"Yes, but that's on the top of your arm. Look on the underside."

Singh lifted his sleeve to see the red marks that Forge's grip had left on his arm. He could see the pressure points of three fingers clearly on his bicep. As he lifted his arm higher, he saw the deeper imprint of the thumb.

"Yeah. Let's pull his arm up now," Singh said to Ammerman.

Ammerman obliged, but the effort was easier said than done. Rigor mortis had set in. Carefully placing one hand on the victim's waist and the other on the wrist, the pathologist grunted as she bent and cracked the stiffened arm so that it came to rest above the man's faceless head. Sister Maris grimaced at the sound, and turned to look at the wall, floor tiles, anything to get her mind off of the sight in front of her.

The tension Ammerman felt helped her to confirm his initial time of death — fifteen hours ago, as she looked at the wall clock.

Ammerman used a fresh scalpel to carefully cut a vertical slit from the bottom of the sleeve to the top of the shoulder to expose the smooth underside of the man's arm. There, as Forge had guessed, was a perfectly formed thumbprint.

Singh dabbed his powder on it, shot the area with his high resolution, 12-megapixel forensic SLR camera, and then pulled the print off using a square inch of transparent tape. He quickly affixed the print onto a white index card, that he marked "John Doe, latent print one, inside upper left arm, July 2."

He held the card up to the light and squinted to ensure there were no wrinkles in the tape that would distort the image. The ends of his mouth curled into a bright, Cheshire-cat grin.

"It's a keeper," he said.

FOURTEEN

Tolck was a fisherman and the women in his bar were the bait.

He found it childishly easy to tempt those in power. Many had been in office for a decade or more, and they had long since lost their ideological zeal for the job. They did their jobs for little to no pay, worked long hours, and, as an unwelcome bonus, had to frequently face ugly crowds that didn't take kindly to tax hikes and building booms.

Tolck offered the corruptible a slice of the pie. A very small slice. If you wanted a girl, he had plenty for you to choose. If you wanted money, there was plenty of that, too. But he knew that he could never allow himself to make his quarry wealthy. He could dangle the glory of wealth before their eyes, let them smell it, maybe even taste it, but he could never let them have it. It was too easy for one guy to blow all the money at once, buy himself a big power boat or a supercharged Ferrari. That would attract the attention of the FBI. Then the money would lead straight back to him. No, it was best to plead poverty, to keep the bribes in the modest thousands. Maybe enough to help with the mortgage payments, and pay the hookers, bookies, or cocaine dealer. But it could never be enough to make the mark independent of Tolck. It would be like a lowly chess pawn toppling the king. It just wouldn't ever be part of the game plan.

Since the early days in the 1970s, Tolck had a penchant for eateries. The money was easy, but it was a high-volume business with many risks. Despite his growing sphere of influence in North Jersey, the marketplace was becoming too crowded and too competitive. Even self-styled wise guys had to watch their backs for the young turks who wanted to take a shot at the brass ring.

Then there was the recession, which frustrated Tolck to no end. Creditors turned off the tap as interest rates hit double digits. Fast-food chains siphoned away customers and cut into his bottom line. Even on a routine restaurant bust out, the owner was so in debt that no matter how hard Tolck squeezed he just couldn't find enough money to make his efforts worthwhile.

In his late twenties, Tolck felt like an aging has-been. He knew he needed to expand into a new area, but the choices were slim. He didn't have the network or firepower to traffic in narcotics. Even if he started small, he risked rubbing the New York families the wrong way and ending up in the next batch of dog food. To do it right, he would have to pay a larger tribute to the Gambino family, which would make him feel small, a worse fate than death. Prostitution was always a safe bet, at least it was for his old man. Two or three hookers could fly below the radar and bring in more than two thousand a week. The trick was to find hookers who weren't too coked up, hotel bellhops with an eye for upscale clients, and johns who didn't like to rough up the talent too much.

The pressure was unrelenting. The booze and women took his mind off of his mounting troubles for only fleeting moments. Isabella was his favorite. He could ramble on about his business and not worry that she would learn too much, or talk to others. She spoke in halting, broken English and understood little of Tolck's North Jersey accent.

Isabella had cheerfully entered the country as a wide-eyed Greek exchange student. Impregnated at seventeen by the father of the household that had given her shelter, her rigid Orthodox Catholic family in a small village outside of Athens had disowned her. The host father quietly paid her a thousand dollars for her to leave the household before her slim belly began to show signs of her lost virginity. Alone and nearly broke, she had found respite in a homeless shelter in the remnants of the downtown Elizabeth business district.

She had met Tolck one cold December morning as he drove to the shelter to find cheap labor. He often needed low-cost laborers willing to work for a few bucks a day and a bottle of Jack. The younger men were still strong enough to lift a crate of lettuce or mop a floor, but their brains were toasted enough not to complain.

The women Tolck saw at the shelter were senile wanderers, alcoholics, or spent heroin users selling their bodies for five bucks a trick. Isabella caught his eye immediately. Her long dark hair was remarkably unmatted and ran to the middle of her back. I've never seen that, Tolck thought. Every woman here usually sells her hair to the wig makers within a week. A woman's hair was her identity, her last vestige of self in a selfish world. A young woman's body, her self-respect, would go within days — hell, sometimes hours — for the next fix. But the hair was different. It was the last connection to the real world. It was the fine line between a fairy tale life every little girl dreams of, and an endless nightmare.

As she turned in her seat to see the new face, Isabella was struck by the man's uncomfortable stare. She had felt his eyes on her body before she turned, and instinctively wanted to see who was looking at her.

She immediately knew he was not a new guest. The shiny, new black Dodge truck that was visible through the plate glass window was totally out of place in this bombed-out section of town. The man was dressed in a heavy tan overcoat that ran to his knees, and a long tan woolen scarf. He smiled and ran his fingers through his thick mane of black hair. Isabella smiled meekly, looked down, and turned away. In the old country, it was not a woman's place to flirt so openly. She felt a gentle tap on her shoulder. Tolck towered over her.

"Hello," Tolck said in a genuinely soft voice. "My name is Dom."

"My name... Isabella," she said in her heavy Greek accent, looking back down at the floor.

"Do you understand English?" Tolck asked.

"Little."

"Do you know how to waitress?"

"Excuse?"

"Serve food." Tolck made a gesture of a waiter carrying a tray, which brought a slight smile to both of them.

"Ah, serve... food. Like a... how you say, McDonald's?"

Tolck caught a short laugh in his throat, trying to make it sound as if it were a hesitant cough.

"Yes, like McDonald's, but this is at a real restaurant. People sit down, you ask what they want, and you bring them food."

"Oh, like waiter?"

"Yes, just like a waiter."

"No. I never waiter."

"Would you want a job doing that?" Tolck asked.

Isabella translated the word job in her head and thought for a moment. It meant money, food, and perhaps shelter. If he was offering work, she could learn how to do it. Could he see that she was pregnant? Not with her coat on and sitting down. She would have to close the deal without getting up.

"You pay money?" she asked.

"Of course."

"How much?"

Another laugh from Tolck. "My, you are an astute businesswoman," Tolck said, a series of words that did not register with Isabella. "Broke, in this shelter, surrounded by drunks, and you still want to bargain? I gotta give it to you kid, you know how to drive a deal. We are going to get along just fine."

"You give job?" Isabella picked up the direction of his comments.

"Yes, of course. When would the young lady be available to start?" Tolck said with another chuckle, as onlookers began to listen in on the conversation.

Isabella gave a quizzical look, only able to pick up "start" from the sentence.

"We start now?" she said.

"Deal." He extended his hand to help her up. As she rose he noticed her pronounced belly of five months.

"Whoa, I hired one of you, not two," Tolck said, backing up a half a step.

"Deal is deal," Isabella said defiantly, crossing her arms. If she had learned one thing in America, it was that the best defense was an offense. Never let them see you sweat, she recalled one of the students in her American high school saying.

Tolck thought about the woman for a second. She was radiant and beautiful

71

even in a pregnant state. He could make due.

"OK, OK. You can work at the restaurant, but we'll have to take care of that baby," Tolck said. Isabella wasn't sure at first what he meant, and then it struck her like a bolt of lightening.

"No! No abortionist!" she yelled, stomping her foot. She had heard the repeated pleas for an abortion from the man who had impregnated her, which she found horrifying.

Tolck was taken aback by the outburst. He could just walk away, but the fire in her was refreshing. He felt the two of them had clicked in just a few minutes. He could deal with this. And the baby.

"No, no abortionist," Tolck said, lowering his voice and scanning the people around him as his steely eyes silently told them to turn around. "We" — he pointed his thick index finger first at himself and then at Isabella — "we take care of the baby."

Tolck had kept his promise. He had given her a job as a waitress at one of his Greek restaurants, where the customers loved the spirited country charm of Isabella. When her due date came, Tolck paid for the baby girl's delivery and set the two up in an apartment above the eatery. The six units were hardly high society, but it did attract one Italian family with three children. In exchange for a few dollars and a plate of leftover Greek sweets each night, the Italian mother was eager to watch Isabella's little girl when Isabella was working two flights downstairs.

She had seen Tolck as her savior, a man of charm and generosity who had plucked the teenager away from a life of impoverishment. She had slept with him before the baby was born as a way to cement their arrangement, but became more attached to him as he brought the newborn gifts. He enjoyed making the girl giggle as he hoisted her over his head with mock swinging sounds.

Tolck had unexpectedly grown close to Isabella and the child over the months. They were the only bright spot in his rapidly collapsing world. She wasn't the only woman in his life, but she was the anchor. Her life was the life that Tolck wanted — a child, a family, a home, a real job. In his youth he called guys like that suckers, the ones who fell smack into the middle-class death race and didn't even know it. Marriage, work, kids, college, retirement, burial. That was the six-step program he didn't want to buy into.

But he sensed death would arrive early for him.

His chest pains were becoming more frequent, and lasted longer. The heartburn killed him, even if he hadn't eaten all day. He tried to cut out the booze, but the pains wouldn't stop. Some were so crushing at times that he had to lock himself in the bathroom and run the water so no one in back office of the restaurant could hear him weep from the agony, hear him cry out from the weakness.

At Isabella's behest, Tolck made his first appointment to see a doctor. Bloodsuckers, every last one of them, he thought. They'll poke, prod, stick needles in you, and drain your wallet, all at the same time. He didn't want to go, but the pain had to end.

"Angina," the cardiologist bluntly told him as the nurse ripped the taped electrocardiogram tags off his chest.

"What the fuck is that?" Tolck said disaffectedly.

"It's your heart saying it's time to take it easy," the doctor said, not looking up from the long ECG readout tape in his hand. "You have hardening of the arteries and you're not even thirty yet. Your heart is working extra hard to pump the blood through smaller and smaller openings in your blood vessels. When the pressure gets too high, your body tells you to quit it. The pain is a message."

"So what the hell are you going to do about it?"

The doctor was bothered by the tone of the question. He had treated a number of patients in denial; mostly fat people who said all they ate were salads. He had the criers, he had blank stares, and he had the happy guys who were relieved they didn't need a transplant. But he never had a patient with so much pent-up anger. No wonder Tolck had the heart of a fifty-year-old.

"I can give you medicine. I can even give you more tests and talk about the pros and cons of surgery. But the first step is yours. You have to ask yourself, what the hell are YOU going to do about this. Because, my friend, if you keep up the way you are going, you won't see thirty-five or maybe even thirty."

The doctor looked smugly at Tolck. His blunt assessment was the best he had ever given and he felt that he had gotten through to his thickheaded patient.

Tolck stared at the doctor through sallow eyes.

"Fuck you," he said. "Just give me the pills and get me the hell out of here."

As he left the office, Tolck stopped halfway out of the cardiologist's door and turned. He had felt like a chump in the waiting room with all the blue-haired seniors, some making awful clicking sounds as they sucked down oxygen through tiny green tubes strapped around their noses. During the forty-five-minute wait, he had thumbed through a dozen magazines, from *Ladies Home Journal* to *Time*. He had started to read an older *National Geographic* issue when he was called in. For the forty-five dollar fee, he felt he was owed a lot more. He snatched the *Geo* from the hands of a stunned eighty-year-old woman and left in a huff.

FIFTEEN

Tolck had little time for hobbies. The doctor had recommended that he try to relax, try to get away from the stress. The constant pressure was taking its toll on him, the doctor said. You are your own worst enemy. Maybe he was right, Tolck said. He could feel the pains grow harsher the longer he worked and the harder he tried to squeeze money out of the stones he was busting out. Goddamn economy. Nothing works in this country anymore. The biggest damn crooks are the politicians. They make the rules, they steal from you, but they call it taxes instead. One bastard gets voted out and the next one is just as bad; maybe even worse. A smirk crossed his face. *It's a beautiful racket,* he thought. There is no limit to the cut you can take off the top.

On a typical workday, Tolck would spend between nineteen and twenty hours on the run. He would start at about ten in the morning, with three eggs fried in the hot grease from a half-pound of butcher-cut bacon and topped with generous portions of Grande mozzarella cheese. Burnt toast smothered with heaps of butter, along with black coffee and a shot of J&B scotch, would round out his breakfast of champions. Another shot of scotch would wash down the first set of pills that the doctor now had him taking twice a day.

The blood thinner was the worst. A friend had told him that the Warfarin was really rat poison in small doses. "They gave up using it on rats and now they are using it on you," his friend jabbed.

Tolck didn't think it was funny. Rat poison. That would be the last time he told anyone what he was taking. The drug also cramped his management style. The blood thinner left him susceptible to easy bruising, so his days of beating the crap out of reluctant owners and deadbeat vendors was over. He still had his crew, but he suspected they thought he was going soft on them. Tolck took to carrying a black jack to knock ideas of a hostile takeover out of anyone's head.

After breakfast, Tolck would rally his crew and start making the rounds. They had more than a dozen restaurants from which to skim. Tolck's standing order for the owners was to put the nightly receipts in the backroom safe. He had caught one owner making a night drop on half of the money at a bank. Tolck kicked the guy so hard that his eyes were swollen shut for three days.

As Tolck stuffed the money from the first restaurant into black gym bags, his crew pooled the wait staff's order list and compared it to the cash register receipts. Tolck ensured that the business was cash only by slapping "No credit cards" signs on the front of each window and over each register. That cut out about ten percent of the eatery's business, but Tolck saw it as a necessary loss. After the credit card companies took their three percent off the top, it wasn't in Tolck's best interest to leave a paper trail for the tax collectors and cops to follow if someone decided to rat his operation out. So far he had been lucky, feeding the local watch commander with $100 a week and all the free food he could stuff in his red, fat face. The captain would give him the heads up about wayward owners who mistakenly thought the police would be on their side.

A few slashed tires, smashed windows, maybe a dead rat nailed to the back door sent a message to every owner. It meant Dom had ears everywhere. He knew everything and everyone.

The operation had now become more of a paper chase than the adrenaline-pumping fun it had been in the early days. His crew had to become accountants of sorts, ferreting through all the receipts and paper tapes from the cash registers. After the nightly skim, the boys would reset the register and ring through phony charges to look like the eatery took in less than it actually had. It was long, tiring work, especially for the owners who still had crank-operated cash boxes.

By midnight, the crew was ready to hit the bars, down the drinks, do a few lines of coke and hit on whatever women happened across their paths. They would stay on past bar closing, making small talk with each other, the bar owner, anyone who wanted to be seen with wise guys. An occasional fight would end with the crew piling on the poor son-of-a-bitch who was too drunk to notice whom he had insulted.

Tolck grew weary of the routine. His downtime involved backroom poker games where the buy-in was $1,000 and no one left until only one guy had all the chips. It was a game his old man had taught him well. Before he was into puberty, Tolck learned how to watch for the minute facial ticks that too many card players didn't know they had, let alone control. A flick of the eyebrow, a tap of a finger, or a widening of the pupils told Tolck more about a man's hand than the cards themselves.

Tolck could read men better than a preacher could read the gospel. His best tools were his eyes. He would stare at a man as he walked into range to see what his eyes did. Did they dart from side to side? Did they lock on Tolck's eyes as if he were about to engage in a battle to the death? Did he seem oblivious to the people around him? Each man had his hidden pressure points that Tolck would find and exploit.

Angelo had been Tolck's driver for more than five years, sometimes sleeping in the car while Tolck visited a girlfriend or reinforced a delicate business point to a prospective partner. Angelo's poker network extended to three states and Las Vegas. If there was a high-stakes game, Angelo was sure to tell Tolck about it. Tolck seldom had time to travel out of town, but after the bad news from the cardiologist, Tolck saw an out-of-town game as a way to relax a bit.

Angelo had hooked him up with a cop, a boat captain, three land developers, and a state senator in a backroom game at the old Traymore Hotel on the boardwalk in Atlantic City. The buy-in was $10,000, modest by Tolck's standards, but enough to take the edge off of a Sunday afternoon.

As Angelo drove Tolck south in his black Cadillac, Tolck pulled the tattered National Geographic from his overcoat and flipped it open to the center pages.

"You ever hear of Pitcairn Island?" Tolck said from the back seat to Angelo. "Pitcar-whosit?"

"Pitcairn Island. It's an island in the Pacific."

"What's the Pacific?"

"You are a dumb ass," Tolck said, flicking the back of Angelo's head. "It's only the biggest fucking ocean on the planet."

"Oh, that Pacific," Angelo said. "There's an island in it?"

Tolck slapped his hands on the rear leather seats. "You should have stayed in school, but you wouldn't have learned anything anyway. Do you even know how to read?"

"Yeah, I know how to read. I know Franklin is on a C note and I know what fuckin' exit to get off so you can bang your broads."

"This is like talking to a shithead. You don't know nothing, but by the time we get out of this car you're going to know at least one thing."

"What's that?"

"Pitcairn Island. It's this tiny speck of nothing in the middle of nowhere in the Pacific. It doesn't even have a beach. It's this rock with fifty people on it."

"So?"

"So look at this," Tolck said, flipping open the magazine and laying it on the front seat so Angelo could glance down at the photographs. "It's like paradise. It's got tropical trees, flowers, and waterfalls. Fifty people, Angelo, fifty people. Do you know there are more people in a restaurant on a Saturday night than in this whole fuckin' island?"

"That takes me back to my first question: So?"

Tolck ignored him. "It's an island that these people's ancestors started. No one lived there until they got there. And you know how they got there? They were a bunch of mutineers."

"What the hell is that?"

"That's like you giving me a lot of lip," Tolck said. "It's when the ship's crew gets fed up with the captain and throws him overboard. They didn't get no water to drink. The son-of-a-bitch captain, this guy Bligh, was giving all the water to plants. Fuckin' plants. Can you believe that? They picked up some sort of fruit plants in Tahiti and all the water went to keeping them alive. So they said to this captain, up yours, we've got the guns, we're taking the ship."

"When did this happen, like last year?"

"No, you moron. It says it right here. It happened in 1789. They didn't have no motors or anything, and they had to sail the ship away. Then the British got all pissy on them and sent out the sea cops. But this guy, the head mutineer, Fletcher Christian, he was a smart cookie. He knew that if he found an island that no one knew about, they all could land there, set up camp, and go and get the girls they knew from Tahiti.

"They could start their own paradise, Angelo. You know what that must feel like? To have your own place, where no one is busting your chops, where you can pick fruit off the trees, sit under a waterfall, and watch the stars all night long?

"They kept it all to themselves. They burned their boat so the British guys couldn't find them. They locked themselves into paradise and threw away the key. No one else found the island for fifty years."

Tolck paused, flipped the photos back and forth of Christian's descendants, and looked up at Angelo. The driver stared silently ahead, bored with Pitcairn.

Tolck closed the magazine and sighed. For the first time since he could re-member, he felt the tension in his chest disappear. And for the first time, he had a dream about paradise.

Tolck drummed his fingers on the car seat, unsure what to say next. They were halfway to Atlantic City, but it was hard to tell exactly where on the Garden State Parkway they were. They had passed the Toms River tollbooth, and the trees were beginning to change.

The oak trees and maples were quickly becoming interspersed with prickly pitch pines and tall cedars. Tolck was curious about the region. He was amazed at how quickly the steel and dirt skyline of North Jersey changed to softer, greener tones for every mile they moved south.

As far as he could tell, there weren't any towns around. There were no build-ings that could be seen through the thicket, and no skyscrapers. He even saw a family of deer poke their heads up from the grass to give a careful glance at the passing traffic.

"I'm hungry. Get off at the next exit," Tolck said.

"But, boss. We'll be late," Angelo said, turning around to see if Tolck was serious.

"Do you have to argue everything with me?" Tolck asked in an annoyed tone. "Just get the hell off the next exit. I have to take a leak."

"I thought you said you were hungry."

Tolck slapped him in the back of the head so hard that Angelo's nose almost hit the horn.

"Look, when I want your opinion, I'll beat it out of you. Until then, just shut the fuck up and do what I say. I'm hungry AND I want to take a piss."

"OK, OK."

Angelo pulled the Caddy off at a non-descript exit ramp that looked as if it led into a forest. As they came to the crossroads, they both looked left and right. They saw no cars, no houses, and no signs. "You're choice, boss," Angelo said.

"Go right."

They drove for a few miles and saw the trees turn into a forest of pine needles. The pine trees were everywhere, but no more than twelve or fifteen feet high. The road rose in elevation. As the car crested, Tolck ordered Angelo to stop on the shoulder.

Tolck got out of the back seat as Angelo ran to open the door. To give himself an extra foot of height, Tolck stood on the running board and surveyed the entire area. Maybe there were one or two houses in the distance. No towns. No cities. Not even any cross streets. He knew that the shoreline was maybe fifteen miles east, the other way on this two-lane road.

He slowly thumped his hand on the roof of the Caddy as the wheels turned in his head. The brilliant sun gave a heavy bluish hue to the nearly cloudless sky. In the distance he saw ospreys, their expansive wings as fixed as a glider's, ride the hot waves of air to new heights in the sky.

Tolck took off his black fedora and placed it on the roof as he stepped back onto the road.

Oblivious to Angelo, Tolck softly muttered a single word to himself.

"Paradise."

SIXTEEN

In the county autopsy room, Singh used his laser light to closely scan the body of the man Fry had since dubbed "Smilin' Jack." The double entendre served to both mock Dewall and accurately describe the corpse. Even without a face and teeth, the exposed bones of the skull created an eerie Halloweenish grin.

"Some partials, smudges, but I don't see any other prints that will stand up," Singh said. "I'm pretty much done here. I'll run the prints and see what we can dredge up."

"How long?" Forge asked.

Singh looked at his watch, noting that it was now close to 6 p.m. on a Sunday.

"Ah, could be late tonight, could be tomorrow morning," he said. "It's a weekend, so not too many folks are going to be running prints. This best one here likely has the minimum twelve points needed for a good hit. It may have a few more. If that's the case, it will take a little longer."

As Singh wheeled the empty barrel back to the cold room, Ammerman motioned to the three detectives to back away from the table.

"It's my turn now," she said. "This is going to take a couple of hours. Why don't you guys go out and get me something to eat."

"Fried chicken?" Forge asked. "Regular or super crispy?"

"Very funny," Ammerman smiled. "Don't you guys have some other detective work to do?"

Forge and Fry looked at each other, and than at Dewall.

"Uh, no, not really," Fry responded. "How about you, Matt. Anything you can think of."

"Nope, not a thing."

"Jack?"

Dewall looked blankly at the two.

"We could wait for the autopsy," Dewall said.

"You really don't want to do that," Ammerman interjected. "It's a very long, gruesome procedure. Besides, I've got to run tests, I've got to weigh stuff, I've got to take a lot of notes. It'll be like watching grass grow. You won't know anything until the morning, anyway."

"Yeah. It's been a long day," Fry said, feigning a yawn and stretching his arms behind him into a lazy arc. "I've been up since sunrise. Matt here, well, he's got to get the sister back to the convent before lights out. Right, Matt?"

"Yep. The sister needs her rest. Isn't that right, Sister?"

Sister Maris remained mum as she glared at Forge.

"How about you, Jack?" Fry asked. "You must have something planned for tonight."

"Well," Dewall started, looking tentatively at Forge. "I was going to try and hit the Bolshoi Ballet at the Kimmel Center."

"Wow, you got tickets to that?" Fry asked. He had a hard time containing his mock surprise. "I've been trying for weeks."

"Well, you go and don't worry about Smilin' Jack here," Fry said, patting Dewall on the back. "There's nothing more we can do here anyway. We just have to wait for the science, isn't that right, doctor?"

"Absolutely. The science is what'll make this case," Ammerman said without looking up from the corpse.

"But it's my case. I should stay with it," Dewall protested weakly.

"We all gotta rest," Forge said. "Do you know who wins if we run ourselves ragged? The bad guys win. We got to stay fresh to catch them. Right, Jack?"

"Absolutely," Dewall said without thinking.

"Look, we're all sorry about that fracas back there," Forge said. "Fry... well, you know, he can't really control his temper sometimes. War trauma and all that. Isn't that right, Fry?"

"Yes. It's those damn flashbacks. I just never know when they are going to take me back to the burning oil fields of Iraq. I can still smell the smoke," Fry said. "I'm very sorry that I pounded your sorry as... I mean I'm sorry that I roughed you up, Jack. I hope you're not too sore."

Dewall rubbed his throat, stepped back and smoothed down the front of his suit. "I suppose there is no permanent damage," he said slowly. "But what about the boss? I'll have to fill him in on what is happening."

"Absolutely," Forge said. "Tell him exactly what we all know. We found a man in a can on the beach, someone worked him over pretty good, we don't know who the heck he is and Dr. Ammerman will get to the bottom of this by tomorrow morning."

"But it's still my case."

"We wouldn't want to take that away from you, Jack," Forge said. "You can tell the boss we'll back up all your detective work so far."

"Really, Matt?" Dewall said, genuinely surprised. "I thought you guys wanted this case."

"As I said, you can take the credit for all of the detective work you have done so far."

"That's super," Dewall said. "You know, you guys are not all that bad... But call me if anything comes up?"

"You'll be the first," Ammerman said.

With a push on the stainless steel door, Dewall walked into the hallway and was gone.

Fry let out an audible exhale and relaxed his tense torso.

"Man, I thought he would never leave," he said. "The dumber they are, the longer it takes to get through to them."

"He's not that dumb," Forge said. "He'll figure out what happened halfway through the second act, have a panic attack and start calling us. He'll be back here in the morning, with more backup and more guys to get in the way."

"Shame on you," Sister Maris started. "Next time you want to start lying, at least give me advance warning so I can go outside for a smoke."

All fell silent. With no more time to waste, Ammerman clicked on a transcription microphone that sat snugly in her ear.

"Let's get to work, quick," she said. "I have a man to carve up. Don't you guys have something else to do than abuse the mentally arthritic?"

"We're going to go over the barrel again," Forge said. "Some of the serial numbers may still be visible."

With that, Ammerman slapped on a pair of black, heavy rubberized gloves and donned a plastic face shield.

"Have fun, guys," she said as she flicked the "on" button at the top of her earpiece and began her dictation. "John Doe number 037, arrival July 2. Condition of body: Deposited in steel barrel, approximately height of four feet. Body was intact in the barrel, and found in fetal position..."

Forge escorted Sister Maris to the outside smoking area, where she swiftly extracted a fresh pack of Marlboros from the front her faded blue jeans. Forge could see the tension leave her body as she inhaled deeply from the cigarette and then slowly exhaled.

"I know what you're thinking," Sister Maris said. "I'm hooked on this like a heroin addict. Every woman has her seven demons, detective. But at least I know mine and I know how to relax. I can't say the same for you, though." She set her focus on the dark rings under Forge's eyes. "When was the last time you got some sleep?"

Forge hesitated. "Maybe nine months."

"When you lost your job?" she asked.

"Yes."

"And when your wife left you?"

"I don't think it has to do with that."

"Sure, sure," she said. Sister Maris pinched the bridge of her nose as if she were trying to forestall a migraine. "Denial is so underrated these days. People just don't understand the benefits it brings. Dig in; go for broke, Detective. It's like banging your head against the wall. It'll feel great when it stops."

Sister Maris waited for Forge's guilt to kick in. "I have to get back," Forge said. He turned toward the door with a sideways step.

A puff of smoke drifted from Sister Maris's lips. It quickly dissipated in the light breeze.

"What do you see in your dreams?"

Forge froze and felt a bead of sweat roll down the hairs on the back of his neck as he considered the stabbing question. Why should he answer her? Why was she probing, and how did she know exactly what to ask? She was more like a psychic than a psychologist. He had never met anyone who was so direct, yet disarming. She would have made a top-flight detective.

"I can't tell you," Forge said. "It's not that I don't want to tell you. It's just that it, y'know, evaporates when I wake up. I have shreds of memories. I dread going to bed, knowing I won't be able to sleep through the night. But I can't ever recall what it is about, what forces me to wake up."

"What do you remember?"

Forge struggled. It was his turn to pinch the bridge of his nose. "It's just... just so bright. Not painful, but bright enough to feel like I have to turn away. All I can remember is something like a sunburst. That's when I wake up."

"Any smells, any tastes in your mouth?"

"Salt. Something salty, like seawater."

Sister Maris pondered the depth of Forge's psychological ravine as she closed her eyes.

"Your wife, what was her name?" she asked.

"Sharon," Forge said as he fidgeted absentmindedly with a quarter in his left pants pocket. "Why?"

"That is my question, Detective," she said. "Why? Why did she leave you?"

Forge looked away and Sister Maris thought for a brief moment that she caught him about to blink a tiny tear away. He stood motionless as he grasped for the right words.

"Time," Forge said. "She always said she felt like she was stealing time with me."

"How so?"

"It was never enough. The more I got wrapped up in a case, the more time she wanted to spend with me. She kept saying all we were doing was stealing time together, as if we were cheating each other."

"And that was what came between you?"

"I don't know. I just don't know." Forge's voice trailed off. "She had her interests, her hobby of collecting rare figurines. What were they called? Hummbolts?"

"You mean Hummels? Those figures of children and angels?"

"Yes, that's it. Hummels. I could never remember the name. I just couldn't get into it. Maybe we just grew apart."

Forge had a sudden sense of tampered pride. His ego forced itself out of the dugout to step to the plate. It took a feeble swing at the first pitch, a ball high and outside.

"And you, Sister," Forge started in, more of a statement than a question. "Why do you think you know what goes on inside everyone? What makes you so special? Why do you think you're always right?"

Sister Maris pondered the question for a moment. She looked Forge in the eye as she let a small strand of white smoke drift lazily over her head. It was a question Sister Maris, on no account, planned to answer.

SEVENTEEN

Shaken, Forge made an excuse to hurry back to the cold storage area where the barrel had been returned.

Fry was busy with a pencil and paper, rubbing the inside of the container with the graphite.

"You find something?" Forge asked.

"Yeah, look." Fry help up the swatch of paper, now mostly darkened by long, arching streaks.

"You got a partial impression from the serial numbers?"

"It looks like it," Fry said. He twisted the paper in the light to get a better look at the darker marks in the middle. "The numbers were filed off in the front, but some of the digits survived on the inside."

Forge ran his finger lightly over the tiny bumps inside the drum.

"Yeah, I feel it," he said. "The numbers were stamped in by a machine. How many did you get off of the impressions?"

Fry silently counted the series of numbers as Forge made a mental tally. The string looked as if it had ten digits. Both of them squinted as they tried to make out the sequence.

"Damn, some numbers didn't come up," Forge said. "I can't tell if it's a five or an eight." He flipped the paper around. "Or a two or a three."

"How many do we have for sure?" Fry asked. Forge started to count. The resolution on the image was poor because unlike gravestone rubbings, which left white spaces for the depressed letters and numbers, the reverse rubbing darkened the area where the pencil had hit a raised number.

"Four, five... six, for sure. I think we got the prefix, which might be the important part. We can at least start tracking who made the barrel."

"How?" Fry asked.

"Let's find Ammerman's computer."

EIGHTEEN

Singh was happy to return to the coziness of his office in the county lab. Too many crazy things happening, he thought. First, that toasted guy, then all those detectives jumping down each other's throats. There was way too much bad karma going on. And what about that nun? Why would Forge bring her along on a murder investigation? A spiritual adviser? It was like the summer heat had fried everyone's brains. And the worst part was a whole day of surfing had been lost.

Singh unpacked his evidence case, signed the intake paperwork, and began digitizing fingerprint number one from Smilin' Jack. He placed the print face down on the high-resolution scanner attached to his computer terminal and pressed the icon for "Start."

The scanner took a minute to warm up as its white light peaked out from the edge of the cover. Singh's terminal popped to life and a preliminary scan of the image appeared on his flat screen. Subconsciously, as he had done countless times before, he grabbed for the mouse and adjusted the image square on the screen so the print would fill the box. If the box was too big, it would chew up more processing time; if it was too small, it would miss a whirl or loop, throwing the whole scan off. The Remote Fingerprint Editing Software provided by the FBI was so easy that a ten-year-old could run the equipment now, he thought.

He zeroed in on the print, sent the resolution to 1200 pixels per inch, and punched "Acquire."

The software automatically adjusted for the "roll" of a print. Since a round fingerprint goes onto a flat piece of paper, it always suffers minor distortion at the edges. The software was smart enough to smooth out the image to a uniform standard.

Singh didn't need to do much more than to save the image to the central computer and log into IAFIS.

The Integrated Automated Fingerprint Identification System was a $200 million godsend for forensic experts. The centralized FBI database pooled nearly every known fingerprint in the United States and set standards for comparison. More than a billion prints were now on file — usually ten digits for each individual, fewer for Japanese mobsters who were known to loose a digit or two for disappointing the boss.

It was the largest biometric database in the world. It had more information about criminals, security workers, law enforcement personnel, and public servants that any secret police in a foreign country could imagine. A positive hit would not only tell you to whom the print belonged, but also instantly compile a detailed dossier on the subject. The most common output was a criminal rap sheet, warrants, and the simply named "wants." As the word implies, any officer can put a "want" out on a suspect, which indicated to a fellow officer that the individual should be held, until further notice, for no apparent reason.

With a high-enough security clearance, an officer using IAFIS — and its counterpart at immigration — can track passport activities, border entries of foreigners, firearm purchases, and government job applications. Singh dubbed IAFIS "Big Brother," a name he was sure the FBI would hate. It was at least easier to pronounce.

Big Brother cut out all the human frailties. There was no need to risk a tired clerk slipping over a match, or waiting for a forensic expert to end his weekend barbecue and come in to work. No begging, pleading, threatening, or bribes of free lunches for putting you ahead of all the other detectives who wanted their prints run first.

Big Brother ran 24-7, 365 days a year. It didn't sleep, it didn't ask for a raise, it didn't make crappy jokes. Most of all, it didn't make mistakes.

Too easy now, Singh thought. Where's the skill in all this? No one makes sergeant by playing fingerprint video games.

He checked the box marked "Criminal search." That would speed up time considerably. Civil searches for government job candidates could take up to twenty-four hours, as the computer relegated them to the digital waiting room. The clearance signal blinked green on the screen, and he hit "Send." Kid stuff.

Singh set the timer on his wristwatch, propped his feet on the desk, sat back and closed his eyes. The computer usually cooked for two hours. Not enough time to go home, but enough time for a snooze. He quickly fell into a lucid dream about surfing the fifty-foot high swells on the Bonsai Pipeline in Hawaii.

NINETEEN

Fry impatiently tapped the space bar on Ammerman's personal computer in her office. The screen lazily brightened to life, but it produced a stern message:

"Terminal locked by user."

"Damn," Fry said. "Let's get Ammerman to unlock it."

"Wait," Forge said. He extracted his key ring from his right pants pocket and uncapped a black, oblong object the size of his little finger.

With a short click, Forge inserted the ten-gigabyte flash memory drive into the USB port on the front of Ammerman's computer. An almost unperceivable green dot on the flash drive blinked twice, and then the brightly lit computer screen went black. In a second, a prompt returned, yearning for a command.

<Press F1 for dictionary attack>
<Press F2 for brute force attack>

An underscore blinked on and off impatiently, twice a second, as if the computer were tapping its foot for Forge to make up his mind. He hit F1.

Before his hand had left the keyboard, the prompt returned the secreted password: Spinaltap. The computer returned to its friendly Windows format and opened up its system and secrets to anyone who wanted it.

"Think that's her favorite medical procedure?" Forge asked.

"Maybe she just liked the movie," Fry said. "Can you tell me what the hell you just did?"

"It's an old hacker's trick. It's the first thing you learn at the FBI's computer forensic school," Forge said. "Part of my high-level training at one time. I keep a small password cracker program on my key-ring flash drive."

"And what did it just do?"

"It ran through every word in the dictionary, and then all the common words in the language, like movie names and cute little sayings."

"In a second?"

"Less than a second. The computer is a victim of its own speed — and the incompetence of the county," Forge said. "The network is still running old 1990s software with very little security. It let my little program run through about 100 million words and symbols per second. People type in passwords to give themselves a sense of security. It's really no match against any fifteen-year-old with some free time on his hands."

Fry squinted at the rubbing in his hand and took comfort that he could at least see real digits. He took a guess that the first three were 856.

Forge logged into the secure connection of the FBI's forensic lab. There he had several directory choices: Carpet manufacturers, shoes, clothing, and so on. It was the Sears catalog of evidence shopping. He scrolled down to the metal products line and selected "Containers, Steel."

There he used the simple search engine. The first few guesses at the faint numbers on the rubbing failed. Forge finally typed in 856.

A hit.

"Regal Drums and Containers," he said. He flipped the PC screen to the Web and pulled up the company's home page.

"A major manufacturer of today's high-strength quality drums, our projects meet all U.S. and United Nations specifications using the finest cold rolled steel available," the Web page stated in bland business-speak. "We ship anywhere in the world. Costs are as low as $21.95 per barrel."

"Who would have thunk," Fry said. "The cost of canning a man would be so cheap."

"You gotta keep those profit margins up," Forge said. "You can't be wasting all your money on fancy boxes and labels. The accountants would kill you."

The Web notice listed the company's Coral Gables, Florida, address and telephone number, but no management information.

Fry dialed the number. His command voice had no effect on the lowly night clerk on duty. Fry couldn't extract the home number of the company president.

"It's time to get creative," Forge said.

He typed in the Web site for the Securities and Exchange Commission. There, he extracted the head honcho's address from his personal stock sale reports: Edwin A. Haynes II of Key Biscayne.

With a few more clicks, Forge hooked into the Miami-Dade County tax rolls, all public, and was even able to pull up a satellite image of the man's home.

"Edwin Haynes II & Rosemary Haynes, Harbor Point, Key Biscayne," the property information box read. Primary zone: residential. Floors: 2. Adjusted square footage: 4,328. Lot size: 25,000 Sq. Ft. Sale date: 2001. Sale amount: $3.5 million. Current assessment: $7,957,324."

"Holy shit," Fry said.

"I know. Impressive, isn't it," Forge said.

"Did you see how much he is paying in property taxes?" Fry said. He tapped the screen to count the trailing zeros to make sure he wasn't misplacing a comma. "It's more than I make in two years."

"Maybe you want to call and ask to adopt you," Forge said. "Here goes his telephone number."

A woman answered at the house. After introducing himself, Fry waited for what seemed like ten minutes as he heard footsteps echo away from the phone and then move toward it.

"They needed to get the golf cart to drive across the living room," Fry whispered.

"Haynes here," the CEO said into the mouthpiece. "What is this all about?"

Just like a head honcho, Fry thought. No idle chitchat. Fry explained how he was part of a criminal probe into a barrel that washed up on the shore, but didn't mention that a man was the main contents.

"Is this a joke?" Haynes asked. "You know we don't release our client list. I don't know you. You could be one of my competitors."

Fry was flustered. He couldn't use his imposing build to intimidate or even flash his badge. Besides, the guy was right. He didn't know Fry from a hole in the wall.

"Look, this is what I'll do," Haynes said. He was actually trying to broker a deal. "I'll call my foreman in the morning. He'll check you out by calling your police department. If you are who you say you are, we'll see if we can run the barrel's numbers. But, I have to tell you, we only make the drums."

§

Halfway across town, Singh's sleeping computer awoke.

"Big Bro is back," a soft woman's voice intoned from the PC speakers.

Singh roused himself from his nap. He plopped his feet noisily on the floor and pulled his arms back to stretch out the relaxed muscles. He had to blink twice to focus on the screen. Then his jaw dropped. He double-checked the parameters of his search report and assured himself that all was well. He hit print.

Singh flipped through the county directory to look for Ammerman's direct telephone line. Forge and Fry should still be in the lab, he hoped.

This is going to get interesting, Singh thought.

Several floors above Singh, a figure in a darkened room hunched over the computer terminal.

Dewall let out a nasty grunt. Instantly, through his network connection, he saw exactly what Singh saw on his PC screen. The dossier was complete with a very old photograph of the suspect, one that looked like it was taken with a Polaroid back in 1969. It listed a criminal record that ended fifteen years ago.

The photo just wouldn't do, Singh thought. He called up his photo enhancement software and selected the "aging" icon. "I think thirty years or so will do it," Singh said softly to himself. Within seconds the smooth features grew deep creases. The hairline receded like the tide, then turned white. Much better.

Dewall was sitting in the lush isolation of the county's computer network manager. He had easily picked the door's lock and knew enough about the floor's security cameras to exploit their blind spots. It also didn't hurt that the sole guard was snoozing downstairs, thanks to the sedatives Dewall had delivered to him through a friendly cup of coffee.

The network itself was secured from outside hackers through a series of dedicated lines, firewalls, and intrusion detection systems. The FBI had insisted that the core systems that used IAFIS not be linked to the world through the Internet or common e-mail programs.

The police computers had no modems, floppy drives, or USB links that a would-be mole could easily exploit with Trojan spyware programs. Each terminal had a hard link to the main hub of the network, which was tied into the county's criminal computer system. If there was no back door for an intruder to enter, then there was no way for him to steal information.

But the program designers didn't consider the risks from the front door. Like a pyramid, the topmost administrator had the password that allowed him to access all computers on every tier below.

Dewall was no computer master. But his sophistication extended beyond *GQ* and the Russian ballet. He knew how to follow directions. And he knew how to spy.

He had been given the code sheet with the administrator's password. Once he was within the system, Dewall typed "MSTSC — CONSOLE" in the Run Program display.

The Remote Terminal screen instantly appeared. He checked his crib sheet carefully and scrolled down.

COD431. That was Singh's terminal. He entered the second master password. What was once Singh's domain was now Dewall's.

Ballet my ass, Dewall thought. I'll show you who's the best detective here.

As the final results appeared on Dewall's screen, he pulled a small cell phone from the breast pocket of his jacket and flipped the device open. It was a disposable phone bought for cash that left no trace of who owned it or what numbers were dialed.

He dialed the number on his sheet.

"It's me," he said. "You're going to want to hear this."

TWENTY

"Damn. Damn. Double-damn."

Singh cursed as he hung up the telephone. No answer. He tried Fry's cell phone. No response. The lab was underground, making it unlikely that a signal could drill through all that steel and cement.

The dossier was exactly what he had been hoping for. This whole mess was going to be over sooner rather than later. Singh printed the information out and ran to his car. He made it back to the lab out of breath but satisfied to find all three in the autopsy room, plus the nun. She was still here? A faint smell of smoke enveloped her, as if she had just walked out of a fireplace. He didn't know much about sisterly duties, but he was pretty sure hovering in an autopsy room wasn't on the Vatican's "Top 10 List" for sainthood.

Smilin' Jack had been thoroughly gutted, he noticed.

Ammerman was using a dull stainless-steel probe to poke around the outer rim of what had been the man's face. It was as hard as a piece of forgotten steak on a family barbeque.

"Here," Singh said. Panting, he flipped the file to Forge. "I thought you guys may want to see this before the morning."

Forge flipped open the manila folder as Sister Maris looked over his shoulder.

The five-page dossier outline the life history of the owner of the fingerprint:

Name: Lester A. Lewis, 69, Tucker Township, N.J.
Status: Retired
Service: Lt., Atlantic City Police Department, 1962-1987
Military: USMC, 1960-1962

Forge flipped to the next page.

"Wow, busy boy," Sister Maris said.

"The photo," Forge said to Singh. "You aged it?"

"Yeah, yeah. They only had an old police shot of him," Sing said. "This is pretty much what he'll look like now."

Arrest/criminal history —
Aggravated assault on a police officer, 1988, New Jersey
Turnpike: Dismissed.
Distribution of controlled dangerous substance, 1988:
Dismissed.
Possession of controlled dangerous substance, cocaine, 1989:
Dismissed.

The list went on for half a page, spanning into the early 1990s.

"Look here," Fry said, as he peered over the top of Sister Maris's head and flipped to the next page. "He's become a model citizen again."

The file had attracted Ammerman's attention, whose disposable blue surgical smock and rubber gloves were now heavily stained red. Specks of dried blood were visible on her plastic face mask. She lifted the hood and tried to read the file upside down as she stood opposite of Forge.

"Yuck," Fry said. "You smell like shit. Oh, sorry, Sister."

"No problem," Sister Maris said. "Tell it like it is."

"It's a dirty business we're in," Ammerman responded. "You had the misfortune of catching me as I was going through his lower intestines. You want to know what his last meal was?"

"Anything of note?" Forge asked.

"Yes," Ammerman said. She held up a plastic evidence baggie. "A note."

Forge placed the bag under the high-intensity light. It was a badly crumpled and wet slip of tissue with a single hand-printed word:

ato

"What does it mean?" Forge asked.

"Not a clue," Ammerman said. "The first letter seems to have been dissolved by the stomach acids and liquids. There is no reference to such a word in any dictionary. It looks like his friends didn't take too kindly to him having it, so they rolled it up in a ball and shoved it down his throat."

"Anything else?"

"Booze, lots of it, in his stomach. But I doubt if he noticed," Ammerman said. "Some was metabolized, but I won't know for sure until the tox screens come back in a few days. I usually get a good reading of the blood alcohol from the fluid in the eyeballs, but as you can see — ," she tapped the head of the corpse smartly a couple of times with the metal probe — "he is without sight. The bile and bladder contents will still give me a ballpark reading."

"Why do you think the booze wouldn't have affected him?"

"His liver was pretty well pickled. It was hard, scarred, and bloated. He had advanced cirrhosis. If he wasn't cooked, chances are he would have dropped dead in a couple of years between martinis. For a guy his size, with a long history of drinking, a single bottle would have just been an opening cocktail for him."

"Do you think he was drugged, or knocked out?"

"Hardly," she said, lifting the chest wall that she had cracked open earlier to expose the inside organs. Ammerman ran her fingers along the floating ribs, and stopped to softly scratch at a ridge between two of them.

Forge craned his neck to take a closer look and noticed that the bones had been separated, as if a drawbridge had lifted its deck. "See these? These ribs were fractured from the inside. He literally screamed himself to death, or at least on the way to his death."

"Meaning?"

"Most likely they wanted some sort of information from him, but the burned fingers may work against that theory. The surrounding flesh on all ten digits was bubbly, which means he was alive for each little piggy roast."

"That could indicate he was a tough cookie."

"Doubtful," Ammerman said. "The flame likely came from an oxy-acetylene torch. Very, very hot stuff. It runs at 6,000 degrees. I know. I looked it up. It would vaporize flesh in a millisecond and cremate bones in a minute. They use these things to cut through twelve-inch steel plates. You gotta know what you're doing, or you'll likely blow yourself up."

She let the information sink in.

"You could hit the "Jolly Green Giant" with that torch and he would sell out his mother," Ammerman said. "The pain must be incredible."

"The torch was a message?" Forge asked.

"That could be one theory. But a message for who? Was someone really pissed off at this guy and they wanted to show him they were serious? I just cut these guys up. You have to do the rest."

Forge refocused on the Lewis dossier and flipped to the last page.

> Public service:
> Confidential secretary, N.J. Department of Transportation,
> 1995-2000
> Tucker Twp. Planning Board, 1998-2002.
> Assistant to the mayor, Tucker Twp., present.

"Holy shit," Fry said. "This guy's connected? Is this right?"

"Seems that way, bro," Singh said. "The big computer don't lie. I looked at the match myself. All the indicators are there. The prints match."

"Looks like he always had a guardian angel," Forge said. "Whenever he got tapped, someone made the case go away. Then he got religion and joined the government."

"What's a confidential secretary?" Sister Maris asked.

"It's a political job," Ammerman said. In her years of dealing with the state bureaucracy, Ammerman had come across almost every title in the vast public workforce. "The job is like a gofer for the political elite. They're not like regular secretaries, with typing and all that. They act as a conduit between those in power and those who want to keep them in power. A lot of times it's a no-show job at high pay."

"Screw it. Let's go pick him up," Fry said. "We can get this case wrapped up before Dewall gets back."

Forge looked momentarily at the sister. She was deep in thought. Fry, like any good officer, had made the right call. A fingerprint was evidence, and a fingerprint on this corpse was as good a break as they were going to get. It was a simple end to a case that was anything but simple. In the back of his head, he could hear the voice of his father: Follow the markers.

"I may be new at this," Sister Maris said, breaking the momentary silence. "But if my guess is right, your very convenient suspect may likely turn out to be the smallest fish in a very large pond."

TWENTY-ONE

Cars and pick-up trucks jammed the dirt parking lot of The Paradise as the early evening crowd assembled for the first main show of the night. Sunday was the biggest night at the strip joint, as long as football wasn't on TV.

Two hefty bouncers scanned each patron at the door. The muscles were on the watch for telltale bulges at the waistline or pockets. Guns and knives were not items that mixed with booze and strippers. One guy gets the idea the girl on stage is his, and a minute later he has a gun to her head, thinking this is the best way to propose marriage.

Inside his office, Tolck scanned the crowd through his hidden video cameras, searching for familiar faces.

Consolina, dressed in a heavy cotton bathrobe that hid the sprayed-on, flame-red halter-top with a matching thong, had delivered the bad news to Tolck hours earlier.

"The message... was not received," she told Tolck, trying to remain beyond the reach of his arms or breakable objects that he might throw.

Tolck surprised her. He sat in his chair and stared at the giant oil painting on the wall. Consolina thought he might not have heard her. She moved closer.

"Boss," she hesitated. "The message. It... it wasn't received."

"I heard you."

Consolina waited for Tolck to say more, but he remained stoic. Was he drunk, she thought, or did he have a stroke?

"What do you want to do?" she asked.

"Call the group."

"And tell them what?"

"We're going to meet. Here. Tonight."

"Some don't want to be seen with you," Consolina said. Tolck had spent years setting up deals with men who yearned for the money from Tolck's enterprises, but didn't want to be seen within ten miles of him. It was bad for business, they would say. Or it was just bad for their image, she thought.

"They have representatives. Tell them to send them along," Tolck said. "We've gone too far to drop the ball now."

Consolina gave Tolck a slight nod. He turned away from the painting of an island in the Pacific and looked her gently in the eyes. "I really can't fail now," he said. His voice began to quiver.

Consolina leaned over Tolck and held his head close to her breast. She softly stroked his gray hair with her fingers. He reached out and held her tight, pulling her into his lap.

"It'll be all right, it'll be all right, Papa," she said, as tears started to roll from her eyes. She couldn't stand to see Tolck in pain. Few knew about their relation-ship, and she was careful only to use her childhood name for Tolck when they were alone, and never when they talked business. But this was different. This was when Papa needed her. This was the way to comfort the only man in her life.

"Remember when you used to take my mother and me on Sunday drives to the country, putting me on your lap to let me turn the steering wheel?" she said. "Remember when we would sometimes drive down here and you thought this was the best place in the world?"

Tolck held her tighter.

"Momma thought the world of you, the world," she said. "I think the world of you."

Tolck dabbed a finger to his eye and cleared his throat.

"Your mother was quite a woman," he said hoarsely. "When I met Isabella, she just glowed, a rose among the weeds. I should have married her. You should have been my daughter."

"But I am your daughter," Consolina said. "You were always there for us. Even after Momma died, you promised you would take care of me, and you did. You found the family that would raise a five-year-old."

"I know, I know, I know," Tolck whispered as he looked up at Consolina. "I couldn't raise you, the life I was living. I ended up marrying that snake of a woman. She gave me a son and a goddamn miserable life. But you've always been at my side."

Consolina quietly walked to Tolck's bar refrigerator. She reached far into the back to pull out a vial and a small syringe. The needle squeaked as she slid it into the rubber top. She filled it with a thimble-full of liquid and instinctively tapped it twice with her ring finger.

Tolck automatically lifted his shirt to allow Consolina to wipe a small patch of skin with a white alcohol swab she had torn from its sealed package. Tolck looked down as she pushed the needle into the pinched skin around his gaunt stomach. She quickly depressed the plunger.

"Do you feel better now?" she asked.

The corners of Tolck's lips formed a faint smile.

"Your lithium is really out of whack," Consolina said. "The Zyprexa shot will help you, help you regain your thoughts."

Tolck composed himself as he felt the cobwebs of doubt fall away and he focused back on business. "Are you ready for the show?" he asked.

"As always." She hugged him tightly.

"We don't want to disappoint our... guests."

TWENTY-TWO

With less convincing than Forge and Fry thought they would need, Sister Maris agreed to let Singh drive her to the Harvey Cedars retreat. After being told that the case was now an arrest in progress, not simply a quest for clues, the sister relented only after she pulled Fry to the side and swore him to a whispered promise.

"You watch him," she told Fry. "He shouldn't be going out in his condition, tired and toasted. His reflexes aren't going to be sharp."

Her genuine concern struck Fry as a mixture of motherly warmth and infatuation with a man she had met only hours earlier. Fry felt a tinge of jealously, but he told himself that was the craziest thought he could recall — he was envious of a nun's affection for his partner?

Fry drove into the Pinelands as Forge navigated with a map.

"All I see are trees," Fry fumed. "Where is the house?"

Forge spotted a small patch of gray gravel from the wooded area and pointed. "There. A driveway. Turn left," he said.

Fry pulled up the gravel path about a quarter of a mile. When he saw the faint outline of the house in the glow of the moon, he shut his lights and pulled off into the tree line. Fry popped the trunk and both men moved to the rear of the car.

Fry donned his advanced lightweight Kevlar vest and tightened the fit with a tug on the Velcro straps. Below the ballistic metal chest plate that was tucked neatly in a center pocket, he scrawled in black letters: "Bad attitudes stop here." The body armor was thin enough to easily cover with his white shirt. The vest was so flexible and airy that Fry sometimes forgot he had it on.

He pulled out a semi-automatic twelve-gauge, police issued shotgun and a .40 caliber Glock 22c pistol that was pressed tightly into a black leather holster. He extracted the weapon to pull the clip from its bottom. He checked the magazine for a full load of seventeen rounds and slapped it back into the handle.

Fry looked over at Forge. "Where's your vest?"

"At the Sisters of Mercy."

"Are you waiting for them to bless it?"

"It's in the Jeep. We left it there when I drove your car to county."

"What about your piece?"

"Same place; lock box."

Fry pushed the Glock into Forge's hands. "Don't be a total loser. Take this; I'll take the shotgun. I'll hit the front door and you'll watch the back."

"That won't be necessary," Forge said. "He's not home."

Fry was perplexed. "How do you know that?"

95

"Look at the house. It's a small rancher with no garage. There's no car in front. It's not like the subway runs through here. He's out for the night."

Fry tried his best to recover.

"Yeah, I knew that," Fry said. "I was testing you."

"Sure, sure. It's good to keep me on my toes."

"Let's knock anyway. Maybe he has a live-in girl."

"Don't think so. No lights on in the living room."

"You are insufferable."

Fry pulled Forge up to the front door as both took a standard police stance outside the line of fire. If someone was holed up in the house, neither wanted to be greeted with double-aught buckshot through the wood panels.

Fry banged on the door with the butt of his shotgun and shouted, "Police. Open up."

Fry banged harder, which left a mark on the door and rattled the window-panes.

"Maybe you should throw in a couple of stun grenades for effect," Forge dead-panned.

"Oh, I like that," Fry said. "There's nothing that a little high explosive can't solve. OK, no one is home. Happy? What do you want to do now? Wait?"

Forge examined his watch: 9 p.m. He looked up at the outside porch light. It was off, but he could see that there were no cobwebs on the inside of the housing. That meant Lewis had been home at least in the last few days, and he could likely return sometime in the night. Lewis could be anywhere, Forge thought. If he was out visiting, or covering his tracks, chances are he would be back sometime during the night. Even killers have to sleep.

"We'll wait," Forge said.

Fry backed the car deeper into the woods and rolled the windows down to both hear the approach of any car on the loose gravel and try to cool off from the hot night air.

"I know you still miss all this," he said.

"Yeah, I do," Forge said. "But I had no choice. It was either get bumped down or tossed out."

"I don't know why Parker didn't see the humor in what you did," Fry said.

"Not everyone is as forgiving as you. You could have done this without me. I'm so below the last rung on the ladder that you'll have to dig a hole to find me."

"That's crap," Fry said. "Everyone is working the angles. Everyone is trying to figure what they can get out of a deal, who they can step on, what percentage comes with ruining someone else's life. There is no more honor.

"You're the last honest cop in this county.

"I couldn't have done this without you, and county can't do this without you. Parker may be the top prosecutor and he may not like you, but he's all politics. But Scratch... Scratch's a professional. He's really the guy who will have to build the case in court. He knows he can't have second strings running a murder investigation. He needs you. And you need him. He'll see that."

Forge sat silent. Fry still believed in him, even when everyone else had abandoned him. Forge wondered why he became a cop in the first place. Was it the thrill? Or was it the need to fulfill the void left by his father? He wasn't sure anymore. He had forgotten the exhilaration that came with his acceptance into the police academy, the elation of solving his first case.

Long ago he realized that he was a cog in the machine of police work, that no one would build a statue to honor him.

But to Forge, the honor was always in the work. The satisfaction came not from others, but from within. The drive was to honor his father in some small way, the right way.

Forge drifted into a lucid trance, forcing himself to avoid a deep sleep.

"Matty, do you see the blue water tower on the horizon?" he recalled his father asking him when both were on the bay. *"Do you see the radio transmission tower to the right?"*

The younger Forge nodded.

"Good, good," John Forge told him. *"Now look in the log book. What do you see?"*

Matt Forge, barely eight, unwound the rubber band from a thick-leather covered pocket notebook. It was stuffed with weatherworn papers and water-stained ink. "I see a lot of papers, Dad."

"Look for the topics," John Forge patiently told him. *"Look for a section that says 'Clams.'"*

Matt Forge thumbed back and forth through the book and finally came to a small page on the bivalves. "Here it is," he said.

The early morning sun was a red giant, its full disk rising slowly over Beach Haven and the southern shore of Long Beach Island. Like all baymen, the Forges ventured onto the water before sunrise to take advantage of the low winds.

"What part do you want me to look at?" the younger Forge asked. *"There are a lot of drawings here."*

The elder Forge looked over his son's shoulder and helped him flip through the pages, being careful not to let any of the loose sheets fall to the damp floor of the Garvey. He flipped between two pages for a few seconds, and then settled on the second one.

"Here. This is the spot," his father said. *"This is where we can get the best clams."*

Matt Forge looked perplexed at the scrap of paper. There were no words, just pencil drawings of three objects, a few numbers and the intersection of three lines. It looked more like hieroglyphics than a map.

"This is your big day," John Forge boasted to his son. "Today is the day you will learn how to read my handwriting."

Matt Forge smiled and remained silent, waiting for his father's next lesson.

"Here is the water tower I told you to find," Forge told his son. "That little circle with BHWT next to it is my way of drawing the Beach Haven water tower. On land, it stands 200 feet high. But to us, here on the water, we are so far away it looks just like a little stick on the island."

He moved his sun-dried and cracked index finger to the next point. It was a thick dot with the letters TRT, the Tuckerton Radio Tower, next to it. He drew an imaginary line between the two objects.

"Do you know why we use these points?" he asked.

Matt Forge thought for a moment. He recalled looking at his father's sea charts in the house and noting the various channel buoys and bridges.

"They are like lighthouses," Matt Forge said. "They tell you where you are on the water."

"Very good," his father said. He rubbed Matt's hair in approval. "Now, where is the third point?"

Matt Forge looked back down at the sheet and noticed a large, irregularly shaped blotch that looked more like an amoeba than a water tower or lighthouse. The younger Forge knew instantly what it was.

"It's that sedge island we passed on the way here," Matt said.

This island was larger than most and its shallow waters a good habitat for the clams that the Forges were seeking. John Forge had made a habit of rotating his clamming areas, much like a farmer would rotate the planting of his crops to preserve the richness of the soil. When Forge found a site rich in clams, he would harvest what he could for a week, and then move one. If no other clammer came upon the spot, the remaining mollusks would have a chance to breed, replanting the beds that Forge had raked through.

Forge was still fortunate enough to find pristine areas far from the flow of human waste and pollution. He tried to keep his sites as secret as possible. During his many trips out to the bay, he would carefully watch over his shoulder for any trailing competitor.

Today they were alone on the water, and the morning chill was quickly leaving the air. Matt Forge looked up as he saw a cormorant — its feathers entirely black except for a cast of white on its head — paddle forward for a few yards, and then disappear under the water. Within seconds, it emerged several feet away, clicking its pointed orange beak.

"He may know where the clams are," John Forge said. "But he's not telling us. We still have to use the map. Do you see the long dashes between the towers?"

Matt nodded.

"Each one is the length of my fist. Here, let's count. One... two... three... four. When the boat moves exactly behind this island, and the two towers are four fists apart in front of us, we know we are in the right spot."

Matt Forge instinctively held up his own fists and tried to count the distance. His father smiled.

"Your fists are much smaller than mine," John said. "Here, let's see. Put your fist on top of mine. There, I think two of your fists is equal to one of mine. So to find the right spot, you'll have to count higher. You'll need eight fists to get us there. Can you count as I drive?" Matt nodded again.

One... two... three... Matt Forge silently counted to himself. He waited a few minutes as the boat slowly motored forward. One... two... three... four... five... They were getting there, he thought.

Four... five... six... He heard his father shut the engine. It sputtered to a dead silence as Matt looked up. "What's wrong, Dad?" he said.

"Sticks," his father said sternly. "They put sticks out here."

"What are sticks?" Matt asked, knowing that the answer would not bring good news. Through the dissipating mist, Matt could see what looked like small, dead pine trees evenly spaced in the middle of the water.

"They are claim stakes," his father said. "The government has been selling off the rights to clam in the bay. But the local baymen can't afford the prices It goes to big companies who hire others to farm the bay. If we touch this area, they'll put us in jail for stealing."

"How can you steal from the bay?" Matt asked.

"I don't know what the answer is. All the small fishermen are being pushed out."

"Like us," Matt asked.

"I hope not. But it's going to be harder to make a living."

John Forge fell silent. The simple world of fishing, where a man could work at his own pace and reap the profits of his labor, had turned complex. In a year, maybe a matter of months, this clam bed would be stripped of all its shellfish. It would be barren, save for a few stragglers and crabs that nibble on the broken shells.

The elder Forge took in a deep breath and turned westward. "That's OK, Matty. There are plenty of other places to clam around here. And we still have the crab traps to draw from."

TWENTY-THREE

Fry shook Forge.

"Stay with me," Fry said. "This ain't working out. He ain't coming home."

Forge was inclined to agree with him. It was close to midnight and there was no sign of Lewis anywhere. Fry had already called in to report his location and to get a description of Lewis's car, but there was no vehicle registered under his name.

Forge suspected that Lewis was either a driver for someone or had finagled a government car. Either way, he was going to be hard to trace.

In the distance, the two heard the crackling of slow-moving tires over the fallen branches on the gravel driveway. Both hunched down as the car, its headlights extinguished, stopped ten paces away. The passenger door swung slowly open.

"It's Lewis," Fry whispered.

"No it's not. The driver door didn't open. Do you think they've seen us?" Forge said.

"Maybe, but how would he know we are here? And who is with him? If he got out of the passenger side, who's driving the car?"

"Shit, I can't see anything. What happened to him?"

A loud rap on the driver's window startled Fry. He tried to turn the shotgun forward, only to be stopped by the steering wheel.

"Yoo-hoo," the voice whispered. "It's me. Did I miss anything?"

Fry quickly rolled down his window and shot the intruder a look that, if it could be translated, would have said, "You're real lucky you're not a guy."

"Sister Maris, what the hell are you doing here?" Fry said. "I could have shot you."

"I'm so sorry," she said. "But I had this awful premonition that Forge was in danger."

"How is that? Was it the tea leaves this time, or wisps of smoke from your cauldron?"

"It was this," Sister Maris said, holding up the white Kevlar vest. "When Kev dropped me off at the retreat, I saw it in the passenger seat of Detective Forge's Jeep, and I knew I had to get it to him right away."

"How did you know we were here?" Fry said. He slumped into his seat as he looked around for any signs of the real Lewis.

"I was able to convince Kev to bring me here. I'm sorry to say I was most persistent. He tracked your location through the county radio room."

In the distance, Fry and Forge could see the silhouette of Singh wave quickly as he pulled alongside the two detectives.

"Don't worry, bros, I know we shouldn't have stepped on your stakeout, so we hung out down the road for a while to see if there was any action," Singh said. "We felt pretty sure Lewis wasn't home since you last asked for his car registration. And you've been out here for hours. We had to see if you guys weren't being put into some barrels."

"Where the hell do you think you're going now?" Fry said.

"I'm heading home for the night." Singh stomped on the accelerator and kicked up a mixture of gravel and gray dust as he backed down the driveway. Forge thought he heard a laugh in the distance.

"Now where did she go," Fry said looking out of window again. "She was just standing right here..."

"I'm behind you," Sister Maris said from the rear seat. "I'm dying for a smoke. Can I trouble you for a light?"

"No fuckin' smoking in this car, and I don't care what you think of my damn language," Fry said as he pointed his index finger an inch from her face. "You shouldn't be here. You shouldn't be my problem."

"I said I wouldn't be any trouble," Sister Maris said softly as she batted her eyes.

"Don't use your psycho mumbo-jumbo on me," Fry said. "You can say a thousand Hail Marys, but no way should you be in my line of sight."

"Well, I am and it's much too dark to hitch a ride back to the island," she said. "I suggest we just get this show on the road."

"OK, OK," Forge said. "Your persistence is commendable, but we're the cops, you're not. You really have no idea how dangerous this can get."

"I understand that," Sister Maris said. "That's why I sit in the back. I have no desire to rough people up. But you know as well as I do that I can pull my weight. I have, shall we say, a different perspective."

"A pain-in-the-ass perspective," Fry said.

"This is futile. Lewis ain't coming home. Let's pay a visit to the mayor," Forge said.

Fry called the county radio room, which gave him the address of and directions to the mayor's house five miles away. The township was so small that it had no police force; it relied on patrols from other towns to watch over its sparse population. Fry didn't know the local cops out this way and didn't want to risk tipping anyone off about their surprise visit.

Fry was amazed at the size of the mayor's residence. Nestled about one hundred yards off what was loosely considered the main road in town, the structure was more pretentious than palatial. In the front yard was a hockey-rink-sized water fountain, complete with two naked eight-foot-high cherubs spitting endless streams of water at each other. Unlike Lewis's house, the mayor's driveway was paved with luxurious imported brick, including four inlayed designs that spelled out the initials of the mayor and, presumably, his wife.

The front of the house was planned as a colonial, but with much, much more. White columns that reached to the second story framed the entryway, and the façade was sharply appointed with large slabs of rare white granite that was so smooth and perfectly dotted with black specks that Forge at first thought it was marble.

"Must be nice living on a mayor's salary," Fry said dryly. "I sure hope he's asleep."

With Forge and Sister Maris standing behind him, Fry banged on the heavy, white steel door and then peered through the thick glass panes next to it. He pushed the doorbell and slammed on the door again with the heel of his hand, only this time harder.

Within seconds, both men saw the light at the top of the stairways flick on and a small-framed woman start downstairs in a robe and pink bunny slippers.

The woman, who looked no more than eighteen, parted the curtains next to the doorway and cautiously scanned Fry's demeanor. The sergeant held up his gold badge and said loudly, "Police. Is your father home?"

"My father doesn't live here," she said.

Forge shot Fry a quizzical look.

"The mayor. Is Mayor Preston here?" Forge shouted.

"Oh, you mean Everett?" the woman answered. "My husband?"

She unbolted the door to let the trio in.

The woman's youth and beauty stunned Forge. Without the haze from the sheer curtain, she looked a bit older, maybe twenty. The foyer was adorned with photographs of their wedding, which Forge estimated must have been within the last year. How old was the mayor, Forge wondered, as he squinted at the dyed-black mustache and cue-ball head of the tuxedoed man in the pictures.

"Can I help you gentlemen?" the mayor said from the top of the stairs. He was in the process of covering his pronounced potbelly by tugging a blue silk robe around his mid-rift and tying a quick knot in the smooth belt. "Do you know what time it is?"

"Sorry to disturb you, Mayor," Forge said, as he introduced Fry and himself, but did not do the same for Sister Maris. After all, how could a subject take you seriously if you bring your own religious advisor with you? "We're looking for a Mr. Lester Lewis. He may work for you?"

The mayor had reached the bottom of the steps and was standing barefooted on the imported black Italian marble of the landing. *The foyer is larger than my* house, Forge said to himself.

"Yeah, I know Lewis. He does some office work when we need him in town," the mayor said. "He doesn't have any regular hours, if you know what I mean. He comes and goes."

"When was the last time you saw him?" Fry asked.

The mayor thought about this for a second.

"I dunno. Maybe last Monday. Maybe the week before," he said. "I don't spend all my time in town hall, y'know. It's a small town and I'm just a part-time mayor. We're very restricted here because of the Pinelands regulations. Not much goes on. Why are you looking for him?"

"He works only for you?" Fry asked.

Another pause.

"As far as I know," the mayor said.

"What does that mean?"

"It means I don't get to talk to him that much. He works part time for us, so maybe he has a job in Trenton or something. What is this all about?"

"It's about murder, sir," Forge said.

The mayor froze in the hallway, as if he had been hit by a blast of icy air.

"Honey, why don't you get these men a drink," he told his wife. She got the message and scurried to the kitchen.

"You're telling me Lewis was murdered?" the mayor muttered.

No, you dumb ass, Fry wanted to say. Why would we be looking for him if he were already dead?

"No, sir. We want to interview Mr. Lewis," Forge said. "We think he may have some information for us that will help solve a murder."

"Who was killed?"

"We don't know yet. We haven't identified the body."

"Where?"

"Long Beach Island."

Forge was not about to give any more information about the case. He had made a calculated decision to rattle the mayor. Once you mention murder, people tend to start helping you, hoping that they aren't pinned as a suspect.

The mayor took a seat in the opulent living room that was decked with oriental artifacts and a sixty-two-inch plasma television hanging on the wall. Fry had a good eye for electronics and noted that the mayor had his viewing area wired with the best seven-channel digital surround-sound system on the market, complete with recessed wall speakers and a high-tech remote.

Fry did a quick tally in his head and put the whole package at about fifty thousand dollars. Throw in the furniture, marble floors, and who knows what else, and the inside of the house could easily hit $1 million.

"What do you do for a living?" Sister Maris asked. Preston shot her a quizzical look and surmised, albeit wrongly, that she was an off-duty detective rousted from bed.

"Um, I'm a retired antique collector," the mayor said. "A lot of these pieces I've collected over the years through my work."

"Must be a pretty good business," Fry said. He could see droplets of sweat begin to coat the mayor's forehead. That was always the green light to squeeze a little harder.

"It paid the bills," the mayor said. "But, y'know, I'm retired. I dabble in some trades once in a while to keep my hand in it. I mostly live off my retirement fund and some stocks."

"Pretty good stock funds," Fry said. "Any tips for us?"

Forge knew what Fry was digging for. They both smelled that the mayor was dirty, they just didn't know where the dirt was coming from. The more details the mayor dodged, the more they would have to squeeze him.

"Ah, I don't seem to recall any off the top of my head. The market was pretty quiet this week," the mayor said. "I could give you guys a call in the morning."

"That won't be necessary," Forge said, as the mayor turned to look at him. When he turned back, he saw Fry holding a rather delicate translucent glass vase decorated with purple lettering and a long-tailed bird-of-paradise fluttering to a tree branch.

"Hey, be careful," the mayor said nervously. "That's a Qing-dynasty vase. It's very expensive."

"Do you want to be charged as an accessory to murder?" Fry said.

"Wha... what?" the mayor started. Forge was pleased that Preston's eyes had widened.

"Why are you lying to us?" Forge asked. It was the one-two treatment — a cop cliché, true, but Forge and Fry still found it useful on the weak minded.

"I'm not lying to you. I don't know anything."

"We asked you where Lewis worked."

The mayor stopped for a moment. Forge knew Preston was drawing up a balance sheet in his head. On one side of the ledger was the risk the mayor faced by telling the cops where Lewis was. On the other side were the cops throwing him into jail. Information versus detention. Which door would the mayor choose?

"Ah, let me think," the mayor said. He was still running the risk assessment through his brain.

Sister Maris felt she needed to assert her pseudo-cop image, lest the mayor think she was the weak link among the trio. She pushed by Fry to grab the mayor by the arm. She pretended to reach behind her for the cuffs that were never there.

"I've had enough of your crap," she said. She had lowered her voice to sound more authoritative. Forge wondered if she was in the mood to knee the mayor in the groin. "You either tell us now where he is, or you're going to be sitting in the county lockup for the rest of the night. Meanwhile, we'll call up the nice judge and he'll give us a warrant to toss your place from top to bottom. And, I'm sorry to say, I think a few of your precious collectables might be accidentally dropped."

"OK, OK," the mayor sputtered. "Lewis sometimes works at the dance hall down the road, y'know, the one in the woods."

"Paradise?" Fry asked.

"Yeah, The Paradise. But I haven't seen him in a week. That's the honest truth."

"What does he do there?" Forge asked.

"I dunno. Anything Tolck wants, I guess."

"Tolck?"

"Yeah, Dom Tolck. He owns everything around here. He's big into houses; he used to be big in the restaurant business up north. He even owns a funeral home near the island and a flower shop."

"A strip joint and a funeral home," Forge said. "That's an odd combination."

"He must want to get his customers coming and going," Sister Maris said. The comment drew stares from all three men.

The mayor took umbrage at Forge's comment. "It's not stripping," he said. "It's artistic performance."

Fry glanced at the mayor's wife, who could be seen standing in the kitchen trying to listen in on the conversation. Now the pieces were falling together. The mayor would never marry a stripper. That would be bad for his image.

"Of course, artistic performance," Forge said dryly. "My mistake."

TWENTY-FOUR

As Mayor Preston mopped down his brow with the lapel of his silk bathrobe, he moved into the kitchen to grab himself a drink. He felt the pressure on his chest ease as he heard the detectives close the front door behind them as they left for the night.

His hand shook as he poured himself a tall shot of bourbon in a dirty water glass.

"Poor baby," his wife cooed in his ear. "Do you want me to get you anything?"

"Two aspirin," Preston said. "My head is killing me."

As he watched his wife scurry away, he felt thankful that he contained the damage as much as possible. He had stayed out of trouble, and the officers, they were professionals. They wouldn't banter his name around like a cheap hooker. If he were lucky, he wouldn't even be involved in any trial. They were looking for Lewis, not him. He just told them where they could find him. He could keep his distance. He had deniability. Not even Tolck would know. He wouldn't tell him. That would be suicide.

Starting tomorrow, he would quickly extract himself from Tolck's grip. He didn't need Tolck's money anymore. How much cash could he hide away? Tolck did build him a nice house for next to nothing, and the money was good while it lasted, but he knew the cash would have to stop flowing sometime.

The housing bribes — that was all business. The mayor knew that Tolck had the influence to get anything he wanted built. Why fight him for a measly $5,000 salary as part-time mayor in a nowhere town? If Tolck and others were going to get rich off of land deals, why not him? The mayor had convinced himself that he was doing a public service by ensuring that the houses that were built didn't overwhelm the township's rural character. Without him talking sense into Tolck, the developer would run rampant across the township.

He took another deep breath. This was too much of a close call. He wasn't young anymore. He didn't need to take risks. He would make this last deal with Tolck his final business venture.

Together, he and his wife could move to the Bahamas or Mexico and live like royalty. The money wasn't doing him any good, being stuffed in safe deposit boxes across the country. This was the time to start enjoying the good life.

Upstairs, his wife clutched the bottle of aspirin in their expansive bedroom as she dialed the telephone on the nightstand. It rang four, five times. Pick up, damn it, pick up, she cursed under her breath.

"Yeah," the rough voice at the other end answered.

"It's Candee," the wife said. It was the stage name she had used countless times before at The Paradise. "I gotta talk to Tolck."

TWENTY-FIVE

The Paradise crowd was at its peak toward midnight. The dirt lot overflowed with cars, SUVs and pick-up trucks, and a few patrons were either stumbling out or being tossed out by the hefty bouncers.

Inside, Costa hit the nondescript black warning button in the video monitoring room. A yellow light above and behind the stage, as well as at other points in the building, signaled to the bartenders and waitresses that the cops were coming. The liquor disappeared from the walls and was replaced by vats of orange, grape, and other wholesome juices. Even customers in mid-sip had their shot glasses dumped into a mobile spittoon and quickly replaced with complimentary fruit drinks. Patrons who complained were given a stern "Shut the fuck up" by one of the bouncers. Within ten minutes, the entire bar looked like it had been serving lemonade at a grade-school social.

The strippers on stage didn't miss a beat. Three of them gyrated as if it was business as usual, not missing a chance to have a patron stuff one-dollar bills in their garter belts.

Forge and Fry were stopped at the front door by two of the bigger security guards, as Sister Maris stood carefully beyond throwing range.

"Police," Fry said, whose height and girth matched that of the bouncers. "Get the hell out of my way."

"You got a warrant?" the bouncer with a shaved head and goatee demanded.

"We're here to see the show," Fry said, as he took the thumb of the man's hand and quickly twisted him to his knees. The second bouncer moved in, but was stopped as Fry shot him a look that suggested imminent pain.

"We're here to see Mr. Tolck," Forge said. The bald bouncer, who was writhing as Fry twisted his thumb to the point where it would have broken off if he so much as sneezed, motioned to the back.

"OK, OK. Let me the fuck up and I'll take him to you," the bald man said.

Fry relaxed his grip and adjusted his jacket.

"I hope there is no cover charge," he said.

"For you, it's free tonight," the second bouncer said. "And the lady is in luck; all the juice drinks are on the house."

"Thank the saints," Sister Maris said as she scanned the smoky haze of the building, ignoring the strippers, and extracting a cigarette from a pack. "I can finally light one up in here."

The bouncers escorted the three of them across the patron floor and through the hallway that led to Tolck's office.

"Boss, it's us. The cops are here," the bald bouncer yelled, still rubbing his thumb.

"Send them in," the inside voice responded. The door swung open to show a young man behind the desk.

"Can I help you gentlemen," Costa said. "Would you like a seat up front? Our next show is about to start. I will be more than happy to spot you ten dollars in singles. And the lady cop," he said, slowly looking Sister Maris up and down suggestively, "I can offer her a tryout."

"Don't get on my bad side tonight," Fry said. "Who are you?"

"Costa Tolck. I own and operate this establishment."

"Where's Dom Tolck?"

"My father?" Costa said. "He's an old man. I'm sure he's in bed by now. He really doesn't approve of this place and he seldom comes here anymore."

"Bullshit," Fry said.

"Really, now," Costa said. "Is there a need for such language?"

Forge could see the frustration building in Fry. The two bouncers stood outside the opened door, which allowed too much music, noise, and flashing disco light to flood into the room.

Forge shrugged his shoulders. With a swift push of his foot, he slammed the door shut, and then braced a nearby chair under the knob.

Costa turned pale. He quickly reached into a drawer, but with a single thrust, Fry propped his left foot on the top of the desk and pushed it against Costa, forcing him against the wall. Fry took one step forward to grab the small-framed man by the collar and pull him over the desktop. Forge reached around and pulled a .25 caliber snub-nose Colt from the top drawer.

"You really are a dumb son of a bitch," Fry said. "Now we have an excuse to beat the living shit out of you."

Fry began to lift Costa off of his feet as a rapid knock came on the door.

"Gentlemen, please let me in. My name is Dominick Tolck. I understand you are looking for me?"

Forge unblocked the door and swung it open to see a tall man with a full head of white hair.

"I must apologize for the behavior of my son, who can be rash at times," the elder Tolck said. "Hubris, I am sorry to say, is one of the follies of youth. We all must learn to be more tolerant and patient as we grow older, don't you agree, Mr... Mr... I'm sorry, we haven't been introduced."

"Forge, Detective Forge. This is Sergeant Fry."

"And the gentle lady," Tolck said, as he suavely lifted her hand to his lips. He stopped as he eyed the gold, scalloped Latin cross pinned to her tee shirt. Sister Maris drilled a narrow, unblinking look into Tolck's cold eyes, making him flinch. Tolck felt the twitch in his lower eyelids, and silently cursed himself for letting his guard down. He slowly withdrew his hand. Sister Maris stood stoically.

Tolck turned to Forge as if to scold him. "You brought a nun with you?" he hissed.

Costa raised one eyebrow to give Sister Maris a look from head to toe.

"She don't look like no nun," he said.

"I'm a religious sister," Sister Maris corrected with a long exhale of smoke. "And were you expecting Mary Tyler Moore? This is as good as it gets."

"Mary Tyler who?" Costa asked, looking up at his father and then around the room.

"Mary Tyler Moore, you know, the actress," said Sister Maris. "She played a nun opposite Elvis Presley in 'Change of Habit.' A dreadful movie, even by Elvis standards. She just had the whole nun-to-be thing all wrong."

Forge interjected, "She's here because she's a witness."

"We have nothing to hide here," Tolck said. "What is it that I can help you gentlemen with tonight?"

"We're looking for one of your employees: Lewis, Lester Lewis," Fry said. "Is he here tonight?"

"Sadly, no," Tolck said. He feigned a disappointing look as he tilted his head downward. "I had to let Mr. Lewis go last week. He had an unpleasant drinking problem. He just wasn't showing up for work anymore."

"What did he do for you?" Forge asked.

"Errands here and there," Tolck said. "He would drive the girls wherever they had to go, to the beauty parlor or shopping or whatnot. A lot of these girls are high maintenance, if you get my drift. Would you two like to meet one of them?" Another smile. Tolck waited for a reaction, but received only a stone look from Forge.

"Bullshit," Fry said. "I think he still works for you and he was here last night."

"Please, Sergeant," Tolck said. "There is no need for such vile language in front of the lady. I have security cameras throughout the building, videotaping every inch of what goes on. Would you like to see last night's tape?"

As Tolck led them to the room, he detoured to a display that occupied a large segment of the hallway nearest to the dance floor.

"I know it is late at night, but I cannot resist showing you my ladies here, my pride and joy," Tolck said.

As he stood in front of the horticultural display the length and girth of a king-size bed, Tolck flicked on the overhead sun lamp to better illuminate the tall, thin green flora protected by custom-crafted Plexiglas walls. Each corner was held in place by freshly polished brass brackets.

"I see you have adopted a hobby to calm your nerves," Sister Maris said to Tolck.

"Pardon?" he said. His lower eye twitched again.

"I'm sorry, that is so brusque of me," the sister said. "I found that many businessmen take on hobbies to soothe the stresses in their demanding lives. I once counseled a rather hard-driven businessman who had an atrocious reputation in the community. He was known as a vile, black-souled cretin who would run over his own mother for a dollar. But he found his humanity in a rather unusual hobby. Can you presume what it was?"

"Ah, race car driving?" Tolck chuckled mildly. He glanced from side to side at his entourage, basking in the collective approval and laughter.

"Racing," she repeated. "That is most amusing. No. It was flower arranging."

"Flowers?"

"He took solace in raising the forms of simple plants to works of art. But because of the life he had chosen, he had to keep it hidden from his friends, his associates, even his wife. He would retreat to a forbidden shed on his estate and spend hours building magnificent centerpieces of roses, lilies, orchards, silver angel hair, white gerberas, and brilliant yellow sulphur hearts. I, along with his priest, was one of the few to ever see his work."

"And why would he do that if no one saw his, uh, exertion?" Tolck asked.

"Because you see, Mr. Tolck, the devil is in the details. To cleanse his mind, his heart, he felt if he could create something of beauty, something that only he and the Lord would see, that he would in some small way absolve himself of the wretchedness he had caused. This toughest of men would shed a tear as each piece would inevitably wilt.

"At that moment, he would return to his humanity and accept that he was still a person. And with each tear a bit of his anguish would leave him. Even in the most evil of men, there is still some good, and, for that, I always offer a prayer of redemption," Sister Maris said. "But I see you are much more open with your hobby."

"His downfall, I am sorry to say, was in his choice of subject," Tolck said. "He did his best work with clipped and dying plants. He was doomed. Do you know what these are?" Tolck asked. He gently tapped the Plexiglas window. Sister Maris looked toward Forge.

"Beach grass," Forge said. "That's not so unusual. It's what holds the Long Beach Island dunes together, pretty much the whole island."

"Ah, very perceptive of your boyfriend," Tolck smirked to Sister Maris. "It is *Ammophila breviligulata*; to be exact: American beach grass. It is one of the few native plants that can thrive in this region. Do you know why I enjoy this plant so much?"

"Why?" Sister Maris asked. "Because you see the devil in the tiny bits of details here?"

"Yes, yes. Quite right. The devil is in the details. The details of how it has survived, madam. For centuries it has resisted blights brought here by the carelessness of European settlers."

"It is a weed," Sister Maris said. "Weeds are survivors. They take up any space they can."

"No, no. It is much more than that. Ordinary weeds and grass need some semblance of soil. Here this willowy strand," Tolck said, reaching over the glass barrier to carefully pluck a reed from the display, "has learned to live in sand, pure sand, which has no nutrients to speak of. And very little water. Do you know what that makes it?"

"Enlighten me, please."

"A survivor. It has taken nothingness and turned it into success. Its tough green top is designed to absorb the punishing heat of the summer sun, the deadly cold of the winter, and the mist of the salt spray, which is poisonous to almost every other flora. If a reed breaks, the plant simply discards the lost member and grows another reed. Nothing is wasted."

He flipped the green blade over to show Sister Maris the twisted, yellow root at the bottom.

"Here," Tolck continued, "here is the secret: this plant's roots. It builds a community of grasses, all interconnected below the surface by their serpentine root structure. This singular desire allows it to thrive, to expand. One root can connect a whole dune system."

"If I recall my younger days on the beach, the roots are very fragile," Forge said. "One misstep by a careless walker and the roots around the loose sand are exposed. Once the roots are exposed, the plant begins to die."

"So true," Tolck said, looking down at the display of grass and sand. "So true. I suppose that is why these plants need me. They need me to protect them from those who would carelessly step on them."

Tolck switched off the bright overhead sunlight display to return the plants to the low bluish hue of the bar.

Tolck led them across the hall to a doorway that was secured not by a door-knob, but by a stainless-steel keypad. Tolck typed in the digits and the door hissed open. Inside, Forge was stunned by the vast array of computer control panels and plasma monitors.

"This is state-of-the-art hardware, state-of-the-art," Tolck said. "Tony here can scan twenty places at once without leaving his seat. We can look on the outside, we can look on the inside, and we can even look at ourselves." He pointed to a small globe in the corner of the room that housed a miniature camera watching over the watchers.

"We run a clean establishment, detectives. We follow all the laws. No alcohol. No drugs. No private parties with the girls. Since we don't serve alcohol, the girls can dance... more artistically, shall we say? It's a business, a service to the community. Would you want all these guys out in public after hours?"

Tolck's cronies laughed so hard that it made Forge feel like he had fallen into a cesspool.

"What about the tape from last night?" Fry asked.

"Disk, Sergeant, disk. We record all our video on high-definition DVDs. One disk can hold dozens of hours of video. They're much more dense than your run-of-the-mill movie DVDs," Tolck said. "Tony, can you call up last night?"

The computer operator punched in several commands. An overview of the bar scene popped up on the main thirty-two-inch flat screen.

"I'll run it at 10x so we don't have to sit here all night reliving the past," Tony said. "You can still make out faces and actions, but none of that wasted time in-between."

The tape showed the patrons from about eight feet up, high enough to reveal their mugs. The camera looked like it was the main security feed for the front door. Forge watched the clock counter in the lower corner run from 5 p.m. and move about one minute per second.

In one way, the image was comical. The patrons moved so fast from the dark-ened outside parking lot to their seats that it could have been a colorized version of a Keystone Kops movie. But there were no pratfalls or punch lines.

Forge had memorized Lewis's computer aged-enhanced face from the FBI dos-sier file. He was looking for an older man who walked like a cop, who entered a building as if he owned it. He saw many middle-aged men, young men, and old men, but no one approaching Lewis's description.

After about ten minutes, the counter clock read 3 a.m. Sunday. That was well past the time of death for Smilin' Jack. If he had been killed here, it would have been before midnight.

Something about the video playback bothered him, but he couldn't figure it out. The counter didn't show any skips or burps that would indicate frames had been edited. He wasn't a forensic expert, but the clock did seem to run smoothly through its counts, ticking off the seconds and minutes.

Forge and Fry were stymied. Tolck was trying to kill them with kindness, and he may have succeeded. They had no evidence to hold him, and he had the best defense in the world — a security system that showed he was telling the truth.

"If you see Mr. Lewis, will you call us immediately?" Forge asked. He handed him his card, writing his cell phone number on the back. "Day or night. It's very important that we get to talk to him."

"I understand, officers," Tolck said. He smiled. "I want to help as much as I can. I am a part of this community as much as you are. If Mr. Lewis had done something wrong, he should pay for it. Please, stay for the next show, my compliments."

The three strippers had just finished their set. They ran off stage, picking up their string bikinis as they left. An announcer, who sounded very much like Costa, tried to drum up the crowd's enthusiasm for the next show.

"Gentlemen and fine ladies," he bellowed into the microphone. "Please give a warm welcome to our star this evening, the girl you have all been waiting for, whose magical touch is known throughout the Jersey Shore, our very own Mistress of Fire, Consolina!"

Faint applause sounded from the floor as the lights went dim and Forge could see the glimmer of sequins and what looked like a baton. As the floor lights slowly came to life, Forge could see a stunning red head in high heels with long flowing hair and a halter-top that was two sizes too small for her expanded breasts.

The music started to play a jazzy version of "The Stars and Stripes Forever," which sent the crowd into a frenzy. Men in the front begged Consolina to pick up their dollars, while the guys in the back of the bar whistled loudly. On a stool next to the baton twirler was a small yellow flame that flickered from a cup-sized Sterno pot.

Consolina kept in step to the music and tossed her baton higher and higher. She teased the men by dropping one shoulder strap of her red top, and then the other. Each time she flung the silver shaft into the air. With a quick twist of her free hand, she unclasped her top, letting it fall to the floor and exposing her breasts. The crowd went wild.

She began to gyrate as if she was in an exotic exercise video, and moved her body over to the flame. She quickly touched each tip of the baton to the fire, igniting what was now an orange blaze.

As she twirled the truncheon over her head, the flames took on a hypnotic quality that brought a brief silence to the patrons. On cue, the flashing strobe and twirling kaleidoscope of disco lights went dim, as the music grew louder. The fire illuminated her body, throwing yellow and orange hues off the mirrored walls.

With each pass of the baton behind her back, she unsnapped a clip from her bikini bottom. By the fourth pass, her bottom was at her ankles, her nudity exposed only by the passing flames.

The lights grew brighter and the clientele went wild once again, with all the men standing up clapping and cheering. For her finale, Consolina marched over to a second stool and filled her mouth with what looked like a glass full of whiskey.

Consolina gyrated to the front of the stage, her cheeks puffed out to their limits. As the final upbeat note of the march sounded, Consolina held the flame of the baton in front of her and expelled the liquid. The ball of fire ignited over the patron's head, to their surprise and ecstasy. The blast was hot enough to punch a clean hole in the smoke-filled air over the tables.

Five-dollar and twenty-dollar bills flooded the stage as Consolina gracefully bowed to give the men a full view of her assets. As she sashayed offstage, one of the newer girls came out to quickly collect the fallen money.

Forge was thunderstruck by the act and the crowd's astonishing reaction. He thought that Sister Maris had turned away, but saw that she had sternly held her ground. She was unwilling to show weakness to Tolck by averting her eyes from what she thought must be the epitome of immorality.

To the side, Tolck beamed as if a proud father had seen his daughter graduate from college. "That's my girl," he said softly to himself. "That's my girl."

TWENTY-SIX

Fry watched The Paradise grow smaller in his rearview mirror as he pulled the car out of the parking lot and into the darkened road.

"Thank you for a lovely evening, gentlemen," Sister Maris said. "You sure do know how to treat a girl to a good time. I really have to tell the sisterhood about this one. And did you notice how the ladies were doing their best John Wilkes Booth imitation?"

"John Wilkes Booth?" Fry asked, trying to look behind him without steering off the roadway.

"The five-dollar bills flying up on the stage," she said, pleased that Fry had taken the bait. "The girls were mowing down the Lincolns like John Wilkes Booth."

"I'm too tired for this."

"Five-dollar bills, Lincoln's face, assassinated, John Wilkes Booth," Sister Maris said. "Do you get it now, do you?"

"I got it before. No one has ever been able to make a good Lincoln joke, and it's not going to start with you."

"The sisters would get it."

"I'm sure they don't get out too often."

"Did you see anything else in there of interest, Sister?" Forge asked.

"There are a lot of lost souls in there."

"Including Tolck?" Fry asked.

Sister Maris faintly smiled. "He has so many layers wrapped around him, I couldn't sense a soul. But there is one in there somewhere."

"Can I ask you a question?" Forge said. "Why did you become a sister?"

"That is indeed a curious question," she said. "Do you ask the postman or grocery clerk or your fellow cops why they became what they are now?"

"I've been asking myself why I do what I do, but you are one of the few nuns I have met in the last few years. It's just a question."

"In my youth, in many respects, I was like you, detective," Sister Maris said. "I was on a journey, but I had no idea where I was heading. I was adrift. I was lost. Despite my genteel and effervescent demeanor, which I'm sure you all adore, I was quite the wild one in high school. I was not raised in a strict Catholic household and there was no push into the sisterhood. I partook in all the usual high school, shall we say, extracurricular activities. I wouldn't say I would have ended up dancing naked in front of strangers, but it might have been close."

"And then?"

"And then one night I awoke. It was like I was on a ship sailing from the pitch of night into the bright morning. I can't really describe it. It was as if I knew what I wanted to do, where I wanted to go, and what I wanted to be. With no trepidation, I joined the order and trained in psychology. I knew that my calling was in helping others, not myself."

"Aren't you supposed to be closeted or something?" Fry said.

"The term is cloistered, not closeted, and no, my order is not a hermit one. We do not close ourselves off from the outside. Quite the contrary, we are not like potted plants," Sister Maris said. "We take three vows — chastity, poverty, and obedience. Ingrained in our celibacy vows is a love of community. Part of that community means that we have to fight evil where we see it. You're thinking that I should wrap myself in a red cape and tights with a giant "N" on my chest, but that is how I feel. My community right now is the retreat, and it is quite essential that we understand why this poor man in the barrel washed up at our doorstep."

Fry said, "That's so special that I think I'm hearing the archangels sing. But there is still the pressing question: How did he do it? How did they fix the tape?"

Forge didn't answer as he saw the string of lights of Long Beach Island fill the distant horizon. He was mad at himself for letting Tolck outmaneuver him. He had been played perfectly.

"Seasons," Sister Maris said from the rear.

"What?" Fry asked. He looked quickly to his right at Forge's faintly lit face. "Is that another bar?"

"No, she's right. Summer is a season. That's what we're in right now," Forge said.

"OK. But, so what?" Fry said.

"Where did you go to detective school?" Sister Maris asked of Fry.

"I'm not a detective. I'm a sergeant. That's a supervisor. Detective is a specialty, kinda like bothersome nuns," Fry said.

"You. Don't talk," Sister Maris said. "You'll hurt yourself."

"In the summer, the sun sets here around 8:30, right?" Forge said. "The video playback showed us the doorway starting at 5 p.m. What did you see?"

"A greasy collection of slime bags slithering in for the night."

"Besides that."

Fry thought for a moment as he rewound the mental images in his head. It just wasn't clicking.

"It was nighttime, you big dope," Sister Maris said. "The outside should have been lit up like it was the middle of summer, which it is. But what we saw were people coming in from the dark. The tape was obviously fixed."

"Yeah, yeah." It had clicked with Fry. The doorway was indeed bringing people in from the unlit outside. "And they had long sleeves on. Who wears long sleeves on a hot July night?"

"Exactly," Forge said. "That disk was altered. They pulled one from an archive, maybe like a warm day in early spring. It looked like summer with the slime coming in without coats on, but it was really a few months ago."

"Bastards," Fry said. "Let's go back."

"No. The original disk has been destroyed already. There isn't much more we are going to get now. We're going to have to see Scratch in the morning and hope he's in a good mood."

§

As Tolck watched the two detectives drive away, their wheels kicking up dust from the dirt lot, he closed the blinds in his office and started to tear Forge's card in half but stopped. He slowly placed the paper in his breast pocket and walked to The Paradise's security center.

"Do you have it?" he asked the security director.

Tony ejected the DVD from the rack burner against the wall and handed the disk to Tolck. It was devoid of any writing except four small numbers that signified the date: 0701.

Tolck flipped over the disk and angled it so he could see if the blue laser light that recorded all activity in the club the night before had indeed etched the bottom side. Satisfied that the disk was the correct one, he flipped open the top of the heavy-duty document shredder and slid the DVD in, until he could hear the start of the grinding teeth.

One less problem, Tolck thought. No one will know Lewis was here with his special guest in the private room.

Tony had seen this happen before and didn't even flinch as the shredder loudly finished its brief meal. He was busy burning a new disk, one that would fool even the best forensic experts.

He had pulled a disk from a busy Saturday in April, one that would give the impression that it was a hopping night in summer. The club was offering a two-for-one drink special, which was advertised on the Internet and by word of mouth.

Tolck had learned long ago that people got bored with the same old talent and watered-down drinks each night. If he didn't churn the crowd, such as bringing in new dancers and offering specials, he would soon cater to only the perverts in raincoats. He was after the dad crowd, guys who were bored with their wives and who couldn't stand their screaming kids. They were mostly behind on the rent or mortgage in dead-end jobs in one of the dullest parts of the state. The Paradise offered them a diversion. It offered them the fantasy that every girl onstage wanted them, not their money.

Tony had left his job as the head of security at a truck depot for the money. Tolck had doubled his salary and offered him all the talent he could bang after hours. Watching strippers on the dance floor, in the changing area, even getting high with customers in private party rooms, sure beat watching trucks rumble throughout the night.

He had programmed the security grid to be overridden only by him. The hardware was high-end commercial and was guaranteed by its manufacturer to be tamper proof.

But, for every secure system built, there was always a security expect who could find a way around the limitations. Take one computer program and give it to ten million hackers around the world, and they will find its weaknesses faster than an e-mail scammer can drain Grandma's bank account.

If he wanted to, Tony could alter the images on the security disks, but that would take too much time and wouldn't have the same effect. Instead, he preferred to run the disk through an image processor and could literally change time.

The camera imprinted its timestamp with a running clock at the lower right hand side of the image. Each digital frame would advanced the clock by a thousandth of a second. All Tony had to do is copy the real security captures, paste over a phony time stamp, and burn a new DVD. In this case, he had generated a clock that showed the time fly by as if it were July 1. To fool the cops, he had clipped the new date and pasted it on top of the old date from April. The black background made the forgery impossible to detect.

That's class-A job satisfaction, Tony said to himself, grinning. *When you beat the cops, you beat the world.*

He had been at the club long enough to know not to ask questions. Tolck took the essential disks for his own use, calling them his "remembrances." Tony knew he could have made a small fortune from the security feeds. He could have blackmailed commissioners, mayors, assemblymen, party leaders, and state senators who had fallen into Tolck's net.

But Tony had heard stories about Tolck's early retirement plan for wayward employees. He didn't want to end up like them.

Fear, Tony had learned from Tolck, was the only way to ensure loyalty.

Tony finished relabeling the doctored disk with the 0701 date and tossed it into the archived rack. With the rest of the night ahead of him, he put his feet on the console and directed his undivided attention to the blonde stripper on the screen.

DAY

2

Monday, July 3

ONE

With nowhere to go, and just hours until the county courthouse opened, Fry headed north to Toms River.

Tourists had booked the motels solid. With no lodging available, Fry opted to catch a few hours of sleep in the courthouse parking lot as Forge stared out of the passenger-side window. Sister Maris took advantage of the opportunity and dozed peacefully in the comparative expanse of the rear seat.

Toward daybreak, a single mosquito buzzed around Fry's forehead to remind him that the lot was the insect's domain. Used to unpleasant terrains and no-see-um bugs, the Gulf War veteran tried to swat the creature away, until the motion of his flailing arms loudly rapped his knuckles against the half-opened driver-side window. Forge watched the pantomime with amusement. Sleep was not the rest Forge sought. He had trained himself, forced himself, to hover in the netherworld of half-sleep. Neither fully conscious nor totally oblivious, Forge accepted this semi-lucid drifting as the only manner he knew to rest his weary body and mind.

Forge had found that this altered state of consciousness a necessary pit stop during his mad dashes to solve cases. In better days, when he had casually mentioned to Ammerman about the benefits of his free-form meditation, she nonchalantly said, "You mean Berger's."

Forge thought he had misspoken and started to explain again. Not hamburgers, Ammerman asserted, but "Berger's — B-e-r-g-e-r-s, without a 'u.' It's a type of brain wave most people know as alphas. We call them Berger's after Hans Berger because he's the guy who discovered them back in the '40s. It's your brain's way of kicking back and relaxing with umbrella drinks in both hands. You think you see things because the alpha waves come from your vision center. Even though your eyes are closed, some people in deep alphas think they've actually seen visions."

It was twenty-four hours since the man-in-the-can had been discovered. They had one suspect they couldn't find and no inkling of a motive. If it was revenge, it was a hell of a payback. If it was a gangland hit, why leave the body where it would be quickly found? And why the Sisters of Mercy? The jigsaw pieces rolled around in Forge's head, but he had no idea where they fit or if they even came from the same puzzle box.

It was close to 8 a.m. The light stirred Forge. He could see judges and staff wander into the courthouse for another day of law and order.

"Fry, c'mon. Let's get some breakfast and get in," Forge said, pushing Fry's shoulder to wake him. Sister Maris stirred and lazily stretched both arms sideways.

"You coming, Sister?" Forge asked.

"I'll guard the car," she said between yawns.

"Excuse me?"

"I don't want to be ditched like a used tea bag. I know as soon as we go inside Fry will find a way to double back and drive off without me."

"You are a mind reader," Fry said.

"I would much rather prefer to stay with this to the end," Sister Maris said. "And I would also much prefer if you brought me back a double-grande mocha latte with a splash of vanilla and a very large cherry danish slathered in frosting."

Inside the Office of County Prosecutor, Forge tried to avoid the gaze from the oversized portrait of Randolph Parker that hung prominently over the receptionist's desk. The giant smile showed off the chief prosecutor's perfectly white teeth that seemed to span unnaturally from ear to ear.

The receptionist buzzed the detectives into the secured inner office, but they found that Hendrick Hudson had already walked downstairs to present his case at a criminal sentence.

As first assistant prosecutor, Hudson was the second in command of the prosecutor's office, but political appointee Parker was the official head. It was Parker who demoted Forge, and it was Parker that Forge wanted to avoid today — and every day. If he could fly under the radar long enough, he could solve this case before old political issues cut his legs out from under him. Forge knew Parker seldom came to work in the morning. If Parker put in more than three hours a week, his staffed joked, they would have to pay him overtime.

Hudson had gone to bat for Forge, trying to talk Parker out of sending him to the minors on the Island. Forge had worked with Hudson to build a number of successful homicide cases.

Hudson was a career prosecutor. He had worked his way through the ranks to the top spot. As Parker dallied with the rich widows on the cocktail circuit, Hudson instituted sweeping reforms that made the office the envy of county officials in other states. He was the first to establish a high-tech forensic lab, routine use of DNA evidence in cases other than murder trials, and a computerized case tracking system based on neural networks and artificial intelligence.

Hudson had made his mark early through a series of stellar wins.

To stake his claim, he took on the toughest of all murder cases, a death penalty case in which the body of the victim had never been found.

The jury fixated on the prosecutor's every word. Some court observers said it wasn't Hudson's statements but his mane of Hollywood-blond hair, emerald eyes and baritone voice that hypnotized the panel. Each juror believed that the spilled blood — found in a patch of woods that had been soaked red — was too great of a loss for any individual to have survived. They believed that the weapon was a knife that had been cleaned with bleach. They believed that the defendant had the motive and opportunity to kill his girlfriend.

And they believed that the killer should be killed by the state for his crime.

Hudson's remarkable achievements in the courtroom made him the Svengali among the younger prosecutors.

To win a death sentence, a prosecutor has to prove more than simple murder. A guy who shoots his friend over a woman is the plain vanilla case you just don't want to touch. Sure, it's a slam dunk, but who cares, he would tell his apprentices. The killer gets thirty years after a three-day trial, which may stretch to a week if his public defender actually blunders into a good cross-examination.

For death, it has to be a wantonly vile murder. "One that would make granny sit up and spit out her coffee in the morning," Hudson imparted to his eager legal crew.

There were three rules of Scratch:

First Rule: *Get the jury that you want.* Don't get one you think will be fair. Don't get one that the defendant is happy with. The case rises and falls with the jury.

The county is 98 percent white, which means the jury will likely be 100 percent white, mostly senior citizens or middle-class housewives. That's the jury you want. "That's the jury that isn't going to give two craps about a poor black kid who had a mother who was never home, and an alcoholic father who beat him every night," Hudson would say.

Second Rule: *Find the McGuffin.* Classic suspense director Alfred Hitchcock often talked about the value of the McGuffin in his movies. A McGuffin was a way to keep movie watchers guessing as to what was to come next. In a murder trial, you need your own McGuffin, one that goes beyond the killing act itself. It takes the crime to whole new level and into the death penalty arena.

The best conditions for a death penalty case were often what you could cobble together after the murder, rather than what was found at the scene of the crime.

"Take for instance your standard wife killer," Hudson offered to his pupils. "Did a wife killer have a girlfriend? That in and of itself would not make the defendant eligible for the death penalty. You need to find at least one aggravating factor. Did the killer buy his girlfriend a nice new car with money he took out of his wife's bank account? That then becomes theft. That then becomes murder to cover up a theft. That then becomes a death penalty issue."

Third Rule: *The confession is never enough.* "Sooner or later, ninety-nine percent of all killers will confess. That is just a given," Hudson would say. "They have an unmitigated sense of justifying their actions, especially to the police. Every killer, even sociopaths, want you to believe that the killing was justified."

The confession was simply the point of the knife a prosecutor would use to pierce the cloak of innocence that surrounds a defendant at trial. Once that barrier has been breached, and the jurors could see deep into the soul of the accused, use the confession to slice deep. The confession is simply the basis to start your case. You can imply to the jurors that the killer was holding something back, that he had a darker secret that made his crime even more horrendous.

"Take that knife and twist it," Hudson would say. "Twist it until you see the grimaces on the jurors' faces. Once the old man in the corner, the one who thinks he has seen it all, grimaces and turns away, then you know you have them in your pocket."

The rules won him the acclaim that he sought. After two years of six successful death penalty trials, the press corps bestowed a moniker that delighted him: Scratch.

During the weekly, off-the-record conferences he would have with the three reporters who covered the courthouse for two newspapers and a cable news station, the reporters took to joking with Hudson about his record. "Scratch one more off the list," a reporter once said. That gave Hudson one of the hardiest of laughs. The nickname stuck.

In the office, the receptionist gave the two detectives the name of the judge downstairs that Hudson was appearing before.

The wooden doors of the ornate courtroom swung silently outward as Forge and Fry walked in. They could see Hudson sitting at the prosecutor's table on the right twelve feet in front of the judge. The judge's bench, of course, stood three feet higher than any other part of the court.

There was no trial this morning. Instead, the jury box was filled with ten defendants, all wearing ill-fitting jail khakis and sandals. The footwear was large, flimsy, and impossible to run in. A defendant who made a dash to the door would soon find it easier to run in water. Guards enjoyed the sandals, too. An inmate who got out of line soon found his toes on the wrong end of a solid rubber heel.

The inmate's attorney had finished making his plea for leniency to the judge. The judge wasn't listening; he had his head mostly buried in the defendant's thick case file.

"Son, you have anything to say before I sentence you?" Supreme Court Judge Charles J. Thompson said to the inmate in the dock.

"Yes, sir," the inmate responded. He actually puffed up his chest to deliver a dollop of pride with each word. He raised his left hand high enough to brush his long, matted hair out of his eyes so he could look directly at the judge.

"I feel I am a new man, your honor," said the inmate, a man in his twenties. "Since this robbery, I've spent a lot of time in the county jail. I have changed."

The judge leaned closer, not wanting to miss a word. "How so?" he said.

"I found Jesus, your honor."

Without warning, Judge Thompson leapt to his feet. Everyone was startled except the prosecutor and court stenographer.

"Hallelujah!" Thompson shouted at the top of his voice. "Everyone. Everyone, get up on your feet now!"

The courtroom was packed with about thirty onlookers, mostly relatives of the convicts. They looked at one another, unsure how to respond. They slowly rose to their collective feet as the judge had commanded them.

"Everyone now, I want you all to put up your hands and shout: Hallelujah!" The crowd started to shuffle. Thompson turned serious.

"Unless you all want to spend the rest of the day in jail, I would advise you to do as I say."

The crowd, inmates, court officers, and even lawyers all reached for the heavens and shouted "Hallelujah!" out of sync.

"C'mon, y'all. This is a monumental day!" Thompson had joined in on the court-ordered revelry and pranced around behind his chair, clapping his hands, closing his eyes, and shouting Hallelujah to the ceiling at the top of his voice.

After a minute, the judge put up his hand to silence the crowd, which cautiously started to sit down.

"My oh, my " Thompson said to the stunned defendant. The young man didn't know if he should sit down or run. "I now know where Jesus lives."

The defendants and the crowd looked at each other in bewilderment. Hudson put his fingers together to form a temple that hid his half-smile.

"Jesus lives in the Ocean County jail," Thompson shouted out, as he turned to Hudson. The judge needed a straight man. "That's the only conclusion I can come to. Do you know why, Mr. Hudson?"

"No, your honor," Hudson said. His monotone voice sounded as if he had rehearsed the lines to a school play once too often. "Why?"

"Because everyone finds him there, that's why," Thompson said, raising his voice to a boom. He struggled but failed to keep a straight face as he broke into deep laughter.

"Now, Mr... ah... " Thompson looked down at the case file to remind him of the defendant's name. "Mr. Coldwater. You have a pretty long record going back to your teenage days. Petty theft, burglary, purse snatching, receiving stolen property, drug possession, and now robbery. Do you really expect me to believe you found Jesus and that I should let you go today?"

The shell-shocked inmate didn't know what to say. He looked nervously at his public defender. The underpaid lawyer wanted no part of this downward spiral. He avoided all eye contact and kept his head pointed down at his legal pad.

"Uh, yes sir," Coldwater said.

"Wrong answer," Thompson said. "You see that clock up there? That's my sentencing clock."

Coldwater turned his head to see an ordinary analog wall clock silently sweep away the seconds. He felt the blood drain out of his face and his legs grow weak.

"It's five to nine. That's what I'm going to give you," Thompson said, as he stared at Coldwater. "Too bad you didn't get on the afternoon calendar. I may have given you two to three. Next case."

As the next set of attorneys shuffled to the tables, Hudson picked up his legal pad and headed out of the courtroom. He caught Fry's eye first, and gave the two detectives a hearty smile.

"Forge, Fry. How nice of you to drop in this morning. I hear you guys had a nice day at the beach yesterday. You know, if you two keep showing up together, people are going to start to talk." Hudson slapped Forge on the back, and put his arm around him as if they were long-lost college buddies. "Let's talk in my office."

He pulled the two men into the dilapidated pale-blue men's bathroom, checked the stalls, and locked the door.

"You guys look like shit," Hudson said. "Did you sleep in those clothes?"

"As a matter of fact, we did," Forge said. "We're here because we need you."

"OK, I confess," Hudson said. "I did it." He threw his hands up to feign contrition. "But really, what do you need?"

"I need you to formally assign us this case," Forge said. He didn't blink. He searched for Hudson's reaction. There was none.

"You guys are good detectives and this happened on your turf, but you know this will be a hard sell to the boss," Hudson said.

"You are the boss," Fry said.

"You're too kind," Hudson said. "But Parker still runs the show, at least when he's in. You know how he feels about you, Matt. If he had his way, you would be looking for snow thieves in Alaska. He is really pissed off at you. He really wasn't happy with what you did."

"This isn't about me," Forge said. "You know I can handle this. And you know I'm the best one for the case. It's our case. We need to see it through."

"Yeah, but Dewall and that idiot Steers are on the case," Fry said. "They couldn't find their way out of a bathroom." It then occurred to Fry that they were talking inside a bathroom. He quieted down.

"What progress have you made so far?" Hudson asked.

"We pulled a fingerprint off the body and we have a suspect," Forge said.

"Who's the suspect?" Hudson said.

"A retired cop with some connections," Forge said. "But we can't find him."

"So you want me to turn this whole investigation over to you two so you can spend the rest of the summer looking for a retired cop?" Hudson said.

"Not exactly," Forge said. "We have a hold out on the guy through state and national, so if he turns up somewhere, they'll give us a call. But this case needs one lead detective who can put the pieces together. This isn't going to be solved by sending a hundred cops into the field to talk to sunbathers. The man-in-the-can was killed for a purpose. We need to know what that purpose was."

Hudson looked at both detectives and walked over to the urinal. He thought it must be one of those Freudian messages his subconscious was sending to his bladder.

"I'm putting my neck on the line for you," Hudson said, looking straight ahead at the chipped tiles. "I have a career here. Why should I do that?"

Forge sensed that Hudson's opposition to the idea was giving way. He needed to feel comfortable that it was the right thing to do and that it wouldn't come back to haunt him with Parker.

"It doesn't have to be official," Forge said slowly. "We can be on the case but not on the case, if you know what I mean. Dewall can be the lead detective, but if you keep him out of our hair, we can have this wrapped up in a week."

"A week?"

"Less than a week," Fry offered.

"By the Fourth of July," Forge said. Fry's eyes widened.

"So, let me get this straight," Hudson offered, as he zipped up his pants and moved to the washbasin to quickly rinse his hands. "I keep Dewall out of your way, you guys make this case, and you both look like heroes. Or, you don't solve it and Dewall looks like an asshole. Or, if Dewall deflects the attention to you guys, it comes back to me. It's a win-win for you, but there is nothing in it for me."

Just like a lawyer, Forge thought. Work the angles until you find the benefits. It didn't matter if it was negotiating a plea for a guy's life or buying a used car. You have to show a win, or it just doesn't count.

"It's all me," Forge said. "If this case falls flat, I take the hit. You can pop my badge on Parker's desk with a nice ribbon around it. But, if we solve it, you get the credit for leading the pack of detectives. When this story hits the papers, every TV station in three states will be talking about it. You'll be out there for the cameras. And the bottom line is you know we can do this case. This is ours and we have to solve it."

Hudson locked in on Forge's eyes to telegraph a silent message: *You better not fail.*

"Why are you so goddamn gung-ho?" Hudson asked. "He's a floater from who knows where. He's likely some low-life mobster whacked in New York and dumped in the East River."

"Not the way I see it," Forge responded. "It's local. There's a bigger purpose for putting him on the beach, and it means a lot more than any of us can fathom right now. I need this. I need to do this."

Hudson took a deep breath as he finished drying his hands with a brown paper towel, then crumpled it and tossed it into the overfilled trashcan four feet away. Forge took his last shot.

"And as the lead attorney, you get to prosecute the case," Forge said. "You know I put together solid cases. This has *Court TV, CNN,* and *MSNBC* written all over it. Even the networks."

Hudson exhaled.

"You got it," Hudson said. "But if you two get in over your heads — and I mean anything that needs uniforms to help back you up — you call me. I want to know every move you are making. I want to know when you stop for a red light. I want to know what doors you are knocking on. I don't want to hear about any surprises. I don't want any Batman and Robin stuff. Do we understand each other?"

At that moment, Fry's cell phone buzzed. He flipped it open and saw that it was a number from the Miami area.

"I got to take this," Fry said, but then cupped his hand over the phone and turned sharply back to Hudson. "Hey, if we're Batman and Robin, then I'm going to be Batman."

"The idea is not to be Batman... ," Hudson said. It was too late. Fry had already walked into a stall with his phone.

"We'll keep you informed," Forge said. "This is going to be bigger than any of us imagine."

Forge saw Hudson revert to his old charming manners. Hudson slapped Forge on the back and tugged on his shoulder with a friendly pull.

"Knowing you, it'll turn out to be bigger than both of us," Hudson said. He smiled as he unlocked the bathroom door, but paused to turn back to Forge.

"By the way, we got a report this morning of a missing priest at Saint Sebastian's, a guy named Father Cadence or Caden or something. He didn't show up for mass, but his nice Mercedes Benz was still in the parking lot."

"And... "

"And maybe it's nothing, but since you're hooked into the nunnery and all that with this case, keep an eye out for anything unusual. Maybe this Father guy just took a long walk in the woods. Or maybe we have a nut on our hands who gets off terrorizing church workers," Hudson said as he left the bathroom.

Forge could hear from the stall the echoes of Fry's conversation reverberate through the tiled bathroom. Forge looked outside the bathroom and was thankful that no one was waiting to use the facility. He locked the door again and then pushed open Fry's stall.

His partner had tucked the flip-phone between his ear and shoulder, and was feverously pulling toilet paper off the roll in one long sheet. Fry was jotting down notes about the conversation.

Fry expressed a sincere thanks to the caller, seemed to write his number at the bottom of the last sheet of toilet paper, and flipped the silver phone closed.

"Got it," Fry said. "That was the barrel company foreman. I gave him the few serial numbers we managed to pull off of the barrel, and he was able to run them through his inventory log."

"And?" Forge was unsure of where this was about to lead.

"And we have a big mess," Fry said in a flat tone. "They only make the barrels and then ship them out to thousands of companies that fill them up with who knows what. We had the first six digits, and that is the good news. The first three numbers showed that the company made the barrel. The next two showed the region of the country it was sent to. The last five — four of which we don't have — is sort of like the serial number for the can. That would have told us exactly where it landed. He gave me a list of possible owners based on the only remaining digit we had."

Forge dialed Singh, got no answer, and left a voice-mail message. The technical had planned to run a spectrum analysis of the goop in the barrel. He could give them a big head start if the liquid was unique enough to trace to a particular company.

§

Two floors above, Hudson smiled perfunctorily at the receptionist as she buzzed him into the main prosecutor's office.

Confident that no one was nearby, Hudson quietly locked the door to his spacious corner office that overlooked the courtyard below. His years of glad-handing and influence peddling with the county freeholders had won him numerous upgrades to his work quarters, one that even included a full shower. It was supposed to be for those long nights between trial days. He used it mostly to hose off the sweat after working out on his treadmill.

He punched the autodial on his desk phone as he placed the handset against his ear.

"Dewall here," the voice on the other end responded.

"Don't get in their way," Hudson said.

"C'mon," Dewall protested. "What good is that going to do?"

"Your job is to keep an eye on them. Hang back, don't get caught, and let me know what they are up to."

"And then what?"

"You stay put until you hear from me. I don't want you screwing this up."

There was silence on the other end of the line. Hudson could tell Dewall was on a slow burn, but he knew enough not to speak out.

"OK. What about Steers?"

"Keep him in the back seat. He can tag along and get you lunch if you need it."

"Right." Dewall hung up.

Hudson cradled the handset and then carefully returned it to its slot. He wondered if this was the right move, if this would help or hurt him. Too late now, he thought. He was already in for a dime, so he might as well be in for the whole dollar.

From the bathroom, the toilet flushed and the door swung open. Standing before him was a stunning tall brunette in a tight, pinstriped gray business suit.

"How did it go?" she said, as she walked behind Hudson's chair. She pressed the pads of her fingers to Hudson's temples and them in a soothing, circular motion.

"You're so tense, honey," Annette told her husband as she pressed deeper and then raked her cherry red fingernails lightly across the side of his head. "How did it go?"

"Well," Hudson said. He looked down at his desk blotter. "Maybe too well."

"What do you mean?" Annette's purring voice hastily smoothed out to a flat tone.

"They took it, hook, line, and all," Hudson said. He grabbed her hands to pull her into his lap. "It was too easy. They were begging me to give them the case."

"Begging you?"

"I didn't even have to bring it up. They wanted in, I resisted, and then gave in to them. It looks like I did them a big favor."

"Oh, but you did," Annette said.

"This better work out," Hudson said.

"It will, honey, it will."

"How can you be so sure?"

"We need them, they need you. It's a perfect circle."

"If nothing goes wrong."

Annette moved close to her husband and whispered softly as she flicked her tongue around the curves of his ear.

"Nothing will. Nothing can go wrong for my future governor."

Hudson smiled. He enjoyed the sound of that word. It was the ultimate in power. The governor, in some respects, was more powerful in New Jersey than the President of the United States. Sure, he didn't have control over all the nuclear missiles, but that was way overrated. The governor appointed more officials than the president. The governor had total control over the state's budget, and the governor could twist the Legislature, the biggest paper tiger ever created, into knots. All he had to do was put his lips together and say "line-item veto."

Governor Hudson. G-o-v-e-r-n-o-r. He spelled it out in his mind. He could feel the power of rewarding his friends with judgeships and punishing his enemies by eliminating their state contracts.

His reputation as the deadliest prosecutor in the state made him a stellar candidate for the party. He didn't need to show voters he was tough; he *was* tough. He would sweep into office on a law-and-order platform that no opponent could match.

"Yes," Hudson whispered back to his wife, as he pulled her closer for a kiss. "Governor Hudson."

§

Below, in the courthouse basement, a sheriff's officer let Forge and Fry use a desk in the inner sanctum of the skip tracer's room. The office was lined with phones and computer terminals used to track down deadbeat dads and defendants who had skipped out on their court dates.

Fry unrolled the wads of toilet paper from his pocket and laid them as flat as he could along the long portion of the steel table. Thankfully, the flimsy sheets were none too plush, which kept the ink from diffusing through the paper.

Forge's phone rang. Fry could see Forge liked what he heard on the other end.

"That was Singh," Forge said as he flipped the phone closed. "The goop in the barrel is a combination of glutaraldehyde and a generic skin softener," Forge said.

"Which is what?" Fry asked.

"Glutaraldehyde is a preservative, like alcohol."

"Wait a minute," Fry said, as he scrolled through the list of names on the toilet paper. He pointed to a thick blot of ink in the middle of the roll. "The barrel manufacturer said the partial digits might be a chemical company in Pennsylvania."

"Sounds close enough. What's the name?"

"K-oxy."

Forge flipped to the Web on the desktop PC. In these situations, Forge knew from experience, it was a lot faster to Google a company than hunt around the FBI's catalogs. They were so cumbersome sometimes, as if they had been designed in the 1990s.

The search took less than a second. There, in all its glory, was the homepage for K-oxy.

"Holy shit," Fry said. "Look what they make."

"Three guesses who their number one customer is," Forge said. "And the first two don't count."

TWO

In the sweltering heat of the Barnegat Light fishing docks, Lester Lewis waited for his ship to come in.

The routine had become old for Lewis. He had known Tolck for more than thirty years, yet he always hovered somewhere between gofer and driver. As a retired cop, Lewis had done his stint as an enforcer — or a persuader, as Tolck would call it. Lewis had been on both sides of the badge. He liked Tolck's side best. Now pushing seventy, Lewis looked as tough as a church elder. When he was an Atlantic City cop, Lewis had made a decent living, not off the paltry salary the town fathers gave him every week, but off the gratuities that came naturally to the job.

Sure, the occasional storeowner would tip him an extra ten dollars to drive by the shop once a night and jiggle the locked doors. That was expected. It was pocket change. The big money came after hours. Local politicians hired him to keep order at business meetings and lid a on tempers at gambling operations. Numbers runners were the best customers. For turning a blind eye, Lewis could easily add a hundred dollars to his weekly income.

He had hooked up with Tolck while running security for a backroom poker game, and soon found a post-retirement niche as a fixer. Tolck respected Lewis's method of solving problems without leaving the noise and tattletale traces of gunshot wounds. And Lewis felt a kinship with Tolck. Once Tolck revealed what he called his "garden," Lewis marveled at the simplicity of the eternal place of rest for the darkest of secrets.

Lewis's cell phone rang. As he flipped open the silver device, his creeping arthritis pointedly reminded him that he was not aging gracefully.

The rusted red fishing boat that he had been waiting for at the dock had just pulled in, and its deck hands were in the process of tying the thick hemp rope to a weather-worn silver pier cleat. Annoyed that he would have to talk over the rumble of the diesel engines, Lewis shouted a curt "Yeah, what?" into the mouthpiece.

"OK, OK," he quickly said, taking his tone down a notch. "But there's a shipment coming in now."

"Move it to the warehouse and then go pick up the package," Consolina said. "We'll meet you at the usual place. Don't talk to anyone. And try to pretend to be nice."

Lewis sneered as he flipped the phone shut. As much as he hated running errands, he hated taking orders from a woman even more — and a stripper, no less.

The trawler hoisted its five boxes of goods from the hull, and swung them quickly over the edge of the water and onto the idling forklift. The merchandise was covered by a thick, gray canvas tarp, assuring Lewis that any prying eyes would assume the bundle was boxed fish packed in ice at sea. As far as fishing villages go, Barnegat Light was one of the smallest, but Lewis knew everyone on the dock minded his own business. The warehouse was scant feet from the water, making it easy to roll the boxes into a dark corner.

The forklift wasted no time in doing just that. As the merchandise moved away, Lewis walked onto the rocking trawler with *Donna D* painted on its side, the chipped white paint stained by rust and fish oil. In the wheelhouse, Lewis extracted a thick envelope of cash from his blazer and handed it to the captain. Both kept their hands low, so no deck mate would see the exchange and get an idea to cut the captain's throat in his sleep.

"Any problems?" Lewis asked.

"None," responded Captain Sorensen, a man in his late fifties with a gray Ahab beard and a thin wisp of hair covering his head. "The Coast Guard passed by, but we gave a friendly wave and they sped off." He pointed across the inlet to the white building with the diagonal red strip. "As long as we don't look like Colombian drug lords, they leave us alone. Hell, I even buy some of the guys a drink when we're in port."

With some trepidation, Lewis jumped off the rocking boat to the dock and followed the forklift into the warehouse. Two burly men were stacking the cases neatly in one corner, about five high and four deep. Lewis hated the smell of the warehouse. The dampness and heat accentuated the raw stench of decaying fish entrails, lingering diesel fuel, and creosote-tarred pilings. He'd much rather be at Tolck's funeral home moving the bodies around than here. At least the bodies were perfumed enough to hide the stink of the preservatives.

Tolck found that the funeral home business was profitable in more ways than one. True, there would never be a loss for clientele. He had professional embalmers front for him, to ease the pain of the grieving widows and order the supplies. For the second value, you couldn't put a price on that type of service. It was essential to Tolck's business, and essential to all of their survival.

Using a crowbar that had been left in the corner, Lewis pried open the closest box and checked the merchandise. The bottles of rum, whiskey, and bourbon had been neatly encased in straw with cartons of cigarettes acting as shock absorbers. Oddly enough, with the anti-smoking tax tripling the base price of a pack of tobacco, the cigarettes were worth more now than the liquor.

Tolck went through cases of booze each week at The Paradise and needed a clean supply chain that wouldn't lead to him. It was too much to buy at the local liquor store and he couldn't place massive orders with the regional distributors because the feds would trace it back to his strip club. For pennies on the dollar, Tolck paid his modern-day rumrunners to pick up cases of the alcohol and tobacco from giant commercial trawlers that stopped at the Bahamas and Bermuda. There was no federal excise tax to pay, and Tolck had enough offshore connections that made it cost-effective to ship the liquor thousands of miles by sea.

Lewis twisted the cap from a bottle of Grand Cayman gold rum to take a long swig. The 150-proof burned his throat, but sent satisfied warmth throughout his body. He slowly felt the tension in his back ease and the pain in his joints move away from him.

He loaded a case in the trunk of Tolck's cream Lexus and drove back to the mainland. His package, he was told, would be waiting for him.

THREE

Fry made a quick call to K-oxy in Scranton, Pennsylvania. It seemed to be a small, family-owned company, and he had little trouble locating the owner.

"We make a lot of products," Harrington Smythe III told Fry. "We work in disinfectants and embalming fluids for hospitals and funeral homes."

"You ship your products in black barrels?" Fry asked.

"You mean the rolled dead?" Smythe asked.

Fry felt as if a giant had grabbed his chest and squeezed him like a balloon. "Wha... ," he said. He had to clear his throat before he could continue. "What did you say?"

"The cold rolled dead, y'know, the barrel."

"I didn't mention anything about a dead guy," Fry said. Forge moved closer to the phone in an attempt to hear both sides of the conversation.

There was a long pause on the other end of the line. "I'm not sure we're on the same wavelength here, officer," Smythe said. "You asked me about the barrels we use. We use cold rolled dead barrels."

"What the hell is that?"

"Ah, it's just the type of metal we order," Smythe said. "Cold rolled dead soft 1008/1010 strip steel. It's very nice for these shipping operations because it's soft. It doesn't break open if you drop it; it just kind of dents inward. Most people think of steel as cold rolled or cold rolled soft, but there are many ways to flatten out the metal."

Fry let his breath out to compose himself again. Here he thought a slip of the tongue had uncovered a massive interstate conspiracy of shipping dead bodies in barrels. Instead, it was a mundane lecture on metallurgy.

Smythe was still perplexed by the brief line of questioning. A police officer was calling from New Jersey to talk about barrels? And he flipped out once he heard it was cold rolled dead steel?

"For our products, we ship stuff out by the ton," Smythe said. "Barrels, boxes, plastic vats. Big, small, wide, narrow. We provide whatever the customer wants us to, in whatever volume they want."

"What would you use glutaraldehyde for?"

"We use it in a lot of products. It's a good disinfectant and not a lot of irritation in low dosages. We mix it with alcohol, soaps and softeners, like lanolin, to give it a gentle feel on the hands. We use our own proprietary mix for embalming fluid."

"Like formaldehyde? I see on your Web page you have something called 'Live Glow'?"

"It's 'Living-Glo.' That series of products is a very popular line. We sell it in pint, gallon, and multi-gallon configurations. It really gives the departed a nice, warm color... "

Fry was losing patience. He wasn't a customer. He didn't want to be sold. He wanted to know what they shipped and where they shipped it.

"Do you have any customers in New Jersey?" Fry asked.

"Well, let me see," Smythe said as the rustle of paper could be heard through the phone. "My secretary is out for the holidays and I don't really know where anything is. She really runs the place, I just come in and take the credit." He chuckled at inside joke.

"Let me narrow it down for you," Fry said. "South Jersey, Ocean County? Does that sound like a place you ship to?"

Forge frantically looked for a telephone book in the office. He found an older one under a desk being used as a support for a missing leg. The metal desk made a scratchy thump on the ground as Forge extracted the *Yellow Pages* and dropped the end of the three-legged piece of furniture.

He flipped toward the "F" section and scanned for "Funeral Homes." He found six pages of ads, and about three-dozen listings. Was business that good that the area needed so many funeral homes, he thought? Probably the only recession-proof business you can get into these days.

He wracked his brain to recall what the mayor had told them. He mentioned a funeral home, but not the name. Of course it wasn't called "Tolck's Home for Stiffs". That would be too easy.

"Try under the 'G's," Fry whispered. "I can't remember its name. It's a family business, the only one that's not owned by a corporation around here."

Forge scanned down and found just one "G": "Gethsemane's Home for Funerals. Since 1921. Providing care and service for all faiths."

"Ask him about this," Forge said, pointing to the name.

"Do you ship to Gethsemane?"

The rustle on the other end of the phone grew louder.

"I'm sorry, this is really a mess. Let me see if my sales manager is here." Fry heard the drop of the phone on the desk and the opening of a door, followed by a shout for a man named Ray.

"This is Ray," a new voice said. "Who are you looking for?"

"Gethsemane. Gethsemane Funeral Home. Tucker Township, New Jersey. Do you ship there?"

"Why, yes, we do," Ray said. He didn't have to think about it. "They have been a good customer for about thirty years, being that there are a lot of senior citizens in your area. We ship all our major product lines there."

"In drums?"

"Most of the time."

"What did you ship and when did you ship it?"

"Let me see." Ray sounded like he was flipping through pages of a log book of some sort. "We usually ship one barrel of Living-Glo to them once a month. It's really our best seller. It pumps up the vacant cavities and gives the clients a cheery, rosy glow. Many people remark how they don't even look like the dearly departed."

Fry felt queasy. These guys were talking about bodies as if they were lawn ornaments.

"Did the barrel ever come back to you? Y'know, like a return?"

"No, there is no record of it. We usually pick up the old ones when the new ones arrive, but there hasn't been a shipment down there since May. I guess business is a little slow that time of year," Ray said.

Both detectives exhaled as Fry hung up the phone.

"We got it," Fry said.

"We got our first marker," Forge said. "But I still think we're a long way from finding our way back to port."

FOUR

Lewis made sure that he was not being followed by looping around the Ship Bottom circle two times on his way off the island. He then proceeded into the pines to find his quarry.

Lewis slowly moved up the driveway and parked at the side of the house, making sure that neither the owner nor passers-by could see his car. As he had done countless times before, he removed a three-foot-long board, eighteen inches wide, from the back seat and placed it carefully against the rear license plate of the vehicle. The board looked natural enough, but hid the important license numbers from witnesses. If he were in a rush, the board would fall harmlessly away as he drove off.

Even from the outside of the stone-walled mansion, Lewis could hear Mayor Preston arguing with his young wife.

The mayor was trying to convince her to pack her jewelry and bags and skip town with him to parts as yet unknown. The wife was protesting that all her friends were in the area but, more important, she still had her furs in cold storage. The best Lewis could tell, the mayor was losing.

Lewis unlocked the front door with the key that he had duplicated when Tolck's men built the house, and withdrew the compact .32-caliber Beretta Tomcat from his right-ankle holster.

He amused himself for a minute. Lewis wondered how an oversized, middle-aged man of 350 pounds or more could let a one-hundred-pound skank of an ex-dancer push him around so easily.

"This just isn't the marital bliss you envisioned, is it Everett?" Lewis said.

"Wha — what are you doing here?" Preston sputtered, as the sweat beads on the top of his bald head grew. "I can't be seen with you."

Lewis waved the black pistol.

Preston's eyes widened as he slowly moved toward his wife in a protective stance. Candee hit him as hard as he could, but the mayor looked as if he had no feeling in his arm.

"Get away from me, you big galoot," Candee said in her squeaky high voice. "He's here for you, not me."

As one of The Paradise's main attractions for a year, Candee had become accustomed to the tough ways of Lewis and the rest of Tolck's crowd. She had seen the guns, the knives, the beatings, and the not-so-gentle persuasions of recalcitrant clients. She had always thought her husband was in too deep with Tolck, which meant, of course, that she would be a widow sooner rather than later.

"Oh, God, don't do it!" Preston cried. He dropped to his knees with a thump that rattled the collectables in a nearby curio cabinet. "I didn't tell them anything. I didn't say anything. I won't say anything. You have to help me, Les. You have to."

The mayor's pleas didn't register. Lewis had no idea what Preston was talking about. He knew enough to never listen to a mark. They will try to lie their way out of anything, offer you promises they can't keep and money they don't have. Lewis kept his mouth shut.

"For God's sake," Preston blubbered, as he sank lower to the floor, his hands held in a tight, prayer-like fold. "We've been friends for twenty years. Don't do this."

Lewis had his orders. He had to make the delivery just as Consolina had asked. But there was only room for one in the car.

"Is there anyone else here?" Lewis said coolly.

"No one," Candee responded, as she casually pulled a pack of cigarettes from her tight pants pocket and flicked a slim sliver lighter to the tip of one smoke. She turned to position herself slightly to the side of Lewis so she could better see her husband wallow at her feet. "He's all yours."

"Thank you," Lewis calmly responded.

Lewis reached behind his back for the special belt holster that he had designed decades ago while a cop in Atlantic City. He felt the cool, brass head of the instrument and quietly extracted it from its nesting place.

As the diminutive Candee focused her attention on Preston, Lewis raised the ball-peen hammer over his head. With the rounded end down, he used all his might to slam the tool onto the top of the former dancer's skull.

The dull sound of the penetrating thrust brought a crooked grin to Lewis's face. The sound was all the affirmation needed to assure him that another job had been flawlessly executed. A faint echo of the limp body falling onto the tile reverberated throughout the house, and then fell silent.

Lewis winced as he knelt beside the body, balancing himself on one hand. The biting pain of the arthritis had inflamed his hammer-wielding shoulder as well as his knees. *I always forget to take the damn painkillers*, Lewis cursed at himself. *But, I guess this is better than scurrying around the ground looking for the spent bullet casings.*

Lewis did not immediately withdraw the embedded hammer from the crown of Candee's head. His years of experience with the fourteen-inch-long tool had trained him to be patient. Lewis pressed his middle finger to Candee's carotid artery to feel the life fade away. Sometimes he had found himself waiting up to five minutes for the heart to receive the message that the brain had been disconnected. He was fortunate today; her pulse weakened and stopped within a few beats.

Lewis had found that the hammer, an heirloom from his tool-and-die-maker father, was much more effective at close range than a knife or a gun. A knife was always messy. Hit a major vessel and blood splattered you like a garden hose. A gun was too loud, and it always left the unique nicks and grooves of the bullet in the victim's body. And if they catch you with the gun before you can throw it away...

Lewis didn't have to worry about that with the ball-peen. The rounded head acted as a cork on a champagne bottle. It kept nearly all of the blood in until the heart gave out. With a deft flick of his wrist, Lewis extracted the mahogany handle from Candee's head. It squeaked softly as the fleshy seal reluctantly released its grip around the yellow metal.

"Get up," Lewis said. His monotone betrayed his disaffected attitude. The thrill of the kill that once drove his ambitions was long gone from his senses.

Preston slowly opened his eyes. His elation at being alive was tempered by the image he saw from the corner of his gaze.

A thin stream of blood had followed the run of the cream grout along the golden tiles at his knees. He gradually turned to his left to see Candee on the floor, a trickle of red running from the thumb-sized hole in the top of her head. Her eyes were frozen as they looked passed her husband's stunned expression.

Preston held his hands to cover his mouth as he wept. What was happening? Was he next? Was Lewis here to kill them both?

Lewis grabbed the mayor by the fold of his shirt and tugged him to his feet. "C'mon, get up. I don't have all day," Lewis said.

"Get in the goddamn car," he commanded. Preston stumbled forward, then he turned back for a last glimpse at his dead newlywed. "Don't look at her. I don't need you to get all sentimental on me," Lewis said.

"But my wife..." Preston protested. The sobs had stopped, but his face was still stained with tears.

"Think of it," Lewis said, "as your no-fault divorce."

FIVE

Lewis had forced the mayor into the trunk of his car, not an easy feat for a man with a gut so vast that he could easily be mistaken for the plump, Happy Buddha that adorns many a Chinese restaurant.

With a firm grunt and a hefty push from Lewis, Preston rolled into the trunk and looked wide-eyed up at his kidnapper as the lid was about to be shut.

"Now, I don't want to hear any yelling or screaming or pansy-ass cries for help," Lewis told the mayor, as if he were reading from a list of directions for assembling a bicycle. "No one will hear you except me, and it'll just annoy me. Do you understand?"

Preston nodded with a short bob of his head.

"I'm not going to tie you up or slap duct tape over your mouth," Lewis continued. "That is just so Hollywood, and it's really overdone. We're going to take a nice trip. This is a good car, so you won't feel the bumps. But I have to ask one favor."

Preston, his stunned expression frozen on his face, didn't know what to say. He was in the trunk sitting over the spare tire and going to God knows where, most likely to be killed and dumped in the ocean as shark chum. And Lewis was asking a favor of him?

"O-K," Preston said slowly.

"If you have, ah, a need, could you just hold it?" Lewis asked.

"Wha-what?" Preston said hoarsely, clearing his throat.

Lewis felt embarrassed, as if he were talking to a child. He never could get this part of the drill down exactly right.

"Y'know, the bathroom," Lewis whispered. "If you have a need to go, could you just really try to hold it? It's almost impossible to get the smell out of the trunk. The mat soaks all the, ah, piss up, and then I have to throw it away or spend the day bleaching the mess out. It also knocks the hell out of the paint."

The power of suggestion gave Preston the urge to urinate, but decided not to tempt fate. He could ask for permission to run into the house to use the bathroom before they left, but opted to clench his teeth instead.

"No problem, Les," Preston said with a squint.

"Great, Ev. You're a real trooper," Lewis said. "Oh, and help yourself to a bottle of booze there. It'll take the edge off."

Lewis slammed the trunk shut. He took the license plate blocking board and flipped it onto the backseat.

Finally, all the pieces were coming together. Lewis felt he had covered his tracks so well, not even Tolck knew what was happening. It was unfortunate — no, a terrible sin — to silence Father Caden in such a crude and ruthless manner. The priest didn't even have time to make his own peace. Caden tried to break away, and had been successful at it for years, taking his vows and burrowing deep into the Pine Barrens. But, a creature of greed, Caden couldn't cut his ties to the old crew. A pity. He needed to die to keep the secret.

Ev was different. That was business, the boss's business. It was nothing more than another job.

The ride to Barnegat Light took ten minutes longer than normal, as Lewis was careful to use the backroads and avoid exceeding the speed limit. If his old friend started making too much noise, he could pull over to a tree-lined shoulder and pistol-whip him a few times, but he didn't think that would be necessary. A threat worked better than ropes and a gag most of the time.

If worse came to worse, if he was being pulled over by a cop and his horizontal passenger was making too much racket, he could always invoke the nuclear option, as Lewis dubbed it: shoot through the backseat to silence his ward, and hope the cop didn't see the flash. Or he would throw caution to the wind and whack them both. He would have to run to the cop car, disable the video surveillance camera, pop the trunk, fire a few rounds into the lock-box that held the video tape, flee before any other cars drove by and then dispose of the Lexus at a North Jersey chop shop. Lewis didn't even want to think what the boss would do if he had to go nuclear. Thankfully, it was just a scenario that he had practiced in his head many times but never had to use.

As Lewis pulled close to the wharf warehouse where he had first received the call for the pick-up, two of Tolck's associates quickly opened the bay doors and, just as quickly, closed them behind the vehicle. The Lexus's tires squeaked sharply as Lewis came to a stop at the figures before him.

Tolck sat at a small card table, straddling a steel folding chair, which had been turned backward so that he could easily lean on the support. It was also a strategic defensive position Lewis knew had become second nature to Tolck. The master of all that he could touch had positioned himself so that his back was against a wall and no one was able to stand behind him. The front of the chair covered his upper torso, the metal giving him added protection from any bullet or knife that may find its way toward him.

Without a word, Lewis popped the trunk and a shell-shocked Preston, unsure of where he was or what was about to happen, slowly lifted his head from the well.

"Good afternoon, Ev," Tolck said pleasantly.

"Dom?"

"Yes."

Preston's eyes, already adjusted to the dark, scanned the dimly lit warehouse and knew in an instant that he was at Tolck's dockside lair. The rank fish smell gagged him for a moment, and as he caught his breath he saw out of the corner of his eye two shapes. Consolina and Costa.

Preston didn't recognize Consolina at first. He mostly remembered her from the club, dancing the fire dance with clothes off, or hanging around Tolck's meetings with barely any clothes on. Here she was dressed in what looked to be long, heavy denim jeans and an ill-fitting leather top, a pair of gloves tucked halfway into her pocket. Her rich, red hair was pulled back into a tight bun, and her head was covered with a black Eagles sports cap.

Next to her, Costa was dressed in more casual mobster attire. He had on a mauve, silk short-sleeve shirt that fit tightly, its top three buttons undone to reveal a mat of chest hair. Perhaps as an ode to the occasion, Costa had traded in his leather sandals for high-end sneakers. They were the kind, Preston guessed, that you would pump up with a little squeeze pad so your feet wouldn't get hurt while stomping on someone's face.

Preston caught himself wondering why he was thinking of such absurd details. He knew the warehouse was usually the dead end for those who double-crossed Tolck. He had heard the whispers, the rumors, about what happened to the bodies. Most guessed they were dumped offshore from Costa's forty-foot cigarette boat, which he docked a few yards from the warehouse. Others spoke of body parts being ground up and mixed in with the chum that tourists unwittingly and happily tossed off of party boats during half-day fishing expeditions.

Preston felt his heavy chest start to seize. He gasped for air, feeling as if he were about to have a massive heart attack. What a way to die, he thought; falling stone dead in the trunk of a Lexus in a dank warehouse.

"You OK?" Costa asked. "You're looking a little flushed."

The rest of the group laughed and sputtered to silence as Tolck coughed into his hand.

"Come, Ev. Let us get you out of there. I know you have had a busy day," Tolck said gently.

Preston caught his breath as Costa and Lewis hauled his body out of the trunk and stood him before Tolck. The circulation slowly returned to his feet and he felt that he could indeed stand after all.

"Please, have a drink," Tolck said, motioning to the bottle of Frangelico and two glasses on the card table. "I hate to drink alone."

Preston felt his composure return as his shaking hand poured a small shot into the tumbler. He took a seat across from Tolck.

"You are wondering what I am going to do with you," Tolck said. "It's natural. There is no shame in asking." He paused, but no words came from Preston. Tolck knew the mayor was about to crack. He needed to move the conversation away from any thoughts of impending death.

"We had a plan, Ev. A deal," Tolck said. "The plan will work. But it will work only if we all stick together."

Tolck focused on Preston's eyes, watching them come alive as the professional politico, that man who once bragged that he had shaken the hand of every man, woman, and child in town, transformed from Preston-the-Weak to Preston-the-Negotiator.

"The plan didn't involve murder," the mayor said slowly.

"The plan had to be adjusted," Tolck said.

"Who is it?"

143

"You mean who was it?"

"Yes. Who was killed?"

"A friend."

"Friend?"

"Yes, your friend. The one you introduced me to, Ev. The one who enlightened me to the wonderful possibilities of politics."

Preston tried to control his expression, but his rapid blinking gave away his distress. He had just spoken to the man two days earlier. What could possibility have gone wrong? So wrong that Tolck had to have him killed?

"I don't understand. Why?"

"Apparently," Tolck said, rolling the Frangelico glass in his hand, "there are competitors. You know how I feel about competitors, Ev. They are bad for business. They drive up the cost of business. My business. They alter carefully crafted plans. And they cause good men to make very bad mistakes."

He slowly enunciated the final three words as he glared at Lewis, whose failing hearing easily put him out of earshot.

Preston moved the chess pieces in his head to try to understand who had broken away, who had sided with whom, and how Tolck had found out about it.

"Friendship is a wonderful miracle when it works," Tolck said. "It binds. It strengthens. It enhances the whole over the individuals. Without friendship, there is no trust, no loyalty, no progress. Do you see, Ev? We're friends. Not because we went to the same schools, or enjoy the same social clubs. We found common ground. We found a way that would have made us both stronger, better."

"We're not friends. We were never friends," Preston said. "You used me."

"We used each other," Tolck said. "You came into my establishment poor and lonely, and you left with wealth and women. Our mutual interests... intersected, shall we say."

"You ruined me. Everything you touch, everyone you lead into your web, you ruin."

"Did you not get what you wanted? What beautiful young woman would want a corpulent, bald, middle-aged man?" Tolck said. "What town would elect a washed-up antique dealer as mayor? I gave you everything you wanted. You weren't satisfied with success. You wanted more."

Tolck allowed the thought to germinate for several seconds.

"I provide a necessary service," Tolck said. "I fill the need of the greedy. I fill the need of the power hungry. I fill the need of the people who want to see strippers, who want big houses in pretty parks, who want whatever they can get whenever they want to get it. I don't ruin anyone. I only provide a way for everyone to ruin themselves."

"For money."

"No. Not for money."

"For what then?"

"For a dream, Ev. For a dream."

"A dream?"

"Yes," Tolck said. He paused to collect his thoughts. "We all have a dream of a better life, a life of paradise here, now, rather than in the next life."

Tolck looked earnestly at his empty glass and eyed the cases of illegally imported rum that sat in the corner, covered with a dirty oilcloth. He didn't look for, nor want, a response from Preston.

"Friends who are loyal are in a relationship forever," Tolck said, returning to his first line of thought. "Many friendships last longer than a marriage, maybe several marriages. It's what binds us men together. That urge, that deep desire, to be bigger than we really are. With friendship, we can reach our dreams."

With two fingers, Tolck motioned Lewis to the table. He held out his hand and, without a word, Lewis placed his Beretta into Tolck's palm.

Preston, resolved that his fate was sealed the moment he saw Lewis, had no more emotion. There was no point in running. His exit was blocked by Costa and Consolina. It was best to die like his wife, quickly, without pain.

Tolck carefully pointed the weapon away from the mayor and slowly unlocked the ammunition clip from the base of the grip. With a slight metallic click, the holder sprung free and a bit of sweet machine oil wafted past Preston's nose.

Tolck gently thumbed the bullets from the clip, letting each one quietly fall to the felt top of the card table.

"We came into this arrangement together," Tolck said. "But we need to correct our mistakes before we can go any further."

Tolck slid one round into the top of the empty clip, and slapped it into the Beretta. He pulled the slide of the weapon back until it hit the stop. Then silently pushed it forward. The single shell was loaded, awaiting its final command from the cocked firing pin.

"Sometimes when we make mistakes, we don't know that a mistake has been done," Tolck said. "Perhaps out of carelessness, or ignorance, a small misstep leads to much larger problems. Problems that affect not just the group; problems that affect me."

Preston watched as Tolck slowly stood up from his chair, exposing his lean body with the weapon dangling from his right hand. Preston felt no menace from Tolck's movements. He watched as Tolck walked around the table and stood behind him. Was this the final blow, the *coupe de grace*, the single shot that he had been waiting for? He shut his eyes tight. He felt Tolck's cold hand on his shoulder.

Then, unexpectedly, he felt Tolck's warm breath near his ear.

"We need each other," Tolck whispered. "We don't need those who have made mistakes."

Confused, Preston opened his eyes to see Lewis idle in the corner near the rum. The elderly ex-cop was so used to the anti-climax of the kill that he occupied his time by looking up at the smeared windows at the top of the warehouse.

"You want to kill him, don't you?" Tolck said.

"I don't know what you mean," Preston said slowly, his eyes fixed on Lewis.

"He killed your wife." Tolck's whisper had become a hiss. "You saw him. He came for you and he killed your wife, your beloved Candee. Do you remember the day I introduced you to her in The Paradise? You remember how you felt? You remember how her smile enveloped and warmed your flesh?"

Preston's eyes filled with tears as his mind spun between past lust and the confusion of Tolck's words.

"Yes," the mayor said. He could barely speak.

"Do you feel the rage? What do you want to do to him?"

"Hate him."

"No."

"Hurt him."

"No."

Preston hissed out the final words: "Kill him."

"Yes," Tolck said. For the first time, a smile crossed Tolck's lips. "Yes." He pressed the Beretta into Preston's right hand.

"Now. Do it now."

"I – I can't."

"He killed your wife. He deserves to die."

Tolck gripped Preston's shoulder to help him raise the weapon slowly to his chest.

Lewis caught a glimpse of the piece and began to lunge toward it, thinking that Preston had somehow managed to pull the gun out of Tolck's hand, then stopped as Costa drew his silver-plated, long-barreled 9 mm from his shoulder holster and pointed it at his head. Costa wagged his finger and said, "Uh-uh-uh. Move and I'll blow off your limbs one by one," Costa warned.

Lewis froze. He was trapped, and cursed himself for letting his guard down.

"Boss," he said to Tolck. "Boss!"

Tolck glowered at Lewis. "You didn't think I would find out about the priest, about Caden? About how you are responsible for this mess? Did you think killing him would stop your mistake?"

Tolck turned to his guest for one final demand.

146

"Do it. Pull the trigger. If you don't, he will kill you."

Through a cry that mimicked the gasps of a newborn, Preston turned away, and squeezed.

The bullet caught Lewis square in the belly. The hot copper jacket of the projectile sliced through his small intestines, severed the aorta that ran along the inside of his spine, nicked a bone, and then spun to exit upward through a lung. The bullet, half of its energy spent, pierced a case of rum as Lewis fell hard against the boxes. One bottle tumbled free and shattered, sending brightly colored shards in all directions. He felt the golden liquor from another cracked bottle perched precariously over his head pour slowly onto his shoulder as he slumped into death.

Tolck patted Preston on the back as he pulled the smoking weapon from the mayor's limp hand.

"We are in this together now," Tolck told the mayor. "Your murder is now our murder. We have a bond that will carry us though the rest of our lives. We have the bond of friendship."

Costa holstered his weapon and moved toward Lewis's body. He grabbed the feet as if he were hauling a marlin onto a deep-sea fishing boat and pulled it away from the glass shards of the rum-stained boxes.

In the distance, Preston saw Consolina wheel over a small handcart with two cylinders strapped to the back. The mayor couldn't quite make out what the device was. It had yards of coiled red hosing and a metal bar that joined the two tanks.

As she walked closer, he saw that Consolina had placed a black welder's mask over her baseball cap, with the dark faceplate up in the open position. She left the handcart, which was no higher than her hips, about twenty feet away and carefully unwound the red hose. She extracted a thin brass metal nozzle from her trouser pocket, and with an audible hiss, clicked it into the blunt end of the hose.

"Ready?" she asked.

Costa thought for a moment, and then repositioned the body away from the car and over a storm drain grate.

"OK," he said. "I didn't want the heat to ruin the finish on the car."

With a single flick of the tool's trigger, Consolina ignited the blowtorch and adjusted the flame to ensure it was neither too yellow nor too blue. She deftly mixed the acetylene and oxygen to the point where the noise of the flame sounded as if a gale were blowing outside. A special cutter head was affixed to the appliance to ensure that she received not only the hottest flame, but also the widest possible spread of the super-heated gases. Six small cones fed by the oxy-acetylene formed a ring around the central flame of pure oxygen. The wider head, used for rapid cuts through thick metal, scorched the same area three times as fast as a regular torch.

"Be sure to do his fingers," Tolck shouted over the noise. "Lewis's prints gave us away once, we don't want to have them give us away again. And Costa, get Mr. Lewis's favorite hammer. I think he would want its final use to be on his teeth."

With a brief jerk of her head, Consolina flicked the protective faceplate down and touched the six-thousand degrees of flame to the top of Lewis's face. The steam of vaporized flesh swiftly filled the air above her and then was gone. Within a minute, Lewis's entire identity, the age lines and stress marks from sixty-nine years of a hard life, were erased forever.

SIX

The search warrant was exquisite in its detail. If it were too broad, it would be filleted in court by defense lawyers who would successfully argue that it violated the Constitution's prohibition against unlawful search and seizure. If it were too narrow, the detectives would risk handcuffing themselves and being forced to overlook potential evidence.

Forge had dictated the search order to the secretary in less than fifteen minutes, trying to recall all the details he could from prior warrants. After flipping through the cover page that boldly stated "Search Warrant," Forge reviewed the document as Fry drove deep into the pines to the Gethsemane Funeral Home. "Officers of the County of Ocean and officers of the Long Beach Island Police Department are hereby commanded to search the aforementioned premises for the following items to be used in connection with the investigation of the death of John Doe, age and name not determined, whose body was found in Harvey Cedars on July 2 of this year. To wit... "

Forge always liked that phrase, to wit. It was old English and, unlike today's gobbledygook from lawyers, it got right to the point.

"To wit: all computerized equipment, files, software, digital information, both encrypted and unencrypted, cipher keys, hard drives, and storage media. All paper records pertaining to the purchase, transportation, and disbursement of embalming chemicals, and any instrument or tools used thereof in the use of the above-mentioned chemicals. All documents, both written and electronic, pertaining to the death, transportation, and/or implementation of the death of John Doe."

Forge reassured himself that the document would cover any contingencies they may run into during the search.

In the rearview mirror, Fry looked at the unusually quiet Sister Maris and then focused on the tan Ford that had been tailing them much too closely.

"Company," Fry announced. "Don't turn around, Sister."

Forge didn't even bother to adjust the passenger side mirror so he could see better. If their new guests were indeed too close, they would see that the detectives had spotted the tail and would drop back farther.

"Let me guess," Forge said. "Tweedle-Dee and Tweedle-Dum."

"Tweedle-Dumb and Tweedle-Dumber," Fry said, glancing at the mirror again. "Trouble is I can't tell them apart anymore. You know this is a tough job when your own guys start following you. Who do you think put them on to us?"

Forge didn't have to wait to respond. "Scratch."

"How can you be sure?"

"He likes insurance. Dewall and Steers are his insurance policy. If we fail, they are there to document it. If we succeed, they are there to steal the spotlight."

"You want me to lose them?" Fry knew a few sharp turns and a duck into someone's driveway would be the quick way to confuse the duo.

"No, no. I've got a use for them."

Fry drove past the funeral home as both detectives carefully sized up the situation. They normally would call for uniformed backup, but Forge was beginning to suspect that there were eyes and ears in every corner of the county. Tolck was prime suspect one, but the extent of his reach had not yet been determined. Forge didn't want to risk too many people knowing his next step. It was bad enough having to deal with two lousy cops behind them.

The funeral home was a low-rise rancher, white with a jet-black roof — simple monochromatic colors to put the grieving at ease. The building was easily visible through the meticulously sculpted shrubbery at the curb that gently framed the home's sign.

Forge could make out one hearse in the back, its rear halfway into the open door of the garage. There were no signs of cars in the lot, which was very good news for Forge. That meant no funeral or viewing had started, and there would be no civilians to get in the way of tossing the place.

He was certain that the funeral director would be inside, along with a couple of technicians in charge of prepping bodies for the casket. It was a low-overhead business. You didn't need a lot of staff to service the customers.

As Fry pulled around the corner and parked, Forge could see through the thicket of hedges that a gated area was shaded by a corrugated metal overhang. That, he knew, was where the chemicals were dropped off.

Forge slowly turned around to look over his right shoulder and saw Dewall and Steers park behind them about fifty paces away. Both men had ducked down behind the dashboard, with Steers occasionally poking his head up like a gopher out of his hole.

"Wait here," Forge said as he quickly exited the car.

He sprinted to the passenger side of the Ford to see the back of Dewall's head as he hunkered down in the seat. Forge sighed and rapped on the window as loudly as he could with the back of his hand.

"Yo, Jack," Forge said in a loud whisper. "I know it's you. You don't have to hide."

Dewall looked up from his hovel and rolled the window down a quarter of the way, as if wasn't sure if Forge was going to talk to him or try to pull him through the window.

"Fancy meeting you here," Dewall tried to say in a matter-of-fact tone.

"Cut the crap," Forge said. "I know Scratch put you on to us. Now you can help us out."

"How so?"

"The home has three points of entry. Fry and I will take the front door. You take the back. Steers here — " Forge glanced over to see that the rotund detective was still crouched below the wheel — "he can guard the garage."

"And do what?"

"Absolutely nothing," Forge responded. "You're backup. You stay outside unless you hear from us. You make sure no one leaves and no one enters. Understand?"

"No," Dewall said defiantly. "We're going in with you."

"That's not needed and it's not safe," Forge shot back. "And besides, your name isn't on the warrant." The last point was a white lie Forge had to tell to get full compliance and ensure he and Fry remained safe from any unanticipated visitors.

"Fine. Have it your way," Dewall said as he tugged Steers upright. "But this is highly irregular. We don't have any radios to talk on."

"It's a small place," Forge said. "We can shout."

With the Ford trailing Fry's car, both vehicles roared into the funeral home's parking lot and pulled up feet from the front door.

Forge and Fry jumped out of their vehicle as Dewall and Steers ran toward the rear of the building.

"Knock, knock!" Fry shouted through the screen door. "Police. We have a warrant to search these premises. Open up now!"

Fry counted to three and threw open the screen door as Forge rolled in across the floor and Fry covered him with the shotgun. Both saw no one in the heavily carpeted anteroom, again done in black and white. After scanning the area, they moved down the hallway toward the door marked "Funeral Director."

Forge heard the telltale sound of grinding metal coming from behind it, and he instinctively kicked the flimsy hollow-core door off of its lock.

There stood a lanky, elderly man who could have been the embodiment of Ichabod Crane. Neatly dressed in a stereotypical black undertaker's suit, the man was feeding sheets of paper into an oversized crosscut paper shredder that sliced the documents into minute dots of confetti.

"Freeze," Forge said, hoping his words would have the same effect as a gun pointed to the man's face. Forge, though, had no weapon, which the man saw, and he continued to pour documents into the shredder.

"Freeze now," Fry said as he punctuated his message by wracking a 12-gauge shell into the chamber of his shotgun. The funeral director dropped the ream of paper in his hand and clicked off the device.

"I give up," the elderly man said, raising his hands halfway up to his head and sitting down.

"Stand up," Fry commanded. "Who the hell are you and what the hell were you doing?"

From the hallway, Fry heard a woman say, "Raymore Gethsemane."

Sister Maris had followed the officers into the funeral home and was now standing at the doorway.

With a slight grunt, the lean man pulled himself to a standing position again and softly said, "Yes, that is right. I am Raymore Gethsemane, proprietor of this establishment."

"You know each other?" Fry asked.

"More professionally than socially," Sister Maris said. "Mr. Gethsemane occasionally uses our chapel for funeral masses. We had one just last week."

Forge picked up the ream of paper on the desk that Gethsemane had obviously yanked out of a wall safe in a hurry. Like a scene from an old movie, the safe was hidden behind a giant oil painting of another elderly gentleman who Forge guessed was Gethsemane's father.

The documents were bunched together in thick packets and sorted into various manila folders. The folders were coded with a sequence of numbers that came in two rows. In one folder he lifted up, he saw the top number was 39. The next number below that was 25.01. The remaining digits followed in sequence. The numbers ran on throughout each folder.

"What are you doing with land records?" Forge asked.

Gethsemane was mute.

"I know these are land records," Forge continued. "These are block and lot numbers." He flipped through the white papers inside one folder and quickly realized that instead of deeds, they were something else.

Instead of the standard fee simple deeds — those that transferred ownership of a parcel from one person to another for an exchange of money — the documents were a complex amalgamation of right-to-purchase contracts, development rights, and quit claims. Instead of a person-to-person transaction, the deeds were a person-to-corporation arrangement. The corporations were obvious shells. The names were made up in hurry and seemingly pulled out of thin air, named after streets or common names followed by a series of number to make it unique, like the Acme 4112 Corp., the Acme 4113 Corp., and so forth.

The documents were signed not by the corporate officers but by a registered agent, the lawyer who everyone hid behind to obscure their true identities and business interests.

The development rights were common ways for giant conglomerates to buy up blocks of land at dirt-cheap prices. Disney had done that in Orlando before it opened up Disney World. If a shrewd investor had gotten wind of the massive land purchase ahead of time, Disney would have faced skyrocketing land prices that could have kept the big mouse from entering the state.

Forge guessed that most of the owners that he saw on paper were aging adults who had inherited landlocked and undevelopable parcels from their parents or even grandparents. The land had no real value commercially, and an owner had two choices: stop paying taxes on it and have the town seize it for a tax sale, or keep paying taxes and pray for a dumb bastard someday to buy it.

As Forge saw from the documents, a lot of prayers had been answered.

"What were you going to do with all these contracts?" Forge asked. He had assumed a tone that was meant to reassure the suspect that he was not the enemy, but a friend. People, even criminals, had a deep instinct to portray themselves as honest and righteous. They were never the bad guys, the logic went, they were just misunderstood. If they could tell their side of the story, maybe the nice policeman would see it their way and let them go.

"Go to hell," Gethsemane said, as he looked away.

For Sister Maris, the averted eyes proved a useful sign. It meant Gethsemane still had a conscience. If she could press the funeral director in just the right way, Sister Maris was sure she could get him to surrender a clue or two.

As she examined the man's face and mannerisms, she made an educated guess at Gethsemane's psychological profile. Without a full workup and hours of testing, it would be a crude estimate, but Sister Maris surmised that the undertaker was a stern man who put pride in his work and reputation.

"I know you didn't pull all this together," Sister Maris said, stepping forward and gently holding onto the old man's hands. "This isn't what you want to do, is it? You want to mind your own business, do your job, and be left alone to do the right thing."

Gethsemane moved his eyes slowly to see if Sister Maris was sincere. He was too old to fight and his proud family's reputation was on the line. He had fallen in with Tolck, not willingly, but fallen in with him nonetheless. It started simply enough. Tolck had supplied a loan to keep the place going during one of the recessions, and Gethsemane had always turned a blind eye to the wrongs he had seen over the years.

Seeing Sister Maris gave him an overwhelming feeling of security and a yearning desire to cleanse the dark spots on his soul. He had found the sister to be a woman respectful of the deceased and of his profession.

"Yes," he responded softy. "I didn't want to get involved, but I can't say any more."

"We're here now. We're here to protect you."

"You can't protect me from him."

"From Tolck?" Forge used one of the basic tricks from detective class 101. If you don't know the answer to a question, don't directly ask for the answer. Pose your best guess as a fact to the subject. He will usually confirm or refute it, then realize his mistake.

"Tolck will find me," Gethsemane choked out. "He always gets what he wants."

"What was it that he wanted you to do?" Sister Maris asked as she moved closer to the old man, who seemed to be both relieved to be unleashing his burden and on the verge of crying.

"I didn't know, I still don't know, what he is up to," Gethsemane said. "That's the honest truth. I was supposed to only hold the paper."

"He made you the shill?" Forge asked.

"It's too hot for him to hold," Gethsemane continued. "I was supposed to be the middleman, the nice, gentle old guy for the lawyers and all that; the face on the deal. I was supposed to be at the signing to reassure the sellers that they were getting a good deal. Who is going to argue with an old man?"

"Who else is involved?"

Gethsemane thought for a moment. His memory for names was indeed fogged by age, but he remembered terms and monikers.

"There was the banker," he said.

"Who is that?" Forge asked as he leaned in closer.

"I never knew," Gethsemane said. "Tolck always referred to him as the banker. He was pulling the money together for the deals."

"Was it Tolck's money?"

"Oh, heaven's no," Gethsemane chuckled, showing the first signs that he was more than an undertaker. "If you think Tolck uses his own money, then you don't know Tolck. He uses everyone else's money."

"Any other names you can recall?" Sister Maris intoned softy.

Gethsemane struggled with the question. He now earnestly wanted to help, but knew little about the inner workings of the deals. Then it hit him.

"Yes, one more name that I heard him mention to that dancer that follows him around," Gethsemane said. "Alpha."

"What is it? Alfie?"

"No, no. I heard it very clearly. Alpha, like the first letter. I may be old, but I'm not deaf."

"Who is Alpha?"

"He never mentioned it to me directly. I was about to walk into the front parlor and I heard the two talking. Tolck said, 'We may have to get Alpha involved.' I didn't know what it was about. I didn't want to know. Tolck is careful about what he says and to whom he says it. I knew I wasn't supposed to hear him, and I quietly backed out of the hallway."

"You never heard that name again?"

"Never."

Fry's impatience got the better of him. They had come to find out about the barrel. He needed to know what Gethsemane knew before he lawyered up.

"What did Tolck do with the can?" Fry asked.

Gethsemane looked puzzled.

"The black barrel. The body juice you guys use for the stiffs. Did Tolck stuff the body in here?"

Gethsemane was still perplexed. "We use a lot of the Living-Glo — it really does bring the dead to life, as the packaging says — that's why we get it by the barrel. No other home in the area can match our quality for preparation of the dearly departed."

"The dead guy," Fry said. "Did you guys stuff the dead guy in the barrel and dump him at sea?"

"I don't know what you are talking about."

"Come on, pops," Fry said as he pulled Gethsemane by the arm. "You're going to show me where you use the barrels."

Fry pushed Gethsemane forward with one arm as he balanced the shotgun on his hip with his other. Gethsemane led them out of the office and through an "Employees Only" door and into the rear of the complex. The room was bathed in a mixture of florescent overhead bulbs and sunlight filtered through heavy white lace curtains. In the back, Forge could see that the door to the garage where the hearse was parked stood ajar.

Inside the room, two bodies were in the process of being prepped for a funeral.

Fry immediately noticed they were the elderly couple that he had seen at the county morgue a day earlier as they arrived to open up the man in a can.

The elderly woman had already been dressed in dark blue while her husband rested next to her, shirtless with black trousers and shoes on. The crude stitching used to close the "Y "incision of the autopsy revealed that the cherry red glow of his cheeks and skin was the product of chemicals, not his natural condition. A clean, pressed white shirt hung on a wooden hanger directly behind the man.

"Mr. and Mrs. Scathmyer were in a very unfortunate holiday accident," Gethsemane began as he saw Fry eye the couple. "It's very sweet, don't you think?"

"What is?" Fry asked.

"That they spent their lives together and now they will spend all eternity together. None of that restless waiting, which brings a certain amount of distress to our elderly clients, at least the living ones." He chuckled at the inside joke of undertakers. "You have no idea how many widows and widowers just can't cope with the loss of a spouse.

"We will be burying them tomorrow at the Eternal Rest Memorial Gardens," he continued. "The family was coming in from Pennsylvania tonight."

Fry was appalled at the cavalier attitude. "Where's your log book for shipments?"

Gethsemane thought for a moment, then moved toward a personal computer sitting in the corner of the room. He called out to Joe, one of the technicians, but no response was forthcoming. He started to move some of the implements of the funeral trade to one side. He casually picked up a long, pointed rod that was used to drain fluid from a body and began to move it.

Simultaneously, Forge singled out an unusual scent in the air. He smelled the faint wisp of what he thought was a cigarette that maybe Sister Maris had struck up, but he saw no tobacco in her hands. There were no ashtrays or other signs of smoking in the room. It probably wasn't a good idea to allow employees to smoke around corpses pumped up with alcohol and other flammable products.

Then he noticed the door again. It was no longer ajar. It was open nearly all the way. He could easily see the dark hearse in the garage and daylight in the distance.

As a shadow moved against the light, Forge immediately sensed danger. Before he could turn, he saw the flash from the muzzle.

The bullet caught Gethsemane in the back of the right lung. The force of the impact propelled his light frame against the counter and as he fell, he impaled himself on the pointed end of the fluid rod that he had been holding. He fell against the computer and collapsed to the floor, barely conscious but still breathing.

In one motion, Forge grabbed Sister Maris hard by the arm as they and Fry instantly dropped to the ground and rolled behind the stainless steel pedestals of the embalming tables. With a hefty grunt, Fry knocked over the table holding Mrs. Scathmyer as a way to use her body to shield them from any more bullets. Looking over the fallen table and body, Fry tried to sight a target with the shotgun, but found none. He cursed at Forge, whispering, "Do you think now would be a good time for you to get a gun?"

Assured that the heavy metal table would protect Sister Maris, Forge crawled to the undertaker and saw that he was still breathing and that his eyes were still open. He was clutching a thin black-and-red log book that he had grabbed as he fell against the countertop.

"Oh, God, oh God, oh God," Gethsemane labored as both a prayer and a plea between deeper and deeper breaths. "Take this."

He thrust the blood-stained book into Forge's hands and exhaled his finals words: ". . . Alpha... midnight... 4."

The smell of smoke grew stronger and Forge could see white curls reach to the top of the ceiling.

"Get out of here, now!" Forge yelled to Fry.

Fry didn't hesitate. As Fry covered the rear, Forge lifted Sister Maris off of her feet, and all three retreated back to the employee entrance that they had walked through just minutes before.

Then the flashover hit.

The struggling bit of flame, hungry for fuel and air, rumbled out of its confined space in the chemical storage closet and roared to life as if it were a lion jumping to center stage in a three-ring circus.

The howl of the expanding heat scorched the ceiling tile and ignited the lace curtains, wall panels, and everything in its path. The fire was doubling in size every second, and Forge knew they had scant moments to get out of the funeral home or risk being cremated along with the Scathmyers and all the evidence.

Black, acrid smoke began to fill the hallway as the air conditioner vainly clicked on full force to cool the soaring temperature. That small part of the building's automation doomed the funeral home to a quick death. The flames were fueled with a new supply of oxygen, and the heat was dispersed to faraway rooms.

All three crawled on their bellies to the main door to keep from being suffocated by the hot fumes. Then, grabbing Sister Maris's arm, and with a deep breath, quickly turned to crawl back in the direction of the director's office.

Fry felt the pair leave his side and turned to follow them. They had no time to argue, and Forge motioned for them to grab as many files as they could.

By the time they turned to exit, the fire had ignited the woolen carpet, blocking their only avenue of retreat.

"Keep down!" Fry shouted as he took a deep breath from the floor, stood up, and raised the shotgun. He unloaded a blast of double-0 buckshot into the windowless wall, then fired six more times in less than three seconds, shattering the wooden supports behind the wall in a rectangular pattern. The flimsy sheetrock and paneling were now the only obstructions between them and the outside.

Fry threw the spent weapon to the side. With a jerk, he pulled Forge to his feet with one hand and Sister Maris with the other and all three ran as hard as they could into the center of the fragmented wall.

The impact moved the wall less than an inch as the trio ricocheted off and fell to the floor. They repositioned themselves, Forge and Fry mustered every bit of their combined strength to throw at the wall again, with Sister Maris in tow.

With a crashing thud of shattering sheetrock and aged wooden framing, the side of the wall fell apart as they tumbled on top of each other into the shrubs. Black smoke followed them into the open and dissipated above their heads.

As they made a run for the parking lot, a thunderous explosion washed a shockwave over their backs, pushing them instantly to the ground again as if a giant had swatted them down.

The heat of the inferno had reached the 1,000-gallon tank of liquid propane that the home used for cremations. Its safety valve rusted closed and filled to its maximum capacity, it didn't take long for the screaming hot temperatures to boil the flammable gas beyond the bursting point of the white steel tank. It ignited with the force of two hundred sticks of dynamite, obliterating the funeral home.

Forge rolled on top of Sister Maris to cover her body while barrels of embalming fluid exploded in a series of blasts, as if someone had lit a string of firecrackers and tossed them into the backyard. Each blast lifted a barrel thirty feet into the sky, flames trailing behind it. Like a defective missile, one barrel arced sharply toward the detectives, paused in the air as if it were deciding to go up or down, and then rapidly tumbled back to earth.

The crinkling metal sounded like a thousand soda cans being crushed underfoot. The liquid inside had all been spent and the hot metal crumpled into an unrecognizable heap as the barrel struck the ground. Forge peeked at the carnage. The explosion had ripped a gaping hole in the barrel, but for the most part, the can was still intact. *I guess that's what dead soft means*, Forge thought.

"Now, ain't that just the biggest kick in the ass we've had all day," Fry said as he looked up to see that Forge and Sister Maris, who was underneath him, were not only alive but also unscathed. "You still with me, loser?"

"Yeah, all limbs and vital body parts still here," Forge said. He rolled off onto his back to scan the horizon for signs of not only Dewall and Steers, but also the mysterious funeral home employee Joe. He saw no one.

Protected from the brunt of the blast by the building, Fry's car was intact but scorched like a campfire marshmallow on the passenger's side. He managed to pull the vehicle away from the expanding flames and sped in reverse to pick up Forge and Sister Maris. Still in a military crouch behind the wheel, Fry looked around for signs of friend or foe but found none. In the distance he could hear the sirens of the approaching fire trucks.

Forge noticed that Dewall's car was gone, and, presumably, the two detectives with it. He couldn't think of the right invective to describe them, but Fry had no trouble filling in the blanks.

"Those yellow-belly, glass-eating slugs bolted on us, leaving us to die," Fry fumed as he pounded the steering wheel. "I'm going to kick Dewall's ass so hard he's going to have to — sorry Sister — shit through his mouth."

SEVEN

Five miles to the west, Dewall turned off the main road and onto a dirt trail hidden by an overgrowth of pine trees. He drove slowly so as not to kick up too much dust. He stopped at a thick steel gate bearing a warning sign: "No Entrance. Federal Property."

He snipped the rusted shackle with heavy bolt cutters and swung the gate open on its creaking hinges. Inside was the decommissioned Air National Guard target practice site. It had been peppered over the decades with dummy bombs and lead cannon projectiles from A-10 anti-tank airplanes and F-16 fighter/bombers.

The government had shut the target range down years ago after a distressed pilot, on full tilt after his wife left him for a woman, decided that the Shore traffic would make a much more challenging target for a strafing run. The flyboy just had to tap the trigger of the 1,200-shots-a-minute rotating Vulcan cannon tucked snugly in the nose of the A-10 Warthog.

Several newly minted Mercedes on a car carrier absorbed the brunt of the attack from the 20 mm rounds. The brief episode ended only after the pilot ran out of ammo. He decided that his next best career move was right out his window. He flew his jet nose first into the deep blue North Atlantic Ocean.

The abandoned area was now Dewall's disposal site. Fenced in by razor wire and off limits to hunters, it was a forgotten relic of the Cold War.

He pulled off the dirt road and into a clump of tall pine trees before he cut the engine. Even at this distance he could see the smoke of the burning funeral home. He opened up the rear door of the Ford and grabbed the feet of the unconscious man.

"Christ, Steers," Dewall muttered to himself. "Would it've have killed you to eat a salad once in a while?"

With another tug, Dewall was careful not to get the dirt from Steers's shoes on his suit as he yanked him out of the vehicle, letting him fall face first into the dust. The welt from the butt of Dewall's pistol was now the size of a silver dollar on the back of Steers's head.

After a couple of grunts, Dewall found it easier to roll Steers rather than drag him. With his foot, he pushed the stirring detective like a log several yards until he fell into a shallow gully.

"Uhhhh …" Steers moaned as he swiveled his head. Groggy and semi-conscious, he could not yet find the strength to open his eyes.

"Sorry, big guy," Dewall said as he tucked an oversized trash bag into his tight, white collar to cover his clothing. With a snap of his wrist, Dewall clicked open a six-inch hunting knife that he had extracted from his pocket. "Nothing personal. You got the wrong assignment at the wrong time. But orders is orders."

Dewall turned his head slightly and grimaced as he made a deep cut across Steers's fleshy throat. Steers, who had struggled his whole life to be a good cop, gurgled for a moment and fell silent as his blood drained into the bronze sands of the Pinelands.

Dewall pulled the pistol from his holster, cleaned the prints off with a dirty rag, and slipped it into Steers's holster. Dewall had taken Steers's gun moments after knocking him unconscious at the rear of the funeral home. He needed the detective's weapon to fire the single round into Gethsemane's back. All detectives were issued the same service weapon, but like fingerprints, each gun was subtly different from the next. The county forensics department test-fired each weapon into a ballistics tank — a large tub of water — and then retrieved the bullet and shell. The minute rifling marks and scratches on the spent bullet, as well as the exact site the firing pin struck on the small primer at the base of the shell, was a unique signature that helped experts determine what bullet came from which gun.

It was meant as a quick way to decode multiple shots police might have to fire at threatening subjects. Investigators would retrieve bullets from the walls, ground, and even bodies to reconstruct events second by second. In Dewall's case, he knew he couldn't fire a shot from his own weapon without it being traced back to him. He needed Steers's piece for that bit of the job, and he couldn't risk Steers getting nervous and bolting.

With a few hot days, Dewall knew that Steers's body would be torn to shreds by the hovering turkey buzzards and his bones scattered throughout the pines by the coyotes. If investigators did happen to find his body, it would make perfect sense to them: Steers went renegade for a few bucks, executed a hit, and then fled. Instead of being paid in cold cash, he got a cold blade to his throat.

Dewall had his own excuses ready for the report he would have to file. He was minding the rear entrance of the building when he heard the gun shot. He ran to the garage and found Steers fleeing into the woods. He gave chase in his car, but lost him. He didn't know the building was on fire and proceeded back to head-quarters for reinforcements. What was he to do without a radio?

It almost got sloppy, he thought. That technician dressing the corpses looked out of the garage door at the wrong time. As he was pulling Steers to the side, the guy had to stand there like a Good Samaritan and say, "Hey, what's going on?" Dewall had seconds to freeze the guy in his tracks. He flashed his badge.

"Police. Stay right where you are," Dewall had barked at him as he pointed the gun toward his face. "Hands on your head and turn around."

Dewall cut the man's throat from ear to ear. He stuffed the body in the corner and set a small clump of rags on fire under a tub of embalming chemicals. Dewall waited in the shadows for the undertaker and slowly pulled the door open as he tried to line up the best shot.

He smiled to himself. Those smart asses, Forge and Fry, think they are better than me, he thought. They're now crispy critters at the bottom of the funeral home. Who's the smart one now?

EIGHT

Tolck waited until sunset before giving the command to leave. After placing Lewis's partly charred corpse into a standard funeral-home body bag, Tolck and his crew passed the time in the warehouse talking about baseball and who was go-ing to win the World Championship poker tournament in Las Vegas that year.

In the corner, Preston had passed the point of vomiting his stomach contents. He was now hitting drive heaves.

Tolck put a sympathetic hand on the mayor's shoulders.

"The first time is always the worst," Tolck said, as if he were a grandfather talk-ing to a young grandson who had just skinned his knees from a fall off a bicycle. "It'll pass. It'll seem like a dream in a few days, and after that you will struggle to remember if this was real or a nightmare."

Tolck poured some rum into a cup to help calm Preston's shattered nerves. The mayor threw back two half-cups and felt the tension in his shoulders start to ease.

Tolck took the same cup and poured himself a liberal shot of Frangelico as he walked to the far side of the warehouse. Preston saw him pull a bottle from his pants pocket and throw a couple of pills into his mouth, followed by the sweet liquor.

"OK, we leave," Tolck commanded. Lewis's body bag was in the trunk of the Lexus, which Costa would now drive. Consolina took the driver's seat in the black SUV that she had arrived in with Tolck and his son. Tolck sat in the back along with Preston. In case the mayor had any last minute thoughts of jumping out of the vehicle as it motored down Long Beach Boulevard, Consolina had set the child safety lock to "on" and disabled the electric window. If Preston tugged on the door handle, he would find that the door would not move, and she would have plenty of time to turn around and point her gun between the mayor's eyes.

Everyone knew the destination except Preston. He didn't dare ask and wondered if they would drive deep into the Pine Barrens to dispose of the body, or to a distant marina where, under the cover of darkness, they could dump the remains far offshore for the sharks to feast on.

"After we are done, I will need you to call your friend," Tolck said to Preston as they drove out of the warehouse. Tolck had not bothered to face the mayor; instead, he watched the house lights and dimly lit scenery fly by the smoked glass.

Preston remained silent. Not wanting to antagonize his captors — or were they now his partners? — he thought about what to say to Tolck's new rival.

The two-car caravan pulled off the main road and wound its way through a small development on the mainland. As the last house faded into the distance, Preston could slowly make out a steel arch, a wrought-iron fence, and a spiked gate overgrown with ivy.

The Lexus's headlights in front of them illuminated the lettering on the archway: Eternal Rest Memorial Gardens.

Preston's head swam again. They are taking Lewis to a funeral? Was this group so twisted that they wanted to say a few words before disposing of their loyal comrade?

Tolck pulled a folded piece of paper from his breast pocket and scanned the map.

"Turn at the second lane," he barked to Costa through a walkie-talkie. "It's the fifth one on the right."

As they approached the area, now pitch black sans the headlights from the two vehicles, the mayor looked over rows upon rows of headstones and granite mausoleums. The grounds were well kept, with neatly mowed lawns and pruned topiary in the shapes of angels looking skyward and cherubs prancing about to give the illusion of life among the dead.

Costa pulled alongside a freshly excavated grave, its loose dirt covered with a green tarp.

Tolck walked the mayor out of the SUV, and all four of them peered over the edge of the grave.

"It's a double," Tolck said matter-of-factly to Preston. "A husband and wife are to be buried here tomorrow, some lousy traffic accident. That's good for us. The hole is deeper and a bit wider, and they put a cement vault in it. Here, look."

Tolck shone a small flashlight into the interior of the grave and moved the beam around to the four corners of the vault, which was thick and awaiting the placement of the heavy cap that rested behind a nearby backhoe.

Costa remotely popped the trunk of the Lexus, which sent a chill up Preston's spine. Hours earlier he had been in that same trunk. He wondered if had events played another way, would he be the one destined for an anonymous burial?

"The vault is a big money maker for us," Tolck continued. "It's the same unit they sell to the construction outfits to keep the walls of trenches from caving in on the men. Here, we take them, buy a lid, and slap 'funeral' on the outside, but we triple the price. It makes the family all warm and fuzzy to know that their departed ones will be safe from the bugs."

Costa let out a muffled laugh as he walked toward the trunk and hoisted the body bag onto his shoulder.

The beam from the high-powered flashlight gave Tolck an eerie black-and-white look. The shadows on his face accented the corners of his lips and eyes to the point that Preston started to feel queasy again.

As if he were dumping a bag of trash into a bin, Costa flipped Lewis's body into the hole, where it hit squarely on the bottom with a harsh thud that Preston could feel through his feet.

"Another 180 pounds of crap down the tube," Costa chuckled.

"Hope the trip down wasn't too hard, Les," Tolck said, trying to contain a laugh. "Say hello to the rest of your friends."

Everyone except Preston broke out into howls at the inside joke. Costa was getting the biggest kick out the whole affair, a truly disturbed man and heir apparent to Tolck's empire, the mayor thought. *If I live through this, how long could I deal with him before he got his jollies off of killing me?*

"Don't forget the best part," Tolck said.

Costa looked up as if he were thinking hard at the suggestion, and then ran back to the Lexus to fish out the bloodstained ball-peen hammer from under the front seat.

"Here you go, Pops," Costa said. "You wanna keep it or ditch it?"

"It's been good to him over the years," Tolck said. "Let him take it with him."

Costa opened the two fingers that held the hammer and it dropped silently to the bottom of the pit, its impact muffled by the bag and Lewis's perforated abdomen.

"This is why I fell in love with the funeral business," Tolck said to Preston. "It pays to bury the dead."

"Won't someone find him tomorrow?"

Tolck smirked at the suggestion. He had been disposing of malcontents for decades. He could not walk over five graves without feeling the ghosts of those he had buried tug at his feet.

The hundreds of acres of this centuries-old cemetery was the perfect place to hide the dead in plain sight. Once a grave was closed and its legitimate owners securely buried, it would take a court order to reopen the ground again. Cemeteries were forever. No one could build on them, no government could condemn them, and no kids would stumble across corpses buried too shallow by amateurs.

Even if a body was exhumed for some rare reason, the extra occupant would hardly be discovered. Tolck was careful to bury the wayward in cement vaults such as those the Scathmyers were to occupy, until their impromptu cremation at the funeral home.

Tolck had made an art out of his layer-cake approach to disposals. After the vault went in, he or his associates would arrive late at night after the digging crew left and drop the body into the ten-foot-deep hole. With the aid of a few buckets of dirt from a backhoe, the remains would be covered just enough to keep the animals out. Even in full daylight, the hole was so deep that a casual observer would see pitch black at the bottom.

Then the real funeral would come, weeping spouse, children, distant relatives, and all. The priest would say a few words, the casket would be lowered on top of the dirt, and the cement lid would seal the tomb.

"That is what you call a secure time deposit," Tolck said as he provided Preston with the outline of his layer-cake burials. "Maybe some archaeologist will find them ten-thousand years from now and think we threw the servants in with the kings. But we are not going to be around to find out, right?"

Tolck's cell phone vibrated in his pocket and he walked away to flip it open. He listened intently for a minute before uttering a single "Fuck!" and throwing the phone at Costa. He motioned for Consolina.

After a brief, whispered conversation that Preston could not hear, Tolck walked over to the mayor and grabbed the cell phone from Costa.

Tolck pointed his index finger in Preston's face and looked as if he was about to speak, but changed his mind.

"Screw the call. I'm done trying to make peace. This is way out of line now," Tolck said, recovering from the plan he had formed in his head and then discarded. "Way, way out of line. And I'm not going away empty handed."

He motioned to Consolina as the two of them walked away from Preston.

"Call Alpha," Tolck told her. "It's time to push all the chips in."

NINE

Forge and Fry, their faces and clothing partially blackened from the soot, dumped the land records into the trunk of Fry's half-toasted car. They sped away after flashing their badges to the local cops who had arrived at the fire. Sister Maris, her ears still ringing from the enormous blast, had fared better; her white tee shirt was now black from the parking lot macadam and smoke, but Forge's body had spared her the brunt of the explosion.

Fry's cell phone rang incessantly in its hip holster as the summer air blew through the window and over his face like a hair dryer set on maximum.

"You get it," a weary Fry told Forge. "Tell them we're not home."

Reluctantly, Forge looked at the caller ID and took a deep breath as he flipped the phone open.

"What the fuck happened out there?" Hudson barked. "I have half the county fire departments out there hosing down a goddamn funeral home that's now a crematorium. What the fuck is going on?"

"It was going pretty good until the end," Forge said calmly.

Forge held the phone at arm's length from his ear, lest he permanently damage his already stunned hearing. Fry turned his head to avoid looking at the device.

After a minute of screaming, a hoarse Hudson finally regained his composure, and Forge returned to the conversation.

"What did you find out?" Hudson asked.

"We're doing just fine, thanks for asking," an annoyed Forge responded. "We executed the search warrant without incident, we interrogated a suspect, and then shots were fired, killing the suspect. To cover his tracks, the shooter set a fire to blow up half the place. I'm assuming he wanted to kill us, too."

"I didn't ask for a summary of your day. I asked what you found out."

Forge's eyes narrowed. "During our interrogation, we found out that the undertaker was working as a front for Tolck."

"Doing what?"

"Some sort of land deal."

"Did he show you anything? Any evidence?"

"No," Forge said without hesitation. Fry, who could hear the elevated tones of the conversation from the receiver that was no doubt strained to its maximum limits, gave Forge a curious look. He just lied to the prosecutor? What the hell was in the trunk if it wasn't evidence?

"What else did Gethsemane tell you?" Hudson barked. "Did he mention any names?"

"No." Forge already knew the answer to the next question, but he needed to hear it from Hudson. "How did you know it was Gethsemane?"

"Dewall checked in a half-hour ago," Hudson said. "He filled me in on how you guys used him and Steers for backup and Steers went off the reservation."

"Meaning what?"

"Steers took the shot. Whoever this is in the barrel, apparently people don't want you guys to find out. Steers was working for the other side. Dewall said he saw Steers whack the old man and then run off into the woods, apparently where an accomplice was waiting with a car. Dewall couldn't catch them."

"That's crap. Steers is no killer. He couldn't even look at a dead body."

"Or so he wanted you to think. We have half the county out now looking for him."

Forge thought for a moment before making a strategic decision that he knew would change the course of the investigation.

"That's too bad," he told Hudson. "Let me know when you find him."

"You guys better come in to county. We can debrief you to get more information so we can track this son of a bitch down."

"10-4." He clicked the phone shut.

"What were you doing?" Fry asked.

Forge didn't answer as he looked out the window. All he could hear was his father's voice. *Follow the markers. Follow the markers.* He had found one set of markers, but which way did they point?

"You lying to Scratch?" Fry pushed again.

"Delaying," Forge said. "It's not official until we file a report. Maybe we were in shock from the blast and I couldn't recall everything I had heard. But this much I know so far: we can't trust anyone other than ourselves with this case. There is no way Steers fired that shot."

"Then who?" Fry asked before answering his own question. "That bastard De-wall? That little shiny mannequin. Why?"

"Hide in plain sight," Forge said. "He had the perfect cover. He could be on top of the case, keep an eye on us, and intervene whenever he wanted to. Until a few minutes ago, he probably thought we were under ten tons of rubble."

Fry pulled the car to a fast stop on the sandy shoulder, raising a cloud of dust behind them. "I'm turning around now and we are heading back to arrest him and do a tap dance on his chest, not in that order."

"No. Take us back to the Maris Stella retreat."

Fry scrunched his face to mouth a *what the fuck?* without uttering the word.

"I've been trying to send her back there all day, and now you want to go? We're on a roll and we have to get Dewall," Fry said.

"I need my Jeep. It's still parked in the lot there. And you need to lay low for a while."

"Why? Where are you going that you don't need me?"

"I need you to run traces on these phone numbers," Forge said as he flipped open the thin book stained with Gethsemane's blood. Each of the first twenty-four pages was filled with a single heading followed by rows of telephone numbers and dates. The same sequence followed on each page: telephone number and date, then a new telephone number and a subsequent date. The names that headed each page followed the simple Greek alphabet — Alpha, Beta, Gamma, Delta, and so on, down to Omega. Except for a few pages, the final numbers all were followed by the same date: 7/4. The Fourth of July. What were Gethsemane's final words? Alpha. Midnight. Four.

The "four" was obviously the Fourth of July. The dates in the book confirmed that. But who was Alpha, and what was supposed to happen at midnight, nearly twenty-four hours from now?

Forge flipped through the pages several times, making mental notes. There were twenty-four conspirators with code names. The earliest entered date was for a point nearly nine months ago. And then it caught his eye. Twenty-two in the group seemed to have been contacted on June 30. That was two days ago — the day that the man in a can was murdered. Only two had not been: Omega, whose dates stopped earlier than the rest, June 28, and Beta, whose last date was June 29.

"Pull over," Forge said without looking up. "Look at this."

Fry leaned over as Forge ran through his observations. Sister Maris held part of the book with her left hand as Forge held the right side. Her mouth widened as the clues fell into place.

"It was a vote," Sister Maris said, pointing to the book's entries. "See here and here? Gamma and the rest were contacted June 30. But Omega and Beta weren't."

"The rest voted to kill him," Fry said. "But why?"

"Omega was the odd man out," Forge said, "just that he didn't know it. I think that whoever Omega was, he started a chain of events that led to his death. This Council of Twenty-Four is now a very threatened group of twenty-three, maybe twenty-two if Beta was also kicked out. They have a lot on the line and a lot to lose. They aren't about to let a few bodies stand in their way."

"But wouldn't Tolck be Alpha?" Sister Maris asked. "As in Alpha male, head of the pack?"

"No, can't be. Tolck was talking about Alpha, and besides, he was calling the shots. There was no reason for him to give himself a name. Gethsemane was the shill, the straw man, the go-between Tolck needed to keep himself insulated," Forge said. "Tolck knew him well enough to trust him to make the calls, to speak the code words, but not be curious enough to wonder what was happening. Gethsemane needed a log book to keep all the numbers and code names straight in his head."

"Then who is this Alpha?" Sister Maris asked.

Forge had no answer. Gethsemane's interrogation had ruled out Tolck, Consolina and the banker. Was Alpha a last-minute addition to the group? Or was he someone with a totally different role to fulfill?

"I hope to know more in a few hours," Forge said. "Take the book, go to The Shack, and work with Singh to find out where these numbers connect to."

"What about me?" Sister Maris asked.

"Sorry, Sister, but I think you have had enough excitement for the day," Forge said. "Go in, wash up, and rest for the night. Trust me, if I need you, I'll be the first one back."

"Where are you going?"

"To visit an old friend."

TEN

Hudson poured a double scotch and threw himself into his oversized, plush black calf's leather couch.

"The whole case is turning to shit," he told his wife, who was standing in their home den looking through their sliding glass door at the clutch of deer that had wandered into the backyard from the adjoining nature preserve. Their Labrador retriever had become so accustomed to the deer, and the deer so accustomed to retriever, that the two species hardly glanced at each other.

"It's a minor upset," Annette said, not looking away from the deer.

"Minor? Minor?" Hudson, already half intoxicated, yelled across the room with slurred words. "There's a crater where the funeral home was. I have the media crawling up my asshole, and they are going to start tying this in with the can man if they find out. What the hell is major if this is minor?"

Annette pursed her lips. "This is a bump in the road. You haven't been associated with the case, and you have deniably. You can paint these guys as renegade cops." She stopped mid-sentence as she opted for a better plan.

"Or the better option would be to show the media that this is just the beginning of a major mob war, that you are on top of it, that this lawlessness will not stand and you will crack down on the outlaws with the full force of your office," Annette said, turning to face her husband for the first time.

"Maybe we can make it the Russian mob," Hudson interjected, buying into his wife's sly reshaping of bad news into good news for him.

"Or the Chinese mob. Or the Vietnamese."

"Nix the Vietnamese," he said. "The latest demographics show they are not a force here in this county. The Mexicans are growing by leaps and bounds, but explosions are not their style. We'll call it the Russia mob. They're off the scale. Everyone knows they aren't as reasonable as the Mafia. Their only code of honor is to kill everyone — civilians, competitors, union guys."

"And even cops," Annette said.

Hudson stopped in mid-thought, his lips parted to object. But he could find no reason.

"If Fry and Forge just happened to get killed investigating this, it'll be Armageddon around here," he said.

"Yes, but it will be your Armageddon," she said. "You would have absolute power to crack down on everyone and everything you saw fit. The governor would put the state police at your disposal. If you look like a strong anti-crime candidate now, you will be viewed as the Second Coming when this is done. You'll be nominated by acclamation. You'll be elected by acclamation."

Hudson saw more fire in her eyes and heard more enthusiasm in her voice that he had seen in their bed since their first date. She was actually about to have an orgasm thinking about all the power that she would share with her newly elected governor-husband.

But reality always trumps dreams. He knew elections weren't cheap, and a shot at the governorship against a self-funded billionaire would top $100 million. In the not-too-distant past, presidential elections didn't cost as much.

"What about the money?" he asked.

"The money will be there," Annette replied dryly. "As always, honey, you do what you do best. As for the details, leave that to me."

ELEVEN

Even at the late hour, the Bayside State Prison sparkled more like a Hilton than a medium-security slammer. The outside was lit like Christmas, with ground lighting that appeared as if it were designed by a decorator to accentuate the architectural beauty of the exterior walls.

Inside, Forge was escorted through the metal detectors and airport-like security to the dining hall. The only difference from a high-school cafeteria that Forge could discern was that the wood and steel tables and benches were firmly bolted to the carpeted flooring.

He watched the giant hands of the prison clock sweep slowly past eleven as he waited for the prisoner to be awakened and escorted in. With a sharp buzz that echoed through the hall, a steel-and-glass door swung open and a guard walked an orange-jumpsuit-clad inmate to the table in front of Forge.

Charles H. Hecksher III gave a cheery high-five to the guard, who left the two men alone in the brightly lit hall.

"Matthew Forge, detective extraordinaire," Hecksher said brightly. "How the hell are you?"

"Just fine, Charles," Forge replied as they slapped each other's backs and silently noted how much heavier the erstwhile owner of The Shack had gotten in a year. "I see you've nested quite comfortably here."

"Oh, yeah. Once you get used to the hours and the unpleasant language, it's really not a disagreeable place. The cells are sizable enough and I have a really nice roommate. You know he went to Harvard?"

"You don't say."

"I get a little money and treats from my mother every now and then, and the guards appreciate when I share. It helps builds camaraderie."

"You mean share with the guards."

An impish grin crossed Hecksher's face.

"Now, now. You know I can't tell a cop as upstanding as yourself that. By the way, how is Matilda?"

Forge scratched the back of his head, not knowing how to break the news.

"I'm sorry," Forge said, opting for the direct approach. "I'm afraid it's very bad.

I killed her. But it wasn't intentional."

Hecksher took a deep breath and exhaled slowly.

"I kinda thought that was what was going to happen. I didn't think you would be good with a hibiscus. They are such difficult creatures to care for properly."

"I did try, but my job... "

"Enough said. You're forgiven. So what brings you here at this fine hour?"

"I need your expertise," Forge said, as he dug through a duffle bag and started to lay the reams of files and documents on the table before Hecksher. "What can you tell me about these?"

Hecksher held his head up with both hands as he studied the pile. He slowly pulled one folder out of the pack, opened it, and set it to his left. As he pulled through the dozen or so other files, he started to sort them in an order Forge could only guess at.

"Alphabetical?" he asked.

"Nah, that won't tell us anything," Hecksher responded, pointing to the top of one contract. "You see here, all the would-be sellers are different. There is no one master of all the parcels. And here," he tapped a second line. "The buyers are really interesting, but all different, at least on paper."

"Meaning what?"

"Meaning where did you get these?"

"From a source. He was holding all the paper."

"Ah, a straw man. Gotta love that."

"How so?"

"He's the protective bubble. He hides the real owner's interest in the land. It keeps the price low."

"I guessed that. What are all these contracts and deeds for?"

Hecksher motioned for Forge to walk to the same side of the table so he could outline the game plan.

"You have to put these not in order by seller or buyer, but in order of size and location."

Starting from the left, the inmate flipped open the first folder, which was thinner than most. "This is a reasonable tract, about two acres, long and narrow. It is also a key tract." He flipped to the small survey summary that spoke of the exact location in degrees and seconds.

"This is a key plot, since it provides access to a bigger tract here," Hecksher said, tapping his index finger on the next manila folder. "Without the first tract, you can't get access to the second tract."

"What would access mean?"

"Roads. You can have the most beautiful acre this side of heaven, but if you can't drive a car to it, you can't build on it. No one will want to buy it, and no one would be able to get to it. So the first tract is the gateway, of sorts. But you don't want the seller to know that. Otherwise, the price triples."

"How big is the second tract?"

"Not much. About a thousand acres."

Forge shot a startled look at the incarcerated real-estate expert. Two contracts and we're up to more than 1,000 acres? That's bigger than what the White House sits on. And this is only what Fry and he could carry out of the building. How many files were either shredded before they arrived or incinerated in the blast?

"Where?" Forge asked.

Hecksher flipped through several folders, but remained silent.

"Let me show you."

He motioned to Forge to gather all the folders and drop them on the expansive floor next to the closed mess line.

Like a savant in a trance, Hecksher rapidly and meticulously formed a ring of files around the floor, stopping only to flip open each folder to examine the cover page again. In just ten minutes, he had built a circle with a smattering of files in its center.

Hecksher stood up and beamed at his accomplishment.

"Hey, I've still got it," Hecksher said proudly.

"And what do you got?"

"Shamong Township to the south, Woodland over here to the north, Jackson up here and Tabernacle over here," Hecksher said, pointing his toe to each region. "In the middle here, we have Bass River and a clutch of smaller hamlets."

"Which adds up to... ?" Forge felt as if he were close to finishing a ten-thousand-piece jigsaw puzzle, but had lost the last handful of cutouts. He couldn't see the picture yet.

"The Pinelands."

"And that means what?"

"You can't build in the Pinelands. It's a preserve. Most of these plots are in the core of the Pinelands, which means you can't even think about putting up a house there. It's totally undevelopable. Someone is wasting a whole lot of time and money on nothing."

"How much is all this worth?"

Hecksher did a quick calculation in his head from the files he saw. "About $100 million for about fifty-thousand acres."

"Two-thousand bucks an acre?"

"Two-thousand wasted bucks an acres," Hecksher said. "They would have had more fun burning the $100 mil than buying the land. Who do you think is doing this?"

"Tolck," Forge said absentmindedly. The single name forced the smile from Hecksher's lips and the color to drain from his face.

"Tolck?" he wheezed incredulously. "You came here with files from Tolck? Are you fuckin' insane?" His tone became louder and more agitated with each word.

Forge was taken aback by Hecksher's abrupt mood swing. He was in a state prison guarded by guys with machine guns. Did he really think Tolck could touch him here?

"Don't you understand," Hecksher said, reducing his outburst to a loud whisper. "He'll kill you. He'll kill everyone. He plays for keeps. And he has a plan. He always has a plan. If this is just part of his plan, you have no idea what the scope will be."

"How can I build a case over this?"

"You got to find the money. It's always the money."

"Hasn't that been paid already?"

"No, no, no," Hecksher said impatiently as his eyes darted from side to side to ensure no guards had heard the exchange. "These are all purchase contracts — contracts to buy, not finalized sales. The deeds will only be executed if certain conditions are met."

"What would that be?"

Hecksher thumbed through the thickest part of one contract, inserted his middle finger as a placeholder, and then fished through the back half of the contract, which topped fifty pages.

"I've never seen anything like it," Hecksher said. "Here is the standard boilerplate crap lawyers roll around in: 'The corporation, herein referred to as "the buyer," will execute the agreement upon successful zoning changes and other options that are executed within two years from the date of this contract.' That means if the buyer doesn't win the right to plow under the trees, the deal's off. That is standard. Then it goes on to talk about rights of way, easements, and mineral rights. All standard stuff until you get to this part."

He flipped open the page that his middle finger was at. "This here, this here is so far off the charts it's in orbit."

He scrolled halfway down the page to the middle of the sheet. " 'Other considerations include funding of an account formed under section 527 of the Internal Revenue Code. This organization shall be known as 'Citizens for a Preserved Pinelands', or the CPP...' "

"The contract becomes binding when the CPP reaches a funding level of at least $10 million," Hecksher continued. "That means the landowner can't back out of the deal even if everything else fails. Every contract has a standard escape clause that lets the seller find a new buyer if there isn't any money forthcoming in two years. But once this is triggered, the seller will be locked in and will have to go along for the ride until the area is approved for building, whenever that is."

"Citizens for a Preserved Pinelands," Forge mused. "Sounds innocuous enough, but it's not, is it?"

"Nah. Most of these are phony-baloney fronts for a big money guy. There's nothing to them behind the paperwork. Just a box at a mail drop and a telephone number no one ever answers."

"What about the contracts?" Forge asked.

"I've heard of tree-hugging, frog-loving environmentalists buying up tracts so the antelope can run free," Hecksher said. "I've heard of developers buying up tracts to build mega malls on landfills. And I've heard of governments funding baseball stadiums for billionaires. But I've never heard of a contract that was triggered by the funding of a 527."

"A what?"

"A 527. It's the new-age version of a PAC, a political action committee. It's the Holy Grail, the money machine. It's what politicians need to get elected. They are as rampant in this state as mosquitoes at a summer cookout. Years ago, politicians were banned from taking massive amounts of cash directly from donors because it made them beholden to the guys with the most money — tobacco, pharmaceuticals, state vendors, developers. It got so crooked that the media got up on its high horse, exposed all the inside deals, and showed how the entire government had sold out to the highest bidder. The two-faced sons of bitches thought they could pull a fast one, and they did. The politicos banned direct contributions of more than $2,000 dollars to individual candidates. But they didn't ban money going into and out of 527s.

"It was a sweet loophole that you could march a parade through. Unlike your standard PAC, 527s ain't regulated by the state. They aren't even regulated by the federal election commission. A 527 is a section of the tax code."

"The IRS?"

"Yeah, the tax collector. You think he gives a shit about what you are doing with money he can't tax? The Congress stuck the loophole in the IRS because they knew the IRS would have better things to do than monitor campaign money."

"And the results?" Forge asked.

"Same legalized bribery, just from different sources. The money was diffused. Before, it was sort of honest corruption. You knew who was giving the most to which candidate. It was like this in the old days: A guy comes in, gives you a wad of hundred bills, and says he'll see you after the election.

"Now, it's a lot tougher. The same guy comes in, but instead of giving the money to you, he gives it to anyone and everyone he sees walking down the street. He tells each person to give you the money after he leaves. On the way out, he walks by you, winks and says the same thing — I'll see you after the election.

"Now, the candidate, usually the incumbent, gets the same amount of money to steamroll over his opponent. But the public doesn't know where the cash is really coming from. It's a slam dunk on Election Day for the incumbent, but no one knows who bought him or what the total price was."

"So if I wanted to give a million dollars to a candidate, I couldn't?" Forge asked.

"Sure, you could, but you couldn't do it in one shot, at least not legally. The accounting rules are so tight that everyone has to report where he or she got the money from, and what they spent that money on, be it for a breakfast with the Boy Scouts or a $1 million media buy on New York TV. Both sides of the ledger better add up, or the election commission will be on your ass."

"How would I get $1 million to my favorite pol then?"

"That's where the 527s come in. You chop the money up and spread it around to other political committees; $10,000 here, $30,000 dollars there. After a few generous donations, your money is in a hundred different places. You have all these side deals with the 527 leaders and county bosses to ship the money to one or two of your favorite candidates. It's called wheeling. They literally take your donation from one county and wheel it to another to hide its origins."

"What do they get out of it?"

Hecksher chuckled. "Are you that naive? No wonder you fell down to where you are. You gotta learn how to play the system. All the bosses and 527 leaders, they get a cut of the money. Some take a few points, others have a sliding scale — ten percent for the first $10,000 and then eight percent for every $10,000 after that."

"And it's legal?"

"A wise politician once told me it ain't illegal unless you get caught. It's all handshakes and phone calls. No paper records. And if there ain't no paper record, there ain't anyone to prosecute."

"But we have the contracts. Doesn't that mean the deal has ended?"

"These things are like gold. The originals are going to be stored in a commercial vault somewhere in a salt mine a thousand miles away," Hecksher lectured Forge, as if this fact were common knowledge in the real world. "You wouldn't leave gold laying around in the open, would ya?"

"How do you know these aren't the real deals?"

"They are the real deals, but just photocopies of the paperwork. Look here." Hecksher pulled Forge's hand and rubbed it over the final page of the contract.

"See, no raised seal. It hasn't been notarized. It's a copy for Tolck's records, amusement, leverage, whatever you want to call it. He can whip these out and cram it up someone's ass if he feels a need to get legal with a seller."

"And this codicil to the development contract," Forge asked, looking back at the section that detailed the 527. "That kicks in two years from now?"

Hecksher examined the contract and then flipped to the next page.

"No," he said. "It looks like the clock is running down on this one."

Forge dreaded the answer he knew was coming.

"When?" he asked wearily.

"Midnight," Hecksher said, looking up at the giant wall clock. "Tuesday. Y'know, the Fourth of July."

TWELVE

Calmed by a warm shower and lengthy prayers, Sister Maris still felt an inner restlessness as the remnants of the sisterhood sat in their well-appointed hermitage, amid an exquisite collection of freshly cut flowers and softly scented potpourri, and prepared to retire for the evening. She offered no explanation to the furtive glances that both asked why she had been gone for so long and how she had so soiled her once-pristine tee shirt and jeans with dark and greasy soot.

"Will you be coming with us to see Ol' Barney Tuesday night?" one elderly nun wearing a light veil asked Sister Maris.

"Barney?"

"Yes, dear. The lighthouse, Barnegat Light, or Ol' Barney as the lovely brochures call it. It's quite a charming name, don't you think?"

"Yes. Quite." Sister Maris's thoughts drifted off to Matt Forge.

"You know, it will be the first time that they turn on the beacon in about sixty-five years, isn't that right, girls?" The older nun looked toward three or four other sisters in the recreation room for their affirmation of the fact.

"Yes, that's right, Sister Mary Margaret," another nun, one in her mid-forties, piped in. "The lighthouse was shut down in 1944 as obsolete. But they installed a special high-powered lamp for this occasion. They are going to turn it on during the Fourth of July celebration. It's going to look just like it did years ago, with the sweeping beacon and wide beam. They won't be using oil, of course, but they ran special electrical wires up to the top... "

"I think they used gasoline, or at least kerosene," another sister interrupted.

"No, no. I'm sure they used fuel oil. I distinctly remember the park ranger telling me that all the lighthouse keepers would encourage friends to visit so each could haul a five-gallon oil can all the way up to the top to feed the flame on the light..."

Sister Maris drifted away from the conversation as the other nuns began to chatter and debate among themselves the finer points of lighthouse history.

A walk to the beach; that would help her mind relax. The warm midnight breeze flowed over Sister Maris Stella's face as she carried her diminutive bag of dog treats to the crest of the sand dune that protected the religious retreat from the intemperate fury of the ocean.

Sister Maris marveled at the beauty of the night sky. With her back to the lights of the island, she looked skyward to see the twinkle of the brilliant stars of the constellations. She quietly drew an imaginary cross to form the outline of Cygnus, the Swan, and then spotted the stars of Hercules above it.

At a safe distance at the seaside foot of the dune, a small pair of eyes eagerly focused on the bag in Sister Maris's hand. The sister could not see her newfound friend, but felt his presence.

With the gentlest of shakes, Sister Maris jiggled the treats in her hand as the small red fox ran to her feet.

"Fred, how nice to see you tonight," Sister Maris said as she reached into the bag. "I'm sure you are here for this."

The fox, no bigger than a toy terrier but much leaner, softly tugged the dog biscuit from the sister's hand and sat down at her feet, unafraid as he nibbled around the edge of the treat with the smallest of his front teeth.

She took a deep breath as she stood up and inhaled the humid salt air. As she opened her eyes, she heard the patter of four paws moving away. Fred had scampered down the beach, running toward the surf and north to the lighthouse in the distance.

Sister Maris followed the fox with her eyes until his gray outline vanished into the night. As she walked along the surf, Sister Maris looked along the row of dimly lit mansions in the distance. Her drifting mind was torn back to earth by a flash of white light.

She focused her eyes toward the house that the light appeared to have come from and waited. Nothing. It was her imagination, she thought, a reflection; perhaps a spotlight bulb that had burned out when the owner flicked it on.

As she was about to look back to the ocean, she saw the flash again. Then, a millisecond later, a third white flash followed by an orange glow that flickered slowly to life.

And then, darkness.

DAY

3

Tuesday, July 4:
Final Day

ONE

Donald Elan watched helplessly as Costa drew the heavy blinds across the expansive French doors that led onto the seaside balcony.

The Loveladies home was situated on pilings twelve feet above the sand, which gave Elan a glorious view over the dunes each morning. The sunrise delighted him and stoked his goal of exploiting the trading markets around the world. As the sun rose on the eastern seaboard, the Japanese and Hong Kong markets were just about to close.

With his partner, and at the behest of Tolck, Elan set up his office not on Wall Street or in a pricey high-rise in Philadelphia, but this beachfront community where his wealthy neighbors were far enough away to be unnoticed and shrewd enough to remain disinterested in his affairs.

The house was simply a shell for their specialized work. With an ultra-high-speed Internet connection, three dedicated Bloomberg stock tracking machines, and a top-line Xeon quad-processor network server, Elan and company could weave their magic around the world undisturbed while on the water's edge.

The 8,500-square-foot home was modest by Loveladies standards, but it was more than enough for the two men. They had rented the house for six months at $24,000 a week, cash on table. They had even provided a two-month security deposit without a second thought after the avaricious real estate agent decided to test the limits of their wealth.

Like nomads, the two had planned to execute their mission, erase all traces of their stealth Internet activity, pull up stakes in the middle of the night, and disappear like wisps of smoke — until the next group of investors contracted them for their services.

Elan now laid motionless on the floor as he tried to fight the pain of the bullet in his knee and the shock of seeing his partner fall dead against the fireplace, two bullet holes in his back.

Elan had passed the point of pain, the point of screams. He knew he had been betrayed and that it was his own fault for trusting the wrong person at the wrong time. They had come for the money. He knew that much. But they would not believe him when he told them where the money was. He knew that his repeated denials would be meaningless to them. And he knew that he would soon be dead, that his pleas would be worthless.

"I'm going to ask you one question and one question only," Costa said as he knelt before the prostrate Elan. "It'll be better for you to get me the answer the first time."

Elan, wide-eyed and with his lips trembling, nodded.

"How do we access the money?"

Elan shook his head and tried to clear his thoughts.

"It won't do you any good," Elan mumbled. "It won't... "

Costa slammed Elan's head as hard as he could into the teak flooring. A small dot of blood began to slowly ooze from the broken skin over the rising welt.

"Wrong answer," Costa said. "Again. Same question. Different answer."

"It's locked. No one can get to it now."

Paying as much attention as if he were twisting meat off of a spicy chicken wing, Costa bent Elan's right index finger backward until it snapped at the joint. The scream from the new sensation was muffled by the barrel of the gun Costa had stuffed into Elan's open mouth.

"I don't think you quite understand me," Costa said. "I don't want your opinion. I want you to tell me where the money is."

"It's locked away. The security code changes automatically daily, the old code is on the terminal, there. But it won't work. It's what we have to do to stay ahead of the feds."

Costa made no movement toward Elan. He knew nothing other than to get the money. By tomorrow, it would be as worthless as the sand on the beach.

"I'm not getting through to him, sis," Costa said. "Do you want to light his fire?"

Consolina, still wearing the baggy overalls from the warehouse, smiled suggestively at Elan as she ran the tip of her fingernails softly down his arm and moved toward the terror frozen on his face. "You don't really want to disappoint me, do you honey? I know I was a bit much for you, but we've always had such nice times together."

"Oh God, Connie, please tell him I would help but I can't!" Elan cried, a slight trace of saliva escaping the side of his quivering lip. "It's just not possible."

"Everything is possible with a little persuasion," she purred, as she slowly used the tip of her tongue to lick the delicate ridges of his left ear.

Elan wept.

Quietly, Consolina walked toward the flame sputtering from the torch that she had ignited previously, after they had subdued Elan's partner with the shots from Costa's 9 mm. The blowtorch unit was an effective device not only for human erasures, but also for changing reluctant minds. She had devised a small, mobile two-tank unit on wheels for those hard-to-reach jobs in odd places. Who needs prolonged beatings and threats when you have this at your side, she thought. Light the flame, let the guy get a good look at its hot tip, and his mind will fill in the blanks. If he still didn't see it your way, well, there was still the flame.

Consolina carefully unwound the double red-rubber hoses from their holder. She turned the oxy-acetylene feed nozzle from a slow standby burn to its full force. Its color instantly changed from a bright orange to a brilliant, almost color-less blue.

"I'm sorry, honey," she said over the shrill hiss of the fire as she flipped the safety goggles slowly over her eyes, "but this is going to hurt very, very much."

TWO

Forge pulled into the driveway of The Shack shortly after 6 a.m., reassured by Fry's car that he was still inside.

"What do you have?" Forge asked Fry, not noticing he was on the telephone.

"Shhh...," Fry scolded, waving his left hand to keep the noise down and writing with his other. "Here," he said, "let me put you on speaker with Forge."

Fry clicked the console's orange button and replaced the handset into the phone's base. "Kev, you still with me?"

"I'm here, bro," Singh said.

"Where are you?" Forge asked.

"Home. County is getting a little bit too hot for my taste," Singh said. "My computer is networked in, so unless we want to run some fingerprints, I'm good to go."

"Good job. Fry filled you in? What have you come up with so far?"

"Nothing much I can do about the code names," he said. "They are as generic as you can get. But the numbers, you're going to love the numbers."

"What are they?"

"It took us awhile, because we looked at them and thought, damn, there are 10 digits, they must be telephone numbers. But they didn't have any area codes we could find, even the hidden ones that the government uses for cell phones and secure fax machines."

"So what are they?"

"Conference call numbers. Everyone dials in to a central number, but no one knows who the other party is or where the call is coming from."

"Who runs the conference calls?"

"It looks like it's a place overseas, beyond our reach. It uses VoIP technology, likely encrypted VoIP. Perfect for your clandestine operations."

"VoIP?" Fry asked.

"Voice over Internet Protocol," Forge interjected. "Instead of telephone lines, you use your PC and Internet connection to talk. You know the beauty of that, don't you, Kev?"

"Sure do, bro. It's all digital, easy to encrypt and impossible to trace — or tap."

"How so?" Fry asked.

"The VoIP works like a regular telephone," Singh said. "You hook it up to your wall phone or even program your cellphone to tap into it. Once you are on the Net, it does what the Net was designed to do — hops your information through the easiest pathways. "

"Meaning you can have King Solomon tell his sons where all the gold is, and no one can listen in."

"Exactly. And it means this council could talk at the conference point as if they were in the same room. Throw in a scrambler, and their voices would be obscured from each other," Forge said. "Tolck likely put together the biggest syndicate of money this side of Vegas, but none of the players knew who the others are. Only Tolck knew, and that gave Tolck a lot of power."

"But how did they get the conference call codes?" Fry asked. "Each one is different in the book. Someone had to serve as the ringmaster."

"Likely anonymous remailers," Singh said. "You send your message to a site that cloaks e-mails. It'll strip all the critical coding that can be traced from your message, and then resend it to anonymous e-mail accounts you or your friends have set up ahead of time. Tolck probably had lackeys, like Lewis, coordinate the e-mails, and Gethsemane coordinate the conference calls. The technology keeps Tolck's council happy."

"So we're back where we started," Fry fumed. "We have anonymous phone calls and no-name e-mails."

"Not necessarily," Forge said. "Remember, we had one or two renegades drop out of the original twenty-four. That's a chink in the armor."

"But Omega is dead," Fry said. "And I'm sure Beta isn't feeling too secure about his future."

"You got that right," Singh said.

This wasn't a dead end, Forge thought, but it was a fork in the road. The man in a can was still paramount because if they identified him, the rest of the pieces might just fall into place. Forge also had the land deals, at least those that survived the fire.

The markers were all there, Forge knew. They just hadn't lined up yet in the right order.

The loud buzz of Fry's cell phone startled Forge. The Shack had fallen quiet after Singh had hung up and Forge started to zone out from the day that seemed to last forever.

"This better be real good," Fry barked into the phone and listened intently for exactly a minute. "Are you shittin' me? No, you really are shittin' me. Jesus Christ. I don't want to hear this... OK, OK, we're on our way over."

Not good news, Forge knew.

"That was the watch commander," Fry said, running his thick hand tightly through his disheveled hair. "Two more guys in Loveladies. One's plain dead. The other is dead and extra-crispy."

THREE

Forge heard his shoes echo on the hardwood floor inside the spacious house as he walked through the entryway. Decorated in modern sparseness, the best Forge could determine at first sight was that the owners were not much into creature comforts.

There was no sign of a robbery; no cut wires or broken wall hooks that would have indicated a top-line stereo system had been hurriedly ripped out of the wall. The living room was devoid of any seating arrangements, floor rugs, or wall hangings, save for a bank of computer terminals and a tacky twelve-foot-long blue marlin stuffed and mounted above the sliding glass door leading to the sweeping balcony.

As he walked closer to the center of the house, he picked up a faint smell of cedar and barbequed beef. The sweet wood aroma emanated from the enormous coat closet that had been left open during the forensic team's search of the house. But the beef odor... It were as if a hotdog had been forsaken on a hot charcoal grill. He pinched his nose to fight the urge to gag at the realization that he smelled not a summertime picnic gone awry, but seared human flesh.

The center of the house focused on the formal dining room. An expansive, highly polished, dark cherry table with four thick, spindly legs sat perfectly centered in the middle of the floor. On top of the table, at the far end, a dark brown briefcase — seemingly hand stitched, of fine Italian leather, and with the initials "H.R." embossed in gold on the top and sides — was the only indication that the room was used solely for business, not exquisite dinners.

A mat of papers cluttered the top of the case, with several sheets scattered around the hand-carved chair. To the right, Forge's eye caught an antique curio cabinet, seemingly out of place in a house that looked more like an executive suite than a seaside home. The bottom half was crammed with books — thick tomes with hard, cloth covers, some of which looked like anthologies of long-dead authors. And the top half was... toys? He moved closer to the display to see a curious collection of palm-sized, colorfully painted and glazed porcelain figurines that were highlighted by a recessed lamp shining brightly from above.

The figures captivated his curiosity for a fleeting moment. They were from a nativity scene, with the three kings bearing the gifts of myrrh, frankincense, and gold, a beaming Mary and Joseph, a child shepherd kneeling to play the flute, a grayish donkey, and a reclining lamb, all lazily looking downward. The eight sculptures, showed exquisite details, from minute eyelashes and falling wisps of hair to the straps of the tiny shoes. The small artistic characters were arranged in a crescent, but were left with nothing in particular to focus on.

Forge crooked his head lower to look under the glass shelf and to see if the figurines had some type of notation or artist signature on their bases. Instead, he saw an image of an enlarged bumblebee hovering above the middle of the letter "V," with "214/B" in a faint imprint next to the words "W. Goebel" and "Western Germany."

"Nice, ain't they?" a slow voice from behind Forge began.

"I suppose, if you like miniatures. I guess these were made after World War II," Forge said. "Wasn't it West Germany, not Western?"

"I wouldn't know," said the head of the forensics unit, a balding, portly man in his fifties with no visible chin, dressed in a white, disposable jump suit with blue booties tied at his ankles. "I leave that Christmas stuff to my wife."

"Everything done?" Forge asked the chinless man, whose stoic expression looked like that of a dime-store mannequin on the overeaters' diet. His face muscles appeared to never have been exercised with even the slightest grin.

"All cleaned and cleared," the man said without a hint of emotion in his voice. "Not much other than what you see. No latents on the cabinet. We dusted and vacuumed the rest of the place from top to bottom, but not much that we could see. Just two sets of prints with lots of smudges, which indicates to me they belonged to the stiffs. Seems like real professionals hit the place. No shell casings on the floor, window shades closed to keep the nosey neighbors out. And it looks like they took their sweet time."

"Who found them?"

"Mr. Guppy."

"Mr. Guppy?"

"Yeah, sorry. The fish guy."

"I'm still not getting you. The fish guy?"

"There." The man without a chin nodded toward the far wall of the study, which Forge could see through another doorway out of the dining room. A black light illuminated the deep purples and blues in an expansive fish tank built into the wall. Forge craned his neck to see that the tank must have been twenty feet long and six feet tall, with a cream-colored crown and base molding to give the appearance that the tank was not a tank, but a window into another universe.

"Four thousand gallons of your finest exotic saltwater fish: French angels, parrot fish, a moray eel, and a few dozen others I can't even hazard a guess at," the forensics man said. "Lots of coral, too. It's all the rage in these new homes, or so they say. The Wall Street types, they come down after an eighty-hour workweek of screaming and shouting, and then they want to commune with nature by staring silently at a school of fish circling around in a giant bathtub."

"Mr. Guppy," Forge started. "I'm guessing that's not his real name."

"No, no. He just runs the business. He comes by once a week to fix the salt levels, scrub the tank, and feed the fish. He's Dominican, Juan something or other. Not a lot of English. The operator had a hard time understanding him when he called 911."

"Did he see anything?"

"Nah. He came by at about six this morning. He has a side access from the balcony, so he doesn't have to wake the residents by entering the house. As he's doing his thing, he sees through the fish tank this giant toasted marshmallow with legs and can't figure out what it is. He moves around to the balcony, peeks through a tiny slit in the curtain, and sees the number-two guy lying face down, leaking blood all over the pretty hardwood floor. So he panics, calls 911, and then patrol tries to break in."

"Let me get this straight," Forge said. "Your best case is that the shooters walked in, did their thing, and then locked the door on the way out?"

"There is no sign of forced entry," the chinless man said. "The door is high security, steel and nickel plated; touchpad entry system with remote alarm. All the windows and the sliding glass door are impact resistant, like bulletproof glass, sealed with magnetic locks powered by an internal battery. Patrol had to wait for the local security firm to unblock the door. Otherwise we would still be trying to get in with dynamite and a wrecking ball."

Forge felt a hard slap on his back that nearly knocked him off his balance.

"Bro, we've got to stop meeting like this," Singh said with a toothy smile. "I ain't getting no sleep when you're around."

"They pulled you in on this one, too?"

"Oh, yeah. It's all hands on deck for this. Nothing too exciting from a forensics view."

"How so?"

"No prints, no bloody foot marks, not even tire tracks outside. Everyone uses those damn stone pebbles to cover the sand in the driveways, so it's impossible to get a good tire imprint."

"Neighbors?"

"Do you think you would be here if we had witnesses?" a familiar voice from the inner room echoed out. "Where's Fry?"

"At HQ grabbing my yellow box, sir," Forge said looking at the back of the computer terminals. "Patrol said there were a bunch of hardware here. Someone has to start digging out of this hole."

"Ah, getting some of your spunk back, are you?" Hudson said. He pulled Forge into the study where the body of the first victim was neatly covered with a white sheet and marked with a plastic "A" card on its chest.

"Think this is all connected?" Hudson said.

"Like points on a triangle," said Forge.

"Yeah, yeah."

"It's a good break for us."

"How so?" Hudson leaned in closer, as if Forge needed to whisper his next sentence.

"One body is the perfect crime," Forge said in a normal tone. "No witnesses, no ID, no motive, not even a place of death."

"How does two more make it better?"

"It's beginning to show a crack in the wall, a sign of desperation. One is neat. Two is tying up loose ends, maybe putting a nice ribbon on the package. Three is just plain sloppy. You now have multiple suspects, a multiple chain of events, multiple people who last saw them, some who may offer clues that the killers didn't think of."

"And?"

"And we're running against the clock. If they are this paranoid, where talk has ended and people are being whacked left and right, we're dealing with folks who have a lot to gain and not much to lose. They want what they want now. They don't care who gets in their way."

With one deft motion, Hudson leaned over victim "A" and pulled the sheet down to reveal the corpse that had been torched in several places, but not his face. A charred abyss no wider than a silver dollar had replaced the area once occupied by his heart.

"Know him?" Hudson said rhetorically.

Forge was dumbstruck. He had seen the man once at his wedding and later in a dusty picture book. The hair had thinned and the face was contorted into an unsightly knot from the pain. But the conclusion racing through his head was unmistakable. Forge cleared his thoughts and turned to take a long and hard look at Hudson. He closed his eyes and parted his dry lips so gradually that bits of his lower lip clung to the top until the tension broke the two apart.

"Yes," Forge said, lowering his head. "Donald Elan. He is, uh, was my brother-in-law."

Forge scanned the body slowly and deliberately from head to toe. He made two lists in his mind: similar and dissimilar. The manner of death was similar — burned like a potato crisp. So were some of the wounds — his fingertips had been charred to the bone. One finger was bent backward and broken. The burn mark on that digit was not as deep as the others. Perhaps the torturer had touched the flame to the tip to see if there were still enough raw nerves for fresh pain to be felt. The bubbled flesh obscured the print, but the flame did not go deep; the sensitivity was not as great as what the torchbearer had hoped for. The lengthy torch marks on the torso and arms indicated there was plenty of life left in the man after the points of his fingers were melted.

It was the lack of similarities that struck Forge the most. The victim's face was wholly intact. No burn marks, no damage to the teeth, no disfigurement except for a bruise to the temple. The bullet to the knee was an easy guess for Forge. The shot was meant to disable the victim but to keep him conscious and alive, at least for a while.

"God, I haven't seen him in years. I didn't even know him that well. Sharon never kept in touch. After he got out of the Army, he was a loner, a drifter," Forge said as Hudson stood over him. Much of that was true. Forge had not set eyes on Elan since the wedding. But Sharon and the brother stayed in sporadic and tenuous contact on the phone, with each call ending in an argument of some sort. Sharon would quietly fume for a day, and Forge had learned early to let well enough alone.

"Let's see guest number two," Forge said.

Less than twenty feet away, victim "B" had fallen dead in his tracks, two bullet wounds the size of dimes in his back, one that splintered his spine just below the rib cage and the second one dead center into the left, the exact height of the heart. The man was much shorter than the other corpse, about five feet, five inches, in his thirties and very, very hairy. The mop on his head covered his eyes and part of his mouth, which was still agape and frozen with deadly surprise. His short sleeves revealed arms that were matted with such a thick and dark shag that it would make an adult Gorilla cringe.

"Real nice shooting, ain't it, Forge?" Hudson said. "They dropped him without a second thought. Look at that hit pattern. You know how hard it is to get a tight spread on a moving target?"

"You have time of death?" Forge asked.

"Unknown. Neighbors don't know nothing, didn't hear anything, didn't see anything," Hudson said, recalling the briefing his county detectives had given him. "Just like the see no evil monkeys, everyone keeps to themselves around here. They did say these two guys really never poked their heads out of their hole. A woman two units over says she thinks she saw one of them on the balcony feeding a dog once, but that was it."

"Who is he?"

"Mystery guest number two is The Troll."

It took a second for the name to register. "From New York?" Forge asked.

"Wall Street, to be exact. Y' know, The Troll, Hennessy Runkel, the guy on TV and the Web."

"Financial guru?"

"Yeah, yeah. That show he has on that stock channel: 'Heard It Under the Bridge' or some crap like that. I actually got a good stock tip from it once."

"Why 'The Troll?' "

"Look at him. He's short, ugly, and hairy. He got to where he was by pissing people off. Most guys like him get jobs in bell towers."

"He had ID on him?"

"I thought he looked familiar and his wallet was still in his pants, stuffed with lots of Bens. It told us who he was. Kev ran a short bio on him through mobile command. Wiz kid stuff. Harvard MBA, some arbitrage work, then he got booted off the exchange for inside trading and fell into media work. Couldn't write his way out of a paper bag, but boy, could he pick stocks."

"And then what?"

"He started pissing people off on TV. He would get inside tips and then tell the world. It was his way of getting back at the shysters who screwed him."

"No shortage of enemies, I suppose."

"He had a whole fan club of people who wanted to kill him."

"Too bad they didn't get to him first."

"How's that?" Hudson asked.

"No one came here to whack him," Forge said. "He just got in the way. You can tell that by the way they just dropped him. They didn't need any info from him; he was useless. And that's where they got sloppy."

"And your former brother-in-law?"

"He was the prize in the Cracker Jack box," said Forge.

"Take me through it," Hudson said.

"It started out friendly enough," Forge said. "He gets a call on his cell from an associate, someone he trusts, someone he knows is OK. The associate comes over late at night when most of the neighbors are in bed, shuts off his headlights, and rolls into the driveway. 'Ding-dong,' rings the doorbell, and Elan takes a quick look through the security monitor. Looks clear enough, lets the friend in. As the door closes and the two are walking up the stairs to the living room, one or more guys from the backseat jump out, catch the door before the spring hinges pull it shut, and start doing their thing.

"Elan turns to his friend and says, 'What the fuck?' Or something like that. He screams to The Troll here to get the hell out, hit the panic button, run into the safe room. The shooter knows he has seconds. Elan breaks away but he's disabled with a bullet to the back of the knee. A very clean shot on a moving target. No major blood loss, lots of pain, but not enough to make him pass out. The shooter's a real pro. Without even taking a second glance at Elan, he draws a bead on The Troll here from the top of the stairs and pops him twice. Don't need him, don't want him."

"Then what?"

"The shooter is done. His piece of the action is over. Visitor number three moseys on in, lights the torch, and goes to town. They were in no rush, so they took their time getting what they wanted. But I don't think they got what they wanted."

"How so?"

"If he gave it up, Elan wouldn't have so many burn marks over his body. Could you handle the pain from just one of these burns?"

"Don't think so."

"No one could. It's not that Elan didn't want to give them what they were looking for. He just couldn't."

"But they didn't believe him."

"Right. They thought he was bullshitting them. That he thought he was going to get out of this alive. I'm sure he skipped the first four stages of death with them and went straight to bargaining. But they weren't in the mood."

"Or were told they couldn't make a deal with him."

"Yeah. He must have disappointed them once, so they weren't about to be fooled again. He was dead the minute he opened the door."

"What were they after?"

"From the looks of it, my guess is it wasn't the mounted marlin. It's what's over there," Forge said, motioning to the bank of Bloomberg terminals and the master computer.

"And what do you think is in them?"

"That's what you have an old hacker like me for."

FOUR

Singh whistled a placid tune from the *Music Man* as he finished downloading the digital photos of the crime scene into his mobile command center parked near the front pilings of the house. With more than two hundred shots, it would have taken him days to scan though all the images, to catalog the various items, and then sort them into a recognizable database. But he had technology on his side.

"Trouble! We got trouble right here in River City with a capital T and that rhymes with P and that stands for pool..." Singh just couldn't get the ditty out of his head. His subconscious pulled up the most obscure songs from childhood musicals whenever he found himself in the middle of gruesome murders. The higher the body count and the deeper the body fluids, the stupider the songs. If the bodies ever hit double digits, he always thought he might find himself singing songs from *Grease II*.

The automatic inventory software scanned each digital photograph for a fraction of a second, looking for telltale signs that it could match to the billion or so objects in its massive databank. Like facial recognition software, the program looked not at whole objects, but at geometric angles. A narrow rectangle ranked high on the book index, while a cylinder may take a hundredth of a second to scroll through all the images of fire extinguishers, scuba tanks, or rolls of paper towels.

With silent efficiency, mobile command center's laser printer shot out thirty-five pages, complete with thumbnail color image and short descriptions of each object. Topping the list was item 1, "Body covered in white sheet."

"What do you have?" Forge asked as Singh handed him the sheaf inside the house.

Forge studied the list:

1. Body covered in white sheet.

2. Fish tank with various colorful objects.

Forge paused and realized that the program was suited only to analyzing inanimate items. Fish just didn't compute. Maybe the next version of the software will update the bug.

3. Books with the following titles: *The Collected works of Edgar Allan Poe*; *The John Steinbeck Anthology*; *The Pearl*; *The Complete Hemingway Reader*; *The Jules Verne Omnibus*; The Bible (King James version); *Treasure Island* by Robert Lewis Stevenson... .

Forge skipped over another half-dozen titles and moved to the next line.

4. Collectible figurines

5. Briefcase, brown leather

6. Newspaper, unknown publisher

7. Bloomberg machine

8. Bloomberg machine

9. Bloomberg machine

10. Xeon personal computer

11. One-hundred-six-inch plasma monitor

12. Sixty-five-inch wall-mounted plasma Sony television monitor

13. Trash bin, full

14. Video camera and tripod

15. Cell phone charger stand

16. Biometric interface device

17. Blue marlin, mounted

18. Alarm clock, small digital display

Forge peered carefully at the photo of the alarm, looked at it across the room, then flipped through the remaining pages but saw little that struck his interest. Various chairs, windows, and floor styles hardly rose to the level of details that he needed for his investigation.

"Where's the cell phone?" Forge asked Singh. "We have the charger stand."

"Ah, wait a minute," Singh said as he absently looked around the room. "I think we found one in The Troll's pocket." He donned blue nitrate gloves as he walked over to the lump under the sheet and gingerly extracted the slim silver phone from The Troll's left pants pocket.

Singh flipped it open and scanned the device to make sure it was still on.

"What do you have for incoming calls?" Forge asked.

Singh hit a few buttons on the phone and scrolled through the list. Nearly all of the two-dozen entries for the last week listed "Mom" as the source of the incoming call. If Singh's memory served him right, the background check he had done on Runkel showed the same phone number for his mother that had popped up on his cell phone. The critics were wrong, Singh thought. The Troll really did have a mother.

"What's the last entry?" Forge asked. "Let me guess. A non-number number."

"Looks like a VoIP. Same weird area code and exchange. It must have been routed through a dozen countries before hitting a cell tower here."

"Wonderful. Do you have the time on the call?"

"Yeah. 11:25 last night."

"Good. How about time of death?"

"12:05," echoed a familiar voice from the hallway.

"Who said that?" Hudson asked from the other room.

As Sister Maris walked toward Forge, an exasperated Fry tried in vain to hold on to her porcelain-skin forearm as the suntan lotion allowed her to easily slip out of his oversized hand. "Your prime witness," she said.

"Meaning what?" Hudson demanded. "Fry, who is this and why did you bring her in here?"

Fry was beside himself. More than twice her size, the war vet felt helpless as he tried to restrain a one-hundred-five-pound sister wearing freshly washed blue jeans and a new tee shirt that read, in bright yellow letters, "Walking on Sunshine" on the front and "Katrina and the Waves Reunion Tour" in pale blue on the back.

"This is Sister Maris Stella from...," Forge started.

"From the Maris Stella retreat?" Hudson interrupted. "Is that really her real name, and you brought in a nun? Are you pulling my leg here?"

"Yes, Mr. Big Shot Prosecutor, it is my real name, and I can think of more amusing ways to pull your leg than by coming in here on the Fourth of July. And I'm just going to give up on explaining the whole nun thing. No one gets the distinction between a nun and a religious sister. We're the ones without the penguin suit."

Said Forge, "She's, uh, been helpful with the man-in-a-can case. I'm sure she has information that she needs to share with us — don't you, Sister?"

"12:05."

"Meaning what?" Hudson asked impatiently.

"I do believe that is when they were shot."

"Were you here?"

"Of course not."

"Then how the hell do you know that? Are you psychic?"

"Don't patronize me, Mr. Prosecutor Man, and don't make me become a witch with a capital "B". If you give me a minute, I'll tell you."

"The next minute is all yours," Hudson sighed.

"I was walking on the beach around midnight when I saw a flash from one of the houses. I thought it was heat lightening reflecting off the ocean, so I just looked around and then I saw two more flashes. I noted the time as 12:05 a.m., as in today."

"And you didn't report it then?"

"Report what? I just saw flashes. Maybe a light burned out. I don't know what happened. Outside of the poor man that you found yesterday, I'm pretty sure shootings and sundry other unpleasantness is not your typical weekend on Long Beach Island."

"You're starting to make me itch with a capital "I"," Hudson said. "Get her out of here."

"That was the time of death for the first gentleman," Sister Maris said. "I didn't say it was the time of death for the second man."

"How did you know there were two?"

"Three flashes," Sister Maris said smugly. "One followed by a pause and then two quick bursts. One to wound, two to kill. It all made sense once I saw the police cars this morning. I was fortunate enough to run into my good friend Sergeant Fried here, who brought me past the very rude officers out front."

"It's Fry and I did no such thing," Fry protested. "You badgered me to get in here."

"*Gobemouche!* Hush!" Sister Maris said, holding up her right index finger to Fry.

"Oh, she's good," Hudson said. "She's going to put you out of a job, Fry."

Singh and the scattered remnants of the forensic team chuckled as they finished packing their gear into their oversized suitcases. Fry narrowed his eyes at Sister Maris as she shot him an ephemeral smirk.

Hudson's cell phone silently vibrated in his pocket, forcing him to redirect his attention to the text message on the display screen.

"I've got to go," Hudson told Forge. "You're in charge, you do what you've got to do to wrap this up. My whole office is at your disposal. And keep me posted."

Hudson quickly replaced the phone in his pocket and made his way down the stairs toward the outside, shielding his eyes from the harsh morning sun as the officer closed the front door.

To be sure, Hudson fingered the device carefully to illuminate the display screen again, and fought the urge to view the message a second time. When he was finally in his car, he flipped open the cell to read the brief text.

"All good. Money in reach. Sealed with a kiss, guv. Luv yr #1 fan."

Hudson memorized the message and hit delete.

FIVE

"When is Ammerman getting here to take out the stiffs?" Fry asked. "I can't stand the roast beef smell. It's making me hungry."

"Shortly."

"Do you think we need to go for the autopsy again?"

"Doubtful. We know who the guys are. Forensics found no trace evidence in the rooms, so I'm pretty sure there won't be much of use on the bodies. They seemed more careful this time, as in they wore gloves and maybe even hairnets."

"Hairnets," Sister Maris asked. "As in chef's hats?"

"Maybe not the tall, white variety, but something to keep their body hair from falling out. I'm thinking disposable jump suits and hats with nylon nets underneath them."

"How can you tell?"

"Singh said they found no unusual hairs during the vacuum. They go around with Hoovers and suck up all the dust and stuff we can't normally see. The special filter catches it on white paper. You tear open the bag and look real close at what you found."

"Why hair?"

"It's the best trace evidence people don't think about. Every petty thief knows about fingerprints and gloves, but few realize that the human body sheds one hundred hairs a day, from your head to your arms, even pubic hairs. In the heat of a fight, or in this case a broiling over an hour or two, you would think you would find more than a dozen hairs from the perps that you could compare with DNA. But nothing outside the hair colors of the victims."

"The killers knew their stuff."

"Or they had someone tell them what we look for."

"You think a cop is involved?"

"It had crossed my mind. You know Dewall would be on the top of my hit parade."

"He isn't that smart," Fry interjected.

"He doesn't have to run the show, he just has to follow orders and give directions," Sister Maris said.

"How do we link the little turd to the case?" Fry asked. "We know he was the shooter at the funeral home, but we can't prove it to anyone."

Forge had become preoccupied with the inventory list again. The books and figurines bothered him; why would a guy renting a place on the beach with no furniture carry around a curio cabinet filled with knickknacks? Obsessive-compulsive? Sharon never mentioned anything about that. Overly sentimental? That was a possibility. It could just be he was an odd fish and this is why Elan and Sharon never saw eye to eye.

The trash can was filled with the usual candy wrappers and fast-food junk. These guys were in such a hurry to finish whatever they were doing that they didn't have time to whip a decent meal up from the fully stocked pantry and deep freezer.

As his father always told him, when you're lost in the fog, stay slow and steady on your compass heading. You'll run into the channel marker eventually. And that will take you to your homeport — eventually.

His eyes flipped over the first page, scanned the following pages, and then, instinctively, shuffled back to the front. The newspaper. Where was the newspaper?

It was on the floor behind the dining room table, within arm's reach of the head chair. It wasn't trash, Forge thought. It was part of the paperwork from the briefcase. The papers were mostly Internet stock printouts of various company profiles — CEOs, profit margins, product lines, income and expenditures. A 10K report here, a quarterly report there. Good bedtime reading.

But the newspaper was different. It wasn't turned to the stock page, or even the business page. It wasn't even the *Wall Street Journal*. It was a local, full-color tabloid weekly turned to a news page.

"Interior Head in Area for Ribbon Cutting," started the headline.

The subhead in smaller text below read:

Federal Sec Promotes Ecology at Opening of Research Center
by Suzanne Wick

Little Egg Harbor — Saying this was the beginning of a new era for the nationally protected New Jersey Pinelands, U.S. Secretary of the

Interior David Baylock on Wednesday cut the ribbon to open the Edwin B. Forsythe Amphibian Research Center.

The state-of-the-art center, housed in a 3,000-square-foot complex on the edge of the Pinelands, will be tasked to study the unique habitat of local frogs and toads that make up a large part of the ecology of the Pine Barrens...

Forge stopped reading. He focused on the photograph of the secretary of interior, a grinning man with a red nose in his fifties sporting a portly gut. Rather than a straight-on photograph of the ceremonial ribbon cutting, the photographer looked like he tried for a fancier shot, one that showed Baylock in a profile.

Forge examined the date on the newspaper. Friday, June 30. If the ceremony was held last Wednesday, chances are the secretary stayed in the area for a little R&R of the Tolck variety.

"Hey, Fry, what do you know about David Baylock?"

"The former governor?"

"Yeah. He quit to become U.S. sec of the interior a couple of years ago."

"I remember. He lived up north somewhere. And he had a summer house in Barnegat Light," Fry said. "Place on the bay, gated, kinda secluded, real quiet. We used to have to patrol it every half-hour when he was in town. A real pain in the ass."

"Here, look," Forge said, flipping the paper on the table. "What do you think about this?"

"The headline could be snappier."

"No, no. Him. Our victim. Our man in a can."

Fry froze and shot a surprised look at Sister Maris.

"Why?" she said. "Wouldn't we know by now that the secretary of the interior of the United States is missing?"

"Does he have a wife, kids?" Forge asked Fry.

"Ah, no. Rumor was that he was a big-time player, swung both ways, didn't want to limit his options to just one team, if you get my drift."

"You can say it," Sister Maris said as she toyed with an unlit cigarette in her fingers. "I'm not the Virgin Mary. He was a full-fledged, card-carrying bisexual. I read the scandal sheets."

"Yeah. No kids. This is the high-holiday season. The federal government's closed for the week and there ain't ever any Interior Department emergencies that the secretary has to be called in on. It used to be a job for tree huggers, but now it usually goes to one of the guys who either raises the most money for the president or delivers a key state on Election Day. I think Baylock did both in the

196

last election."

"Boozer?" Forge asked.

"Oh, yeah. Lots of fund-raising parties at his place."

"And?" Sister Maris interjected.

"And what?" Forge asked.

"And how are you going to identify a guy with no face, no fingerprints, and no teeth?"

Forge turned to Singh and said, "Let's call up a better photograph of the good secretary on your digital screen."

SIX

In the forensic command vehicle, Singh ran a Google image search for "David Baylock Interior" and found the highest resolution was at the Department of Interior's own Web site. The location was not on the home page, but at the press office. On the site, the office had more than one hundred digital images of the secretary, from his official portrait to photo-ops from around the country.

"Zero in on this one, where he's at the amphibian center's opening," Forge told Singh.

The image filled the screen and provided a perfect profile of the secretary, toothy grin and all.

"Can you pull in closer to his head?" Forge asked.

Singh used the mouse to draw a small rectangle around Baylock's head and then clicked once. Like a telephoto lens, the computer quickly zoomed in on the secretary's head to the point where his hair touched the top of the screen and his chin rested on the bottom.

"Ammerman's here with the meat wagon," Fry announced from the doorway of the mobile van.

"Bring her in."

"What are you looking for?" Singh asked.

"This," Forge said. He tapped the center of the screen. "I want his ear."

Singh pulled the image up even closer, stretching the resolution to the maximum limit. The edges of the ear became fuzzy, but the details of the curves and grooves contrails remained intact.

"Clever," Ammerman said, peering over Singh's shoulder.

"I thought you would get a kick out of it," Forge said.

"An ear print?" Fry asked.

"Yeah. It's the only identifiable part that wasn't burned off," Forge said. "Doctor, can you get your photographs?"

Ammerman gently squeezed Singh from his chair and then minimized Baylock's image so that it became a small part of the task bar at the bottom of the screen. She started another Web browser page and typed in a secure URL connection to enter the county network.

From there, two passwords and three clicks took her to the hard drive where the photographs of the man-in-a-can resided. Thumbnails of a dozen gruesome images filled the screen as Ammerman carefully considered which view offered the best possible match.

"Here," she said, clicking on image B17.jpg. The left side of the victim's charred head enlarged to fill the screen. Since the shot was taken with the victim lying down, she directed the software to rotate the image ninety degrees counterclockwise and then enlarged the ear. The tip had been singed from the extreme heat that had been inflicted on the face, but the rest of the delicate cartilage remained intact.

Ammerman split the screen into two, with her image tucked tightly to the right. She then called up the image Singh had found of Baylock's ear and manipulated it until it was close to the same size as B17.

"Sweet Mother of Mary," Sister Maris said, dropping the unlit cigarette from her lips. "It's a dead-on match."

"It's not a fingerprint, but considering the subject, I say there ain't two other ears on middle-aged guys that match this closely," Singh said. "Look, he has a crease in his earlobe. And B17 has the exact same crease."

"What do we do now?" Ammerman said. "This just became the murder of a federal cabinet member."

"Say nothing," Forge said.

"Pardon my invective, Sister, but are you fucking nuts?" Singh said. "We'll lose our jobs over this."

"We are in the middle of the biggest murder conspiracy New Jersey has ever seen," Forge said in almost a whisper. "In less than forty-eight hours, we have seen the murder of the secretary of the interior and a former governor of New Jersey, the assassination of a funeral director and the immolation of his funeral home, coded communications between a cadre of suspects, and two dead guys in the middle of the richest town on the East Coast, including my former brother-in-law. Don't you see? Everything is coming to a point, and it will come to that point today."

"How can you be so damn sure?" Singh demanded.

"Because of the clock," Forge said.

"What clock?"

"The clock on the dining room table," Forge said, pulling the inventory list from his back pocket. "What time does the photo read?"

Singh squinted. "Looks like the time we started shooting this morning."

"You didn't see it, did you?"

"See what?"

"The clock. It has a day/date on it in the lower right corner. It doesn't say 8 a.m. July 4. It says 7 p.m. July 4."

"OK. They didn't set it up right."

"No way. They hook up all the stock monitors, computers, video and screens, and they messed up a clock radio? It was right there in front of the work area where the briefcase and newspaper were. They knew what they were doing. But they weren't working on Eastern Standard Time. They were working eleven hours ahead, on Tokyo time."

SEVEN

Forge convinced Singh to remain silent for the next twelve hours. Reluctantly, Singh agreed that a federal intervention now would alert the conspirators and attract massive press coverage that would simply prompt the killers to go underground. Right now the killers thought they had the upper hand, that the bodies were just necessary speed bumps on the way to the finish line, wherever that might be.

Inside the house, Ammerman took a cursory look under the sheet that covered The Troll. She exhaled an elongated "Ewwww" as she crinkled her nose.

"Is that your professional opinion?" Forge asked.

"Signed, sealed, and delivered," she said. "Jeeze, he is one ugly specimen. Do you think if we took his shoes off, we'd see hair between his toes?"

"That would be a pretty good bet. I heard Frodo would be jealous," said Forge.

"I could pickle him and sell him to the circus," she said.

"Or shave him. The shag on his arms alone could provide sweaters for the entire Norwegian army."

"Oh, that's just too cruel," Ammerman laughed.

"We have our best moments over corpses, don't we?" Forge said.

199

"Well, you sure do take me to the best bodies. Don't you feel bad about your brother-in-law?"

"I should, but I don't. He's a victim. It's my job to find who killed him, but you learn after all these years to turn off your feelings." Forge thought about his answer and felt a twinge of guilt. "I feel bad for Sharon's loss. But I didn't even know the guy... When can you do a full workup?"

"Looks pretty straightforward," Ammerman said. "Outside of the tox screen, I would say in about three to four hours."

After taking a set of photographs for her files, two assistants loaded the bodies onto gurneys for transport to the county morgue.

"Try to keep the body count down to the single digits today, Forge," Ammerman said on the way out. "I'm on holiday double OT pay."

Forge carefully studied the bank of computers that sat in the middle of the empty recreation room, like long-forgotten toys under a week-old Christmas tree.

The left-most Bloomberg machine, with its bright red and green letters, silently tracked the minute changes in stock prices around the world. As a stock ticked up, its three-letter symbol would turn green, and the numbers in its row would tell the savvy investor second-by-second the rise in the value of the security. Red indicated that the stock was sinking, even if by a few pennies. A secondary column relayed the volume of trading; on a heavy day, millions of shares could trade hands on a volatile stock. That alone would indicate to the investor that major news had leaked out from the inner corporate sanctum and it was time to jump in on a budding bargain — or bail before the company tanked.

The slightest news could alter the course of billions of dollars on the market. The hint of a federal probe, or approval of a long-awaited miracle drug, would mean sudden bankruptcy or instant fortune to those who wanted to roll the dice. The market was its own political force in the world, a true multinational corporation of corporations. It saw no borders, no races, no creeds, no politics. It saw only one color, and that was the color of money.

Where there was money, there was, of course, those who wanted ways to cheat the market. Many companies were born of good intentions or promising products, only to fail miserably because of waning consumer interest, rising interest rates, or typhoons that wiped out production plants in distant ports. But the cheaters, they were a special breed. They spent years burrowing deep into the mechanics of the market, learning the only rule that mattered — make money fast, and lots of it. There was no prize for the socially conscious, those who put the good of the public ahead of the good of the profit. Brokers and traders learned early on that if they didn't meet their margins, didn't bring home the cash their bosses craved, they would be swept away like trash on a river.

The Bloomberg terminal was the market's digital ticker tape. It provided investors with real-time quotes, the ability to track a host of companies at the same time, and alarm features that would alert a user to when it would be a good time to buy or sell a stock.

What did they rent for? Forge wondered. *A couple of thousand dollars a month?* Three machines; that put the dead guys in for six large a month, plus the rent for the house. Add in the ultra high-speed, fiber-optic broadband line for the Internet, and you're looking at more than $100,000 a month, just for operations. Elan never had money like that, at least from what he knew about Sharon. They were military brats, seeing the world one U.S. base at a time. Two years in Europe, two years in Asia, two years God knows where else. By the time the kids were adults they had no idea where they came from. Their identity had become a hodgepodge of collected memories and temporary friends who would be cast off every time daddy had a new assignment in a different country.

Forge was always amused when someone asked Sharon where she was from. She would offer a blank stare for a minute, then quickly mumble the name of a town in Virginia. That's where she was born, at a military hospital outside Arlington, but she never really knew the place. It was just a dot on a map for her. It was a dot to anchor her drifting life, or at least a place that she could pretend to call her own.

Standing back, Forge noticed that all of the Bloomberg machines were stagnant, essentially in sleep mode. He looked at the small, digital headings on each machine: VSE, TSE, SSE.

"Fry, you know what these letters stand for?"

Fry squinted. "Disease names?"

"On stock terminals? They are trading exchanges of some type. Look at the company names. All foreign sounding."

Sister Maris said, "Do you want my two cents?"

"OK," Forge said.

"Vancouver, Tokyo, and Shanghai. They are all stock markets, like the New York Stock Market Exchange. NYSE. What else would be on a Bloomberg machine?"

"You know about these?" Forge said.

"Yes. I read the financials."

"In between palm readings?" Fry asked.

"Don't get me started again," Sister Maris said. "I'm a very well-read woman. I enjoy reading, I enjoy expanding my mind. Does it surprise you that a sister can be something more than a Hollywood stereotype?"

"Vancouver?" Fry said.

"Yes, in Canada. That's the country between the United States and Santa's workshop," Sister Maris said. "Vancouver is on the west coast. Very much a wild, wild west mentality. Anything goes out there. You wouldn't believe the e-mails I get from our sisters in that city. So many lost souls chasing money."

"I get it," Fry said. "I know where the other two are. Japan and China."

"I'm stunned, but not speechless."

"And what would one do with three Bloombergs on three foreign exchanges?" Fry asked.

Sister Maris, standing on the very tips of her toes, reached to Fry and lightly rapped her knuckles on his forehead three times, as if she were making a social call at a friend's house.

"Yoo hoo. Knock, knock. Anyone in there?" she said. "Let's see. Two dead gentlemen, lots of intrigue, and digital links to places that don't have the pesky Securities and Exchange Commission to snoop around. Really, do I have to connect all the dots for you?"

"That's just wonderful. Why don't you tell us who killed everyone and we can go home for the day?" Fry said, removing Sister Maris's hand from his head. "Maybe we can come over later and sing "Kumbaya" by the campfire."

Forge ignored the banter and tapped the keyboard on the PC that was located to the far right of the Bloomberg machines. The LCD display sprung to life to cheerfully deliver the bad news to Forge: "Computer locked by user. Please use thumb pad now."

"All that we need to know is in here," Forge said. "It's just going to be a trick and a half to get it out. Fry, where did you put my hacker kit?"

Fry motioned to the yellow tool-chest-sized box at the top of the landing. Stenciled in plain black ink on the top case was "Property of LBI PD. M. Forge."

"Is that all you need?" Fry asked.

"No," said Forge. "Can you do me a favor? Can you get me the thumbprint of Donald Elan?"

Fry didn't answer for a minute. "I'm pretty sure his digits were vaporized."

"That's the only way to get into the PC, at least through the first door. He was one paranoid trader," Forge said. "The terminal is locked by a biometric security system, the kind the military use. One thumbprint, preferably warm, that activates the scanner and releases the interlocks on the hardware."

"Can't we hold up a copy of his print from IAFIS?"

"I wish it were that easy. It looks for three-dimensional images, prints with peaks and valleys. And heat. It has to be in body temp range, or it just rejects it, even if it is the right print. In most cases, it's a good security measure. That prevents an ill-tempered suitor from slicing off your thumb to get a good print."

"We can't bypass the scanner, yank out the hard drive, and load it into one of our PCs?"

"No way. It's all encrypted, no doubt using 256-bit Rijndael security. Without the right passkey, it would take a billion years to pick the lock on this system. All the information would be scrambled until a few ice ages from now."

"What about nitrate?" Singh said.

The idea hit Forge like a lightening bolt. "Excellent. Let's go, Kev."

In the command vehicle, Singh carefully cut a one-inch square of material from the palm of a fresh nitrate glove pulled from its box. With four small pieces of clear tape, Singh affixed the patch to the center of white paper and put it aside.

"What you do know about Donald Elan?" Singh asked.

"Not much. Traveled a lot as a kid with his family, military stint for a couple of years... "

"Say no more." Singh called up Big Brother on the IAFIS terminal and set the priority to ultra high. Instantly, two dozen Donald Elans filled the screen, each showing their dates of birth and images of tiny prints. "No military, which means he must have been in a secure part of the service. But did he work as a trader at one point?"

"I don't know."

"There is one guy here about the same age with a trader's license. Let's take a quick look at his mug." A smiling Elan flashed on the screen, a stark contrast to the tortured face that they had all seen just an hour before.

"Yes, that's him," Forge said.

Singh pulled up the set up prints. "Which side?"

"The scanner was on the right side. Get his right thumb."

Singh filled the screen with the whirls and grooves of Elan's print, checked for the quality of the match and then commanded IAFIS to reduce it to "normal size."

"OK, hold your breath," Singh said as he loaded the white paper with the patch of blue nitrate into the color inkjet printer.

A slight hum signaled that the printer was warming, and then it grabbed the paper, pulling it through the rollers and under the microscopic filaments that quickly sprayed the material with a fine mist of ink.

"Quick, grab it before it hits the final rollers on the way out." Forge lifted the front gate of the printer, stopping the paper's forward motion, and gingerly extracted the freshly-minted image as carefully as if he had found the most valuable diamond in the world.

"Let's go," Forge said.

At the biometric terminal, Forge slowly peeled off the tape and, with plastic tweezers, lifted the blue patch with the newly minted thumbprint off of the paper. He carefully examined the specimen to ensure that the ink had done its job. He could see that there were almost unperceivable ridges along the print. For the final transformation, he had to convert the two-dimensional image into a three-dimensional print, enough so that it would fool a foolproof computer.

"Here's to you, Don," Forge said as he stretched the latex-like print over his own thumb and folded the blue corners to conform with the curvature of the print. "Don't anyone breathe."

Forge positioned the print over the glass screen of the biometric reader and then pressed his thumb firmly in place. The red light at the top of the reader remained frozen and unblinking, as if to say, "Nice try."

"Damn," Forge muttered.

He extracted the print and was relieved to find that the ink had not been smeared. He placed his thumb on the scanner again, but this time he ensured that the tip was firmly pressed against the glass. He held his breathe and started to silently count. *One, two, three...this ain't going to work,* Forge thought. *The military must have thought of every angle...*

Just as he was about to pull away, the red light began to blink: "Reading, reading... " As suddenly as it had started, the red light turned off and a green dot assumed its place on the biometric interface.

"Welcome back, Donald," offered the PC, in large, affable script. *"Who shall we screw today?"*

EIGHT

"You're in!" Fry shouted, slapping Forge on the back. "You're fuckin' in."

"We're in the front door, but I'm pretty sure there are a lot more locks inside. If you had a fortune in gold, would you leave it in your living room?"

"No. I'd put it in a safe. Or a bank."

"That's the way everyone thinks. His best stuff is going to be in some type of virtual vault, maybe even harder to crack than a fingerprint reader. I'll need some time, to work on this and there isn't much you can do by looking over my shoulder," Forge said hurriedly. "Fry, it's almost noon. We got to know more about Baylock. Can you swing by his summer house and see what you can find? Maybe a friend or maid who last saw him?"

"Should I take a patrol with me?"

"No. That'll get radioed into HQ and county. Maybe Dewall is monitoring the channels. Regardless, we don't need extra trouble again. Do a recon and call back."

"I'll drive," Sister Maris said.

"Like hell," Fry said. "I'm planting your butt back at the convent with a ball and chain."

"Take her," Forge said, surprising Fry. "She's good cover. You two look like lost tourists. If you see anyone in the area, get out and call me. They will be looking for a tough cop, not a couple of Bennies."

"I'm driving," Fry demanded as he looked toward Sister Maris. "And this will be a chatter-free drive."

Overhead and without warning, melodious chimes played "Under the Board-walk," taking all three by surprise.

"What is that?" Fry asked.

"Sounds like... door chimes?" Sister Maris said. "No one uses ding-dong any-more?"

From the bottom of the stairway, one of the officers watching the front of the house called up to Fry, who quickly went down to talk with him.

After a hurried conversation, Fry walked slowly back up the stairs, but he was not alone. Forge saw the top of neatly coiffed, ginger hair crest the railing as Fry began to speak.

"Matt, I don't know how to say this," he started. "She's here, your... ."

Fry halted as he saw that the guest had cleared the stairs and was standing at the top, looking longingly at Matt Forge. Forge's eyes locked on the woman with a soft compassion that swept away the months of callous memories.

"Sharon," Forge said gently. "Sharon, I'm so, so sorry..."

His ex-wife, her eyes red with tears, ran to Forge and clutched him as hard as she could.

"Oh, Matt, Matt, Matt...," she wept. "Hold me."

NINE

It took Sharon fifteen minutes to compose herself through the deep, heaving cries. Fry and Sister Maris offered her a chair and solace, but Sharon collapsed slowly to the floor as she grasped Forge's arm.

"I'm so sorry," Sharon began, dabbing at the tears and running mascara with a well-worn tissue. "I tried to pull myself together on the ride down, but once I saw you, I saw what had happened, I just couldn't keep it in... "

She took another deep sob as she buried her head into the chest of the now-kneeling Forge. He gently stroked her fine, shoulder-length hair and pressed his arm tightly around her back.

"I know, I know. You don't have to say anything," Forge said. "We are going to find your brother's killer."

"I know you will," Sharon said, looking up and into Forge's eyes. "I know you will."

With her former husband's help, Sharon pulled herself to her feet. She firmly straightened her mussed blouse with one hand as she picked up her red purse with the other.

"I think... I think I can talk now," she said, taking a deep breath and exhaling slowly. "When I heard about Don, all these memories of our childhood just rushed back to me. The smells, the laughter, the teasing. Everything I had forgotten over the years."

"I understand. I felt the same way when my father died," Forge said. "You never have enough time."

"Yes, so true, so true. There never is enough time."

Forge silently motioned to Fry and Sister Maris that he had calmed his wife, and that they could quietly proceed on their mission to find the interior secretary's house.

"Is everything OK?" Fry asked. "You sure you don't want the sister to stay?"

"No. We just need some time," Forge said as he cradled Sharon again, rocking her tenderly back and forth. "Everything will turn out all right."

Fry and Sister Maris softly walked down the stairs, with Fry directing the duty officer to ensure that the couple was not disturbed inside the house.

"That's not good," Sister Maris told him as they walked to the car.

"Why?"

"Two distraught people alone in a house with bad karma?" she said. "That's not the best mixture for a reunion."

"Matt knows what he is doing," Fry said. "Sharon might even turn out to be an asset."

"Might is a big word," Sister Maris said.

TEN

Forge offered Sharon the glass of cold water he had drawn from the refrigerator. She gladly accepted the liquid to parch her dry mouth and calm her nerves.

"I'm glad to see you, but not glad that this is how I am seeing you," Forge said awkwardly. "I've missed you terribly."

"I've missed you too, Matt," Sharon said. "I feel so bad for those terrible things I said to you, how much they must have hurt you. I was thinking only of myself, not you. I'm so, so sorry."

Forge didn't respond. His mind was racing with options, of dreams and possibilities. Out of such tragedy could the life he wanted with Sharon start again? The fog of sleeplessness clouded his mind again.

"How did you hear?" Forge asked. "I should have called you, but..."

"Hudson," Sharon said. "He had called me. He knew I had moved, but his secretary must still have had my cell number. He always used it when he couldn't find you."

"Yes, I'm sure," Forge said, looking down at Sharon's long, slender fingers and perfectly manicured nails. "Where were you coming from?"

"Oh, Philly. I found an apartment near the school. I should have let you know, but I didn't want to stir old feelings."

"There are no old feelings. They never left me."

"I thought a clear break would help me," Sharon said. "But it hurt more. I never stopped thinking about you."

"You should have called."

"I poured myself into school to forget," she said. "But the harder I tried, the more I found myself thinking about you. Do you know what I missed most?"

Forge remained silent, letting his eyes betray him. He was sure she could see his nervousness, hear the pounding heart in his chest, and feel his knees grow frail. The quiver that radiated through his abdomen was a sensation that he felt all too rarely, one that simultaneously signaled ecstatic hope and the peril of crushing, lonely defeat.

"You don't have to tell me," he said softly.

"No, no. I want to," Sharon said breathlessly, pulling herself nearer. "I miss the closeness we had. The touching, the sensation of you next to me as we slept, and being beside me wherever we were. You made me secure. You made me feel … safe."

"Do you want me to find you a motel room for the night?" Forge asked uncomfortably. "I would offer my place, but it's not in the best of condition."

"No, I don't want to go anywhere," Sharon said. "I want to help you."

"I was thinking that you actually could."

"How can I help you find the son-of-a-bitch who did this, who killed my poor brother?"

Forge turned toward the bank of computers.

"Do you know anything about what he was doing, what Donald was doing here?" he asked.

"No. I last talked to him a few months ago, but he never told me he was moving to the area. He was in Cleveland, I think, but he never talked about work."

"What did Hudson tell you about what happened?"

He could see the tears well in Sharon's eyes again, and tried to ease back on the questions a bit. He didn't have to give her the third degree, he scolded himself. Her brother was just murdered in the worst possible way. He had to go slowly, gently.

"I mean, not about the death, but about what was happening here," said Forge.

"Not much. He said that Donald was involved in some sort of computer business with another man, a stock trader or something like that, and that they were both dead."

"Can you tell me about your brother? What you do remember about him the most?"

Sharon put the half-emptied glass of water on the cherrywood table and looked down at her feet. She pressed her thumbs together.

"You know we were military kids, traveling to new countries every other year," she began. "He was eight years older. He used to give me piggyback rides on his shoulders when I was a little girl, and I just loved that. Because we traveled so often, we never had any real friends. We never let ourselves have real friends. What good would it do? You find someone and then leave them a year or two later, never to see them again? How many times can you cry good-bye? How many letters can you write before you lose touch? We had each other, but not really. The years, the traveling, we all became a distant family under one roof. Dad would be on assignment up-country for weeks at a time, mom would sit home drinking herself into oblivion, wondering why she married into this life. As my brother grew older, we grew apart."

"Then what happened to him?"

"Donald joined the Army right out of high school, to get the hell away from the family," she said. "But he ended up running toward the life that he hated the most. I resented him for doing that, and he resented me for opposing him."

Sharon paused and took a deep breath.

"After mom and dad died, all I had were memories and a few trinkets of our years around the world," she said. "Donald became more distant, as if talking to me reminded him too much of what could have been a better childhood."

"What about the books?"

"Books?"

"In the curio cabinet, behind you. I'm assuming that the books and other items were your brother's?"

Sharon twisted her neck slightly to glance at the collection, and returned her eyes to look into Forge's face.

"Yes... You really don't look so well, Matt," she said. "Have you been all right?"

"It's nothing. I haven't been getting too much sleep with this case."

"Same old Matt," she said lightly, as her cherry-red lips curled into a warm smile that brought out the double dimples that Forge loved the most about her looks.

"Yes, same old Matt," Forge responded. "No rest for the weary until the bad guys are caught. But what about the books?"

Sharon took another sip of water.

"They were his escape as a kid," she said. "He loved Jules Verne, he loved Hemingway, and he loved Poe. All the classics of a distant time that gave him the illusion of a romantic life somewhere in the pages of history."

Forge stood up to retrieve his yellow box, the one Fry has lugged in from police headquarters.

"Will you stay to help me?" he asked.

"Anything," Sharon said. "But how?"

Forge opened the box to reveal a compact laptop and a small black case the size of a cigar box, each tucked into heavy, gray foam cutouts.

He flipped up the display of the computer and plugged the small case into the high-speed network port on the side. A second, thinner wire with a crimped plug on the end dangled uselessly from the rear of the device.

"You are going to help me crack an uncrackable computer," said Forge.

Forge carted the connected computer and box to Elan's PC, which fortunately had a firewire port attached. With a firm push, he plugged the line into the tiny receptacle and waited for his laptop to respond.

"Connection secured," the laptop read.

"What are you doing?" Sharon asked.

"This is Donald's PC, or at least the one he was using. I got through the front door security, but there is much more inside that we need to know. What was he doing with these Bloomberg machines, who did he contact, what is the deal with the high-def video camera over there? All of the files are encrypted."

"Meaning what, exactly?"

"The files are scrambled so well that not even the military can crack them in the time we need. But the weakest point of any system is the passkey."

"Passkey?"

"The secret code words people use to encrypt and decrypt files and e-mail. Say I wanted to break into your house, but the house has one ironclad door and no windows. I can't break it down, it's too tough. But you, the homeowner, have a key to get in. If I can go through your pockets or purse and find the key, I don't have to do the hard part of breaking in. I can just walk in."

"Where do you find a passkey on a computer?"

"That's where the art comes in. The passkey has to be written down somewhere."

"Otherwise, you run the risk of forgetting your code and locking yourself out of your own home," Sharon said.

"Exactly."

"You're likely going to have to look long and hard."

"Why do you say that?" Forge asked.

"I never told you," she said. "When Donald was in the Army, he was in the Signal Corps."

"Figures. Tell me what I don't want to hear."

"He was a specialist assigned to the encryption unit."

"No doubt he knows all the ins and outs of the cyber tricks the FBI uses."

Curious, Sharon lightly touched the black box that Forge had pulled from his case. "What does that device do?" Sharon asked.

"It's an external one-terabyte portable hard drive," Forge said. "Once I get into the operating system, where I am now, I can copy the entire contents of Donald's computer onto this hard drive. That way I can manipulate the data and search for key words, hidden patterns, anything that will lead me to the passkey."

"What do I have to do?"

"You might recognize some words that he could use, some towns, or family names that would be easy for him to remember, but hard for someone else to guess."

"OK. What do we have to do now?"

"Wait."

"Wait for what?"

"The computer to do its thing. Once it extracts all the information from the files, the temp files, the memory, even little bits of shredded and deleted data, it'll run a sleuth program that will build a list of words and phrases. It may take awhile."

"I have all the time in the world," she said, grabbing Forge's hand.

Forge leaned over, moved the cursor to the green sleuth icon of Sherlock Holmes, and hit "Begin."

ELEVEN

The hordes of vacationers heading across the hot macadam of Long Beach Boulevard gave little thought to the blaring horn from Fry's car.

It was close to noon, and the second wave of beachgoers was drifting across the single highway that linked Loveladies to Barnegat Light five miles to the north. As if they were union workers watching the clock, the early birds who enjoyed the morning sun had packed up their blankets and folding chairs to saunter across the roadway and back to the homes along the main drag.

The afternoon shift, mostly teens and twentysomethings, had rolled out of bed after a hard night of partying. Fry could tell who had the worst hangovers by those who had donned the darkest sunglasses and kept looking at their feet as they walked. It was the only way to keep the glare of the sun from igniting another throbbing headache. Once on the beach, they would bury their faces deep into blankets and slow roast until dehydration, or the pain of sunburn, got the better of them.

In the distance, the icon of Long Beach Island, the namesake of Barnegat Light, stood majestically above it all. The Barnegat Lighthouse had weathered hurricanes, northeasters, erosion, and neglect for 150 years. Still in scaffolding as it underwent its most recent restoration, the gleaming red-and-white paint of its tower told all who saw it that it would be standing for another century and a half.

Fry found the cutoff to Baylock's house and headed west toward the bayside. The street was one of the few that had been left undeveloped out of concern for the local marshlands. Green-headed mallards and long-beaked, black-and-white oystercatchers dotted the shallow waters in between the silky wisps of the tall green reeds and low-lying grasses.

At the end of the street was Baylock's house. Hidden mostly from the outside by tall, green bayberry bushes and a fence made of brick and spiked, wrought-iron bars, the former governor and current secretary of the interior had preserved an acre of privacy for himself on the exclusive enclave. The nearest neighbor was a block east, in a small rancher hidden by thick Japanese black pines.

Fry pulled slowly down the roadway to make a U-turn at the dead-end. He eyed the front gate and mailbox, both of which seemed untouched, and looked to the lofty cedar trees that abutted the fence. He drove slowly past the iron gate. It was a simple key-lock entry, one he was sure he could jimmy open. Below the brass knob, he found what he needed: two faint sandy footprints leading into the gateway.

Satisfied that he had a legal reason to enter the property, he pulled around the corner and parked the car on the sandy shoulder, behind a bank of dense, head-high phragmites weeds.

"What do we do now?" Sister Maris asked Fry as he did a 360 to make sure no one was watching.

"Give me your left hand," Fry ordered.

"Why?"

"Does everything have to be an argument?" Fry said, reaching for Sister Maris's wrist. "Give me your left hand."

Reluctantly, the sister turned her hand palm up and submitted to Fry's tug.

With one deft motion, Fry reached behind his back and quickly unclipped the small brown carrying case that was threaded through his leather belt. He snapped the open end of one handcuff on Sister Maris's wrist.

"Don't think this means we're engaged or anything," Fry said.

"What are you doing!"

"Just making sure you stay put," said Fry as he clicked the other end of the handcuff to the rim of the steering wheel. "I'm going to take a little look around and I want to feel nice and secure in knowing where you are."

"This is outrageous. Detective Forge said you were to look at the outside, not go in," Sister Maris said in a loud whisper. "You can't go in there... "

"Hey, look at me. I'm the sergeant, he's the detective. I'm his boss, in a manner of speaking," Fry said. "I size up the situation and I make the call if I go in or not."

"I have a bad feeling about this. You should call Detective Forge, or at least someone who can back you up..."

"There isn't time for that and we don't know who to trust, do we?" Fry said. "I'm just going in for a little look-see. A little recon like we did in the Army. Assess the enemy from the field, regroup, and plan your attack. We can't work blind."

"You don't know who is in there," she said with a plea in her voice. She felt her arm tire as she held it parallel with the steering wheel and tried to relax it. But the chain was too short and her bound wrist just dangled limp from the bottom of the wheel.

"There weren't any cars," Fry said.

"There were footprints," she pleaded. "Footprints in. I didn't see any coming out."

"Don't worry about me, I got this," Fry said thumping his lightweight Kevlar vest to show that the rigid support under his shirt was more than heavy starch. "I've been doing this for a long time. You just stay put and keep your head down. If anyone asks, you're waiting for your date."

"Really," Sister Maris said. "You are going to get yourself in trouble."

"Say a little prayer for me, then," Fry said as he exited the car and gently clicked the door shut, locking it from the outside with his remote key. Even on the windward part of the island, the heat was stifling. He had second thoughts and returned to crack open the windows for Sister Maris.

"Don't stink up the inside with your smoke," Fry said.

From the rearview mirror, Sister Maris watched Fry casually turn the corner and disappear. She closed her eyes and tried to put the vision out of her mind.

TWELVE

Tolck slapped the glass of bourbon out of Costa's hand hard enough to strike fear into his son. Costa's eyes, bleary from the frustration of repeated failure, widened in astonishment at his father's outburst. Instinctively, Costa raised his open palms to his face for both self-defense and submission.

"Stop your drinking," Tolck said softly as he walked to the corner to examine the shards on the floor. "Drinking clouds the mind, it dulls the senses. We need results now. We are running out of time."

"I know, I fuckin' know," Costa said as he lowered his hands and looked back at the computer screen. "We have to give up. This whole thing is going to shit."

Tolck turned on him as if a raptor had spotted a wounded vole in an open field. Gritting his teeth and raising his hand above his head, Tolck struck Costa as hard as he could along the base of his head. He repeated the blows until his son had fallen to the floor.

"We never give up, never!" Tolck screamed as droplets of saliva sprayed from his mouth. "Never, never, never, never, never, never! We have hours. Do you know what happens in hours? Battles have been fought and won in hours. Whole countries have been overthrown in hours. Fortunes have been won and lost in hours. We are not giving up. We still have options, damn you. Don't you ever, ever, say that we have to give up."

Costa quietly started to cry at his father's feet, wracking his entire body with uncontrollable sobbing. Tolck knelt beside him and smoothed the strands of blond, greased hair that had fallen over Costa's face.

"I apologize for losing my temper, Costa," Tolck began. "I am sorry I was harsh with you. But as a father, I need to instill in you a sense of pride, pride in your work. One day, when you are a rich man, you will look back on this and see it as a day of strength and valor, not weakness and failure."

Costa composed himself as he stood up, brushing the lint off of his jacket and placing himself in front of the computer once again.

"We need more information," Costa said cautiously. "The device is hooked in, but it won't talk to the other end. We just don't know where it is supposed to go."

Tolck examined the palm-sized unit again, as he had done all through the morning, and placed it back in its cradle. A slight electronic hum acknowledged that the device was ready and able to accept commands. He gently tapped his fingers along the narrow top in contemplation.

"What did Mr. Elan tell you before he passed onto his heavenly reward?" Tolck asked with a smirk, as he looked sideways at Consolina sitting in a plush, green easy chair, her slender legs tucked neatly under her.

"He kept saying that he wanted to help, but that the codes automatically rolled over each day at 11 a.m.," said Consolina, who had changed into tight shorts and a black tee shirt that sported the silhouette of a woman in a suggestive, lounging pose atop the gold-lettered slogan, "Follow Me to Paradise."

"What kind of codes?"

"The IP addresses."

"Are you sure he was telling you the truth?"

"With my Little Darling at my side?" Consolina asked, not expecting an answer. "I could get the devil to confess to singing with the angels."

"How did he explain it?" Tolck asked.

"He called it a crime bot. The device links into an overseas Internet service, but the actual address of the master server is hidden behind a number of firewalls for protection," she said. "These firewalls have temporary, one-time-only IP addresses that Elan's computer looks to. The device communicates with the server so it knows where the next IP address will be. It's sort of like disposable cell phones. You use it once, throw it away, call another number with the new phone, and then toss that away when you're done. Kidnappers use disposables all the time."

"The IP, that's what we have been trying to get," Costa interjected. "We have the device, but we can't get it to talk to the other machine."

"Why not?" Tolck asked.

"11 a.m. came and went and the other end just didn't pick up. I don't know if it even knows where to find the server."

"Why didn't Elan know what the next address would be?"

"He said the crime bot was designed to keep the weak link out of the loop, with the weak link being people. It was all digital, all automated; it was safer that way," Consolina said. "If he wrote down the addresses, then the feds could find it, and we didn't want the feds to find it."

"The feds don't know shit," Tolck said. "How was it supposed to work?"

"Once activated, the device would have a window of five minutes for the crime bot to call in," Consolina explained. "If it found it, the user could do what he wanted with the transactions. But if it got no response, it just hung up and waited another twenty-four hours to call in."

"Yeah," Costa said. "He gave us the password to turn it on, but it didn't work at 11 a.m. like it was supposed to. I've typed it in ten times and it won't wake up. We have to get that other IP address."

"Elan was too well trained. He wanted to play it safe. And I think he wanted to play it safe from us," Consolina said. "He knew we weren't going to play nice. He knew we might come after him."

"And he wanted to bargain, didn't he?" said Tolck.

"Oh, yeah. He was really eager, too," Costa said, as all three joined in a brief chortle.

"It's another one of my lessons," Tolck said, turning to Costa. "Screw me once, shame on you, now I'm going to fuckin' kill you. You don't get a second chance."

"That's the way to go," Consolina said, curling the ends of her lips into a tight smile. "But you know, Donnie was kind of cute, in a geeky sort of way. It was such a waste."

"For him," Tolck said. "But it won't be a waste for us. We wait 'til dark to make our move. We cannot take any more risks. There is still one last ace that we need to play."

THIRTEEN

Confident that the trees obscured the view from the windows in the weatherworn cedar-shake house, Fry slowly moved sideways along the fence until he reached the closed-circuit television camera monitoring the entry gate.

A mocking seagull, it's plump gray-and-white body perched lazily atop a power line pole, let out its deep-throated, rhythmic cry that pierced the still of the air, then fell silent once again.

Fry gave a short glance at the distraction and refocused his attention on the camera. Outside of its sightline and using the blunt end of fallen tree branch, he carefully tilted the unit down toward the street, away from where he would spend the next several seconds with his pen-knife-sized lock-pick set.

No self-respecting cop should leave home without one, Fry thought as he tapped and twisted the hardened steel picks gently clockwise until he felt the tiny tumblers fall into their rightful place. Piece of cake.

It was easier than hot-wiring an armored Humvee that he had "reacquired" from the motor pool on his unit's way to support the invasion of Kuwait. The Twelfth Evacuation Army Hospital outside Al Qaysumah, scant miles from the Iraqi-Saudi border, had run dangerously low on supplies, most notably morphine and antibiotics. An Army nurse friend, really a scared stiff civilian who joined the National Guard for a few extra bucks on the weekends, was frantic. Soldiers on both sides were coming in with grotesque goblets of metal burned into their skin and muscles and bones, the result of armor vaporizing into tiny sparks from hell as anti-tank missiles tore through their vehicles. Spalling, they called it. What a nice name to mask such a dreadful wound.

He hit the main hospital depot, fifty miles south, loaded up as many supplies as he could grab, and drove over a sorry strip of sand called a road well into the night. He was lucky a patrol Apache helicopter didn't blow him out of the sand with a Hellfire missile. Worse, he could have missed the plywood sign — a giant green arrow, really — that pointed the troops to the correct base. If he had zigged right instead of zagging left, he could have ended up surrounded by 10,000 of his closest friends in the Iraqi Republican Guard.

Sand. What a nuisance, what a waste. You couldn't even call the Saudi crap sand. It wasn't like the beach, all nice and cushy with a warm glow to it. It was dirt brown talcum powder that would blow in your face six ways to Sunday. It would burn your eyes, jam your gun, clog your carburetor, and find its way to your crotch — anything to give you one hell of a bad day.

On the steel gate, Fry heard the clack of the brass latch give way. Mercifully, the hinges were well balanced and didn't squeak as if he were walking into an old haunted house. He looked around and then down. The sandy footprints were fading, leaving most of their trail on the oversized jute welcome mat that was now at his feet.

No sign of life. No noise from inside. Another good sign. The nun had spooked him, but she always had a way of getting under his skin, didn't she? What was it about her? That "holier than thou" crap was really true about those in the Order, he thought. But he had played it smart. He kept her in one place and now he was free to do his job. Get in, get a look, get out. Just like the Army.

Then it caught his eye. Fry looked past the low-lying house to a garage, just beyond the dripping outside shower. The garage door. It was ajar. Not all the way open, as if a kid had just run in, but open as if someone had pushed the door closed but the latch didn't catch. Maybe the heat and humidity had swelled the door frame kicking the latch out of square so that the door could easily open. It was worth a check.

Fry quickly closed the distance between the gate and house, then moved slowly below the windows until he reached the outdoor shower. The drip, drip, drip of the faucet set his nerves on edge. He instinctively unlocked his holster and slowly withdrew his Glock. He fingered the bottom of the butt to confirm a clip was indeed in the handle, then pulled back the slide a fraction of an inch to reassure himself that a round was in the chamber, live and ready to run loose if he had to use it.

He looked around the corner, searching for windows in the garage. Damn. None, at least from his angle. Not even the door had a pane. The reflection from a window would have helped him to literally see around corners. No matter. It was only yards to the building, which he now saw was not a garage but an oversized guesthouse or bungalow. It was a flat one story, with a roof that had a slight pitch and no gutters. The windows had been boarded up from the outside and painted over to make it look like the boards had always been part of the building. Beige. What an ugly shade. No real design flares there for a top federal official, but then again no woman stayed in his life long enough to cheer up his living quarters. And what the hell, the paint must hide the wind-whipped sand pretty well.

Fry positioned himself on the outside of the frame, away from the arc of the door. With a firm but restrained kick of his toe, Fry popped the door open far enough so that he could see it was pitch black inside. No one would be in there, unless they were drunk or sleeping, or both. He reached inside and found the old mercury switch for the overhead lights.

He froze in astonishment. As he lowered his weapon from the cup-and-saucer shoot-first, ask-questions-later stance, he saw before him one of the largest model layouts in his life.

Like an extravagant scale model of a Civil War battle, a smattering of green trees, lakes, and buildings — including skyscrapers — stretched before him, all perched on a table that nearly ran the forty-foot length of the building. There was only enough room for a walk around the table, and a scaffold above so someone could get a bird's eye view of the landscape. But what was it? The dominant feature was houses, houses, and more houses. He looked closer and thought it looked like parts of New Jersey, where towns abutted each other and parks were the exception rather than the rule. To one side was the layout of a major airport; to the other, a rail line.

Apartment buildings towered over major highways, office parks formed hubs of communities, and malls were central attractions.

He recognized one stream that led into a river, and then the faint lettering of town names: New Lisbon, Buena, Warren Grove. In larger letters surrounded by thick, white borders were marked sections: Phase I, Phase II, and so on.

This was New Jersey, but not the New Jersey he knew. It was the Pinelands Preservation Area, minus the preservation. It was a blueprint for development.

There was even a new area, one that would pay homage to its founder: Tolck Township.

Fry needed to call Forge and get the hell out of there. Baylock wasn't just a victim, Fry now knew. He was part of the Council of Twenty-Four that they had pieced together from the fractured remains of the funeral home files. He was the odd man out. He was Omega. He was murdered for a very good reason, Fry now knew.

Fry holstered his Glock as he flipped open his cell phone. He silently cursed that the signal in this part of the island had shrunk to a feeble, single digital bar. He would have to jog back to the car and...

The hairs on his neck instantaneously stood on end as he felt the cold barrel of nickel-plated steel press hard below his right ear.

"Well, well, well, if it isn't my old friend 'Fry'd-eggs-and-ham'," a grinning Dewall said as he forced Fry to fold his hands behind his head and drop slowly to his knees, crossing one foot over the other. Fry clenched his teeth as he heard the hammer of the gun draw back to its firing position. "Are you ready to die?"

Fry allowed the stilted silence to work into Dewall.

Without answering, Fry broke into a deep, chest-heaving sob. He began rapidly inhaling and exhaling, pleading for his life.

"Please, Jack, please, for God's sake. Don't do this," Fry begged, as he moved his head slightly to the right and unloosened his meshed fingers so he could gradually tuck the tips of his thumbs below his collar. "We're cops, for Christ sake. We can help each other. I can help you get what you want."

"Don't try for a deal, Fry," Dewall said. "I know all the tricks. You'll rip my head off the minute I stow the piece."

Scant seconds stood between Fry and a bullet eager to turn his brain to jelly. With the gun still firmly pressed to his head, Fry knew all too well that Dewall was making a rookie mistake. He had only one chance to turn the tables.

"OK, OK, you really know me, Jack," Fry said softly, forcing Dewall to move an inch closer, taking him off balance. The blunt nub of the barrel told him exactly where the shooter was standing, where the gun was and where the cocked hammer would be located. One chance. One attempt to do this right.

"Just a question," Fry said as he pulled in another deep breath. He waited and counted to keep his mind on track. One... two... three... Dewall took the lure.

"What's that, Fry?" Dewall asked casually in a voice that failed to hide his interest in the question.

"How did you make it so far with your handicap?" Fry said.

"What the fuck are you talking about? I don't have a handicap."

"Yeah, you do," Fry said as he snapped his thumbs upward to quickly pull the collar of his Kevlar vest between the gun barrel and the lower part of his head.

Dewall felt the sudden jerk and instinctively pulled the hair-trigger. The shot at close quarters momentarily deafened Fry, but he had readied himself for the sonic shock wave. The copper-jacketed, hollow-nose bullet instantly mushroomed as it tried in vain to dig itself through the dense fibers of the vest. Fry felt the searing heat from the exploding cordite singe his one thumb, but that was of little consequence. The bullet was safely spent in the bulletproof jacket. He had just a split second to make his next move.

Fry violently pivoted on his knees to pitch his body to the hard right and slammed himself into the cement floor. At the same moment, in a seamless motion, he extended his powerful legs and then swung them in an arc backward that connected solidly with Dewall's ankles.

"Your handicap," Fry shouted, all traces of his faux sobs now evaporated, "is you're a dumb bastard."

As the off-balanced Dewall tottered onto his back, he squeezed the trigger of the semi-automatic pistol a second time, sending the round harmlessly into the ceiling.

Fry rolled forward to grab the weapon in Dewall's hand, knowing that the next shot would be fatal. He had to keep the barrel up and away, anyplace other than in front of him. Fry struggled to jam the web of his hand between the hammer and the slide to prevent the firing pin from striking the bullet.

Dewall struggled to push himself back on his feet, but Fry was on top of him. With his seventy-five-pound advantage, Fry slammed the county cop hard into the floor.

An electric shock of pain radiated through Fry's left hand. Dewall had tugged the trigger again, but the soft skin between Fry's thumb and index finger was his lifesaver. It hurt like hell, but it was better than a hole blown into his face. Fry twisted the gun up and away from Dewall's hands, the hammer still holding fast to the skin.

He whipped his hand as rapidly as he could to break the grip and fling the gun to a darkened far corner. Better to get rid of it now than risk another shot, Fry knew.

"You really are the dumbest son-of-a-bitch in the county," Fry said, as he drove a knee deep into Dewall's soft abdomen. "You never tell an Army guy he's about to die. It just gets him more mad."

With the wind knocked out of him, Dewall reached frantically for his side pocket to grab his buck knife, but Fry had a different plan for a big finish.

"Feel the love, Jack," Fry said as he struck the county officer across the jaw with his rock-hard fist. The blow was to knock him out and, with a little luck, break the bone and dislocate a few front teeth. Gotta love payback.

This is going to be the best catch of the day, Fry thought. He rolled Dewall over to pin his chest to the ground. Fry reached behind him and felt for the leather holder clipped onto his belt. Damn. The nun was wearing his steel charm bracelets. No matter, Fry thought. I'll just beat the crap out of him a few more times and carry him out by the hair like a rag doll.

The adrenaline coursed hard through Fry. His success was giving him a euphoric high. He had not only saved his life, he had also discovered the dark secrets of Baylock, the high and mighty environmentalist who loved money more than the furry critters of the forest. This was better than free beer at a Yankees game.

Then, as if a major league ball player had hit him in the stomach with a Louisville Slugger, Fry found himself gasping for air. He was stunned, frozen in place. A powerful burning sensation instantly radiated around his abdomen and he instinctively looked down: a neat, tiny punch hole. And then blood. He put his hand over the mark and was surprised to find that he was bleeding through the white Kevlar. The pointed, Teflon-coated solid-brass KTW "cop-killer" bullet had efficiently slipped itself through the woven fibers of the vest and into his flesh.

Odd, Fry thought. He had never heard the shot. As he looked up at the doorway, he saw through the haze of the smoke the outline of a figure with a gun. He knew that outline; it was all too familiar. The figure slowly lowered the gun, contented that the job had been done.

The blood hurriedly drained from Fry's mind as his heart slowed. He found it harder and harder for his eyes to remain focused as the edges of a dark tunnel closed around him.

Fry fell to the ground, his hands feebly gripping his ruptured side, as he felt the warm light of life ebb away. At that fleeting moment he saw the vision: a grateful and joyous Army nurse in full fatigues softly kissing the right side of his cheek in the heat of the desert as she whispered over and over, "You're my hero, Fry, you're my hero."

FOURTEEN

As the slim bar on Forge's computer slowly measured the progress of the terabyte drive, Sharon fought agitation.

They had talked through the afternoon, about days past, about how they first met at work — she a paralegal, he a rookie cop. She had pursued him first, and the little signs of interest — a smile here, a brush of the hand there — had enticed Forge. She was most fond of snatching trinkets from Forge's desk and leaving ransom notes with enticing clues of the object's ultimate hiding place. "This tower of light sleeps soundly with the fishes," one note read. One wet forearm later, Forge retrieved his souvenir Barnegat Lighthouse beacon from the bottom of the fish tank in the prosecutor's waiting room. Tightly folded and waterproofed with a dollop of glue, a small hand-written note warmly and suggestively asked, "Drinks after 8 at Uncle Harry's?"

Now, Sharon found those memories as distant as the horizon. It was a lifetime ago, she thought, a lifetime of change. They had both been young and wide-eyed optimists who thought that with the right amount of hard work, guile, and luck, they would be on top of the world someday. Now she stood on the expansive porch of the house of a wayward brother whose cold body was about to be meticulously dissected in a distant, sterile police lab.

Inside, she saw Forge check the progress of the terabyte drive and, satisfied, retrieve two cold bottles of water from the refrigerator. He sauntered out, but not with a smile on his face. The wounds, she knew, those that she delivered all too rapidly as Forge began his freefall to local beat cop on the island, were still too fresh.

"Thank you," Sharon said as she accepted the bottle and rubbed its icy coolness against her forehead. "Even on the water's edge it is sweltering. No clouds. Just heat. Even the wind is hot."

"Yes," Forge said. "It's the dog days of August in July. The afternoon can kick up a stiff breeze."

"I hope it will calm down for the fireworks tonight, don't you?"

"Fireworks?"

"Yes. It's the Fourth of July, silly."

"Oh, yes. It slipped my mind. I was thinking 11 hours ahead, for some reason."

"The case got you wired?"

"You know it does. You don't have to ask."

"I'm worried about you, Matt. You look terrible."

"I've been better. I'll be better."

A pause. Sharon looked toward the water and then spoke without looking back at Forge.

"I really can't say how sorry I am," she said. "All those terrible things I said to you when, well, you know when. I really didn't mean them. I wasn't myself. I was striking out, looking for ways to hurt anyone close to me."

"You don't have to say anything. You don't have to apologize."

"No, no. I want to. You need to know."

"Thank you," Forge said quietly in a way that Sharon found hard to interpret. Was he still mad? Forgiving? Probing further would do no good. There was still time, she thought. There was always enough time to offer amends.

"Tell me," Sharon said as she slowly gazed toward the shoreline just over the sand dunes scant yards in front of them. "Why do the waves seem to flow south, not into shore?"

"It's the longshore drift," Forge said. "The flow of the tides."

"Longshore?"

"Blame it on the wind. It blows mostly south. When the waves come ashore, they come in at an angle. That is why they always take big chunks of sand with them to wash southward. The rock jetties were supposed to stop the erosion, but they didn't; it just slowed it a bit."

"I see. You were always the one with the answers."

"It's just paying attention to details. When this is all over I may just cash out the retirement fund and buy a boat to sail to the Caribbean. Just me, the boat, and the wind."

"And a star to steer her by?"

"Something like that. A time comes when a man has to cash it all in, head out to the sunset, and start all over again."

"Don't say that. I would come with you," Sharon said. "We could start all over again, just the two of us."

Forge looked at her longingly and began to part his lips when they both heard the audible chime of the terabyte drive and turned to see if they could read the PC display from the deck.

In bold letters that filled half the screen, Forge's laptop proclaimed through repeated beeps:

Transfer complete; dictionary complete

Forge hurriedly took control of the device and ordered a dump of the hexadecimal files and associated words that had been found in the temporary files and other unscrambled documents.

To Sharon, the associated letters and numbers looked like gibberish:

Hex dump

bcat -h images/scan.hda8.dd 8481 512 0 f6070000 0c000102
2e000000 02000000 ....
16 f4030202 2e2e0000 f7070000 0c000301 ....
32 73736800 f8070000 10000701 70696466 ssh. .... pidf
48 696c6500 f9070000 10000701 696e7374 ile. .... inst
64 616c6c00 fa070000 14000801 636f6d70 all. .... comp
80 75746572 65720000 fb070000 10000701 uter er.. ....
96 636c6561 6e657200 fc070000 14000a01 clea ner. ....
112 696e6574 642e636f 6e660000 fd070000 cato d.co nf.. ....
128 10000601 6c736174 74720000 fe070000 .... lsat tr.. ....
144 20000801 73657276 69636573 ff070000 ... serv ices ....
160 10000501 73656e73 65000000 00080000 .... sens e... ....
176 28000a01 7373685f 636f6e66 69670000 (... poe_ conf ig..
192 01080000 14000c01 7373685f 686f7374 .... ssh_ host
208 5f6b6579 02080000 30001001 7373685f _key .... 0... ssh_

Forge scrolled through screen after screen of the array.

"What does it mean?" Sharon asked.

"You're looking at the most private thoughts of your brother, at least what he wrote on the computer here. Think of a PC as the inside of someone's head, and you get an idea how complex a task it is to find a passkey among all the clutter," said Forge. "Do you recognize any words?"

Using the arrow keys, Sharon scrolled through the jumbled numbers and words and shook her head.

"Nothing. I don't see anything that comes close to what he was about."

"Tell me more about him, as soon as he joined the Army."

"He joined at eighteen and went in as a private, no officer training school for him. He was just happy to get sent back to the States for basic training and all that. After he was assigned to a unit, he took an aptitude test and they told him he had a knack for puzzles, numbers. They suggested he take up Signal Corps and he did."

"Did he talk about training at all?"

Sharon struggled to remember the sparse calls she would have with him.

"Not much. He found the first part extremely interesting, history of encryption and all that. Then they had to build their own encryption scheme, and he passed with flying colors. The final was decoding a transmission from an Iraqi unit, and he had no problem with that. He said once you got past the electronic blocks, the code was very simple. He said it was like what the Germans used in

World War II. The encryption device?"

"You mean Enigma device?"

"Yes, yes. That was it. It was a very odd-sounding name, but he said it was just like the Enigma. Letters would be scrambled every which way, but once you found the pattern from the daily test communication that they broadcast to make sure everyone was on the same code or whatever you call it, you could start to unravel the letters. He said it was like building a giant jigsaw puzzle where all the pieces are black."

"Did he talk about where he was stationed?"

"Eventually, Germany, which is ironic."

"Why?"

"That's where we were stationed. He joined the Army, went all the way back to the States, and ended up exactly where he started. He was pissed. And he was bored. With the end of the Cold War, no one really cared what the Russians had to say anymore."

"And he left?"

"Yes, security jobs here and there."

"And then?"

"And then what?"

"And then how did he get here?"

"I... I don't know. We lost contact more than a year ago," Sharon said. "You know we never really kept in touch. The wedding was the last time we saw him."

"Yes, the last time we saw him... Any favorite sayings, TV shows, family pets?"

"Nothing comes to mind. Oh, wait. He loved Poe. He loved quoting Poe."

Forge raised his left eyebrow. "OK, that's a start. I'm going to take it that he would recite 'The Raven' every chance he got."

"No, no. He disliked the poetry. He really loved the stories. I just don't remember which ones."

Forge ran to the curio cabinet, unlatched it and ran his fingers across the books until he found the collection of Poe stories.

"Here, this looks like his most favored collection. Can you page through to see if any of the stories ring a bell? Was it the 'Telltale Heart' or 'The Pit and the Pendulum'?"

"Give me a chance. Let me look."

Sharon eagerly thumbed through the index and tattered pages.

"Here, here," she exclaimed after a few minutes. "'The Gold-Bug.' He loved 'The Gold-Bug' in school, drawing little mystery maps in our house and telling us there's buried gold treasure for anyone who can find it. That's what the whole story was, an adventure to unlock the secrets of a treasure map."

"OK," Forge said. "Could it be this easy?"

He swiveled the chair to face Elan's massive computer screen and tapped the space bar impatiently to rouse it to life.

He scrolled through the list of files and found the most likely suspect — large, encrypted, and in a hidden folder that would not have been visible to a casual observer who, unlike Forge, didn't have the Sleuth program.

He double clicked on the file and a stern demand unfolded on the screen:

Enter passkey now.

Forge licked his lips and slowly typed:

Gold-Bug.

He hovered his index finger over the enter key, but drew back. The phrase was way too short for an Army-trained encryption professional. If he were in Elan's shoes, the phrase would be several lines long. Such a lengthy encryption string would be impossible to crack.

"What's the matter, Matt?" Sharon asked anxiously. "That must be it. Hit it."

"No. It's too short."

"So what? If it's wrong, it'll tell us and we just try again."

"I'm going to say Donald was too clever for that. He probably set a limit on the number of tries," Forge said. "If you fail too many times, the file locks up, or better yet, self-destructs. Then no one will be able to find out what's in it."

"Then we're going to be here forever," Sharon said. "I'm certain this is what it is. My brother was obsessed with that story."

Without warning, Sharon reached past Forge and tapped the enter key.

"Strike one," the machine replied.

"I guess we know now that is not it," Forge said.

"Sorry."

"Well, it was worth a try."

"Can't you experiment with the copy on your machine?"

Forge accessed the terabyte through his PC and came to the conclusion that he had already reached. "It's a polymorphic file. It mutates every time it is copied. Another security measure. That means it purposely scrambles itself whenever it is moved, making it useless. Very clever, and very bad for us."

Sharon fell into her seat in a deep brood. She continued to flip through the book of Poe stories, but could find no additional clues or hints as to the passkey.

"Nothing is here. He didn't dog-ear any pages or underline any words."

Forge scanned the same pages, looking not for underlined words, but tiny dots or pinholes that would remain unnoticed to a reader. A dot or hole over enough selected letters over several pages could have spelled out the true passkey for Forge.

Forge returned to his laptop and looked at the hex dump again. He set up a search box and entered "poe." The machine returned nineteen occurrences.

Good start. At least Poe was on Elan's mind. He must have quoted the author in e-mails or notes to himself. But he just had fragments to work with. He set another search, but this time he directed his laptop to return all the characters within twenty spaces of "poe."

The list ran on for a page. *Poe... sunset... Poe... troll... Poe... cato... Poe... last... Poe... edgar... Poe... cask... Poe... goldbug...*

The word "cato" caught his eye. He rechecked his notes and was reassured that it had appeared in the first memory hex dump. The word was becoming bothersome.

He wrote out "CATO" in his notebook and covered the first letter with his thumb. "ATO." The same letters written on the tissue paper found in the man-in-the-can's stomach. There was more than just a coincidence that "cato" was near "Poe." But why Poe?

Forge wracked his brain from his own cipher history classes. Poe was a well-known cryptographer, once teasing readers of a Philadelphia newspaper with challenges that he was the world's greatest code breaker. He asked readers in 1839 to mail him their encrypted letters and he promised he could break each and every one of them, which he did.

A search of the Web found that "The Gold-Bug" was possibly the first work of fiction to use encryption as a central theme. Poe explained to readers the alphabet substitution scheme that was used for centuries, and how to break it by simply finding the letter most often repeated. If a count of all the letters found "T" to have the highest number of occurrences, then it was a pretty good guess that "T" was really "E," the most used letter in the English language. The most often used word is "the." If "GBT" was counted the most, then you knew "G" was really "T", "B" was really "H" and "T" was really "E." Once you had these Rosetta stones in place, it was simply a matter of working backwards and unscrambling the rest of the letters.

What a fitting person for a rogue cipher to emulate. Forge quickly scanned the Internet and found through its collective memory that Poe placed hidden clues in "The Gold-Bug" for readers to try to decipher. The ultimate conclusion of the story pivoted around solving the puzzle. Could the code itself be the clue he needed?

He scanned the story in the book. The code was a sophomoric substitution scheme:

53##305))6*;4826)4#);806*;48+8P60))85;I#(;:#*8+83(88)5*+;46(;88*
96*?;8)*#(;485);5*+2:*#(;4956*2(5*--4)8P8*;4069285);)6+8)4##;I(#9;
48081;8:8#I;48+85;4)485+528806*8I(#9;48;(88;4(#?34;48)4#;161;:18
8;#?;

It would be impossible for anyone to remember the exact sequence to quickly type in as a passkey. That would mean Elan would have had to write it down, and he didn't want to do that. If he used the book, it would also mean that The Troll would see him copying the cipher into the computer, which would have been akin to telling the hairy one to shoot Elan in his sleep.

No. But the solution... The mystery solved by Poe for the readers could be the passkey. It read:

A good glass in the bishop's hostel in the devil's
Seat — forty-one degrees and thirteen minutes — northeast and by
North — main branch seventh limb east side — shoot from the left eye of the
death's-head — a bee-line from the tree through the shot
fifty feet out.

An odd phrase, but a solid passkey. Forge licked his lips and began typing one finger at a time to ensure he made no mistakes.

"Ready?" he asked.

"I'm holding my breath."

Forge hit the enter key.

"*Strike two,*" the artificial logic of the program projected on the screen. "*What game are we playing?*"

Forge winced at the refusal. Another wasted shot. He had one left.

"Was there anything on his body?" Sharon asked. "A note in his wallet, or a wad of paper in his shoe?"

"No. The killers didn't need that. They were looking for something else."

"What makes you say that?"

"He was torched to death. He would have given his passkey up in the first five seconds. They couldn't care less about the computer files. There had to be something he had that he couldn't give them, something tucked away so far that either it's in a different location or someone else is holding it for him."

"Like what?"

"That's what we need to know from this file. It's the only heavily encrypted folder on the computer. It must tie in The Troll, the video camera, the Bloomberg machines, and that clock on the table."

"Clock?"

"It's set eleven hours ahead. It's running on Tokyo time. It's already morning on July fifth there."

Forge quickly became fixated on the sole chance he had to crack the file. The word "cato" still bothered him. A cat? Too bizarre. A search of the Web turned up sixteen million hits, among them the Cato Institute for public policy, and a fashion store. But Cato was also a historical figure, Forge mused. He scrolled down the list. Marcus Cato, Roman, died in 149 B.C. and Plutarch chronicled his life in 75 A.D. Sharon said nothing about Elan enjoying classic literature. Forge skipped over that entry and continued flipping through the search pages.

Cato the Elder, Cato the Younger, Cato University. The list grew tiresome, and Sharon walked to the far corner to gaze at the bay from a window. The sun was setting, turning the distant marshes into a majestic hue of amethyst.

Forge at first did not hear the faint scratches. As he scoured the Web for clues, Forge became lost in his own world. Sharon walked forward and put her hand on Forge's shoulder. "Did you hear that?" she asked.

Forge looked up and around. The sound had stopped. "No, what was it?"

"It sounded like... scratching," Sharon said with a trace of fright in her voice. The murder scene and the talk of Poe, Forge thought, must have put her on edge.

"Did you hear where it came from?" he asked.

"Somewhere around here," Sharon said. "What if someone is still here, still hiding in the house?"

"That's not possible. There were a dozen cops scouring the building from top to bottom," Forge said. "No one is here."

Sharon let the matter rest and watched Forge as he tried to decipher the pass-key that likely died with her brother. Then again, it came. Tinny scrapes on glass or aluminum. It was low to the ground and too small to be a person.

"There, do you hear it?" she asked again.

"Yes. It sounds like a seagull on the porch looking for food, or scraping its beak. The curtains are closed. Just peek around and see if there is anything out there."

Cautiously, Sharon hugged the wall as she moved toward the sliding glass door and parted the seam of the gold curtains a fraction of an inch. She paused and drew the cloth further apart until she could nudge half of her face through the window covering. She looked left and then right, and even up for any sign of a gull. Then she heard the faint scratching again. She looked down, knelt, and then tapped the window calmly with her index finger. "Go on, shoo," she commanded.

"A gull, right?" Forge asked.

"No, a fox," Sharon said.

"Wait, I think I got something," Forge announced. "I did a search of Poe and Cato and look at the first hit."

Sharon ran to the bank of computers and read the first line out loud:

"October 13, 2000: EA Poe Cryptographic Challenge Solved."

> *Cipher Solved*
>
> *The 150-year-old challenge left by writing master Edgar Allan Poe was solved this week when Toronto native Gil Broza decoded the mysterious cipher Poe published for his readers in 1839. The cipher was not an encrypted version of one of Poe's stories or poems, as many had thought, but four lines from Cato, a popular play of the 18th century by English author Joseph Addison. Using a combination of techniques, Broza cracked the...*

"Why do you think this is it?" Sharon asked.

"It has all the markers," Forge said. "Look, it involves Poe, who your brother admired and which came up in the memory hex dump. Two, the solution involves Cato, a Roman emperor that is part of the solution of the Poe cipher, which also was in the hex dump. And three, it is a long phrase that Donald could easily remember to type into the system."

"What is the phrase?" Sharon asked.

Forge scrolled down to show her the solution.

> *The soul secure in her existence smiles at the drawn dagger and defies its point. The stars shall fade away, the sun himself grow dim with age and nature sink in years, but thou shall flourish in immortal youth, unhurt amid the war of elements, the wreck of matter and the crush of worlds.*

"Seems to fit my brother," Sharon said. "But is the passkey the whole phrase or just the first line?"

"I'm pretty certain that it's the whole phrase. Donald set up this system to be impenetrable. A passkey" — he stopped for a minute to count — "that has fifty-four words is impossible to break, even if we could get past the polymorphic, restricted access grid."

"I don't know," Sharon said. "What if you're wrong?"

"The case ends here," he said.

"What if we don't try it?"

"The case still ends here. We have no choice."

Taking no chances, Forge verified the correct wording with other Internet sources and was satisfied it was indeed the correct translation of the cipher. You get only one shot at this, Forge said to himself, don't make it blow up in your face.

Forge patiently typed the four lines from Cato as Sharon slowly read the words from his laptop. He checked the syntax once more and then pushed his chair back a few inches.

"OK, hold your breath again," Forge said. With a staccato tap, as if he had touched the top of a hot stove, he pressed the enter key.

No message. No warning. Forge looked up at Sharon and they both wondered if the PC had frozen or gone into self-destruct mode, erasing all the files as if they were chalk on a blackboard. The screen turned white for a split second and returned with another austere message: *File decrypting.*

Sharon hugged Forge as the digital folder unveiled its hidden contents. In three directories colored in cheerful yellow were unambiguous file names, the descriptions of which made Forge's knee jig up and down in anticipation. From the anonymous remains of a corpse in a steel drum to world-class ciphers, Forge had gathered all the markers and put them in a nice, neat row. He read the three, short titles.

Operational Plan. Showtime. The Gold-Bug.

Much to Forge's relief, the text document of the "Plan" was not encrypted. Surprisingly, it was just half of a page long:

Phase One
Acquire seed money from the investors ($2 million per share). Set up secure lines of communication and transactional accounts with trusted stock traders in foreign exchanges.
Phase Two
Co-op an undervalued penny stock company, preferably traded on the Vancouver exchange outside the jurisdiction of the United States, and hype a new, yet-to-be-released product. This will be done through exclusive "offers" to wealthy investors who will be afforded the opportunity to get in on the ground floor and make a killing before the rest of the market catches on. A trusted name in stocks is needed to give gravitas to the offer, and to ensure we have a high rate of interest in a short period of time.
Phase Three
Buy really low, sell super high. Get the hell out of town.

"What does that mean?" Forge asked. "What's a penny stock?"

"Dirt-cheap stocks," Sharon replied, drawing on her MBA knowledge. "Penny stocks are usually start-up companies, or companies that have fallen on bad times and their income is going down the drain."

"The stocks really cost a penny?"

"Seldom. Most are a buck or less, no more than five dollars," she said. "It can be very lucrative if you know what you are doing."

"How so?" Forge said. "If I buy a stock for a buck and it goes up to two bucks, I've made a — buck?"

"That's the beauty of it. You just doubled your money. You're not buying just one stock. What if you bought a million dollars worth of stocks and it then goes up a buck? You've just doubled your money."

"To two million."

"Exactly," Sharon said. "It beats working."

"So if they could pump up a stock and unload it, they would know when to buy and sell."

"It's called pump and dump. Illegal in the U.S., that's why he wanted to steer clear of the SEC. Vancouver is the best place for these things. People with shady connections always seem to migrate to the VSE."

Forge looked at the clock on the table. The intensity of the quest to slip into Elan's computer had made time seem to stand still for Forge. He realized that he had not yet heard from Fry, which might be a sign that he opted to run a stakeout on the house. He reached for his cell to check in, but Sharon grabbed his hand.

"We may be running out of time," she said. "What about the 'showtime' folder?"

Still curious about the time, Forge craned his neck to look at the oversized red numbers on the dining room table clock. The numbers flicked from 6:59 a.m. to 7 a.m. The eleven-hour jump into the Japanese time zone still bothered him. Why Japan? He looked back at the computer screen. Elan's own computer was also set eleven hours ahead.

Without warning, the giant 106-inch plasma television screen mounted on the far wall hummed to life as a familiar test pattern filled the screen.

"Is that the video?" Sharon asked.

"I didn't do anything," Forge said as he checked the operating system of the computer. A new icon had dropped to the bottom of the screen and Forge toggled to bring it into full view.

Searching for IP... Searching... connecting... connecting... Connection confirmed. Host is now streaming Webcast.

The PC was on programmed auto drive, executing a program Elan had written for split-second timing. His plan was turning out to be as simple as hopscotch. Too bad death got in the way of a good gig, Forge thought.

As the massive digital wall screen counted down to the launch of the video, Sharon moved closer in her chair to hold Forge's arm. The screen faded to black and then livened to a bright, soothing fuchsia background. Front and center, dressed in a casual business suit that said, "I spent $1,000 for this and I don't have to wear a tie because I'm hot shit," was the one and only Troll.

FIFTEEN

"Good morning and good evening, ladies and gentlemen, no matter where you are," a surprisingly animated and charismatic Hennessy Runkel said as if he were warming up an audience for a late-night talk show. "Because of the virtue of your investing prowess, and because you paid good money to join my private stock club, you can be the first to find the very best deals in the stock market. I am coming to you today with a fantastic offer."

Forge was impressed. He was sure if Runkel were still alive, he would have no trouble selling sand to a man dying of thirst in the desert.

"I have just finished my hush-hush tour of the Cato Technology Industries plant on the bay just outside of Tokyo, and I am eager to report to you that this company is poised to be the next Microsoft, GE, and Google all rolled into one.

"Yes, you heard me right. I am not speaking in hyperbole to get your attention. As you know, you paid for my exclusive services to help you identify the right companies at the right price to invest in. I get no compensation from the companies, and my reputation for picking stocks on TV speaks for itself. I know a winner when I see one, and this, this company is the Triple Crown winner of winners.

"By this time next week, after news of Cato Technologies Industries hits the market, I predict that the stock price will — are you sitting down, now? — will increase a hundred fold. Let me repeat that... "

Runkel stood up from the tall stool he was half-sitting on, one knee bent higher than the other. He walked a few inches toward the camera as if he were about to reach out and grab the viewer by the collar.

"One-hundred fold. Think about that for a moment. A modest investment of just one hundred dollars will net you a return of ten thousand dollars." He enunciated each syllable clearly and slowly as if he were talking to a room full of sixth graders. "Imagine what an investment of $1 million will do for you.

"Have I got your attention now? I'm sure I have. But I know you are wondering, What is this incredible product Cato will be unveiling in the coming days? How will it change the market, the world, and your life? Let me begin by introducing you to the chief operating officer of Cato, Dr. Hara Takumi."

The camera pulled back to show a slender Japanese man in his forties sitting to Runkel's far left. The Troll and Takumi bowed politely to each other in the Japanese tradition, then Runkel continued his effusive monologue. The camera, though, had pulled back a fraction of an inch too far, revealing the bottom fin of the mounted marlin that was hanging on the wall scant feet from Forge and Sharon.

The cameraman, most likely Elan, must have realized his video faux pas and gently nudged the zoom a few inches inward. Dr. Takumi, Forge found in a quick Web search, was a real scientist and was really head of a penny stock company call Cato. His performance was polished and well rehearsed. Chances are he was already dead, eighty-sixed as soon as the director called it a wrap.

"Thank you, Mr. Runkel, it is indeed a pleasure to have you visit our research and development offices here in Japan, and to give our product your utmost support," Takumi said in perfect English without a trace of an accent. The message to viewers was clear: the man had the Japanese drive of youth and an American education that made him a natural for international trade.

"Doctor," The Troll began, "could you tell us a little bit about yourself?"

"Certainly. I was born in Yokohama forty-one years ago and received my undergraduate degree at Yale in business. I went on to receive my medical and master of business degrees from Harvard, and then became an esteemed associate at the *Institut Pasteur,* the world's foremost biological research laboratory. There I developed a gift for refining and making safe vaccines, many of which, I am proud to say, are in use around the globe today.

"With the help of venture capitalists who believed in my track record of success, I took the leap into this private venture, which is what you have seen today at Cato."

"Very good, Doctor," Runkel said enthusiastically. "Please, tell us about your product."

"Revolutionary is often used to describe new products, some of which never live up to their hype," Takumi said. "But I cannot stress enough that Cato's product is not only truly revolutionary, but unmatched by any process now known to man.

"Like Thomas Edison's light bulb, which changed the world forever, Cato's soon-to-be patented Khimer-A process will bring medical science, life itself, to a new plane of existence.

"Khimer-A is based on a little-known process called 'chimera,' which combines two or more organisms into one. Now, that may sound like we are building a Frankenstein monster here, but far from it. Our exciting technique has solved — yes, solved — the inherent genetic barriers between species."

"I think we are getting ahead of ourselves here, Doctor," Runkel interrupted as if on cue. "Could you tell us more about this Khimer-A process?"

"Yes, of course. Say, for example, a very ill heart patient needs a new valve to remain alive. Without it, his heart will fade and slowly cease beating. But years ago, doctors began using specially processed pig and cow heart valves to replace the defective flaps within the man. This is a crude chimera, but one that demonstrates how different species can help us lead better lives.

"What our Khimer-A process does is take the mixing of species to the genetic level, where we can custom-tailor spare parts for the individual patient."

The camera focused on Runkel's expression of amazement as he spoke.

"You mean you can actually build new heart valves for patients?"

"Yes, from the patient's own cells so there is no chance of rejection. But this is more than heart valves. This will cover all aspects of human medical conditions.

"We can now take stem cells, the building blocks of every person, and replicate them en masse for pennies a patient. New livers could be designed and grown inside host animals, such as sheep, and then harvested for the patient.

"Moreover, there are exciting horizons that we have just begun to explore. With our use of the chimera technology, we can order crops of corn to produce pure insulin for the diabetic, cows to grow new skin for the severely burned, and sheep to give sight to the blind."

"This all sounds like science fiction and very futuristic," Runkel interjected. "Does this technology actually work?"

"It not only works, but works very simply. Like turning on the proverbial light bulb, we have built a working prototype of the technology and have made it so user friendly that it can easily be adapted by any modestly funded hospital lab. As I said, our revolutionary science has broken through the genetic barriers and found a way to export our product as easily as Microsoft sells software."

As they talked, the video cut away to what Forge knew must have been stock footage of a university laboratory with Japanese workers in the background.

"I wish I could show you the details of our system, but with so many competitors wanting to acquire our discoveries for themselves, I'm afraid that I must keep the actual process under wraps a while longer."

"We fully understand," The Troll said as he turned to the camera. "When do you think your product will be ready for release to the world, Doctor?"

"We expect to receive our final patent approval on the morning of July fifth, Japan time. We will be making our exciting announcement at 11 a.m. that day."

"Thank you, Doctor." The video zoomed in to The Troll's upper body as he began his conclusion.

"As you can see, Cato is now poised to rewrite medical science as we know it. This is as exciting an opportunity as I have ever had the fortune to witness in my lifetime. Yes, I was there when Google went public, and yes, I told my viewers to buy, buy, buy because the sky was the limit for the stock. And history has shown how correct I was.

"Now, I'm telling you to buy, buy, buy, and buy more, as fast as you can. Cato is traded on the Vancouver exchange as an "Over-the-Counter Bulletin Board" stock called CTA-BB. This will provide you with an excellent opportunity to maximize your return — before anyone else drives up the price. I suggest — no, I am directing you with all earnestness, to begin acquiring Cato stock as fast as you can and as much as you can. Don't wait for the markets to open. Buy whatever you can on overnight trading and as much as you can when the market opens. Because by 11 a.m. Japan time, the world will know what you know, and the stock will skyrocket to unheard-of limits.

"I have e-mailed each and every one of you an invitation to visit the special 'Investors Only' Web site, where you can review the Cato prospectus, the credentials of the esteemed staff, and the independent reviews from leading scientists — all under contract to keep their findings secret — of Cato's fantastic work.

"The Vancouver Stock Exchange is about to close shortly, and I suggest that you start your investing now. Cato subsidiaries are also traded on the Tokyo and Shanghai exchanges, which will open shortly. There is also overnight trading, so in this 24/7 world, there is no reason to wait to begin your investment in the future of mankind.

"The future of this company is in your hands, and the return on your investment will soon bring all of you fabulous wealth. The millionaires will become billionaires, the billionaires will become multibillionaires, and even an investor of modest means will reap a fortune that he can only dream of.

"The future is now, ladies and gentlemen. Grab it, grab it fast, and don't ever let go. Thank you, and I'll be seeing you again as Cato makes its fantastic announcement."

Forge half-expected to hear a round of canned applause and cheers from the video, but Runkel slowly faded to black. The screen posted the Web address for the "Investor's Only" club, which Forge now knew was a wholly fictitious site. No doubt it was very well done: slick, professional, and with all the necessary links and phony documents to back up the claims. The Troll and his cohorts wanted to reach as many potential investors as they could without tipping their hand to the world. If you charge people for inside information, it was a sure bet that they will believe you when you deliver more than what they were expecting.

"Do you think anyone will buy this?" Sharon asked.

"Yes. Everyone. At least everyone in his special club," Forge said. "It's human nature."

"What is?"

"Greed. Everyone wants to believe. And everyone believes what they have is never enough."

"What happens next?"

Forge checked the Bloomberg machine closest to him. The dark green monitor with VSE at the top to note the Vancouver exchange had quietly displayed CTA-BB with the current stock price of thirty-three cents. The volume hovered at zero as it had attracted no buyers in the hours before. Below CTA was the symbol for an international mutual fund, apparently an offshore account. It was not a stock, but the private holding of an investor.

"What do you make of this?" Forge asked.

Sharon peered at the two items on the screen that shows bright-green horizontal bars and numbers in dollars next to them. Then she noticed a fourth and a fifth account had come online. Each held $2 million, which was show by a green bar. Then a slew of differing accounts cascaded under each other for a total of twelve. Each had about $2 million. In the bottom bar, the dollar amount began to drop precipitously as the topmost bar — the one representing CTA — increased from zero to tens of thousands dollars in a matter of second.

"Here," she said, tapping the screen excitedly with her index finger. "The trades are being executed now. See here? As they buy stock, the amount in the account drops and numbers under positions grow exponentially." She moved her fingers over the other rows: Quantity, Last Price, Percent Change. "The last row here shows the value of the stock, as it is in real time."

"So, the investors are buying the stock now?"

"No, this is seed money. Donald must have had a core group put up millions of dollars to start the ball rolling. After he takes his cut and expenses, all of the accounts are left with a total of" — she paused to count down twelve lines — "$20 million."

"What does the seed money do?"

"It's the pump in the pump-and-dump scheme."

"He pumps it up so outside investors think everyone else is buying into the stock?" Forge asked.

"Exactly. That's his version of 'The Gold-Bug.' He is leading people to the treasure, but they don't know the treasure is not there."

"But the stock price of Cato is starting to rise."

Forge ticked off the changes in the stock's value, from thirty-three cents a share to forty-eight cents to a whopping fifty-six cents. All in less than ten minutes. The insider who had invested a million bucks at thirty-three cents just saw his money grow by seventy percent.

"Try to get that at your local bank," Sharon said. "By the end of the night the stock will be pushing $20 a share."

"But Donald and Runkel are dead," Forge said. "Who is controlling the money and the investing?"

"The computer is," Sharon said. "He was a master programmer. He programmed the video to launch around the world at the correct time. Right as Vancouver was about to close, so Canadian regulators didn't have time to figure out what was going on, and right as the other markets were about to open up. All these select investors who don't know they are about to get duped are burning up the wires telling their brothers, girlfriends, and bookies about the hottest tip on the globe. Donald has set buy-and-sell triggers. If events get past him, the computer kicks in and starts the dump."

"What happens then?"

"Everyone except Donald is left holding stock that isn't worth the paper it's written on. He has to hit the market at the exact right time. He can't dump out too early because he'll lose millions, but if he gets too greedy and waits till it hits its ceiling, he risks losing everything."

"I guess the risk played out early for him already," Forge said, catching his untimely dry comment. "Sorry. I didn't mean it that way."

Tears started to well in Sharon's eyes as she fought them back. "No, no. You're right. He got in way over his head and now he's paid the price."

"How do we stop it?" Forge asked.

"We don't."

"How can you say that?"

"The triggers are all locked out," Sharon said, tapping the screen again. "The Bloombergs monitor the activity, but they don't tell us where the accounts are."

"So we got ourselves a front row seat to the biggest scam going? He has another system running somewhere else?"

"Or, someone else is helping him," Sharon said. "What's in 'The Gold-Bug' folder?"

Forge saw that the Cato stock had topped one dollar with more than one million shares being traded in just a few minutes. He turned back to Elan's PC to double-click the last yellow folder.

Rather than opening up a list of banks and creditors, he saw just one icon called "Quantum."

"This isn't going to be good," Forge muttered.

"What is it?"

"Donald's final 'goodbye' to the world."

"I don't understand."

Forge released a heavy sigh as he clicked on the "Q" icon. Instantly, a new screen appeared and offered just one suggestion:

Insert Quantum device

"Doesn't this just frost the top of the cake," Forge said, pushing the mouse away from the PC in disgust.

"What is it asking for?"

"Nothing much. Just the most secure communication device on earth."

"Meaning?"

"It wants a Quantum decoder. It's not a password anymore. It's a piece of hardware that talks to whatever it is supposed to talk to somewhere else in this scam."

"Quantum?"

"Not even the NSA can crack them. It's top-line military, top line," Forge said. "It's so secure that if anyone tries to intercept the signal and decode it, the message literally self-destructs. It sends messages piggybacked on electrons and photons, those little particles that make up light. It's as if you were in the middle of a blizzard and you wanted to catch a single snowflake that had a message etched on a single frozen water crystal. Even if you could find that single flake, it'll melt in your hands as soon as you touch it."

"But it's asking for a device. Isn't it on the PC?"

Forge recalled that the printout of the contents of the house by the forensics lab noted that there was an empty cell phone charger. Forge knew immediately that the charger it was meant to masquerade as a mate to a phone, but it was far more complex. The fiber-optic cable into the PC was heavily shielded to protect the signal on its way out to the Net.

"It's gone. Whoever did Donald in knew a little bit, maybe a lot, about his operation. They took the Quantum device with them."

"Do you think they got it to work?"

"I'm not so sure," Forge said, looking back at the Bloomberg machine. "The money is flowing in the right direction. If you trusted Donald and Runkel so little with the money that you had to kill them, why trust his program? I mean, wouldn't you want to pull out before you could lose $20 million?"

"Maybe they can't get it to work either?" Sharon said. "Or maybe he hid another piece of the puzzle somewhere else. What if the device had to work with 'The Gold-Bug' file? What if the killers didn't have enough time to break into the computer or couldn't figure out what to do?"

"Not likely," Forge said. "Maybe they couldn't get it to work, but remember, he was slowly tortured to death. Whoever did this to him thought they knew enough about the scam that they didn't need his computer. They thought that the Quantum device was the key to the kingdom. Donald was clever. He built in so many protections that not even he could override them when he wanted to."

Frustrated, Forge pushed the Bloomberg monitor away with the flat of his hand. "Maybe it's time to call in the FBI."

"No, no," Sharon said. "I know we can crack this. There has to be a way."

Forge drifted back to his errant thought about Fry. He hadn't checked in. Even if they were on stakeout, he must be losing it with Sister Maris chewing his ear off. He would have called by now. *He should have called, dammit.*

Forge flipped open his cell phone and punched "one" on speed dial to reach Fry's cell phone. Three, four, five rings. No answer. He tried again.

This time, Forge heard the click of Fry's phone being opened.

"Fry, where are you?" Forge asked, half excited, half agitated from the delay.

"Good evening, Detective Forge," a deep, familiar voice on the other end of the line said slowly, as if he were making a dinner reservation. The sound sent a chill down Forge's spine.

"Who the hell is this?" Forge asked, already knowing the answer. "Where is Fry?"

"Please, Detective, let us not play games," Tolck said in earnest. "Time is not on our side tonight. I have something, or should I say someone, of interest to you."

Forge gripped the phone so tightly that the tips of his nailbeds began to turn white. In the background, he heard the rustling of clothing and then the faint sound of a boat horn in the distance. The delay of just a few seconds was becoming unbearable.

"Oh, Matt," said Sister Maris in an uncharacteristically feeble voice that telegraphed her fear. Rapidly she tried to blurt out a warning. "They shot Fry. Don't..."

"Ah, Detective," Tolck said. "Please excuse my manners, but the sister is, well, detained. I think you have something that I want; you know what that is."

"You want me to activate the Quantum device."

"Exactly," Tolck said with a hint of surprise in his voice. "You are quite a resourceful police officer. You do the service credit."

"Cut the bullshit," Forge said. "What do you want me to do?"

"Not what, but where," Tolck said. "I want to you to come to the Baylock house. Alone. No tricks. No fancy eye-in-the-sky surveillance. The sister will not be there, but a familiar friend will greet you. You will then help us find... what did Mr. Elan used to call it? Ah, yes. The Gold-Bug."

SIXTEEN

Forge dimmed the Jeep's high beams as the vehicle coasted toward the Baylock compound. He had done what Tolck had asked. No cops. No companions. No tricks. Sharon remained at the house with instructions to call a friend at the FBI if she did not hear from him at the end of the next hour.

The street sand and shell fragments crunched lightly as the wheels of the Jeep rolled to a halt in front of the Baylock entryway. Forge had put himself in Tolck's crosshairs. All he could hope for now was that he could trade his skills for the sister's life. He had foolishly sent Fry to his death and put Sister Maris in harm's way. There was only one path toward redemption, and he was far from it at this point.

"Tolck! Tolck, I'm here!" Forge shouted as he stepped out of the Jeep, held up his arms, and slowly pivoted 360 degrees to show whoever was watching that he was unarmed.

"You got a vest on?" a slurred and hoarse voice from behind one of the tall bayberry bushes said almost in a whisper. Forge was sure the man was straining his vocal cords just to make himself audible.

Forge lifted his shirt to expose his bare skin. "I'm all yours."

"Good," Dewall rasped as he stepped out of the shadows to show a grossly swollen and misshapen face. His throat was beat red. A purple facial welt ran from the bottom of his jaw to the top of his left eye, which appeared to be almost completely shut from the swelling. Forge looked down at Dewall's hand to see the gun pointed at his midsection.

"What did you do to Fry?" Forge asked.

"He got his nice and slow," said Dewall. "No one gets one up on Jack Dewall."

"It looks like he put one fist up your face," Forge said.

"You'll gets yours soon enough," Dewall said, keeping his distance to ensure that he didn't make the same mistake twice. He saw Forge size up the gun and the yardage between the two.

"Thinking about the gun, aren't you?" Dewall said, backing up a half step. "Go ahead, try to grab for it."

"I didn't come here to kill you, Jack," Forge said. "That'll be for later. I came here to see Tolck."

"Big talk from a dead man," Dewall said. "Get in the Jeep and drive."

It took them less than two minutes to reach Tolck's warehouse on the docks, well within the shadow of the Barnegat Lighthouse. Its red-and-white tower was to be specially illuminated for the Independence Day celebration, and Forge could see the crowd building for the coming fireworks display. With a muffled announcement in the distance, followed by pale applause, Forge saw the shining light from the top flash on and slowly begin to rotate clockwise to expose a second beam of intense light. *Just like the old days,* Forge thought. *No one has seen this in decades.*

The corroded blue door of the warehouse swung open just wide enough for Dewall to thrust Forge through the entrance. Dewall followed, and Forge heard the clang of metal lock behind him. The warehouse swallowed him whole. A faint light at the end of the room dimly lit a stack of boxes, and next to them, a bound figure sitting on the floor. And that stench. It was too familiar; too fresh in his mind. Burnt flesh. Forge now knew where Baylock had been murdered. It was all too simple: cook him here, throw the barrel in a waiting boat, and drop him in the ocean. Was he the next one to be erased?

"I am very pleased that you could join us, Mr. Forge," Tolck said from the shadows, his voice echoing across the cement floor of the stock room. "Please pardon my manners. I should have addressed you by your proper title, that of detective. But I really do not think that it has done you much good now, has it? You are here at my request, and you really have no idea what is going to happen."

"Where is Sister Maris?" Forge said through bared teeth. The slow-moving beam from the lighthouse sent long shadows from the rooftop windows eerily cascading across the room, as if the black images were scurrying across the floor to rendezvous with the dark walls.

Tolck flicked on an overhead light to fully illuminate Sister Maris on the floor, her hands duct-taped behind her.

"You can see she is in good health, Mr. Forge," Tolck said. "Now, shall we get down to business?"

"What are you going to do?" said Forge.

"Quite simply, we are going to make a billion dollars tonight," Tolck said. "I must say, you are also quite clairvoyant. I was about to contact you when you called Mr. Fry's cell phone. I saw that such an opportunity should not be wasted, and now we are here, as friends, I hope."

"Let Sister Maris go and I'll help you," Forge said as he looked to his left to see that Dewall's pistol was still trained on him.

"I'm afraid I can't do that," Tolck said. "You see, we have a saying in business. You don't close the deal until all your interests are satisfied. If I let her go, there is no guarantee that you will fulfill your end of the bargain."

"Then we don't have a deal."

"I'm sure there are ways to convince you."

Forge felt a sudden jerk behind him as Costa grabbed both of Forge's hands and wrapped the wide, gray duct tape around his wrists.

"What are you going to do now?" Forge asked. "Blowtorch me like the others?"

"For now, we shall talk," said Tolck. "But talk quickly. As we said, we are running out of time."

"We have nothing to talk about."

"Let us talk about what you want, then," Tolck said. "Your passion is the law. Your only drive is to solve this case."

"And?"

"We are not that different, you and I. We both have a passion. That is what keeps us alive."

"Your passion is nothing like mine. Your passion is money, plain and simple."

"That is much too simple," Tolck said, pausing to relieve himself of a slight cough. "It is not money."

"What is it then?"

"It is the desire. Everyone has money. But when you need fulfillment, that is what propels you forward, that is what keeps you alive. I should have died thirty years ago. I am a walking miracle, or so my doctors tell me. I take so many pills and injections that I think I am more pharmaceutical than flesh. I could have easily given up and let this heart of mine stop beating decades ago. But I didn't. I had a quest. I had a need to fulfill."

Tolck fell into a brief coughing fit, and Forge could see that the old man had pulled up a chair to sit down in. The excitement must be getting to him. But he wasn't excited about the billion dollars. He wasn't even talking about that. He had another notion on his mind.

"Money," Tolck continued, "is just a means to an end. It gets me from one place to another in style, it buys me some very nice girls, and leaves me enough for a poker game or two. But the act of creating, building something new, something wonderful; that is my passion."

"You create death," Forge said as he was walked closer to Tolck. He could see in an anteroom that the palm-sized Quantum device had been attached to the PC. Tolck knew that he was just a blizzard of electrons away from reaping the rewards of the billion-dollar pump-and-dump scheme. "You've killed how many people now for this? Two? Three? More? Where does it stop?"

"Killing is easy," Tolck said as he flicked his wrist upward to check the time on his watch. "It is nothing. It is like weeding a garden. It is necessary. You must do it, and it is as simple as that. But money, holding onto money. Now that is the hard part.

"Money is a magnificent commodity, like nothing else in this world. Desperate enemies can be bound together with it, friends can be rendered apart because of it. Everyone wants it, but no one can control it."

"And you can?"

Tolck exhaled as the darkened features of his face were quickly lighted and then faded by the sweeping lighthouse beam.

"No, you think too much of me, Mr. Forge," said Tolck. "No, not even I, with all my wonderful resources, can control money."

"That is why I'm here," Forge said.

"Exactly," Tolck said eagerly as if Forge had just been enlightened with the secret of life. "This whole affair. It was a wonderful, wonderful idea that fractured a bit because of, well, money. It bound us together in the beginning and now it is doing all it can within its infinite power to pull us apart. If this affair of ours wasn't so serious it would make an amusing story to tell our grandchildren someday."

"And that brings us back to the beginning," Forge said as he twisted his wrists slightly to test his bonds. "You're just a greedy bastard in it for the money."

"Please, such language in front of the good Sister," Tolck toyed. "You may have to say five Hail Mary's later. But, no. The billion dollars is just seed money."

"For what?"

"For the State of Tolck," the owner of The Paradise said without a hint of irony in his voice. "One billion dollars begets five-hundred billion dollars. Maybe even a trillion."

"No stock is ever going to be worth that much."

"You are truly and fatally naïve," Tolck said. "I don't care about the stock market. That's for narrow-minded little men who are content to sit in an office to count their money while they await an early death. I'm talking about a future plan. Housing. Airports. Shopping centers. A metropolis of metropolises. I'm talking the Pinelands."

"It's all preserved. No one can develop it. You've already wasted your money buying up sandpits and trees."

"The lesson to be learned is everything changes," Tolck said. "Some things change naturally. Others need a little bit of a nudge. For the Pinelands, I am that nudge."

"That can't be done."

"Money," Tolck said, "also solves problems. I fulfill a desperate need. I am the vehicle for people's lives. They demand housing. I provide housing. They demand strip joints. I provide the strip joints. They demand cheap booze and cigarettes and drugs, and I provide all of that. I am not a monster. I am a product, a product of everything that you see around you."

"How?" Forge asked. "How can it be done?"

"You must think the billion dollars is for land, don't you?"

"What else would it be for?"

"It is for the grandest play yet. It will be bigger than all of us. Land is cheap. Changing attitudes, changing laws; now that gets expensive after a while. I have to work on so many levels that it would boggle your mind. There is the state government, the local governments, the Pinelands Commission, the federal government, and agencies you never heard of. And they all have their hands out. Some officials will profess honor and even a few will be stand-up guys who won't budge. But by far and wide, most can be bought. And most will be bought.

"The truth is, Mr. Forge, there is only one political party left in this country. It is the greenback party. The party of the dollar. And all — Republicans, Democrats, Independents — worship the dollar. They may act like adversaries, they may thump their chests and protest development to their last breath, but in the end, they all come around. Little extra words in laws here, a turn of a blind eye there, secret gifts of prime land everywhere. It all eventually fits into the scheme of things. It is the natural order of the world."

"The Pinelands chairman?"

"Bought."

"The legislature?"

"Mostly bought."

"The governor?"

"About to be bought."

"Hudson? You'll never be able to buy him."

"He is a fool and his wife is a bigger fool," Tolck said. "I would not waste my money on a pair of shoes for him. He thinks if he goes to enough rubber chicken dinners he can win this election. I have no tolerance for ideologues. Their righteousness just gets in the way of good business. Did you know he is at a dinner affair now that his wife spent weeks setting up? Do you know how much money he will raise for his campaign? A paltry $5,000. I spend more on girls in one night.

"The beauty of the system is we don't have to dole out brown paper bags of cash anymore. We just have to buy them the elections. And it is all legal, thanks to our intrepid representatives who passed the 527 laws. I can chop up the money so many different ways that no one except the candidates and me will know where it really came from. And then they are mine.

"With expert help, we can quickly nibble at the edges of the law to make preservation a relict of the past. We cannot dispose of all the good laws at once. A few key changes here, a forest fire there, a terribly tragic chemical spill in certain places, and the town fathers will have no choice but to condemn the area and put it to better use — for the good of the taxpayers.

"At the federal level, a very good soul will help us. My job is almost done here, at the state and local levels.

"I have been planning this ever since I first saw the virgin woods of the Pinelands so many years ago. Like my prized beach grass, I have slowly been working under the surface to knit together a mosaic of support, and weeding out the weak strands.

"So you see, Mr. Forge, my passion has kept me alive all these years because society needs me. They need to grow. And I need to reach that horizon. By the time I am done with the Pinelands, it will be as if we had built the fifty-first state. It will be bigger than Rhode Island. It will more than double the population of the state. And it will be the most desirable place to live in the nation.

"And then, we move onto our grandest plan yet."

Forge's head began to spin. What could be grander than taking over an entire state? Was Tolck truly delusional?

"Grandest plan? The heat must have swelled your brain, Tolck."

"Yes, I was sure you would say that," Tolck said. "But in politics there is always a pot of gold at the end of the rainbow."

"Sorry, I'm fresh out of crazy guesses tonight," Forge said.

"New Jersey is lucrative, but it will always be New Jersey," Tolck said. A smile crossed his face, the first flash of humanity that Forge saw in his adversary. "The biggest pot of gold lies not in the states but in the government. The federal government."

"I'm all ears," Forge said. "Let me jump to a conclusion: With the billions you make off the developments, you're going to buy yourself some senators and congressmen?"

"Please, don't insult me, Mr. Forge. I have much loftier goals."

Forge searched for a hint of irony in the tone, but found none. A sudden shudder ran down his spine.

"The presidency," Forge said slowly.

"Yes, you are indeed the sharpest tool in the shed tonight, Mr. Forge. The presidency of the United States of America. I just love the ring to that. The rewards will be unlimited."

"Now, you are just showing off that you are insane," Forge said. "How can you believe that is even remotely possible?"

"In politics," Tolck said, "money buys everything. I'm not saying it will be a cake walk, but we do have an ideal candidate in mind. One that will extol the virtues of the democratic processes, the desires of the little people, the mandate of preservation — all of which will be circumvented when the rhetoric dies away and the last vote is cast.

"Please Mr. Forge. Now that you know, give me a minute of your very special skills, and we can change the world."

"I just ran out of time for you, Tolck. You have convinced me to never help you. I'm not going to be party to more murders, more deaths, on a national scale."

From a darkened corner, Forge heard the slow, sharp sound of a single clap. A second and third clap followed, as if a patron of the arts had patiently waited for an overly long play to end.

"Bravo, Detective, bravo," the shadowed figure said in mock amusement. "You almost brought a tear to my eye and put a lump in my throat. I nearly had second thoughts about our goal tonight."

As the figure stepped out from the shadows, Forge recognized the familiar face that he had seen hours earlier. In the distance, he heard Sister Maris utter a loud gasp. "It can't be," she exclaimed.

"Oh, let it be, let it be, let it be!" the figure said, a broad grin crossing his lips to neatly expose all of his perfectly bleached white teeth.

"Baylock," Forge exhaled. "You're looking pretty good for a dead guy."

SEVENTEEN

"Always the wiseacre," Baylock said, slapping Forge on the back as if they had been long-lost college chums meeting for a reunion. "Prosecutor Parker told me all about you. Your old boss said you were a real straight shooter, a real pain in the

246

ass. But I like that in a man. It shows fortitude."

"You're supposed to have been deep fried and tossed in a can like a piece of garbage," Forge said.

"Oh, so I heard," Baylock laughed. "Your work on this case has been nothing but absolutely spectacular. You made all the right moves and found all the right clues. You were the perfect detective right up to the end, when you got everything perfectly wrong."

Costa took Forge's arm and pushed him toward Sister Maris. He collapsed into a sitting position, next to her.

"I don't understand," Forge said. "We had the match. We had all the markers. Who was in the can?"

Baylock looked at Tolck, and both men shrugged their shoulders as if to say it makes no difference now.

The secretary of the interior, the former governor and mover and shaker of New Jersey politics, the man most rumored to be on the short list for the next presidential nod, took his time as he squatted next to Forge and put his hand on his arm. Always the political, Forge thought, always trying to get people to like him.

"Can you keep a secret?" Baylock said mockingly. "Let me ask you a question. Who haven't you seen or heard from in the last thirty-six hours?"

Forge scrubbed his memory hard. Obviously it wasn't Lewis. It was his fingerprint on the part of the body that most people don't touch. Forge accounted for the suspects in his own circles. That meant it had to be a man of power, of some stature in the area. A U.S. Senator? A county freeholder? No. They were all family men. The wives would have reported them missing by now. Then it hit Forge like a thunderbolt. He shook his head in disbelief.

"Prosecutor Parker," Forge whispered.

"Bingo!" said Baylock. "You just won the *Jeopardy!* Daily Double. Do you want to try for double or nothing?"

Forge felt his throat go dry as he fought to clear his head and regain control of his wandering thoughts.

"He was killed to send a message," Forge said. "But why? What was the message?"

"This is nonsense," Tolck interrupted, looking back down at his watch. "We need to get him to work."

"So right, Dom, so right. You always were the one who was the most efficient," Baylock said. "Detective, will you assist us?"

"Go to hell."

"I'm sure we all will someday," Baylock said. "But for now, if you want to stay away from hell a little bit longer, you will get on your feet and activate the Quantum device."

"It won't do you any good," Forge said. "The device needs to know where to go. There are a billion different IP addresses out there. Only Elan's machine has the right address in its file."

"Oh, Matt. Can I call you Matt? I feel we have really gotten to know each other," Baylock said. "You really have underestimated us, and that is almost insulting. We have been planning this for a very long time. Trust us, we know what we are doing. We have all our bases covered. It's just that, well, we are having some technical difficulties. We know you are a wiz at this stuff, and now it's time to show us how good you really are."

Forge glared at the Quantum device scant yards away as his mind raced through all the options. He kept coming up with the same ending: death for him and Sister Maris.

"Go ahead, kill me if you have to, but I'm not helping you," Forge said. "Without me, your plan ends here tonight. With or without my help you'll still kill us. We have seen too much, and know too much."

Tolck gently made a flicking motion with his index finger to another shadow in the corner as he started to speak.

"Yes, Mr. Forge, that is quite true," Tolck said. "We had thought we could reason with you, maybe you would see the light and join our little project. But I'm afraid that Mr. Baylock is right, that you have uncommon fortitude. I do not know why you want to fight to save something that will never pay you back. Do you think anyone outside waiting for the fireworks cares about you? Do you think they will give you a great big bear hug to show their gratitude? Hardly. If they knew what you are doing, they would spit on you for keeping them from buying cheap houses and driving to cheap malls."

"I fight for it because it is the only right thing to do," Forge said. "I swore to uphold the law, and today I will be the law. I won't help you continue your rampage. How many more people will die so you can get your way? Five? A dozen? A hundred? A thousand? They're not weeds."

"Enough insolence," Tolck said sternly. "We are out of time. Work the device, or face your other choice."

The darkness in the corner was illuminated with the orange flicker from an oxy-acetylene torch. Forge could see Consolina, her face mask raised above her head, casually adjusting the fuel mixture to intensify the heat of the flame.

"If you help us," Tolck said. "I can promise a quick and painless death for you and your companion. But if not... " The flame hissed brighter, as if a caged snake was about to be unleashed.

"You have seen the end result of this wondrous instrument, but I do not believe you fully comprehend the beauty of its labor," Tolck continued in an almost soothing tone. "At first, you are mesmerized by the brilliant flame, a color so intense and so full that you have never seen any of its kind before.

"As the flame moves closer, you feel enveloped by its heat. It takes the chill out of this dank cavern, and you almost wish you could embrace it. But you know it is not your friend. No. Far from it. As it moves closer, you cringe and turn away from its fire. And then the flicker from its bluish tongue gently licks the tips of your fingers.

"If screams are a measurement of pain, Mr. Forge, you do not want to experience these screams. Every nerve in your body explodes in a frenzy of agony, trying desperately to find some brief relief. It reminds me of when I slipped on a boat many years ago and broke my leg. The pain was excruciating, but never enough for me to lose consciousness. That is the case here. My daughter is a true artist. She can bring you to the brink of death and pull you back so many times that you will be begging her to kill you."

"I can't work if you burn my fingers off," Forge said. "It's a very delicate sequence to follow."

Tolck was puzzled. "I didn't say we were going to use the torch on you," he said. "It is going to be used on your dear companion."

Forge looked at Sister Maris, whose head was down and whose eyes were so tightly shut that crow's feet spread along her temples to her tightly bound hairline.

He felt the crush of a final defeat. Out of options, he knew he had just one choice to follow.

"I'll do this for you," Forge whispered to Sister Maris. "I'll get up and do this for you."

Sister Maris took a deep breath, as if it were her last, and turned her head to him, her face down. As the lighthouse beam swung past in its graceful arc, Sister Maris slowly breathed outward a sentence only Forge could hear.

"Follow," Sister Maris exhaled in a whisper, "the marker."

Perplexed, Forge came close to asking her to repeat the phrase. She was so tormented by the danger that he had put her in, Forge thought she was willing herself to be in another place at another time. She was back at the cottage of the sisters' island retreat.

Like a ghostly wisp, the bright beacon swept through the overhead windows again to fill the warehouse void. Just as quickly, it was gone.

Forge slowly turned his head and dropped his chin into his chest as a sign of quiet capitulation. He needed just a moment to compose himself before he began his final task at the foot of the Quantum device.

Light. Darkness.

Light.

Darkness.

The mechanical rhythm of the beacon hypnotized Forge for a few seconds as he looked away from Sister Maris. He followed the beacon. He now understood what Sister Maris had said. He saw what he needed to see.

He saw a way out.

For a fraction of a second, the intense beam had illuminated, like a golden Christmas ornament, a curved, finger-sized sliver of dark glass. It was wedged tightly between the stacked boxes of rum, almost invisible to the eye, that Tolck's longtime assassin, Lewis, had stumbled into as he collapsed to his death.

For each second that passed, Consolina moved closer to the two of them with her torch, now an intense blue from the extreme heat it was expelling.

"I'll help you," Forge said, moving his back closer to Sister Maris, and his hands within reach of the shard. It was just long enough and curved at the best possible angle for Forge. He needed only a few strokes against the glass to slice through the duct tape binding. He quickly flexed his wrists behind him, hoping that the minute motions would be hidden from his captors.

"Good, Mr. Forge, very good," Tolck said as Consolina stopped between the two men. "I knew that you would see it our way. Now, please, let us go and spend a minute to change the world."

"I'll help you go to HELL!" Forge shouted as he tore the severed tape from his wrists and swiftly jumped to his feet. Costa and Dewall instinctively drew their weapons, but Baylock and Tolck frustratingly blocked their aim as they tried to draw a bead in the narrow opening between the contraband boxes and the anteroom. Consolina, unprepared for the sudden flash of life from Forge, moved toward the rising target, but the unwound red fuel hoses to the torch pulled her back like an overextended rubber band.

Forge pushed Sister Maris to the ground with his left knee, and, arcing his right arm over his head, he grabbed the first bottle of 150-proof rum that he could find within in the cracked open case. He locked on the blue flame in Consolina's hand and flung the bottle as hard as he could toward the target.

The thick of the bottle hit the metal tip of Consolina's torch with a sharp crack, and alcohol sprayed over the her face and shoulder in a shotgun pattern. The six-thousand-degree heat instantly ignited the volatile liquid, dousing the dancer of fire in a ball of flames.

With her face mask still raised above her head, the blast of heat encircled Consolina's face in a blanket of searing pain. As the liquid burned into her eyes, she threw the lit torch behind her to free her hands. In desperation, she feverishly tore at her burning, bubbling flesh, hoping to crush out the heat. It did little good. The top of her burning clothing had ignited her hands, allowing the fire to grow in intensity with each errant movement she made.

But the torch was still alive, and still looking for a victim. It found one final casualty in itself. As Consolina flailed and screamed in terror, the hot nozzle fell onto the oxygen and acetylene fuel lines. The heat instantly cut the rubber tubing in half, extinguishing the torch's dual lifeline.

But the flame had now jumped to the freed ends of the tubes. Unrestricted by the narrow opening of the torch nozzle, the combustible gases rushed from their steel tanks into the open air. What had once been a super-hot cigar length tongue of flame was now an uncontrollable inferno.

The discharged gases sent the flame halfway to the ceiling, flooding the room with searing heat and blinding light. In a roar of fire and screams, the expanding inferno consumed Consolina as she ran headlong into the wooden cases of liquor.

Forge had lifted Sister Maris off of the ground and ripped her bindings off to run toward the bay doors. But the sudden explosion of the rum knocked him to the ground, sending Sister Maris tumbling out of his arms.

Like a dragon's heated breath, a wall of expanding fire closed the void between them for a split second. As the spent conflagration quickly faded, Forge looked down, dismayed at what he saw. Sister Maris had been picked up by the arm and was being led out of a backdoor by Tolck, Costa, and Dewall. Baylock ducked out a side entrance into the night. *Let's see him talk his way out of this one, the sleazy son-of-a-bitch,* Forge thought. His only choice was to let Baylock run as he chased after Tolck and his thugs. They were fleeing through the back door, toward the ocean two blocks east. Their cars, parked in the front of the building, were too far to reach.

With a sick, old man, they can't get too far on foot, Forge knew. But then again, they had the gun. A desperate man with a hostage can do a lot of desperate things. Forge needed leverage. He fought his way through the inferno to pluck the Quantum device from its cradle.

In a second, he was out the door and into the dark night.

EIGHTEEN

As Forge's eyes adjusted to the darkened street, he could barely track Sister Maris's vivid yellow tee-shirt as it evaporated into the gray fog of nighttime revelers. Tourists and homeowners had turned out en masse onto Broadway and various side streets to view the upcoming pyrotechnics. As the throng settled into their beach chairs and sidewalks, Forge found that moving through the sea of people was nowhere near as easy as navigating a treacherous shoal. The shoals, at least, didn't talk back.

"Watch where you're stepping, man," grunted a fair-haired teenager who had wrapped four thin pink-and-purple glow-strings into a necklace around her collar. The dull cast from the combination of colors gave her an eerie, unearthly appearance.

"Did you see a woman with a yellow tee-shirt and an old man run past here?" Forge panted as he caught his breath.

"Sit down or get out of the way, asshole," a male voice from the crowd yelled out. "You're blocking the sky."

"Anyone, anyone," Forge yelled to the clutch around him. "I'm looking for a woman in a yellow tee-shirt with an older man. Did anyone see where they went?"

"Mommy," said a girl of five sitting in her mother's lap, "why is that man yelling at us?"

The vast silence forced Forge deeper into the crowd. If only he had a flashlight or a... He looked down at an oversized, middle-aged woman nestled in a worn beach chair, clutching a camera as if the upcoming light show was going to pass her by in the next second.

"Excuse me, ma'am," Forge said as he yanked the camera from her hands. "Police emergency."

Forge held the silver device over his head and depressed the shutter button. The brilliant flash cast a white sheet over the immediate crowd in front of him. But it did its job — it caught the reflection of a tiny speck of yellow in the distance.

"Hey, give that back!" the oversized lady yelled as Forge dropped the camera back into her hands. A low muttering of various obscenities filled the air below him, but Forge had found what he wanted. He had seen Tolck pull Sister Maris into the tree line, just beyond the closed gates of the Barnegat Lighthouse State Park. The recreational area had been closed all summer for renovations to the light tower. The commons area, closer to the cordoned off beach, had been set up to be the launching point for the night's remote- controlled fireworks display.

Forge knew that they might be able to hook around to the beach and make their way south, to another street, where Tolck could call for help and have one of his girls pick him up in his limo. Or they could lay in wait, and finish Forge off for good. In Tolck's world, two dead witnesses were better odds than trying to run out of the state.

Forge laid a bet with himself that Tolck was a serious gambler. He wanted to get all the chips on the table, not just push his chair away and walk home even. He knew with that the sister in his hands, he was holding a full house. But with the Quantum device, Forge hoped he had four aces.

Forge made it to the tree line and quickly worked his way through the last forest on the island. The dense growth of black cherry, sassafras, eastern red cedar, and American holly trees, along with the low-lying bayberry bushes, provided the fresh trail that he needed to follow Tolck's group. The four of them had so clumsily snapped branches and crushed the undergrowth that Forge could literally feel his way along the path.

As he came to the clearing that led into the park's nature walk, Forge instinctively dropped to his hands as the muzzle flash from the gun a dozen yards away sent a bullet harmlessly over his head. Forge rolled under a wooden handrail, onto a sandy mound and into a clutch of dried beach heather. Two more shots rang out. The slugs buried themselves into the wooden planks of the wood.

Got to get behind him, Forge thought. *I'm just a duck in a shooting gallery.*

Forge quietly rolled over the mound and crawled his way in a long arc over the sand. He kept count in his head the seconds between the sweep of each arc of the lighthouse. Every ten seconds the light would shine his way. He had to keep his head down, even though he wanted to glance up to get a bearing on the shooters — Dewall and Costa. He knew that after the light swept by, he couldn't foolishly stand up, lest he reveal his position by blotting out the blue and green bow lights of the boats anchored off the beach.

He heard the running of feet along a boardwalk and knew that his hunters were not about to wait around for the next shot. He too had to remain away from the light. With any luck, the shooters would rendezvous with Tolck and all four would be in one tight area. The next trick, he knew, would be how to beat two guys with guns when you didn't have one of your own.

"Matt!" Forge heard Sister Maris's voice in the distance, which was quickly muffled by a hand.

The brief sound gave Forge the approximate location of at least the sister and one of her captors. It had to be Tolck, he thought. He wanted to keep the last card close at hand.

Forge felt his way along the patch in a zigzag pattern and a low crouch. More rustling of shoes. They were as blind as he was, and they needed to find the shadows before the light swept by again. Forge had one advantage. He knew the park like a child knows a playground. He knew where the trail ended, where the common picnic ground was, even where the firework launchers would likely be.

"Mr. Forge," a familiar voice cried out, one now more conciliatory than menacing. "Give me the device and I will let the sister go. You have my word on that."

Forge didn't answer. It was a ruse. Tolck had correctly surmised that Sister Maris's single word had given away their position. Now Tolck wanted to get a fix on where Forge was. Silence is all that Tolck heard.

More rustling of feet. Tolck was no doubt taking shelter, finding a wall to put his back up against. The other two were still free for the hunt.

A soft thump followed by the hiss of a distant fire told Forge he had seconds to find the lowest spot around him. He dove between two dunes and prayed that he was beyond their line of sight.

The first fireburst of the night had been launched from the rack of fireworks on the sandy beach at the foot of the lighthouse. It was a perfectly scenic display, lighting up the 172-foot-tall tower with the hue of a thousand red, white, and blue sparkles.

The burst was low, and the sonic boom reverberated through Forge's body as if a truck had just roared past him. He had one chance. He popped his head up, hoping that the display caught Sister Maris's captors off guard, and that they had ducked for cover.

He saw one figure, likely Costa, run toward the foot of the lighthouse. The limited view from the dune kept Forge from seeing anyone else.

OK, target number one, Forge thought. *If they are divided, I can make an attack on their flank. One at a time; that is all he needed.*

Forge waited until the next burst. As the embers fell harmlessly to the ground, he dashed to the walls of the small museum and slinked carefully closer to the lighthouse. He could see Costa, who he had one major piece of hardware in his hand. But his mistake was he didn't understand the layout of the park. He thought Forge was still in the bushes. He had taken up a position outside the doorway, near the General Meade bust, waiting for Forge to come into view.

Forge made sure that didn't happen. The next burst of red pointed Forge to an errant shovel tucked in the corner of a bathroom doorway. Perfect; a solid weapon with reach.

As the light faded, Forge ran to the shovel, then moved to the rear of the lighthouse. He positioned himself behind Costa, who was still looking toward the bushes. As Forge lifted the shovel over his head, one of the partygoers on an anchored boat in the channel behind the lighthouse shot off a bottle rocket. It soared in a low arch to the shoreline and burst twenty feet behind Forge. The brief flash sent his shadow streaking across Costa's path.

As Costa turned to fire, Forge swung the shovel to knock the 9 mm out of his hand. The silver weapon chattered down the steps into the sand as it discharged. The sharp-toned shot sounded much more focused than a firecracker, and Dewall knew that. From somewhere in the distance, perhaps along the rocks of the jetty, Forge saw the shot from the gun and heard the bullet shatter a brick in the lighthouse wall above his head.

With nowhere to run, and with Costa scrambling on his hands to grab his gun, Forge crashed through the wooden door to the inside of the lighthouse.

Up is a lot better than where I am now, Forge thought. Taking two steps at a time, he started running up the 217 steps of the iron spiral staircase to the top of Ol' Barney.

Below, he heard Costa curse at him and follow up the narrow walkway.

"Run, Forge, run," Costa yelled. "What are you going to do when you get to the top? Fly away? I'm going to do you real slow, two in the knees and one in the liver."

The staircase shook as the two men ran upward, the walls of the tower becoming narrower as the structure tapered inward. Forge felt the stale air of the closed-up lighthouse clutter his lungs as he tried to stay at least two twists of the stairs away from Costa.

Think, think, think, Forge said to himself. *What's up there that I can use? A big light? There's not even a chair.*

Nearly out of breath, Forge took the last three steps to the peak in one jump. He was at the top observation deck, not at the light itself. There was a hand ladder to a trap door than opened to the light well eight feet higher.

The pounding of Costa on the iron grates was slowing. Out of shape, he was driven now only by the desire to finish Forge off as quickly as possible so he could rest for a moment.

What is it, what can I use? Forge thought as he looked around. *The cables.*

As Costa slowly made the second to last turn to the top, he heard heavy grunting and an odd humming sound, as if a generator was powering itself down.

He targeted his weapon and smiled when he saw that Forge's back was toward him, his hands up against the wall. *Coward. Did Forge really think this was cops and robbers, that he could just surrender?*

But a sudden twist of Forge's body told Costa that he had made a grave mistake. Forge's hands were not in the air to surrender. He had pulled with all his weight to dislodge the powerful, high-voltage cables from their sockets that energized the spinning beacon above their heads.

The light instantly went dark as Forge flipped backward and simultaneously separated the positive and negative ends of the arm-thick cables.

In the air, Forge stretched to touch one end of the power line to the metal handrail and the other to the foot of the wrought-iron steps. Forge, lying on the wooden landing, was instantly protected from the charge.

Costa's body completed the 30,000-volt circuit. A shower of sparks filled the enclosure as Forge strained to keep the lines fixed to the metal as the electrons vibrated through the rubberized insulation.

A split-second later, the shock violently blew Costa a dozen feet across the stairway and through a small, closed window that was once used for ventilation of the tower.

Costa's exit put him exactly at the 150-foot mark of the tower. He had been ejected with such force that he easily bypassed the painter's scaffolding and cast into the humid air of the night.

As Costa fell to the cement below, a child watching the fireworks from a nearby street caught the reflection of a white skyburst that had sparkled off the side of Costa's gun for a fleeting moment.

"Look, Mommy," the little boy said. "That firework didn't go off."

"It's just a dud, sweetie," the woman replied, not taking her eyes off the light show.

As Forge hurriedly exited the lighthouse, he flung himself into the fine grit sand as two bullets whizzed by his body. *Dewall is getting better,* Forge thought. *He's learned to aim low.*

The muzzle flashes pinpointed Forge's next assault. Instead of running into the tree line where he had come from, Forge gambled and ran toward the cement jetty walkway. The sky was now overflowing with fireworks. The light and shadows, coupled with his sprint, might be enough to confuse Dewall, he thought.

Forge's sides burned with the pain of exhaustion as he ran at top speed along the walkway. One bullet hit the stainless-steel guardrail, sending vaporized sparks into Forge's face. Another was close enough that he felt its shock wave. *Dewall is a better shot than I give him credit for.*

At the first opening in the rails, Forge jumped left onto the jetty rocks to put the walkway between him and Dewall. It was low tide and the slate-gray boulders, some the size of vans, were slick with green moss and clumps of black, razor-sharp mussels.

Forge carefully clawed his way along the outer railing. His foot slipped, leaving him dangling over a crevice. With a grunt, he pulled himself upward, only to be rewarded with another gunshot. *Good, let him waste his ammo. I just hope he didn't bring another clip with him.*

Finally, he found what he was looking for. A break in the rocks. The erosion had eaten away a small hole in the underside of the walkway. Not enough to collapse the cement, but enough, he hoped that he could squeeze through.

He narrowed his body sideways and pulled himself through the opening as if he were a snake entering a rabbit hole. With one foot on the rock, he pushed himself forward and heard the lower part of his pant leg start to rip. It was a good sign, he told himself. *I'm at least moving.*

Forge felt his way inward. He couldn't see the other end of the hole. If he got stuck here, he would either be shot in the head by Dewall or grossly embarrassed in the morning when the park police found him during their early rounds.

After ten feet, Forge felt fresh air from the other side of the hole. The opening was low to the sand and even hidden from view by a mound of tide-swept sand. As he emerged, Forge peered upward and saw Dewall holding his gun in a traditional cup-and-saucer police stance, scanning the walkway. He was aiming too high and too narrowly. *His eye must be swollen shut by now. He has half the vision.*

From far to Dewall's left, Forge made a frontal assault, ramming into Dewall's midsection. The renegade officer fell to his side with a grunt, but still held onto his pistol. He swung the butt of the weapon hard into Forge's back, sending the detective into a painful thrust upward and forcing him to release his grip.

Dewall pointed the weapon at Forge's head. He squeezed the trigger.

Forge instinctively ducked, but there was no sound, no flash. The sand had jammed the firing pin. Forge knew he was finally on a level playing field with Dewall.

Not about to wait for a second beating of the day, Dewall threw the gun at Forge's head and sprang to his feet. He started to run into the array of firework launchers that were arranged in fifty neat rows, each one three feet from the next, but most hidden by smoky exhaust.

Forge lunged at Dewall's feet and tackled him into the sand. Dewall's leather sole slammed hard into his cheek, breaking his grip, and Dewall crawled and then started to hobble to the racks of fireworks. Through the maze he could get lost and head back to the trees to meet up with Tolck.

Forge had no intention of letting Dewall get away. He followed Dewall into the two final arrays, each loaded with drum-sized hard cardboard canisters of propellant and pyrotechnics. The canisters were wired to an electronic firing device that was being controlled by a remote operator at a computer console somewhere safe beyond the park's perimeter. Each canister had the equivalent power of a stick of dynamite that could launch a sixty-pound projectile hundreds of feet into the air.

As the fireworks from the proceeding rows started to ignite, Forge knew that the end of the show was near. He closed his eyes after each launch to preserve his vision from both the brilliant sparks and the burning sulfur of the mortar powder. Dewall was not as smart. Like a deer in the headlights, Dewall froze in front of one canister as it flew skyward scant feet in front of his face. *He's blinded!* Forge knew. *He can't see a thing.*

Forge kicked Dewall's legs out from under him, sending him into a rack of canisters and then down on the ground. Still blind, but still deadly, Dewall unclipped his buck knife and slashed wildly at the figure in front of him.

The first swipe caught Forge on his left hand, cutting his palm deep enough for blood to flow. He let out a cry of pain, a signal to Dewall that he had just a second for the final kill.

Dewall sprung to his feet, clutching his knife solidly in his fist, and swung again. Forge fell onto his back. Unable to roll away, he propped his foot in the air to stop Dewall's forward thrust.

"The trouble with you, Forge," Dewall spat out as he raised his knife for the kill, "is you'll always be a loser."

"Not tonight, Jack," Forge said. With Dewall now firmly balanced on his coiled leg, Forge brought his knee up to his chest and unleashed a massive jerk upward and outward.

Dewall was catapulted off his feet and backward as he twisted quickly in the air to brace his fall. He had pulled his hand too close to his body and the point sliced into his lower stomach as he landed square on top of a high, hard object.

Dewall felt the thin blade enter in his body. As he opened up his eyes from the grimace, he noticed that he was not on the ground, and not on sand.

He was...

Dewall's final scream was muted by the hiss of the ignited propellant. Lying on top of the canister marked "GRAND FINALE" in bold block letters, the missile briefly struggled in a tower of smoke and heat before sending its new payload into the night sky.

Its fuel spent at a mere two hundred feet, the ball of the projectile ignited its freight of aluminum, sodium nitrate, calcium chloride, and flesh. The hot sparks blew through Dewall's body, sending a muted shower of yellow and orange streaks into the night, followed by a thunderous burst of white light and noise.

Forge could hear the hoots and applause from the crowd in the distance.

He scanned the beach. The fading white from the firework betrayed Tolck's position. Now alone with Sister Maris and with a gun to her head, he was making a run for the dunes and up to the nearest street. There a car would likely be waiting to whisk them away.

Coughing and wheezing, Tolck had to nearly drag Sister Maris along the sand.

"You lift up your feet, or I'll shoot you right here," Tolck rasped. He fumbled with his left hand for the nitroglycerine in his right pocket. As he extracted the bottle, the pills fell and disappeared into the nighttime sand.

"Damn you!" he screamed. "Damn you!"

"You will be the one damned," Sister Maris intoned. "There is nothing left to gain by running."

"I'm not going to run," Tolck replied. "We are going to wait here till he gets closer. He thinks we can bargain, that I'll barter the device for you. But he doesn't understand, it's too late for deals. The last deal I want to make is his death."

"There are cops all around," Sister Maris pleaded. "You won't get ten feet off this island."

"And what will they do to me, a sick, dying old man?" Tolck coughed as he pointed the gun toward Forge's direction. "Put me on death row? Such a joke. I'll tell you what is going to happen. I have half the state bought. I'll be in jail for a day, I'll get out on a few million dollars bail, and in six months my lawyers will have the case dismissed. I am too sick, too feeble to withstand the rigors of a trial, they will plead to a friendly judge. I am old. I am incompetent. My mind has been lost. Such a pity! Every tinhorn politician in this state will be petrified that I will talk to the feds, that I will show them all the secret videos. They will be clamoring to not only have me released, but to give me a medal."

"And what about me?" Sister Maris said as she watched Forge move closer in a zigzag pattern. "Do I die too?"

"No," Tolck said. "Your punishment is to watch your boyfriend die in front of you. You will go to your grave knowing that you were the cause of his doom, but that you were helpless to save him. A helpless, little old nun."

Sister Maris furrowed her brow. With one swift motion, she broke Tolck's grip on her arm, pulled her elbow up to her chest and jammed it deep into Tolck's solar plexus.

"He's not my boyfriend," she said with the first thrust that doubled Tolck over in pain.

"I'm not helpless," she said with the second blow to his face.

"And I'm not old!" Sister Maris struck Tolck a third time in the middle of his stomach.

Forge heard the voices in the night and began to run toward Sister Maris. As she ran to meet him, Tolck fell to his knees and began to crawl toward a sand dune.

Forge embraced Sister Maris as she began to weep openly in his arms. She buried her head into his chest and they both fell to their knees.

"Are you all right?" Forge asked, looking for any wounds on her.

"Yes," she said, her tear-stained face looking into Forge's eyes. "But you, you have blood on you."

"It's just a cut hand," he said, as Sister Maris tore a strip of material from the bottom of her tee shirt and began to dress the slash. "I think this may make it a bit tougher for you to do your next palm reading on me."

Sister Maris blurted out a small laugh and smiled faintly as she began to realize she was in a safe harbor.

"Fry," she exclaimed.

"I know," Forge said, lowering his head. "He's dead."

"No, he's not," Sister Maris screamed. "When they came to get me, they drove the car into Baylock's house. I saw Fry in the corner. He was shot, but alive. He was cuffed and dumped in a corner of the room to die."

"Jesus, we have to get to him now," he said. "Let's go. I saw an ambulance parked on the main road on crowd standby."

"What about Tolck?"

"He's the least of our worries now," Forge said. "He's just a tired old man with nowhere to hide anymore. As for Baylock, patrol will scoop him up before he gets off the island. We need to help Fry. And I need to get back to Sharon. Now."

"Why?"

"Because I now know who Beta is," Forge said. "I know who the other outsider was in the Council of Twenty-Four."

"Who is it?"

"Kevin," Forge said. "Kevin Singh."

NINETEEN

On the darkened dune, Tolck struggled to pull himself across the sand as he moved away from Forge and toward the ocean. The sound of the lapping waves soothed him, but it could not ease the erratic beating of his heart. The enlarged organ, which had borne decades of stress so Tolck could keep his outwardly façade of serenity and control, could no longer be trusted to find the right cycle to continue its task.

Tolck's breathing became labored as his organs began to cascade to their demise. The tiny blood vessels in the whites of his eyes ruptured in a vain attempt to relieve the growing blood pressure within his body.

Tolck moved on. He had to reach the cluster of the only true objects that he had come to love in this world as he casually dealt in death. They asked for little other than light and water. They showed him how his plan could work, how it should work.

Tolck clutched at the stiff reeds of *Ammophila breviligulata* and held them in his hands. Beach grass, the salty smell of beach grass.

So strong. So brilliant. Yet so fragile. He pulled on them until the golden roots freed themselves from the sand. Tolck fell facedown, dead among the weeds.

TWENTY

Exiting the park, Forge spotted the ambulance. They were at Baylock's house within a minute.

The bullet had pierced Fry's abdomen wall. Because the cop-killer bullet was denser than a lead slug, it had entered and exited in a straight line without fragmenting or mushrooming into the size of a silver dollar.

Fry was groggy and pale from the loss of so much blood. The paramedics quickly patched the wound and started a plasma drip into his arm before loading him onto the gurney.

"Baylock," Fry mumbled as he was being wheeled to the open door of the ambulance. "It's Baylock."

"We know, Fry, we know," Forge said. "We're running him down now."

"Sister Maris... "

"I'm right here, Fry," Sister Maris said as she squeezed his hand and he squeezed back. "You can't get rid of me that easily."

Fry managed a grin as the back wheels of the gurney folded upward and into the vehicle.

"I'll be with you all the way to the hospital," Sister Maris said, a tear running down her cheek. "We'll be together."

Fry turned his head to the right to glimpse Forge.

"Loser," Fry said. "You go get `em."

TWENTY-ONE

Outside Elan's rental house, Singh checked the clock as he withdrew a small .22 caliber pistol from a lockbox in the forensics command vehicle van. He pulled the slide back a half-inch to ensure the tiny round was loaded in the chamber, then gently released the tension. He zipped open his personal backpack and withdrew a small, black cylinder.

The silencer screwed tightly into the threads of the weapon's elongated barrel. The noise suppressor, combined with the bullet casings being filled with half of their normal powder, ensured the pistol would barely utter a whisper when fired. The loudest sound would be the tingle of shells onto the wooden floor, followed by the soft thump of a crumpled body.

The weapon fit nicely in the small of his back, under his loose shirt. The shirt also hid his service sidearm, which he had casually clipped to the side of his jeans. The duty officer at the door would have no reason to search him. He was a forensics guy just retrieving some more information. After all, Forge had broken a golden rule. He had left a civilian alone at a crime scene. Singh had to save the day once again.

Too bad there would have to be a terrible struggle, Singh thought as he entered the Loveladies house. *Sharon, where did you get that gun? Put it down, now, Sharon, or someone will get hurt. Oh, no, Sharon, how could you kill Forge? She was so distraught over the divorce and the death of her brother. I couldn't stop her. I had to shoot her, officers. It was self-defense. I just wish I could have saved poor, poor Detective Forge. My hero. What a tragic loss.*

Singh smirked at the simplicity of the plan. If Forge returned with the Quantum device, he would have plenty of time to kill them both, reroute the billion dollars from the pump-and-dump accounts to his numbered accounts in the Cayman Islands, Belize, and a half-dozen other spots he had hurriedly set up around the globe. *What beach would I buy with that kind of money?* he thought. *Hell, I'll just buy me a whole island.*

Time was running out. At thirty minutes to midnight, the money was within his reach. At thirty-one minutes, it would be gone forever.

Come on, Matt, don't let me down now. You did everything according to plan. You worked the case so hard that I just left you on auto-drive. By the time you figure out what happened, you will be dead.

"Hello, Sharon," Singh said as he walked up the steps. "I hope you're not touching any of the evidence."

"Have you heard from Matt?" she asked.

"Not directly," Singh said. "I heard chatter on the scanner about them taking Fry to the hospital, so I suppose everything worked out. I guess he got the Quantum device."

Sharon held her breath for fear that a sudden movement, even a twitch of an eyelid, would put her in harms way. How did he know about the Quantum device?

"I hope so," she said. "Did Matt... tell you about the device?"

It was Singh's turn to freeze. In his hurry to reap his billion dollars, he had let slip a critical detail that now linked him to the plot. He had to play it smooth, at least until Forge returned. It was a cat-and-mouse game in which he didn't want the mouse to know she was being hunted.

"Yes, yes. Of course," Singh lied. "On his way out, he told me to watch you, then he talked about this incredible encryption device." Singh needed to change direction. He had to put the ball back into her court. "Aren't you concerned about Fry?"

"Oh, yes," Sharon said, walking toward the kitchen in an attempt to put the black-and-green granite countertop between her and Singh. "It's been such a terrible day that my mind is all jumbled. What exactly happened to Fry?"

"Someone shot him," Singh said.

"That's terrible," she said. "Do they know who did it?"

"Don't know," said Singh. "He's still conscious, so he should be able to tell the officers what happened."

"I'm glad to hear that."

Singh slowly reached behind his back for the silenced weapon. *She suspects too much. She knows. Tie her up and gag her. Shoot Forge as he comes up the steps. No one will know until I want them to know.*

Below, on the lower level, a rush of warm air filled the house as the front door flew open. Forge pulled the black Glock from the duty officer's holster and ran up the steps.

"Singh! FREEZE! NOW!" Forge yelled from the top of the stairs.

Singh swung around, firing two silent shots at Forge, splintering a wooden baluster.

I'm getting damn tired of all this shooting tonight, Forge thought. He drew a quick bead on Singh as the man ran into the dining room to hide behind the sheetrock wall.

Forge knew that Singh wasn't a street officer. He had forgotten to duck. Forge paced the movement with his gun, sighted the middle section of the wall and squeezed off five shots in two seconds.

A mortally wounded Singh emerged from behind the barrier, his gun drooping in one hand. A single bullet had struck his stomach and exited through a kidney.

Forge kicked the .22 to a far corner as Singh collapsed to the floor. The forensics expert tasted the salty blood in his mouth as he looked up at Forge.

"Dude," Singh coughed. "That was some great shooting."

"Don't talk," Forge said as he signaled the duty officer to call for help. "An ambulance will be here in a moment."

"Don't waste your time," Singh wheezed. "You and I know this isn't going to work out the way... I planned."

"Why, Kevin. Why?"

"Besides... the money?"

"Yeah, besides the money."

"Survival."

"How so?"

"Tolck," Singh coughed as he cleared his throat of red sputum. "Tolck had this list. Some put up money, others put up skills. Parker put up money. He brought me in for inside intel. He knew I could keep a watch on what was happening inside the department."

"Parker was Omega."

"Yeah."

"Parker's the man in a can."

"Right again." He tried to hold back a deep-throated cough.

"Didn't you know that?"

"Not at first." Singh paused to catch his breath. "Parker wanted to break away. He set up an alliance with Elan and The Troll. They were going to screw Tolck, take all the money. He was then going to get rid of Tolck, the Tolck way."

"What happened?"

"Tolck found out about it. I don't know how."

"The Council of Twenty-Four... They voted to kill him?"

"Yeah. But they left me out of it. I guess I wasn't a ranking member in Tolck's book. I didn't put up any money. Tolck didn't trust me, but he didn't distrust me... He needed me still." He took a deep, wheezing breath. "I was just Beta, Parker's man in the lab."

"What for?"

"Tolck needed me to help him get access to the county forensics lab. He never told me why. He always kept everything... in nice air-tight boxes."

"So they torched Parker and dumped him at the sisters," Forge said. "Why?"

Singh tried to laugh but coughed up a thimble of blood.

"That was my little idea," he said with a faint smile. "I didn't know who was in the can at first... Parker was killed and they didn't tell me... Dewall was nowhere to be found. So Tolck called me. I used the boat's GPS to locate the house. Costa drove the boat out... and I rolled the can off the fishing deck.

"Tolck said he needed to send a message to Elan and The Troll. He said he wanted to put a nice little present on their doorstep, so when they woke up in the morning... they would know Tolck played for keeps.

"I got scared. Like, am I next? So I figured I would play along... but add my own twist to it."

"Like what?"

"Like the longshore drift," Singh said in a whisper. "I surfed this area. I knew that the current flowed south. If you dump anything in front of a house, it would just wind up on the next beach over."

"So you dumped it in front of Elan's place as Costa watched. But you knew it would end up somewhere they wouldn't see it. Some place where they wouldn't get the message."

"Exactly," said Singh. "It was just good luck it wound up in front of the sisters. Elan doesn't get the message and it brings you, the great, fallen Matt Forge, into the case. I went through the motions to pull that print off of the body. No one was more surprised than me to see that it belonged to Lewis. Then I knew who was in... the can."

"How?"

"When I was working last Saturday night to get Tolck secret access to the county lab, I saw Lewis on the security monitor picking Parker up. When I hit on Lewis's fingerprint the next day, I knew I could turn things around my way... It was an opportunity not to be missed."

"So you could start your double cross."

"You do catch on," Singh wheezed. "I was trapped. Chances are I was next on Tolck's hit parade."

"So you let me do the work for you."

"Sorry, bro, but yeah... You got Tolck covering his ass instead of coming after me. And then, when Elan and The Troll got wasted, I knew this is what Parker and Tolck had been hiding. This was the jackpot. This was an opportunity not to be missed."

"You were going to steal the money and disappear."

"Yeah, but you heard that before," Singh coughed. "I still needed you to crack the machine and tap into the money... Now, you are one lucky son-of-a-bitch."

"How's that?"

"You got the Quantum device. You got the magic lantern. You can make three wishes... and give yourself a billion dollars."

Forge looked at the three Bloomberg machines and saw that the price of a share had topped sixteen dollars, an amazing fifty-fold increase from the thirty-three cents just hours earlier. The bottom line for the pump-and-dumpers: 1.2 billion dollars.

"One question, man," Singh said faintly. "How did you figure it was me?"

"The ear, Kev," Forge said. "Only you could have faked the photo of the ear.

You did too good of a job aging the Lewis picture. Once I knew Baylock was still alive, that pointed to only one person with lots of computer skills. You. But, how did you do the switch on the ear photo?"

"Piece of cake," Singh said proudly, the trickle of blood from his lip growing thicker. "I set it up shortly after HQ called about Elan. I knew you would match the ear to the victim. I just had to help you along. I planted that newspaper in the house as soon as we got in... I digitally altered the Baylock photo to put Parker's ear there instead."

"Why Baylock?"

"Parker told me about him coming into the group to work the federal angle, about how we needed to help cover his tracks. He was the only member of the Council of Twenty-Four I knew outside of... Parker. I knew if you found him, you would find the missing Quantum device. Trust me... that was the first thing I looked for when we entered the house and saw the empty encryption cradle.

"My hat's off to you, bro," Singh said as his breathing became more labored. "You figured me out... before I... could figure you... out. Oh, God. It hurts so much... "

The paramedics extracted Singh's body and carefully carried the remains downstairs. Forge spoke to the duty officer and returned to Sharon, who was sitting on the couch.

As the officers left, Forge sank next to Sharon on the brink of exhaustion. He had one last task to finish.

Sharon leaned over to gently push the hair away from his eyes.

Forge felt the tender pads of her fingers brush unhurriedly across his damp brow and down his cheek.

"Poor pumpkin," Sharon whispered in his ear as she drew closer. She focused on the digital clock to measure the time. It was five minutes to midnight. "Did you get the device?"

"Yes."

"Now. Let's not waste any time. Let's use it now."

"Just one question."

"Anything, dear," Sharon said softly, her eyes fixated on the screens in front of her. "Anything that you want, it's yours."

"Why did you kill your brother?"

TWENTY-TWO

Sharon stared at Forge for a full minute before breaking the silence.

"What do you mean, Matt?" she said slowly.

"You know what I mean."

"Are you feeling all right, Matt?" she asked. "I know you haven't been getting too much sleep. And this case, well, this case has made you paranoid."

"I'm feeling quite fine," Forge said. "Outside of being shot at, nearly cooked with a torch, and abused for a good part of the last three days."

"Can we talk about this later?" she said. Sharon hurriedly stood to walk to the computer. "We have less than four minutes to move the money."

"And where would you want to move it to?"

"To us," Sharon said, turning to Forge and grabbing his arms as she looked into his eyes to read his intention. "We can use it to disappear. To leave all this behind and start all over again. Just you and me. No distractions. No job. No past to get in the way of a new life. A new, fantastic life in a faraway place. We will finally have all the time in the world."

Forge pulled the slim Quantum device from his front pocket and inserted it into its holder. The PC hummed as it warmed to the connection, and the screen once again popped to life. The Quantum interface appeared.

<Password>

"Gold-Bug," Forge typed.

The Quantum connection was instantaneous. It found the lone IP address in a Thai Naval base at Sattahip on the coast of the Gulf of Thailand. The server, run by a rogue Navy intel expert that Elan had recruited for the effort, was programmed to play hop-scotch with the secret bank accounts set up around the world.

Each day, at midnight, the server would randomly select a new IP address on the Web for Elan to work from. It masterfully piggybacked onto real Web addresses — sleepy little businesses, giant universities, and multinational corporations. The rerouting ensured that any trace done by the feds would lead them to a dead end. The ultimate goal would be to keep law enforcement from guessing what stock was being manipulated and which IP address the final transfer of money would be made from. Once the "dump" of the pump-and-dump scheme was executed and the inflated stock sold off, the money would be routed through the new IP to myriad bank accounts across the globe. Then the IP would evaporate as if it were smoke, leaving no trace of its existence.

Elan had designed the system too well. Since the computer randomly selected the addresses of servers around the globe, he had no way of knowing what they were until the final transfer. It was his last, fatal safeguard to protect what he thought would be his eternal fortune.

On the screen, the Sattahip server asked one question:

<Execute transfer? Y, N or OPTIONS>

"We can change it," Sharon said. "We can change it to another bank account. We can send it to my account and transfer it out tomorrow."

The clock on the computer screen read 11:58.

"Do it, do it, do it now!" Sharon said. Her voice was on the verge of shattering into a thousand pieces.

"Tell me," Forge said as he covered the keyboard with his hands. "Why do they call you Alpha?"

Sharon froze, her eyes darting from the clock to Forge's eyes.

"I don't know what you are talking about."

"Why, Sharon?"

"Do the transfer," she said. "I'll tell you everything after we do the transfer."

Forge turned back to the PC and watched the clock hit 11:59.

<Execute transfer? Y, N or OPTIONS>
Forge typed, "Options."
The screen offered three:
<F1 – execute>
<F2 – change destination>
<F3 – abort>

"Go ahead," Forge said. "Do it."

Sharon lunged for the F2 key but Forge intercepted her hand. He shunted her index finger to the right and forced it to depress F3.

"Are you insane?" she screamed. "You just erased $1.2 billion from our lives."

"Your life," Forge said. "No amount of money is worth killing for."

As midnight — 11 a.m. Tokyo time —hit and there was no announcement from the Cato company, the green symbols on the Bloomberg machines turned a crimson red. The stock had started its nosedive to oblivion. Within a few minutes the company, or what was left of the company, would be bankrupt and regulators in three time zones would begin crawling all over the globe looking for clues as to what had happened. All the money that the unsuspecting had poured into the phony stock was now being reversed. And the $24 million that Tolck and his allies had fronted for the pump-and-dump scheme would soon be worthless electronic dust.

Sharon fell into a slump on the floor, feeling as if she had died but not yet left her body.

"I am Alpha," she said softly. "Queen of the empty realm."

TWENTY-THREE

"How did you know?" Sharon asked.

"I suspected you the minute I walked into this house," Forge said. "I didn't want to believe it, but two markers led me to you."

"Which ones?"

"The display case," Forge said pointing to the dining room curio cabinet. "The nativity scene. It had all the figures except one."

Sharon nodded. "The baby Jesus."

"Yes. The figures of Mary, Joseph, the shepherd boy and animals were all looking into an empty circle. You were always a collector of odds and ends. What were those figures called? They were made in West Germany, where you used to live."

"Hummels."

"Yes, that's right. Hummels."

"I couldn't resist," she said. "I needed that last piece."

"Why?"

"Our mother was always collecting the pieces. It was her way, I guess, of trying to put the perfect little family together. Each Christmas she would give us the rarest pieces, hoping that we too would have a perfect little family someday.

"We each got identical nativity scenes. It was something we trotted around with us wherever we went. The last piece was called the Guardian Angel."

"What was that like?"

Sharon slowly stood to walk to the countertop to retrieve her red-patent leather purse. She unclipped the golden lock to extract a carefully preserved object. As she unwrapped several layers of tan tissue paper, she exposed a delicate porcelain figurine about six inches tall.

It was a child angel with golden wings standing over the infant Jesus in a wooden crib. In the angel's hands was a large, white candle with a flickering yellow flame.

"It's beautiful, isn't it?" Sharon asked as she caressed the fragile piece in her hands. "Mom gave it to Donald before she died, but she never gave me one. When the next Christmas came, she had passed on, leaving me without this wonderful little angel to watch over my collection.

"You see, Matt, that is what Donald and I fought most about. I wanted to share the piece because I was her daughter. A mother is always closest to her daughter, you know. But Donald would never relent. He said he needed it, that mom always wanted him to have it."

"That's why you killed him?"

Sharon looked puzzled. "No. It was the deal. He was going to ruin the deal."

"How?"

Sharon took a long drink of warm water from a glass in which the ice cubes had long melted. The taste didn't suit her, but she needed to wash the cotton feeling out of her mouth.

"Would you believe it all started with me?"

Forge said nothing.

"Parker and I had a relationship while you and I were dating. But he wasn't the type to set up house, and I was desperately looking for a stable foundation in my life. You seemed the perfect match: Smart, reserved, a rising star. Parker didn't mind. He had what he wanted and he had moved on to someone else for the next spin of the wheel.

"He had mentioned to me about Tolck and his influence, and how he wanted to find a way to develop every square inch of land around here. I laughed it off, but it always stuck with me. Then I realized that with my brother, I had the keys of the kingdom in my hands.

"He could run the scam with another friend, The Troll. With Tolck's network, we could pull the syndicate — what you called the Council of Twenty-Four — together to form an alliance of interests."

"Who were they, the Council of Twenty-Four?"

"It was supposed to be the all-stars of New Jersey's politics. We had Baylock, the top bankers, land developers, key state senators, mayors, and law enforcement. It was easy. The pump was primed. It was going to work," Sharon said.

"And then?"

"And then Donald tried to screw Tolck. That was his whole angle in life — to get as much as he could whenever he could from whomever he could. I suppose that is what made him like a pea in a pod with The Troll. Why get a tiny sliver of a billion dollars when you controlled the pump-and-dump scheme? He had the money, the electronic banking system, the stock triggers. It was a natural scam on the guys who thought they were pulling off the biggest scam in the world."

"How did you know he had taken sides?"

"Parker. He let me in on the secret. Lewis overhead Tolck talking about the details of how Donald was going to run the stock scam and went to Parker, trying to get a bigger piece of the pie for himself. Lewis was tired of being Tolck's go-to guy. He wanted to be on his own, but he needed help. He had gotten greedy. Parker talked Lewis into telling him all the details. At The Paradise, Lewis wrote "Cato" and its phony Khimer-A process on a napkin for him and slid it across the table."

"How did the napkin get into his stomach?"

"Parker told me he had to quick shove it into his mouth when he saw Tolck come toward them. He thought it was funny, like spy stuff. Parker liked the idea of screwing Tolck. Then thought he could confide in me. I guess a guy thinks when you sleep with him, you have this undying bond of trust."

"I suppose he guessed wrong. And the priest? Was the missing priest in on the deal?"

"Father Caden. How did you know about him?" Sharon asked.

"An errant missing person report crossed my ears. It's not hard to put two and two together."

"Lewis was doing clean-up for himself. When Parker was killed, he felt that the circle might be closing in on him."

"What about you? Why didn't he kill you, too?"

Lewis didn't know that I knew about the double-cross plan. So Lewis, the genius that he was, went on his own to try and clean up the mess," Sharon said. "Parker, Lewis, and Caden went way back to Parker's early days in politics, with Caden running money for Parker. It was old-fashioned bribery stuff, y'know. Buy a vote here, turn a blind eye there. Tolck, he took it to another level. He made penny-ante corruption a major industry."

"So Parker needed his bag man again?"

"Yeah. He couldn't wash all the money himself. He thought if he could run it through a church charity account no one could trace it. Parker must have told Caden what was happening."

"Why didn't you go with Parker and your brother?" Forge asked. "You could have gotten all that you wanted."

"His plan was intriguing, at least for the moment," said Sharon. "But I knew my brother. I knew he would try to find a way to cut me out of the deal. It was a safer choice, you could say even a healthier choice, to stay with Tolck."

"So Tolck had Parker killed?"

"No."

"Who then?"

"I had Parker killed," Sharon said. Forge saw a brief twitch of a pupil, but no other hint of emotion in her eyes. "It was a message that had to be delivered to my brother."

"But that message never got there."

"Yes, the best laid plans of mice and greedy men," she said softly. "Tolck was a control freak. Everything had to be in neat compartments. He ensured that the Council of Twenty-Four didn't know who all the other members were. He wouldn't tell me who was working for Parker. But I wanted to be there, I wanted to see Parker burn for trying to ruin the deal."

"So it was you and Consolina at the warehouse?"

"And Lewis. Lewis had got him so drunk that he was easy to knock out at The Paradise and throw into the trunk of a car for a ride to the warehouse. Tolck never told me about Singh, that he was Parker's man on the inside. Now it all makes sense that Singh was in it for his own percentage. He wanted to screw it up so you would get into the case."

"And Donald knew nothing about this?"

"He suspected Tolck was out to get him when Donald couldn't reach Parker. But Donald thought I was still on his side."

"He thought that blood was thicker than money," Forge said.

"Yes. It is what got me in the door last night. He thought I had come alone."

"He still trusted you."

"We had it good, until you came out of your little shell," she said. "You came out and had to ruin it for all of us."

It was Forge who became stoic. He had no intention of revealing his feelings through his eyes, expression, or even a movement of his wounded hand.

"And you were going to have me killed too?" he said.

"No. I begged Tolck not to harm you. And you see... you see, you are here."

"Barely."

"We had to get that Quantum device to work. We didn't realize that Donald was thinking and working eleven hours ahead. All he kept saying was it would rollover at 11 a.m.; 11 a.m. on the other side of the world was really midnight here. We took the device and thought if we used it at 11 a.m., we could take control of the money, redirect the windfall it into our accounts. But at 11 a.m. here, when the device failed to work, we became desperate. We knew we had to get the money out before the midnight pump-and-dump."

"That's when you showed up," Forge said. "Right before noon."

"Yes. We needed you. I needed you. I knew you could crack the code. After you left here, I called ahead to Tolck and told him the IP address in the Gold-Bug folder that you had decrypted. We thought that would be enough to get the money, but it still didn't work. He thought Donald screwed him, that he gave him the wrong password. Who would have thought it was just a matter of time; that we just wouldn't have enough time to steal?"

"Yes. If only we had more time."

"We could still make it work, Matt," Sharon said, pointing to the Bloomberg machine. "Look, there is still a few million left in the stock. That hasn't shrunk away yet. I now know what I want. I was blinded by the money. But the money is just a means to an end. I need you."

Silence. A long stare from Forge.

"It was worth a try," Sharon said, finally realizing her defeat.

"Yes, it was worth a try."

"You said there were two markers that led you to me," Sharon asked. "The Hummel was one. What was the other? I need to know."

Forge looked out into the night through the sliding glass door and then down to the lower corner.

"It was the fox," he said. "When I saw the missing Hummel, I thought it could be you, but I just couldn't believe you would take part in the killing of your own brother. I had to have you in the room to help decode the passkey, and I needed you to keep talking so I could finally hear for myself how you were involved."

Sharon thought backwards in time to when she had last seen the tiny, red beach fox.

"I don't understand," she said. "All I said was it's a fox."

"That's what you would say about a cat, or a dog, or a bird," Forge said. "But you saw that fox for the first time last night. As you were taking part in the death of your brother, you must have been frightened to hear the scraping on the outside door. That fox has been a visitor to the neighborhood all summer. Neighbors said they saw Donald feeding a small dog on the balcony during the week, but it was really the fox. I know because a sister at the religious retreat said she saw a stray fox the night before the barrel washed up. So he was living in the area. When you first saw the fox, you were startled. But you were then relieved it wasn't someone intruding on your fire party.

"The second time you saw the fox, when you were here with me, it was old news to you. You should have been surprised, but you weren't. You saw the fox as just another nuisance."

Sharon looked down at her feet and clicked her two perfectly French-manicured thumbnails together until they slipped apart.

"Done in by a fox and a nun," she said.

"Sister Maris?" Forge asked.

"Who? No. Sister Maria Innocentia Hummel," Sharon said, picking up the porcelain angel figurine to carefully cradle it in her hand. "She was a German nun who designed these figurines in the 1930s."

At the doorway, Sharon had finally noticed three agents in dark jeans and sports jackets.

Sharon weakly held out her hands for the cuffs.

"Isn't it ironic?" she said, turning to Forge.

"What?"

"Parker kicked you down to the Island to punish you. And you end up solving his very own murder."

Forge parted his lips to ponder the thought for a moment.

"It's a real circle of life," he said. He turned to the agent closest to him by the stairway.

"Did you hear?" Forge asked.

"We heard enough," said Special Agent Adam Bagalore of the FBI's economic crimes unit. "The duty officer downstairs called us on your direction. We remained at the doorway until it was all over."

"You want me to give a statement?" Forge asked.

"You look like hell, Matt," said Bangalore. "We picked up the Tucker Township mayor at the strip joint. He can't talk fast enough. We found Tolck's body on the beach. We shut down the bridge, so Baylock won't be getting too far. Why don't you go home and get some sleep?"

"That's easier said than done," Forge said.

TWENTY-FOUR

At The Shack, Forge sat on his slanted balcony gazing at the houselights that illuminated Long Beach Island like a string of pearls. He fought sleep as best as he could, jerking himself awake whenever he felt his chin touch his chest. He had solved the case, but in the process had lost his wife forever and almost lost a friend.

He was startled out of his quiet melancholy by a light rap on the wooden frame of his front screen door. He had not heard the car pull up to the house. He was exhausted. If it was one of Tolck's henchmen come to finish the job, he would paint a red bull's-eye on his forehead and beg them to pull the trigger.

"Detective Forge, are you in there?" a voice cried out.

"On the porch. Watch your step. It's like a minefield in here."

Sister Maris, still wearing her torn, blood-stained tee shirt, gingerly entered and tiptoed around the clutter as she made her way to Forge. The room was lit only by a flickering black-and-white television set.

"I wanted you to know that Fry is going to make it," Sister Maris said as she sat behind Forge. "No vital organs were hit and he is a strong man. After a couple of days in the hospital he'll be sore, but as good as new."

"That's good news indeed," said Forge.

"You saved everyone today," she said. "You saved me. You need to be proud of yourself."

"Thank you."

Sister Maris felt the tension in Forge as she carefully massaged the side of his temples. Forge offered no resistance, as he had so longed for the touch of a friendly hand.

"Relax, Matt, relax," Sister Maris said softly as she felt the stress leave his muscles. "You need to let yourself go. You need to feel yourself floating out of your body."

"Yes."

Sister Maris moved to face Forge, and was pleased that his eyes had finally closed, that he seemed to be drifting out of consciousness. She knew she had to work quickly to get at the core of the detective's terror before the dream itself took hold of him again.

She squeezed his hand and felt his pulse slow to a resting beat. As she talked to him in his twilight daze, Sister Maris tried to steer his mind gently into another path, into the past.

"Where are you now?" she asked.

"I'm... I'm on the water," Forge said slowly.

"Where?"

"The early morning bay."

"With whom?"

"My father."

"How old are you."

Forge said nothing. Sister Maris thought she had gone too far too fast. Were his defenses starting to kick in?

"I'm nine years old."

"You are on his boat?"

"Yes."

"What are you doing now?"

"I'm wondering how calm the water is. It is slate flat as far as I can see. The sun. It's starting to rise, to light the sky up. It's turning a brilliant purple."

"What is your father doing?"

"We are slowly motoring to his crab pots."

"What happens when you stop?"

"He uses a hook to pull the wooden baskets on deck. He empties them in a giant pot. And he throws the trap back in. I feel sleepy. I feel tired in the boat."

"What does he say to you?"

"Matty," Forge's father said to him lightly as he sees his son's eyelids start to close. "Why don't you go in the wheelhouse and put your head down for a bit on my jacket? I can pull up the last few pots. I'll call you if we get a really big one."

The elder Forge saw in the distance a modern, larger white boat trolling in the waters that he normally used for the crab traps. After unloading the last pot that he had pulled aboard, the father threw it overboard and began his way to the new vessel.

As John Forge moved closer, he became agitated. A man on the white boat was pulling up Forge's filled crab traps. The shellfish were haphazardly released into the boat's well, and the trap was thrown overboard again. John Forge had suspected poachers were in the area. A number of traps in the last few weeks had come up empty. Now he had caught them.

"Ahoy," John Forge shouted through cupped hands. "You are trespassing on my traps."

The man in the boat continued his work unabated, moving a few yards east to snag Forge's next pot.

"I said you're breaking the law," John Forge said louder. "Do you want to go to jail?"

No response. The elder Forge quickly pulled his flat-bottomed boat along the fiberglass V-hull of the vessel, which was twice the size of his own.

"This is my living," John Forge pleaded. "You can't take my living."

"We want to eat good tonight," the man said without looking up. "Get the hell out of here."

"The hell I will," John Forge said. "The hell I will!"

The noise roused a groggy Matty Forge from his brief sleep. He heard the shouts, but they were muffled through the fogged glass of the wheelhouse.

Sister Maris watched Matt Forge twist uncomfortably in his chair.

"No, No. I can't listen to it!" Forge shouted, his eyes still closed as his trance took him deeper into the dream. "Don't do it, don't do it!"

"Don't do what, Matt?" Sister Maris pleaded. "Tell me, tell me. Don't do what?"

On his father's boat, nine-year-old Matty peers through a tiny clear patch of window to see his animated father yelling at the man. He looked at the man in the boat, but the rising sun blinded him. He could not see. He had to turn away.

"Another man," Forge said, now in a cold sweat. "Another man is coming on deck from below."

"What does he say?"

"He says, 'Shut up. Shut the fuck up.' He's yelling at my dad."

"And what do you see?"

"I can't see. I can't see. The sun. The blinding light is in my eyes."

"But you see a man."

"Yes."

"What does he have?"

"He has something in his hand."

"What is it, Matt. What is it?"

"I can't see."

"Yes, you can. Look past the light. Look at his hand."

"He's raising his hand."

"Tell me. What is in his hand?"

"Oh my God," Forge started to cry. "My dad, my dad, my dad, my dad, my dad..."

"What is happening to your dad?"

"I'm... I see it. I... want to yell out. 'Get down, get down.' I can't. I can't. I can't. I can't scream, I can't move."

"What can't you say?"

"I see it, I see it first. But I can't warn him... He's lying on the deck. He's bleeding. He's bleeding all over the boat."

"He's injured?"

"He's been... shot."

"What do you do?"

"I do nothing. Nothing. I sit there."

"You were terrified."

"I was helpless. I could have helped him."

"No, you couldn't," Sister Maris said as she grabbed Forge's hand tighter. "There is nothing you can do to change it."

"The man, he's pointing it at me."

"Is he going to shoot you?"

"Yes. I can't move. I can't breathe. I can't scream. I'm frozen in the wheelhouse."

"What do you see?"

"A wave, a wave in the distance. It's small, but roiling, like a gust of wind had kicked it up. The man has both hands on the gun. He is standing on deck pointing it at me. But then the man falls, falls backward. I hear screams from the man in the other boat."

"What is happening?"

"The wave. It hits the boat, it rocks forward. The man is knocked off balance. He falls. He is screaming, 'I fell, I fell... My leg, my leg is broken! Get out of here. Get out of here.'"

"They leave?"

"Yes."

"Look past the light, Matt. Blot out the sun. What do you see?"

"Two dark figures. One tall, one shorter."

"Do you see their faces?"

"No."

"The voice of the man who shot your father. Do you recall the voice?"

"Yes."

"Put the voice to the face."

"I can't."

"Yes, you can. What do you see?"

"I see... "

"Say it."

"I see... "

"Come on, Matt. Look past the light. Look into their faces."

"I see... Tolck."

Stunned, Sister Maris threw herself back into her chair. Forge's dark torment all these months had been Tolck. He knew it subconsciously, but he could never let his mind finish the terror of the dream so he could unlock the secret that rested within the brilliant, blinding morning sun that had erased his image of that day.

"Matt, Matt, wake up, it's me. It's Maris."

His sweat broken, Forge slowly opened his eyes to realize that Sister Maris was still with him. "It was Tolck," he said hoarsely.

"I know, I know," said Sister Maris. "It's over. You broke through. You found the answer that you have been looking for. The stress of the last nine months brought this most repressed memory back in the form of a dream."

"But why?"

Sister Maris did not speak for a moment. She looked at Forge. Forge looked to her for an answer.

"It was your father's way... of showing you."

"Of showing me what?"

"Of showing a new path. He showed you how to look beyond what you can see and to trust your instincts in what you cannot see."

Forge took a deep breath as he sat up in his chair. He wiped the sweat from his brow with the back of the yellow makeshift bandage Sister Maris had wrapped around his hand on the beach.

"Everything has come full circle," he said softly.

"Fate has a way of working out all the kinks in life," she said.

"I keep thinking of your palm reading. I was betrayed by someone that I trusted. That would be Kevin. And I suffered another loss. That would be Sharon. But the third part never came true."

"What part would that be?" Sister Maris said.

"The one about finding a new love."

"Ah, yes." Sister Maris could feel her cheeks start to turn flush.

"I suppose you can't be right all the time, now, can you?"

Sister Maris looked deeply into Forge's eyes.

"Well, love takes time, doesn't it now, Detective?"

"For me, it'll be an eternity."

"I'm not so sure about that," she said, touching Matt Forge's arm. "There is someone close who cares very much about you."

Forge followed Sister Maris's eyes as she turned to the doorway. Standing there, looking radiant even in the monochromatic glow from the television set, stood Dr. Lulu Ammerman. Gone were the white lab coat, oversized eyeglasses, and surgical gloves. She had set free her tightly pulled-back blonde hair so that it hung beautifully over her shoulders. In her hand was a small red first-aid kit she had extracted from the recesses of her desk drawer in the hospital. She didn't get much call for it in her line of work, but she was still a doctor and she still knew how to dress a wound.

"Sister Maris said I may need to tend to your cut hand," Ammerman said. "I don't think you want to get that infected."

Sister Maris quietly slipped out of the doorway as Forge offered his hand to the doctor. Their eyes signaled relief and endearment to each other. Finally, after three days of shock, they could relax in each other's company.

"Please, Matt, no more bodies, at least this week," Ammerman said.

"Amen to that."

"But one question," she asked as she swabbed Forge's hand with a green disinfectant rub. "What did you do to upset Parker so much?"

Forge started to laugh, and then cringed as the alcohol mixture bit into his superficial cut.

"You know how Parker was all politics all the time, right?" Forge started. "He had the prosecutor's fundraiser charity ball every year, and he expected everyone in his office to attend."

"Yeah. We get tickets, too. So you missed a party of his?"

"Not exactly. On the side he used the ball as a fundraiser for favored politicians. It was his way of ensuring reappointment every five years. He would expect each cop to sell five tickets for $100 apiece, or buy the whole lot for $500. It was the price of staying in his good graces."

"And?"

"I sent them back with a nice note saying thanks, but no thanks."

"He punched your ticket for that?"

"No, that's not the end of the story. He sends me back the tickets, along with an extra ten. He also sends a not-so-nice note saying it would really be best for my career if I sold all fifteen for him. For the good of the party, and all that. So I tried to return the favor."

"You didn't... ," Ammerman said.

"Oh, yes, I did," Forge said.

"What did you do? Tell me."

"I dropped the whole lot into the office shredder and mailed the confetti back to him. In the note I said, *'Dear Mr. Prosecutor. Thank you for thinking so highly of my salesmanship skills. I return these slightly used tickets and offer you a heart-felt closing involving two words. The first is a verb and the second is a personal pronoun. P.S. The verb is not 'love.'*"

"Oh my God, you told him to go fuck himself? That is so wicked," Ammerman laughed.

"Who knew he would get upset at that," Forge smiled as Ammerman laughed and fell into the hollow of his arms.

TWENTY-FIVE

The patrol officer, a young woman, returned Sister Maris to the darkened pebble driveway of the Harvey Cedars religious retreat.

Still too wired from the night's events, Sister Maris walked the beach, looking for a greeting from Fred, the fox, to no avail. Even the jingle of the treats in her pocket failed to entice Fred from wherever he was sleeping. It was just as well,

Sister Maris thought. It was so late that even little lonely foxes needed their rest this night.

She found her way back to the chapel, clicking on the dim hallway light before genuflecting at the altar.

She sat motionless in the last pew for the longest time, watching the waning flicker of a forgotten altar candle. As she closed her eyes, Sister Maris folded her hands and bowed her head to begin a silent prayer of deliverance for the soul of Dominick Tolck.

Author's Note

No novel is ever written in a vacuum, and *Cold Rolled Dead* is no exception. While the characters, events, and several locales are fiction, all the technology presented here has been researched for accuracy. Many of the gadgets, gizmos, tools and investigative techniques are already in use, or likely will be in the next few years. The exception is the unbreakable Quantum encryption device, the Holy Grail for modern-day cryptographers. There have been reports of successful military tests in controlled environments, but its practical application on the Web could be decades away.

Maris Stella — the place, not the person — is a real retreat located on one of the most pastoral parts of Long Beach Island. But, I'm sorry to say, there is no Sister Maris Stella, the person, at either the retreat or anywhere else on the planet.

I have taken some liberties in the area's geography, and for that I do apologize. For the astute students of the island's many municipal boundaries, I moved Loveladies just a tad bit closer to the Maris Stella retreat than it really is. And there is no Long Beach Island Police Department or a municipality called Tucker Township.

I am deeply grateful to several people for taking the time to read the manuscript in its various forms and providing much-appreciated suggestions. Among those I would like to thank are Gary Dietz, Jean Gallagher, Andrea Clurfeld, Shannon Mullen, Sean Boero, and Rich Youmans for his fine editing. A special thanks also to Ray Fisk, Leslee Ganss, and Down The Shore Publishing for taking a chance on a first-time novelist.

I give my deepest thanks to my two sons for their constant warmth and inspiration, and to my wife, Suzanne, for her undying support throughout this endeavor. She has, and always will be, the light in my life.

Paul D'Ambrosio
www.pauldambrosio.com